"Yep. . . . my p . . . occul . . . he warra . . . ey were facing serious charges from the law and even bigger threats from Luxe. There was no way out—they had to run."

"You too."

"Me too," I agreed, remembering the panic and fear . . . the sudden loss of my family. "I don't know how Luxe got their fingerprints, but it was rigged evidence. It was a demon, not a knife, that did the dirty work."

"The albino demon?"

I nodded.

"But they didn't summon it?"

"No. We think it was either someone from the Luxe group who was trying to sabotage our order, or a rogue magician trying to take over all the orders. If I can find the demon, I can force it to tell me who did it. My parents can be exonerated, the person who summoned the demon and killed three people can go to jail, and the Luxe Order will leave me the hell alone."

"You need me to find it fast because the police will be looking for your parents?"

"Well, that doesn't help matters, but it's more because the Luxe Order has given my organization a mandate to turn over my parents—or me—in two weeks."

His eyebrows shot up. "What would they do if you turned yourself in to them?"

"Kill me," I said very seriously.

Turn the page for rave reviews of *Kindling the Moon*. . . .

Praise for Jenn Bennett and *Kindling the Moon*

"Jenn Bennett has written a great off-beat debut novel with a likeable heroine and a fun, original storyline. . . . I thoroughly enjoyed it and am eagerly awaiting a sequel—hopefully to come out soon!"

—Karen Chance, *New York Times* bestselling author of *Death's Mistress*

"*Kindling the Moon* engaged me from page one. I loved it! I immediately adored the heroine, Arcadia Bell. This book is packed from cover to cover with unpredictable twists, heart-pounding action, and heated sexual tension. . . . Jenn Bennett has definitely made my 'To Buy' list, and I'm looking forward to the next book in this series."

—Anya Bast, *New York Times* bestselling author of *Cruel Enchantment*

"*Kindling the Moon* rocks like AC/DC on Saturday night. This book has it all: great writing, action, romance, a strong heroine, a unique hero, and the best teenager ever. I can't wait for the next one."

—Ann Aguirre, national bestselling author of *Shady Lady*

"Debut author Jenn Bennett takes the familiar ideas of magic, demons, and mythology, and she gives us something sexy, fun, and genuinely unique in *Kindling the Moon*. Arcadia Bell is a sassy, whip-smart addition to the growing pantheon of urban fantasy heroines, and Bennett an author to watch!"

—Kelly Meding, author of *Three Days to Dead*

"Fantastic magic, nonstop action, and hot romance make *Kindling the Moon* a not-to-be-missed debut. Arcadia Bell is a tenacious and savvy heroine who had me hooked from the start."

—Linda Robertson, author of *Arcane Circle*

"Delicious characters, fun twists, and fiendish risks. . . . This smart, stylish debut really delivers. Loved, loved, loved it!"

—Carolyn Crane, author of *Double Cross*

This title is also available as an eBook

KINDLING
THE MOON

AN ARCADIA BELL NOVEL

JENN BENNETT

POCKET BOOKS
New York   London   Toronto   Sydney

Pocket Books
A Division of Simon & Schuster, Inc.
1230 Avenue of the Americas
New York, NY 10020

This book is a work of fiction. Names, characters, places, and incidents either are products of the author's imagination or are used fictitiously. Any resemblance to actual events or locales or persons, living or dead, is entirely coincidental.

First Pocket Books paperback edition July 2011

POCKET and colophon are registered trademarks of Simon & Schuster, Inc.

For information about special discounts for bulk purchases, please contact Simon & Schuster Special Sales at 1-866-506-1949 or business@simonandschuster.com.

The Simon & Schuster Speakers Bureau can bring authors to your live event. For more information or to book an event contact the Simon & Schuster Speakers Bureau at 1-866-248-3049 or visit our website at www.simonspeakers.com.

Designed by Esther Paradelo
Cover design by Tony Mauro

Manufactured in the United States of America

10 9 8 7 6 5 4 3 2 1

ISBN 978-1-4516-2052-8
ISBN 978-1-4516-2054-2 (ebook)

For my mother, who first suggested that I write a book,
and my father, who later urged me to write another one.

1

I knew better than to be preoccupied when Tambuku Tiki Lounge was overcapacity. Crowds are ugly; it doesn't matter if they're human or demon.

Our bar held a maximum of sixty-five people per California fire code. My business partner treated this rule as more of a suggestion on Thursday nights, when *Paranormal Patrol* made us a midtown hot spot. Easy for her; all she had to do was sweet-talk the county inspector out of a citation. She wasn't the one being expected to break up drunken, demonic brawls.

"Hey!" My eyes zeroed in on a college kid stealing a drink off the bar. "Did you pay for that? No, you didn't. Get your grubby paws off."

"That woman left it," he argued. "Possession's two-thirds of the law."

"Nine-tenths, jackass," I corrected, snatching the ceramic Suffering Bastard mug out of his hand. An anguished face was molded into the side of the classic black tiki mug, half filled with a potent cocktail bearing the same name. When I dumped the contents in a small bar sink, the kid acted like I'd just thrown gold in the trash. He glared at me before stomping across the room to rejoin his broke buddies.

If I were a bartender in any other small bar in the city, I might be encouraged on occasion to double as a bouncer. As the only trained magician on staff at Tambuku, I didn't have a choice; it was my responsibility. After two years of sweeping up broken glass and trying to avoid projectile vomit, I'd seen enough demons-gone-wild behavior that would make a boring, corporate desk job appear attractive to any normal person. Good thing I wasn't normal.

"Arcadia? Cady? Hello?"

Amanda leaned across an empty bar stool, waving her hand in front of my face.

"Sorry, what?"

"I said that I need another Scorpion Bowl for booth three. Jeez, you're distracted tonight," she complained, unloading two empty wooden snack dishes from her tray before circling around the L-shaped bar top to join me.

"How wasted are they?" I craned my neck to see the booth while scooping up Japanese rice crackers from a large bin.

"They've passed over the halfway mark, but they aren't there yet. No singing or fighting." She wiped sweat from her forehead with a dirty bar towel. Amanda was one of three full-time waitresses we employed at Tambuku. Tall, blond, tan, and permanently outfitted with a stack of worn, braided hemp bracelets circling her wrist, she looked like the stereo-typical California girl.

Her family had lived on the central coast for several gen-erations in La Sirena, a small beach community thirty minutes away from the city; it captured its bewitching namesake with photo-worthy vistas of the rocky coastline and the blue Pacific that bordered it. Her parents had a ceramics studio there, and we'd commissioned them to make most of our tiki mugs and bowls, which now sat in neat rows on bamboo shelves behind the bar.

"I'm more concerned about the couple at hightop three." Amanda peered into the cracked mirror over the cash register that allowed me to watch the bar when I had my back turned; she poked a few stray wisps of hair back into her braid.

Keeping our specialized clientele happy without sending them into a drunken frenzy was difficult at times. I strained to get a look at Amanda's hightop couple, two women who were red-faced with laughter. One of them had dropped something under the table and, after retrieving it, was having trouble getting her ass back up onto her chair. They were verging on sloppy drunk, so I made a mental note to cut them off. Still, my money was on the obnoxiously loud group at booth three.

Amanda waited while I constructed the four-person Scorpion Bowl from brandy, two kinds of rum, and fresh juices. When no one was looking, I smuggled in a few drops of a tincture derived from damiana leaf, one of my medicinals that I kept stashed away in a hidden compartment behind the bar. Most of these were brewed from basic folk recipes, steeped herbs and macerated roots. They soothed nerves, calmed anger, or sobered the mind. Nothing earth-shattering. Well, mostly . . .

A few were intensified with magick. Spells in liquid form, I guess you might say. Just as perfume smells different in the bottle than on a person's skin, magical medicinals react with body chemistry and produce unique results; the same medicinal that creates a mildly lethargic feeling in one person might put someone else in deep sleep. Sometimes I had to experiment to find the right one for the job. The one I was using now, the damianatha, has a calming effect that usually wears off pretty fast; I often use it to quell potential bar fights.

I didn't feel guilty about dosing people without their permission. I had a business to protect, and the sign at the entrance—marked with the two interlocking circles that formed a Nox symbol, identifying us as a demon-friendly establishment—*did* clearly say ENTER AT YOUR OWN RISK.

After putting away the damianatha, I strained the enhanced concoction into a serving bowl. Inside the ceramic volcano that rose up from the center, I floated a sugar cube soaked in 151-proof rum on top of an orange slice. When we first opened Tambuku, I'd light the Scorpion Bowls right there at the bar, until Amanda once caught her hair on fire during the trek to the table. Now I make her light it herself once she gets there. Not as dramatic, but much safer.

"Almost time for the show," Amanda noted as she searched her pockets for a lighter. "I think there's only that one table of savages to get rid of before it starts. Can you check?"

Savages. Slang for humans who didn't believe in anything paranormal . . . which would be *most* humans. Savages didn't believe in magick, and they certainly didn't believe that a small but growing group of the population was made up of demons.

I double-checked to make sure Amanda was right about the lone table of savages, and she was. Just a group of women dressed in corporate-gray suits, probably trying out the "wacky" tiki bar down the street from their office. "They'll leave. Shouldn't be an issue." And apart from them, Amanda and I were the only nonsavage humans in the bar. I tossed four extra-long straws into the Scorpion Bowl, and she whisked it away on her tray.

Now, when I say demons, I don't mean big, bad evil creatures with horns and tails and rows of bloodstained teeth.

Don't get me wrong, those kinds of demons exist, safely tucked away on another plane; Æthyric demons can be summoned by talented magicians, such as myself, with the proper rituals and seals. Nevertheless, the Earthbounds that patronized my bar were much lower down on the supernatural food chain.

Apart from their minor demonic abilities, which vary from demon to demon, the only distinguishing feature of an Earthbound demon is a glowing arc of light around the head: a halo.

Yep, that's right. Demons have halos. Everything preternatural does. Not a static, detached ring like you see in religious paintings, but more of a diffused, colorful cloud. Surprised? I might have been, the first time I saw an Earthbound, back in Florida, when I was a kid . . . that is, if I hadn't already seen my own halo in the mirror. I'm not demon. Just different. My conception was kinda weird. Okay, it was *really* weird, but the point is that my parents weren't all that surprised to discover I had a halo; they were just surprised that I could actually *see* it. They couldn't, but that's because humans can't see halos. They are basically color-blind when it comes to detecting preternatural visual markers. But just because you can't see ultraviolet light doesn't mean it's not there.

My small, silver halo didn't *quite* look like the nebulous green and blue halos on the demons who frequented our bar, but it still came in handy; most demons wouldn't normally come near a practicing magician with a ten-foot pole, much less frequent a bar owned by one, but my strange halo granted me a wary trust.

I checked the clock. Almost time for our weekly TV addiction.

After I made a couple of Fog Cutters for another order,

I wound my hair into a twist on top of my head and pinned it in place with a plastic swizzle stick. Then I turned off the tropical exotica bar music—classic Martin Denny—stood on a stool at the end of the bar, and tugged down my snug 1982 Iron Maiden concert T-shirt, a triumphant two-dollar score from the Goodwill down the block.

"Listen up," I yelled across the room as eighty-plus pairs of eyes turned toward me. "It's eleven o'clock. Most of you know what that means here on Thursdays at Tambuku."

"PATROL TIME!" The group reply echoed around the bar, followed by a series of cheers and whoops.

"That's right," I said with a grin after they'd calmed down. "It's *Paranormal Patrol* time. For those of you who aren't familiar with Tambuku's weekly TV ritual, you might want to get out while the gettin's good. Because it's about to be *really* loud in here—" Two whistles and a couple of indistinct shouts interrupted me. "Yeah, like that, only worse, and with lots more profanity. If you want a quiet drink, go across the street to the Sunset Bar. You have now been officially warned."

A respectable round of applause ended my speech. The lone table of savages began gathering their purses and left a tip on their table. Worked every time. As they headed out the door, I climbed down from the bar stool, readied the DVR, and started the show.

When the *Paranormal Patrol* logo moved across the screen, Tambuku's regulars began singing along with the theme music, substituting an alternate, rude set of lyrics. I spotted Amanda and the table busser gleefully joining in and smiled as I cleared away a couple of empty tiki mugs and wiped down the bar. Amanda's laughing couple at the hightop were getting a bit rowdy. Maybe she was right after all; I kept my eye on them.

This week's episode of *Patrol* took place in Charleston, where the intrepid crew of professional hunters—all savages—were investigating the hundred-year-old ghost of a nun. After they set up their equipment, the so-called expert began his introductions to the so-called ghost: "Hello? I'm trying to speak to the ghost of Mary—can you hear me? Give me a sign if you can. I come in peace."

So funny that humans waste money on ion counters, night vision cameras, and all the rest of the junk that purports to "detect" the paranormal. Because halos and other supernatural markers show up plain as day on most modern cameras if you have the right eyes . . . and Tambuku's patrons did. So when a small glowing head poked up over the shoulder of the ghost hunter, our customers began their call-and-response game and all yelled in unison, "*Look behind you, asshole!*" Around the bar, everyone downed a drink in tribute to the first on-screen imp appearance.

Rocky Horror fans had nothing on us.

The ghost seeker's eyes watered as he sat down on an old bed where the ghostly nun was murdered years ago. "Oh, God . . . I think I feel something," he whimpered into the camera. He felt something all right; it was the same imp they filmed the week before in Chicago. Looks like they had themselves a hitchhiker.

Even savages who dismiss most paranormal phenomenon love to entertain the possibility that ghosts exist; too bad they don't. Sorry to burst your bubble, but if you think your house is haunted, it's most likely just everyday, run-of-the-mill imps: small transparent demons that humans can't see. Imps are pretty much harmless, but they're fond of creating minor havoc. Moaning, turning the lights on and off, lowering the temperature of a room, and this was exactly why imps had made the Earthbounds who produced *Paranormal Patrol* very, very rich. Sending a group of unsuspecting and gullible humans down in buildings known to be infested with imps? Damn fine TV.

Everyone in Tambuku was enjoying the imp in this week's episode until the second commercial break; that's when I heard breaking glass. Amanda's laughing couple at the hightop was now kissing. Not them, then. My eyes flicked to the table with the dosed Scorpion Bowl, but they were all staring at the booth behind them. Amanda and I had both been wrong.

"Oh, holy Whore of Babylon." I muted the TV and reached for my caduceus, a carved wooden staff entwined with two snakes and wings at the top. It wasn't some mystical ceremonial object; it was made in China, like, last year. Despite this, it *does* have a real graphite core that conducts energy, and that was the important part. The only ritual objects I use are practical ones. Robes and candles and sacred temple spaces? Forget it. Just useless, bullshit trappings.

Caduceus in hand, I abandoned my post behind the bar and strode in the direction of the offenders. But before I could make it there, a low gasp spread through the crowd and everyone in front of me began backing up.

"Move it." I pushed people out of my way until I made it to the problem table. Broken glass crunched beneath my lowtop sneakers as I approached.

There were three Earthbounds at the booth: Kara and her boyfriend, both regulars, and some other guy I didn't know in a red flannel shirt . . . whom Kara was choking. Well, not choking so much as freezing the skin around his neck. Beneath her hands, a network of blue lines formed on his skin as she screamed, "Motherfucking liar!"

"Did you sleep with him, Kara?" her boyfriend asked, sitting at her side. His face was stroke-red. *For crying out loud, no ambulances tonight*, I thought to myself as the choking victim knocked a ceramic coconut-shaped mug off the table with his flailing arm. It shattered into ragged snow as it hit the floor. The crowd behind me jumped back as an errant ceramic shard ricocheted and pegged me on the arm. It stung like hell.

"Hey!" I yelled, rubbing my injury. "That's handmade. We've only got a few of those mugs left in stock. You're paying for that."

Kara's victim paid no attention to me as two other mugs, the rice cracker bowl, and all the napkins began rising off the table. I'd heard that her boyfriend was telekinetic, and apparently he had a hard time controlling it when he got upset. Awesome.

I double-checked that the bar was still savage free. It was.

"Tell him that I didn't sleep with you! Tell him!" Kara spoke in a frantic, high-pitched voice as the blue lines erupting on his neck began spreading up into his face.

Enough. I gripped my caduceus and struck the floor in front of the booth, right on the triangle point that was painted on the hardwood. It was a binding triangle. There was one under every table in the bar. Risk management.

Eyes closed, I tapped into electrical energy from the bar, reeling it into me with care and precision. Amanda once asked me how magick like this worked. Different spells called for different kinds of magick, but the energy I needed to power a binding like this had to be amplified, or "kindled." The easiest way to think of magical energy—Heka—was to picture it as a wood log in a fireplace. Just as wood burns when you put a match to it, Heka transforms into a more intense energy when it's been kindled by an outside source; electricity was just one of several ways to do that.

As I pulled, the garish tropical-themed lights inside the bar wavered and dimmed. I mumbled a short binding spell and, in one massive push, released the kindled Heka through the caduceus, into the binding triangle.

My stomach lurched like I was riding a roller coaster. Depending on the spell, the accompanying nausea could last for a couple of seconds, or it could make me so sick and exhausted that I'd have trouble standing. Fortunately, this time, it wasn't bad.

When I reopened my eyes, a low moan rose from the crowd behind me. They were impressed, as usual, but I wasn't; the binding triangle glowed with kindled Heka, but it wasn't bright like it should be—it was dull and popped with static. It must've been because of my mood. Whatever. It was working, and that was what mattered. The objects crashed back down on the table, rice crackers scattering everywhere, as the three drunken demons in the booth finally looked up.

"Shit." Kara released the man across the table and dropped her fading blue hands to her side. He fell back into his seat and coughed, reaching for his wounded neck.

"Seriously, Kara, this is the second time this month. I told you last time that if it happened again, I'd ban you from the bar."

A lock of dyed orange hair fell across her cheek. "I didn't mean to get so out of control. Give me another chance. I promise—"

"Please unbind us," her boyfriend pleaded. "It raises my blood pressure and I don't feel so good right now."

Amanda pushed her way through the crowd. "Wait! They started a tab. They owe us, hold on." She fumbled in her pocket, then flipped through several scraps of wrinkled paper until she found the right one. "Sixty-three dollars and forty cents. Oh, and Kara didn't tip me last week when she came in." She clicked her tongue at Kara and winked. "Don't think I didn't notice."

"There's also the broken barware," I noted.

"Here!" Kara's boyfriend pulled out a hundred-dollar bill. "Please, unbind us now."

As Amanda snatched up the money, her foot crossed the triangle and inadvertently broke the binding spell. Kara's boyfriend slumped to the table, heaving, as the other two gasped in relief.

"Oops, sorry, Cady." Amanda winced at the dead triangle as she pocketed the money.

A table busser appeared with a broom. I scanned the crowd for one of our regulars and quickly spotted him. Bob was a short Earthbound in his thirties with dark, slicked-back hair and a lazy eye. He was dressed in his usual attire, a Hawaiian printed shirt with repeating hula girls. Unlike half the people in the bar, Bob's demonic ability was useful. He was a healer. Not a miraculous one, but good in a pinch. He also had a thing for me and would probably set himself on fire if asked.

"Hey Bob," I called out. "Will you take a look at that guy's neck? Make sure he's okay."

"No problem." Bob trotted off behind the wounded man, who was making a beeline toward the door along with Kara's boyfriend.

"Am I banned?" Kara asked as she scooted out of the booth.

"You're banned on Thursday nights for the next month. No *Paranormal Patrol*."

Her face fell, but she nodded in acceptance and made a drunken attempt at a short curtsy as she left, her blue hands now fully reverted to their normal color.

Low whispers hummed around the bar as the crowd dispersed and people returned to their seats. Someone asked if I could rewind *Patrol*; we'd missed several minutes during the ruckus.

After I made my way back behind the bar, I picked up the remote and started to hit rewind when I noticed what was on the screen and froze. A special news report had interrupted the program. I took it off mute and ignored the murmured complaints about another delay in the evening's festivities. A petite Latina reporter spoke into a microphone beneath a red umbrella.

"I repeat, local authorities here in Dallas are trying to confirm whether the couple in the parking garage are indeed the notorious serial killers, Enola and Alexander Duval, who made international headlines when they were charged with the deaths of three rival occultists seven years ago, known collectively as the Black Lodge slayings. The footage we're about to show you was just released to us, taken this morning from a gas station near the airport."

A clip from the surveillance video played. Clear as day, there were my parents getting into an SUV. What the hell were they thinking? They weren't supposed to be in the States; they hadn't been here in years.

Right after we faked our deaths and went into hiding, I saw them every few months. Then a few months turned into a year, and a year into three. I didn't think about them much, unless I heard their names mentioned in some true-crime-exposé rerun on basic cable.

The reporter continued. "The fact that the killers are still alive and in Texas after all these years is astonishing. There's speculation that their daughter, also a member of their former occult order, could still be alive too. Now, back to the studio for Tom's commentary. Tom?"

I stood stiff as a soldier and stared at the screen. I was dimly aware that my hands were trembling. My vision tunneled, then everything went black.

2

When I came to, I lay on the floor inside the Tambuku office looking at two pairs of feet; one was wearing purple sneakers . . . Amanda. The other feet were bare and belonged to my business partner, Kar Yee. She never wore shoes at work. She would begrudgingly put them on if forced to meander past the bar, but that was her limit. No threat of broken glass and spills or health department requirements would sway her; she even drove her car without shoes.

The two women were arguing. Amanda was trying to convince Kar Yee that she could stand in for me at the bar, begging her not to call in a replacement bartender.

"I won't screw anything up," Amanda promised.

"You're too slow mixing drinks," Kar Yee said. "*Too. Slow.* Do you know why? You talk too much." A petite Chinese Earthbound, Kar Yee had perfect skin, catlike eyes, and a chin-length bob with severe, straight bangs. Two long, thin locks of hair framed her face, several inches longer than the rest of her bob, and she sculpted these into sharp points that dangled to her shoulders. All of this was surrounded by a stunning aqua-blue halo.

I cracked my neck and pushed myself up off the floor as

the two of them continued to squabble. "Give me a few minutes, then I can finish my shift."

"Oh, you're awake," Kar Yee noted without emotion.

Amanda groped my clammy forehead. "Are you okay? What happened? Are you sick?"

"I'm fine," I said, pushing her hand away. Then I remembered what caused the blackout. A pang of worry tightened my chest. "I mean, uh, yeah. Probably getting sick, that's all."

"You want me to mix drinks for a few minutes?" Amanda asked me. "Mika can handle my tables."

Kar Yee made a perturbed noise and folded her arms across her slender chest. Amanda often played us like a mom and dad. If one said no, she'd corner the other to get the answer that she wanted. Still, running the back office was Kar Yee's responsibility; managing the bar and our small staff was mine. My call, not hers, and I didn't feel like wrangling someone else to come in and sub for me on their night off.

"Who's watching the bar?" I asked.

"Mika, and Bob's helping her guard the cash register. Can I mix drinks? Please? I won't touch your potions this time, I swear."

"They aren't potions . . ." Well, technically that's exactly what they were, but whatever. "Ugh. Fine. Go. Don't let people talk you into adding extra shots without paying. Buzz if you need help."

"Thanks, Cady!"

Amanda sprang away as Kar Yee handed me a glass of water and leaned against her desk.

"What's really wrong?" she asked after Amanda was gone. "You look like shit. Your halo is all . . . bleh." She made a sour face and wiggled her fingers. "In trouble, maybe? It better not interfere with business. There are two big concerts down the street at the Cypress Club this weekend that are going to keep us slammed."

Kar Yee's no-nonsense way of thinking made her a great business partner, but not a warm-and-fuzzy friend. Most of the time this worked out well for me because she didn't pry into my background too much. Sentimental friends were a liability for someone in my situation.

"It's probably not a big deal. Just something that I need to sort out. Tomorrow's my night off, so hopefully I can take care of it before Saturday."

"Hmph."

Her usual response. It meant, I know you're lying to me, but I'm not asking.

I met Kar Yee at college in Seattle, a year after going into hiding, and right after I had assumed my current identity. Before that, I'd been traveling around the country under several other aliases in an attempt to elude our rival magical organization and any stray FBI investigators with nagging suspicions about my parents' faked deaths.

Kar Yee's parents lived in Hong Kong. She came to the States to study international law, but ditched the law program for a degree in business. During her second year in school, she decided that she didn't want to go back home, so she married an American boy to get her U.S. citizenship, then divorced him after INS lost interest in them. Even though they'd never consummated the sham marriage, her fake husband seemed genuinely upset to see her go.

After college, it was her idea to move to California. Most Earthbounds prefer a Mediterranean climate near a large body of water, which is why there are so many living in our area. (If you want to avoid demons, try the Midwest—virtually demon free, at least from what I've heard.)

Once we got to California, it was my idea to start up the tiki bar. We traveled up and down the northern coast for almost a month before we settled on the city of Morella. Bordering the Big Sur region, Morella is the fourth largest city in the state, half an hour from the ocean, and a couple hours south of San Francisco, if you drive fast. And there were Earthbounds aplenty here; you can't swing a dead cat without hitting one. The blocks surrounding Tambuku are lined with demon-friendly businesses. So when we found this location for lease—half underground, the entrance at the foot of a short flight of cement steps down from the sidewalk—we knew it was perfect. We'd been in business for almost two years, a success from day one.

Amanda's voice came through the speakerphone on Kar Yee's desk. "Uh, Arcadia? Is there more white rum out here somewhere? I kinda tipped over the bottle you were using and I can't find—oh wait. Never mind. Crap. A big group of people just came in the door." A loud chorus from the bar rattled the speaker before she hung up. *Paranormal Patrol* was still going strong.

"Can you help her?" I gave Kar Yee a pleading look. "I need a few minutes alone to make a phone call."

She shot me a suspicious look, then nodded silently and complied, closing the door behind her. I locked it before pushing up the sleeve of my T-shirt to reveal a raised design on the inside of my arm, between my wrist and elbow.

Inked in white with a thick needle, the tattoo isn't noticeable unless you're looking hard—a long, oval Egyptian *cartouche* that contains seven hidden sigils, which I can identify like Braille from the scarring. Most of them are protective wards: instant, ACME-style spells for protection and stealth. Having them permanently affixed to my skin allows me to avoid hand-drawing the symbols in a pinch and could mean the difference between life or death . . . or between staying hidden and being caught.

One of the symbols, though, contains a homing sigil for my personal guardian, an Æthyric messenger spirit that can be called for information or help. Known as Hermeneus entities, these beings are coveted by magicians. To petition their aid, you have to woo them in a special ritual. If one of them takes a liking to you, it might offer up its services—either a onetime deal or a more permanent situation, in which they form a link to your Heka signature, something as unique to each person as a fingerprint.

Once linked to you, a guardian will be your loyal eyes and ears on the Æthyric plane, able to glean bits of hidden knowledge, warn about Æthyric disturbances, and monitor spirits who are linked to other magicians. The magician's equivalent of the witch's familiar.

These Hermeneus spirits don't physically cross over from the Æthyr to our plane. Instead, they use Heka to transmit a kind of noncorporeal hologram of themselves. Because of this, they aren't much use for earthly tasks. All they can really do here is relay information from one magician to another. Before the phone was invented, this was probably helpful, but now? Not so much.

Unlike the binding triangle I'd just powered up in the bar, my guardian's homing sigil didn't need to be charged with Heka that had been kindled with electrical energy. It required a more passive, personal energy gained from bodily fluids. Might sound a little odd, but magicians have used fluids to charge spells for centuries: blood, saliva, sexual fluids, tears. Inside all of these is raw, unkindled Heka. The amount of raw Heka varies by fluid type—blood has more Heka than saliva, for example—and it also varies person to person. Not that there's some lab test available to verify this, but I was pretty sure that my blood had a hell of a lot more Heka than the average person's. And this definitely gave me an advantage, magically speaking. Just as anybody can learn how to draw, anybody can learn to do magick; however, someone who lacks natural artistic talent might take twice as long to master the basics. And let's face it: that person might eventually learn to pull off a decent landscape, but they'll probably never be Michelangelo.

Ready to call my guardian, I stuck my finger in my mouth, extracted a small amount of Heka-rich saliva, then wiped it on my guardian's sigil. "Priya," I whispered. "Come to me."

A familiar wave of nausea rolled through my stomach. The air in front of me shuddered, and a wispy, glowing figure pulsed into view. Like other Hermeneus spirits, Priya has a birdlike head and a unisex body, too rugged to be female, too soft to be male.

Priya nodded at me, bending at the waist. *Command me*, it said inside my head.

"My parents are in trouble. They've been spotted by authorities in Texas and are no longer hidden. The Luxe Order will soon know that they're still alive, if their wards haven't already alerted them. Contact my parents' guardians in the Æthyr and relay this message. Wait for a response. I need to know what they want me to do to help. Go."

Priya nodded and disappeared.

My guardian was my solitary link to my parents. Only in an emergency was I supposed to send it out to contact their guardians; I thought this qualified.

When I sent Priya out on these errands, the return time

varied. Sometimes the spirit would come back to me with a report after a few minutes, sometimes several hours later, I could never tell. So I plopped down on Kar Yee's chair and hoped it would be a short trip.

Opening one of the desk drawers, I reached toward the back until my fingers skimmed a stash of hand-rolled valrivia cigarettes. Calming like nicotine, but with a mild euphoric kick, valrivia doesn't trash your lungs the way tobacco does and is about as addictive as caffeine. Half the demon population has a valrivia habit. I picked up mine from Kar Yee in college. I'd already smoked two that day—my self-imposed limit—but under the circumstances, I thought I deserved another. I dug a lighter out of my jeans pocket and lit up.

It was hard for me to believe that it had been seven years since the so-called Black Lodge slayings had thrust my parents into the public spotlight, making them villains in the lead story of every news organization, half a dozen true crime novels, and God only knows how many television investigative reports. They even got their own trading cards, part of a collectible set of serial killer profile cards that included Charles Manson and John Wayne Gacy. Classy.

Their sensational story was everything that the American public craved: gory murders, witchy ritual occultism, and a Bonnie and Clyde escape from the law with their daughter that ended tragically in their deaths.

Only, the three of us weren't dead, and my parents weren't guilty.

A repeat of an *American Killers* episode played on the muted television screen on the desk. It had been only a few hours since they'd been spotted, and already the stations were rearranging their programming to capitalize on the news story.

I turned off the television in disgust and took a few drags off my cigarette before my guardian reappeared.

May I show myself? Priya's voice inquired in my head.

"Yes." I crushed the remainder of the cig into a chipped ashtray shaped like a monkey head.

Priya's form took shape again in front of me. *Enola's guardian confirms that they are aware of the situation. The Luxe Order will try to hunt you down. She suggests you ward yourself. She will contact us when they are safe, and will give you a place and time to meet them. She also said it would be unwise to pursue any other communication with them at this time. It's too dangerous.*

After years of little to no contact with my family, I was finally going to see them again? My heart fluttered, but I was still puzzled. "Why did they come into the States without warning me?"

I do not know. Enola's guardian was closemouthed.

I exhaled in frustration. "Was there anything else?"

Your father's guardian refused my request to communicate.

"They're probably just being cautious. The Luxe Order has been able to intercept communication between guardians in the past."

Yes, it would be logical for your parents to be heavily warded at this time.

A I tried to make sense of everything I caught myself chewing my fingernails; all of them were down to the quick, so not much left to bite. I wondered if the local branch of our magical order knew more than my parents were saying; it wouldn't hurt to check with them.

Do you require anything else?

"Just keep your eyes open in the Æthyr and let me know if you see anything unusual."

Priya nodded and began fading. Before the spirt vanished, it added, *Be careful.*

Right. And now I had to walk back out into the busy bar and pretend that I really was Arcadia Bell, bar owner. Not the daughter of two alleged serial killers being hunted down by the FBI. For the first time in years, I was genuinely afraid that I couldn't keep up the lie.

3

After my excruciatingly long shift at the bar ended, I spent the remainder of the night holed up in my house, watching for additional news reports and waiting for my local magical lodge to open its doors the next morning. They officially opened at nine, but sometime around seven I became impatient.

Morning traffic made a fifteen-minute drive twice as long and strained my already frazzled nerves. I parked my gunmetal gray Jetta near a warehouse two blocks away from the lodge in an area called Wildewood Park, an eclectic neighborhood composed of abandoned factories and a mixture of low- to middle-income ranch houses built in the 1960s.

Though I felt pretty confident about the security of my current identity and didn't believe I was in immediate danger of being tracked down by the Luxe, walking into the local lodge in broad daylight made me slightly paranoid. For all I knew, people could be staking it out. I mumbled a quick spell and charged one of the sigils on my arm to further obscure my identity, just to be safe. I tugged my purse higher up on my shoulder after the nausea subsided, then slunk down the cracked sidewalk.

Ekklesia Eleusia, or E∴E∴ as it is known in the magical community, is an occult order founded in the late twelfth century in France, which makes it the longest-running esoteric society in the world. Like every other order, it's a nonprofit, tax-exempt organization, and dedicated to the "Study, Knowledge, and Advancement of the Arcane Arts." Kinda like Hogwarts, only with fewer wands and more nudity.

The order moved its operational headquarters from Europe to the States in the early twentieth century, along with two other occult orders. There were a couple thousand E∴E∴ members scattered around a handful of U.S. lodges. The main lodge in Florida, where I grew up, was impressive; the local lodge here in Morella is not. Fewer than a hundred members attended regular ritual services and classes here.

The morning sun was blinding as I stepped out of early-autumn shadows and made my way to the side door of the lodge. Two scraggly, underwatered palm trees flanked the entrance. I rang the doorbell and noticed a couple of rental cars in the back parking lot. This made me a little nervous, but before I could think about it too much, a short man with cropped blond hair opened the door: the Grandmaster's assistant. He gave me a nasty little smile as he greeted me by my birth name.

"Soror Seléne, my . . . *heart* expands in your presence."

I rolled my eyes and begrudged a formal acknowledgment. "Frater Kantor."

"You look as if you didn't get much sleep either last night, Soror. Too bad we couldn't have stayed up together." His eyes lingered over my breasts.

"That will never, ever happen, Frater."

"A shame. With my brains and your bloodline . . ."

Ah, yes. My freaking bloodline. My order called me a

Moonchild. Heralded as a kind of saint, I was conceived during an elaborate series of secret magical sex rituals between my parents. At best, the expected result of these rituals was to create a new godlike being, something between Jesus and *Rosemary's Baby*. At worst, it was just selective esoteric breeding between two powerful and once-respected magicians.

Apart from my preternatural vision, the small silver halo—that nobody but me and Earthbounds could see—and an innate knack for kindling Heka, I was pretty sure the rest of it was a crock of shit. Still, before the Black Lodge slayings changed everything, the occult community was buzzing about my potential. I was eighteen and just coming into my abilities. I was a big deal. Now only a handful of trusted people in my organization acknowledged my existence; how the mighty have fallen.

"Speaking of my bloodline, Frater Kantor, if you continue to harass me every time I come to the Morella Lodge, I'm going to pull rank and get you kicked out of the damn order."

"My apologies, Soror." He couldn't have meant it less. "Perhaps you'll be happy to know that Caliph Superior from the Florida lodge is inside waiting for you."

The rental cars outside . . . this was serious. I hadn't seen Caliph Superior in person since I'd gone into hiding. We'd only communicated by phone and email, occasionally through our guardians.

I pushed Frater Kantor aside and walked into the lodge, the heels of my boots clicking on the tiled floor in the darkened, cool hallway. Frater Kantor locked the outside door, then hurried to get in front of me as I made it to the back offices. Before he could announce me, the local Grandmaster stood up. But I couldn't have cared less about her; it was the man behind her I wanted to see.

"Seléne, my darling," he said. "It's so good to see you again."

A swell of emotion caught me by surprise at the sight of him. It took me a moment to answer. "Godfather."

He held out his arms to me. I stepped forward into his embrace allowed him to kiss me, once on each cheek. He smelled familiar and earthy. Safe.

Caliph Superior was in his early seventies. His once long, white hair was now short and thinning. Apart from wearing a large gold ring bearing an engraved unicursal hexagram, you wouldn't have a clue that he was the leader of one of the most powerful magical organizations in the Western world. In his expensive suit, he looked more like a retired lawyer or someone's rich grandfather—both of which he was. He had seven children by four different women, and a slew of grand-children, all of whom could claim a lineage extending back to beginnings of the order. One of them would take over as leader when he died.

"Soror Yolanda," I said, nodding my head toward the Grandmaster. She nodded back and motioned for me to take a seat in a cracked leather armchair that was grouped with several others in front of an unlit fireplace. A painting of a Sumerian war goddess hung above the mantel between a William Blake print and an engraving of John Dee and Edward Kelley evoking a spirit. Caliph Superior sat down next to me while the Grandmaster shooed away her wormy assistant.

"I can't believe how much you've changed," Caliph Superior said. "To see you in person instead of photos . . . ah, my goddaughter became a woman." His eyes glazed over with emotion as he reached to touch my face.

"You cut your hair." I smiled at him while brushing away a stray tear before it could fall.

"You grew yours out. It's lovely."

The last time I'd seen him, my hair was cropped short. Now it fell to the middle of my back. Naturally a dark brunette, I started bleaching the underside white-blond; Kar Yee said it made me look like Pepé Le Pew's girlfriend.

"Contacts?" he asked.

"Yes." Blues were now brown.

He sighed and withdrew his hand.

When the three of us were alone, the Grandmaster sat in front of us and gave me a grave look. An attractive woman in her fifties, she had severe, thin lips that seemed out of place on an otherwise round face and plump body. I hadn't had much contact with her since I'd moved to Morella two years ago; I did my best to avoid the E∴E∴ in my new life.

"What's going on? Why wasn't I informed that my parents were coming to the States?" I looked between the two of them. Caliph Superior spoke first.

"We didn't inform you because we ourselves didn't know."

"They haven't contacted you?"

He shook his head. "No. Nothing has changed. You know that when all of you went into hiding I agreed not to contact your parents, even through our guardians. As far as the authorities go, I'm sure Elona and Alex have hidden themselves well by now. There's no way to authenticate their identity on the video footage. The FBI will give a cursory search, then move on to something more important when the scandal dies down. You shouldn't worry about that."

I nodded. He was probably right.

"Right now," he added, "we have bigger problems than the FBI."

"Luxe," I said in a low voice. "They know, don't they?"

Based out of San Diego, the Luxe Order was a rival occult organization that boasted a membership of five thousand. Though the E∴E∴ could claim only about two thousand members, we were older and more elite. The two organizations were the largest and most respected of all the international esoteric orders, but often butted heads on philosophy and had a long history of fighting—with both public lawsuits and private magical sabotage. So when the Luxe leader pointed the finger at my parents and cried "killers," no one in the E∴E∴ was surprised; Luxe would do anything to discredit us.

The Grandmaster crossed her legs and answered. "All the organizations know, but Luxe has taken the lead on this, as usual. Your parents will have to do some deft maneuvering to get away from their spies . . . but that's not why we want to talk to you."

"It's not?"

Caliph Superior put his hand on top of mine. "Seléne, darling, the Luxe head is demanding that we turn your parents over to them for retribution."

"Retribution? For crimes they didn't commit?"

"Yes, but that's of no consequence at this point. It took us a long time to negotiate and make peace with all the other orders after the killings—especially Luxe. Now that they know we lied to them about your parents being dead, they've banded together with the lower orders and they've all agreed that they want compensation for their . . . losses."

"Losses? What did Luxe lose? No one was even killed in their order. And since when do any of the orders band together for anything?"

"Since now, I suppose. Luxe is the biggest and strongest, so they are the ones chosen by the smaller orders to flex

muscle. They've issued us a mandate. We have two weeks
to hand over your parents to the Luxe Order in a special
council they are arranging, or they are declaring magical war
against us."

My chest tightened. Occult societies have a tendency to
operate outside the law. I hadn't lived through a magical war
myself, but I'd read accounts of past conflicts. Each order has
its own military of sorts, an elite group of magicians proficient
in summoning and controlling godforms and Æthyric elder
demons—the big, bad immortal kind. Ancient demons that
could be bound to kill on command . . . like the demon that
someone had summoned seven years ago, that killed the three
rival magicians, whose deaths were pinned on my parents.

The Black Lodge slayings consisted of three separate
murders that occurred over six weeks' time. The first killing
was the head of a small hermetic order in England. The second was the head of a similar order in Boston, and the third
was the head of a slightly larger order based in Portland.

The fourth and last attempted murder of the leader of the
Luxe Order, occurred in San Diego. Only, that attempt failed.

"Luxe has given us one other option," the Grandmaster
said as she toyed with a small charm that dangled from a long
silver chain around her neck.

"Yes?" I prompted.

"Give you up as payment for your parents' alleged sins."

Alarmed, I stiffened and straightened in my seat.

"Darling, we would never do that," Caliph Superior assured me, cutting his eyes at the Grandmaster. "You're far too
valuable to our organization."

"Is that the only reason?" My voice was more acerbic than
I intended.

"Of course not," he replied with a calm tenderness. "I

love you as if you were my own flesh and blood. I would give up your parents before I—"

"Caliph!"

"Calm down, child. I'm not suggesting that we do that, either, for the time being."

"What are you suggesting?"

Caliph Superior held up one finger against his lips then looked at the Grandmaster and made a circular gesture. She got up from her seat and picked up a worn piece of paper off her desk. I recognized the silencing ward drawn on it as she carried it over to the door. Setting it on the floor, she pulled a small lancet out of her pocket, pricked her finger, and squeezed out a single drop of blood onto the spell.

She could have used saliva; whatever they were going to tell me, they really didn't want anyone else to hear. She lost her balance for a second, then steadied herself. Probably had been doing warding spells all night and needed a rest.

When she'd finished charging the ward, she returned to us and sat down.

"Listen well," the caliph warned. "Your parents believe that the demon that killed the three Luxe mages was very, very old. Primordial. As you know, they've been trying to identify it for years. We've long ago exhausted our own library and resources trying to help them find it."

I crossed my arms in front of me as a resentful anger bubbled to the surface. "I offered to help summon it years ago, but they always refused to give me any details about the demon. I understand their being overprotective of a young girl, but I'm not a teenager anymore."

"Yes, I know that," the caliph said with a gentle smile. "To be honest, all we have ourselves is a description of the demon and a knowledge of how he killed the victims. It's not much to go on, but if we could find new resources, perhaps we could locate the exact class of demon and, more important, the summoning name."

Hell, yeah, it was more important. There are a finite number of seals used for summoning Æthyric demons to earth. Each type of demon—Jinn, Kerub, Shedu, Oni, Asura, et cetera—requires a seal specific to its class. The variable is the addition of the demon's name. Without the name, the demon can't be summoned.

"And if you could find the demon's name," the Grandmaster added, "then, with your summoning abilities, you could certainly control him, and bind him in front of the Luxe council. Like every other demon, he can be forced—"

"To tell the truth," I finished. "Yes, I'm well aware of the reason they've been searching for this demon all these years." It would be the perfect witness to the murders. If he could be found and bound, he would tell everyone who really summoned and commanded him to kill those three people. It would exonerate my parents. Problem was, nobody knew what demon they were looking for. "How can we find the demon's class and name in two weeks, when you've been working on it for years?"

"There is nothing more that I can do personally, but perhaps there is something *you* can do. We've protected you from this for too long. Like you said, you're an adult now, and a powerful mage. I know you've been studying and working with other magicians outside the order—"

"What else could I do?" I snapped, knowing this was prohibited.

"You did what you had to. But if I'm guessing correctly, I think you may have contacts and sources that could bring a fresh perspective to the hunt."

My brain began firing as I assembled a short list of options I could try. "If you can give me some more details about the demon in question, maybe."

"Well, my dear, 'maybe' is all we have right now. If the demon can't be identified conclusively . . ."

"Then what?" I challenged.

"Then," he replied after a long sigh, "we're going to have to comply with the Luxe Order's mandate and give up your parents."

A strangled protest got caught in my throat.

"I know this is hard to hear, but we really don't have another choice. We can't afford a war right now. Times have changed, society is sharper and smarter than it was a hundred years ago. The savages won't look the other way if more people are killed, and there's been too much harsh light shed on our organization over the murders as it is. A magical war could mean the end of the E∴E∴ and, as its leader, I can't allow that to happen."

I heard what he was saying, but I couldn't accept it. We argued for several minutes, going around in circles, until I acquiesced and shut up. He gave me the description of the demon and what little information he had on the seal; it wasn't much to go on.

"This is happening so fast." I felt like I was being sucked into a whirlpool with no chance of escape.

He grasped my hands together in my lap. "If there's anyone to blame in this, you can point the finger at me. Your parents insisted on keeping you out of this mess, but I should have fought them. Even now, I'm sure they wouldn't approve of my asking you to do this for them."

"Well, since no one can contact them right now, I guess they don't get a vote."

"Darling, you're a better magician than either one of them—even better than me, and that's the truth. Maybe that's due to your special conception, but even without it, I know in my heart that you're strong. If anyone can help them, it's you."

I stared at the fireplace, hearing his words, but inwardly making plans.

"Do you have a place in mind that you can begin your search?" the caliph asked. For the first time since I'd arrived, I noticed a little worry in his face and wondered if he really believed that I could do this.

"Yes," I answered with as much certainty as I could muster.

In the middle of the chaos swirling around in my head, one local resource stood above everyone else who might help me, someone that no member of the E∴E∴ or any other magical order would ever consider asking, because of centuries-old prejudices and mistrust: a retired priest. One who wasn't a savage . . . or even human, for that matter.

4

Father Carrow lived down the street from me. I met him a year or so ago when he was walking his dog past my house. Unfortunately, at the time I was in the middle of binding some imps for my elderly Earthbound neighbor. But instead of freaking out and calling the cops on us or damning me to hell, Father Carrow was quite interested in what I was doing. And I was quite interested in *him*, because he was the first Earthbound priest I'd ever met. We struck up a fast, if not odd, friendship.

It had been ten years since he'd retired from the priesthood. Back in his heyday, he spent a good bit of time studying demons, from both religious and ancestral angles. He definitely had a few personal ideas about the subject that weren't exactly church-sanctioned. But he never had a problem distinguishing what his faith labeled "devils" from demons, and he was comfortable with his spirituality and his place in the world. And maybe that's why I trusted him. He didn't know my real identity, of course—no one did—but he knew I was different, and he was okay with that, because he was different too.

I called Father Carrow after my meeting with the caliph

and told him that I urgently needed to get my hands on some rare books that would have descriptions and names of primordial Æthyric demons. Just as I'd hoped, he knew someone who might help: a former demonologist who lived nearby in Amanda's beach town, and who was able to meet with us that afternoon.

After a quick lunch, I picked up Father Carrow and we headed out to La Sirena for our meeting. "So, what's this guy's name again?" I asked after we'd merged onto the highway leading to the coast.

"Lon Butler. A trustworthy fellow, but he's not chatty. He was a little reluctant to meet you, so I had to tell him that you practiced the dark arts."

I groaned and shot him a dirty look. "I'm not a black magician and you know it. I don't worship the devil or sacrifice animals, nor do I molest children . . . which is more than you can say about some of your colleagues."

He muttered something under his breath that sounded more like a curse than a prayer. "You said this was important. I had to hook him somehow or he wouldn't have come. He prefers to keep to himself."

Great. Probably some antisocial religious hermit.

Father Carrow's fingers straightened the band on the black fedora that he was holding in his lap. He always wore a hat, which I often told him was a shame; it covered up a nice head of thick, gray hair that matched his eyes. But no hat could cover up his halo, thankfully, which was a delicate pale cornflower blue.

"So," I said, "this Lon Butler studied demonology like you did, but he didn't become a priest. Why?"

"He was kicked out of the seminary a year into his program. A scandal. And it didn't involve molestation, before you're tempted to go there again. He's a famous photographer now. I'm surprised you haven't heard of him."

I sped up when a car tried to pass us on the two-lane highway, but they got around anyway. "Photographer? Nope, can't say that I have, but I want to hear more about this salacious scandal. What did he do?"

"The records are sealed."

"Really?" This piqued my interest. "Maybe it involved a woman. Oh, maybe even a nun—ooh! Wouldn't *that* be scandalous?"

"Indeed, but no. I'm afraid you'll have to ask him yourself. It's not my place to gossip about another man's troubles. Or a woman's." He glanced at my halo to hammer home his point. Well taken. How could I ask him to spill someone else's secrets but keep mine?

He paused for a moment, then cleared his throat. "However, what I *can* tell you is a bit of information that's public knowledge. Several old books went missing from the seminary after his dismissal. They were on loan from the Vatican— very rare. The church had no proof that he was to blame, and he denied that he had anything to do with them going missing. Still does."

"Do you think he's lying?"

"Not sure, he's . . . hard to read. A good poker face."

"Were they goetias, the books that went missing?" Goetias were my primary focus for researching what I needed to summon my demon witness. They're archaic demonic encyclopedias that usually feature crude drawings of Æthyric demons, along with a list of their abilities, summoning names, classification seals, and any problems that previous summoners had uncovered when dealing with them.

"Bingo. That's why he may be your guy. One of the

goetias should have never been sent out on loan. No other known copy exists. It could fetch hundreds of thousands of dollars—possibly more—from the right buyer. The content inside the book is listed as being extremely unusual, so I'm guessing it may contain listings of Æthyric demons not found in other books."

I must admit, I got a little excited about this bit of information; I had a thing for rare occult books, and with the pressing matter of my parents' lives on the line, that made it even more enticing.

Father Carrow didn't offer much more about the scandalous Lon Butler, and after the thirty-minute drive, I was starting to lose the caffeine buzz I'd pumped myself up with at lunch. I needed sleep or a strong cup of coffee. But when we finally made it to the small beach town, I got a second wind.

La Sirena is a strange place. Only a few thousand people live there, half of whom are bohemian artists; the other half has money, and lots of it. The heart of the small town includes several square blocks of buildings with Hansel and Gretel fairy-tale exteriors, known collectively as the Village. None of the buildings have addresses, just names. There also are no streetlights, and neon signs are prohibited. The sidewalks are irregular due to the abundance of beautiful Monterey cypress trees lining the cobblestone streets, whose gnarled roots have pushed the pavement up.

If you're in the market for art, the Village contains a wealth of shops and galleries that sell paintings and ceramics from local artists. Between these, a plethora of restaurants and cafés dot the winding streets, along with quaint old-fashioned candy stores. And once you've had your fill of shopping and seafood, the rocky beach is only a few blocks away.

Father Carrow and I arrived at a small coffee shop in the

Village several minutes before our designated meeting time, so we ordered inside—quad espresso for me, tea for him—and staked out a shady table in the back of a tree-filled courtyard at the side of the shop.

When Lon Butler rounded the corner and raised his hand to us, I was taken aback; he was not what I expected. I stood up from the table when Father Carrow made the introductions.

"Lon, this is Arcadia Bell. Cady, meet Lon Butler."

Tall and lean, the man looked to be in his forties. Wavy, light brown hair fell to the tops of his shoulders and was neatly tucked behind his ears. A slender mustache trailed around his mouth and down his chin, matching the patch of hair below the center of his bottom lip. He reminded me of a pirate. A very attractive one.

He was also an Earthbound.

"Mr. Butler," I said as he offered his hand to shake. I took it, and tried not to squint too hard at his halo. Usually Earthbound halos are green or blue, but his was unusual—green near his head, changing to gold toward the outer edge, with small, shimmery bits suspended inside like glitter in a souvenir snow globe.

"Just Lon is fine," he replied in a low monotone.

I stopped staring at his halo, only to find his own eyes fixed above my head. When Earthbounds first meet me and see my small silver halo, they're usually wary or nervous. He wasn't. Matching my gaze, bold and direct, he discretely lifted one eyebrow.

"I think you'll both find," Father Carrow said with a kind smile, "that the three of us have some concerns that intersect. Isn't it wonderful when we can learn something new?"

Wonderful? I wasn't sure about that. But it was certainly

compelling. I wondered if Lon was the reason that Father Carrow had never pressed me too hard about the origins of my silver halo. Next to his, mine seemed almost pedestrian.

After Lon let go of my hand, I realized we'd been shaking far too long. My palms were hot and sweaty; I wiped them on my jeans as I sat down. Instead of taking the more convenient chair across the table, Lon sat in the empty seat next to me. A little too close. I didn't like that.

"I'm afraid Cady isn't a photography aficionado," Father Carrow said as he pulled his chair closer to the table. "She owns a bar back in Morella. It's got an interesting reputation."

Lon's eyes darted to mine, but he didn't say anything. Tambuku Tiki Lounge wasn't the only demon-friendly bar in Morella. Okay, maybe it was the only one with binding magick being used, but still, I doubted he'd heard of it way out here, and I *definitely* would have remembered seeing him in my bar.

I wrapped my hands around my coffee cup. "I didn't think you'd be . . ." What? Another Earthbound, like Father Carrow? The first person I'd ever met with a halo weirder than mine? So good-looking? "So young," I finished.

"You either." His eyes trailed away as he pulled a silver cigarette case out of his denim jacket pocket.

Unsure whether that was a barb or not, I tried to keep my face blank to mimic his. He held out the open cigarette case in offering—valrivia. Its pungent, earthy scent was inviting. I hesitated, then gave in and took a skinny cigarette. He offered the case to Father Carrow with an inquiring chin nod.

"No, no," Father Carrow said with a shake of his head.

"I've told you before, it doesn't get you stoned. It's just calming. I don't think God would count it as a sin," I teased.

"You're probably right, but I just don't understand the

attraction." He waved the case away. "I have trouble staying awake as it is at my age—I don't need anything to make me calmer."

I leaned forward while Lon flicked a sleek, engraved metal lighter for me. His hands were tan and muscular. From that and the golden strands of hair at his crown, I assumed he spent a lot of time outside. Maybe for his job. I scrutinized him while he exchanged a few pleasantries with Father Carrow. He had a reserved, proud look about him. Long, hollow cheeks sat between deep-set eyes and an angular jaw. Good bones.

"So," Father Carrow said, getting to the point, "as I explained on the phone, Arcadia is looking for information on a rare Æthyric demon. Tell him what it looks like, dear."

I repeated what the Caliph had told me. "It's an albino demon—white skin and hair, light pink eyes. Four arms, each with long talons. Twice the height of an average human. Long tongue that rolls up like a party favor and hangs outside its mouth, and a large set of spiraling horns."

I took another drag from my cigarette.

"Do you know the class of demon?" His small eyes were narrowed. Distrustful. "I've run across drawings and descriptions of many albinos. It's a congenial pigmentation disorder that could occur in any class. Just like humans."

His flippant attitude irritated me. *Famous photographer*, I thought. *Arrogant bastard.* Even though he was dressed casually in an ink-stained T-shirt and a denim jacket with a tear in the pocket, he was also wearing a wide silver watch on his left wrist that looked expensive. *Snotty, too*, I added to my mental list of his probable sins.

"I don't know the class of demon," I replied with forced patience, "but I do have a little information about the seal." I perched my cigarette on the edge of the wrought-iron table and dug around in my purse until I found a pen and an old envelope that I tore up for paper. After sketching a few characters and letters, I slid the paper over to him and put the cap back on my pen. "I'm not sure how familiar you are with summoning seals, but I know them pretty well, and this symbol here"—I pointed—"narrows it down to about fifty or so classes of demon."

He studied it for a few seconds, then gave it back to me.

"You can keep it," I said.

"No need. I've already memorized it."

Show-off. "Then the only other thing I know is that the demon uses his talons to gut his victims from breastbone to pelvis—rips the torsos open in one, clean swipe."

He gave me a blank look. No emotion whatsoever.

"Can you help her?" Father Carrow asked as he cradled his paper cup filled with hot tea.

"Don't know."

"She's a good gal, Lon. I wouldn't get you involved in this if I didn't trust her."

Lon tilted his head to the side and slowly rolled his cigarette between thumb and index finger. "Why do you need to locate this demon?"

Because my parents' lives depend on it, and maybe mine too. I couldn't say that, though. I ran through several excuses in my head and answered, "I just do. It's important."

"You planning some sort of revenge against someone?"

"Just the opposite."

"What does that mean?"

For God's sake. "The demon . . . has some information that I need."

Lon stared at me for several moments until I became

uncomfortable and had to struggle not to look away. Then he pushed back his chair and got up. "I'll think about it."

"Think about it?" I repeated in disbelief. "I'm asking for your help, Mr. Butler. I'll pay you, if that's what you want."

"It's Lon, like I already told you, and I don't want your money."

"Then what do you want?"

"I just need to think about it."

"Why do you need to think about it?" I asked, thoroughly exasperated by his blasé manner.

"You sound like a parrot, repeating everything I say, Miss Bell." A strange, rather unkind smile attempted to hoist the corners of his mouth, but didn't quite succeed.

Attractive or not, he was pissing me off. I definitely felt insulted at that point, and probably looked it as well.

"It's *Arcadia*, not Miss Bell," I mocked. "And if you want me to beg, you can fucking forget it. I can find someone else to help me." Aware that Father Carrow was displeased by my nasty outburst, I grabbed my purse off the back of my chair and ground out my cigarette on the side of a nearby metal trash can before tossing it inside.

"Can you, now?" Lon's smile was getting bigger. I was furious, but he had a point. My back was against the wall, and I couldn't afford to let my pride get in the way.

I blew out a frustrated breath and attempted to calm down. "No, not really," I admitted. "Will you help me?" I tried to say please, but I just couldn't.

It took him several seconds to answer. "I'll consider it. Whom should I contact?" His eyes flicked between the two of us.

"Cady," Father Carrow said gently, "why don't you give him your number, dear?"

I grumbled and dug the pen back out of my purse, then scribbled my cell number on the back of the torn envelope paper that I'd tried to give him earlier. We locked gazes as I stiffly offered it to him again; he took it without looking at it—just stuck the paper under the flap of the torn breast pocket of his jacket, valrivia cigarette dangling between his lips.

"I'll be in touch either way. After the weekend," he said, then turned to leave.

"Wait! I need the information sooner than that."

He stopped and stood in place, but didn't turn around.

"Please," I finally said, caving in and gritting my teeth.

With a brief nod, he slowly walked away, rounded the corner of the building, and was out of sight without a proper answer.

5

Lon's nonexistent sense of urgency ate away at me for the remainder of the day. I spent the early evening scouring my own private library for the albino demon. I called my guardian to ask if it could find any information in the Æthyr about the classification (a bust). I even strengthened the protective wards over the doors and the windows on the first floor of my house. After I ate dinner, my neighbor—Mrs. Marsh, an elderly Earthbound with an ongoing imp infestation—asked me to get rid of an imp, which I chased around her kitchen for several minutes, only to have it escape at the last moment.

But none of that could curb the rising resentment I was feeling toward Lon. And my sour mood nosedived when three quick raps at my side door told me that my pesky neighbor had returned. I cursed under my breath and briefly entertained the ideal of physically harming her on the way to answer her knock; in my defense, it just hadn't been a good day.

Mrs. Marsh's frail frame stood in my doorway. "I'm so sorry, but it's back. The same one—I can tell because its left ear is torn." Dressed in a pale blue quilted housecoat that

zipped up the front, Mrs. Marsh gave me a pleading look behind thick glasses.

"Hold on, let me put on some shoes."

Flip-flops it was. I grabbed a rolled-up piece of canvas
and a small caduceus, then followed Mrs. Marsh across my
dark driveway and through a narrow hole in the shrubbery to
get into her side yard.

"Where is it now?"

Before she could answer, one of her two large cats sprang
from the hood of a rusted barbecue grill at the side of her
house. Mrs. Marsh groaned as she bent low to scoop the cat
into her arms; it nestled against her neck with its arms lazily
dangling over her shoulder.

I hate cats. I try to tell myself that it's because of their
contemptuous attitude, or their sneaky manner, but in reality
it's probably just that I can't control them. Demons I can bind,
humans I can outrun with spells, dogs I can call and they
come, but cats . . .

The tinny sound of something metal crashing on Mrs.
Marsh's patio startled both of us. Our heads whipped around
in unison toward her backyard.

"It's outside on my patio," she whispered loudly.

We walked past the rusted grill and slowed at the corner
of her house. I held my hand up to tell her to halt while I
peeked around the corner. My eyes scanned the night shadows made by the oak trees; they cast a black, lacy pattern on
her lawn until they ended abruptly at the small, yellow circle
of light that radiated out from the bug light at her back door.
Her green city-issued garbage can stood inside the yellow
circle.

An empty can of cat food came to a slow, rolling stop on
the cement patio nearby.

The sooner this imp was gone, the sooner I could get some sleep. I unrolled the worn canvas square, revealing a small circle bordered by runes and symbols that had been stained into the cloth with a mixture of red ochre and pig's blood. No, I did not kill the pig, thankyouverymuch. I bought a small jar of blood from a local occult shop that gets their supply from a slaughterhouse across town. Working with animal blood isn't something I savor—I'm sure there are plenty of things about *your* job that you don't enjoy—but that particular kind of circle requires it.

Triangles are commonly used to bind, but the circle on my canvas has a little something extra. Once charged, it creates a generic gateway leading into the Æthyr. A quick, one-way portal back home, otherwise known as a banishment.

She who summons must banish. That's the unchangeable cosmic law that applies to most anything summoned from the Æthyr. If a magician summons any demon from one of the hundreds of Æthyric classes, that very same magician must send it back. No one else can step up and do the job for you. That's why there are so many Earthbounds running around the States these days. Some idiot magician working for Queen Elizabeth summoned a group of lower-echelon Æthyric demons and trapped them in human bodies, thinking they'd make pliable subjects when America was being colonized. However, the newly invoked Earthbounds lost their ticket home when the magician died of smallpox before he could send them back. A few hundred years of breeding, and here we are. At least, that's how the story goes.

Imps, though, are different.

The cockroaches of the supernatural world, imps slip in and out of the Æthyr at will. Since no one summons them, anyone could banish them; they're fair game, and my spiffy canvas portal worked like a charm. Sure, the imps that I trapped could still come back to earth on their own, but not for several days—or weeks, depending on the strength of the charge that I gave the circle—because my portal left an imbedded blocking spell on the imps. It took me several years of experimentation to find the right combination of sigils that would accomplish this, and I was damn proud of my ingenuity.

I tiptoed around the corner, staying in the shadows as I approached the patio, then laid the entrapment canvas on the cement in front of me. A single scratching noise emerged from the garbage can several feet away. Maybe this would be easy.

I retreated back to Mrs. Marsh again and reached for her cat.

"No!" she whispered. "Not Tiddlywinks!"

"I need bait, Mrs. Marsh. He won't be hurt, promise." Well . . . hopefully.

She reluctantly handed over the cat, which I held at arm's length in front of me like a baby with a dirty diaper. Tiddlywinks began growling at me, so I rushed to put him down near the canvas portal before he tore my eyeballs out. After sniffing the canvas and retreating a few steps, he settled down and began licking his butt without a care in the world. Plumped with cheap cat food and content to live his life in a near-coma state, Tiddlywinks barely had a pulse; with any luck, he'd stay put.

Mrs. Marsh and I stood together behind a bush and waited, our eyes fixed on the garbage can. *Come out, little imp. Get the nice kitty cat.* After a few seconds, I thought I spied some movement behind the garbage can, then a clammy chill ran up my arms. I looked down as Mrs. Marsh yelped, only to see the wispy trail of an imp dart out from between my legs.

"Motherfucker!" I yelled. Tricked again. For a brief

moment, I pitied the people on *Paranormal Patrol*. I ran after the imp, rounding the corner of the house with as much speed as I could manage wearing flip-flops. Tiddlywinks was in a compromising position, with one leg up in the air, paused midlick. His ears were cocked in my direction as I ran toward him at top speed. Then I realized the imp was stopping in front of the cat. He wasn't going to bail; he took the bait.

I slid across the damp grass. To avoid running into the imp and the cat, I half fell, half lunged near them in an awkward dive. I tried to pull an action-movie stunt roll. Big mistake. My upper arm hit the edge of the cement patio. As I cried out in pain, the caduceus flew from my hand and landed somewhere in the shadows. Smooth move.

I curled up into a ball on my side. When I glanced toward my feet, I was surprised to find Tiddlywinks still there, ears flattened and the hair on his back standing on end. The imp was circling the cat like prey. Only a couple of feet tall and mostly transparent, he was tubby, with rolls on his arms and legs like a pudgy baby. He had a bulbous nose and floppy ears, one of them torn, as Mrs. Marsh had noted.

Ignoring the pain in my arm, I reached for the canvas entrapment portal, grabbed the edge of it, and slung it over the imp. And the cat. I couldn't help it; he was in the way.

Without time to find the caduceus, I'd have to release the kindled Heka without a filter. The danger of electrical shock wasn't in the pull as much as the release. As long as I had the caduceus to even things out, the release was relatively painless. Without it, I risked burning myself up from the inside out.

I quickly tapped into the current from Mrs. Marsh's house. Too fast. The raw surge of electricity mixed erratically with my inner Heka; my body stiffened and began shaking.

Ever been shocked with electrical current? I mean, *really* shocked, as in a jolt up the arm, can't let go, can't breathe, life flashing before your eyes kind of shock? Not something most people would want to willingly do. You have to be a little crazy to practice hard-core magick: It's not for the weak. The only thing in my favor was the high electric resistance that Heka-rich bodies tend to possess. Current flows differently in me.

But not so differently that I was indestructible.

At this point, all I could do was release the Heka, but it wouldn't be pretty. I gathered all my willpower, flung myself up and over toward the imp, and muttered the entrapment spell as my hand came down on the canvas and released the energy.

My teeth clattered as the kindled charge left my body, hit the canvas, and exploded into a small fire.

"Shit!"

A muffled howl came from underneath the burning canvas as Tiddlywinks shot out and sped off toward the front yard. Before the entrapment portal could burn away, I said one more spell and banished the imp back into the Æthyr.

"Tiddlywinks!" Mrs. Marsh yelled as she ran after her cat.

I leapt over to the canvas, removed one flip-flop, and used it to beat the fire down. It took several slaps to extinguish. Putrid-smelling smoke trailed up into the air from the blackened hole in the middle of the cloth. Smoked pig's blood. Disgusting.

As I slid back on my soot-smeared shoe, Mrs. Marsh appeared with Tiddlywinks in tow.

"Guess you'll have to make another circle, sweetie," she said as we both looked down at the smoking cloth. "But at least I'll be able to sleep tonight."

And at least I wasn't wasting my magical talent on supernatural pest control. Oh, wait—I was. I found my caduceus in the grass and stalked off toward my house, one charred corner of the barbecued canvas dangling between the tips of my fingers.

6

Exhaustion set in as I locked my side door. On the way upstairs to my bedroom, I gathered up my pet, Mr. Piggy, a rescued hedgehog. Not much bigger than my hand, Mr. Piggy is a cute thing with a petite pink nose and dark, beady eyes. I scratched him on the underside of his little pointy chin and he yawned. At times he can be downright grumpy, but as far as roommates go, he's a pretty good one.

Sleep. That was what I needed. Once I got to my bedroom, I maneuvered my bra from underneath my shirt, dropped it on the floor, and ditched my jeans before crawling under the bedcovers. The small, sagging mattress felt like heaven. Mr. Piggy huffed and puffed as he climbed the set of pet stairs that I kept at the foot of the bed; he waddled across the covers and stopped when he found an acceptable spot to settle near my feet. Then he turned three slow circles before finally plopping down.

My hair stunk of smoky pig's blood, but I didn't have the strength to care. At that moment I just needed rest; I figured I'd wash off the funk when I woke up.

I drowsily made plans for the next day. First I'd contact Father Carrow and ask him to put some pressure on Lon for me. Then maybe I'd call Kar Yee to arrange for a part-time bartender to take a couple of my shifts. My thoughts roamed and faded. Just when I was at the cusp of succumbing to the heavy pull of sleep, a loud knock sounded from downstairs.

"Are you fucking kidding me?" No way on God's green earth was I getting out of bed to run after another damned imp for that woman. All my charity and goodwill were gone. If I didn't answer the door, maybe she'd go away. I waited and heard nothing, then settled back into my pillow while Mr. Piggy grumbled his own protests.

Not for long.

Another knock came, this one louder and more insistent. Furious, I threw back the covers and stomped downstairs. I really didn't think I could be nice this time. I made my way down the side hall, turned the lock, and flung the door open with nothing short of malice.

"Mrs. Marsh—" I hissed.

It was not Mrs. Marsh standing in my doorway. It was Lon Butler.

"Expecting someone else?" he asked with an amused look on his face.

"What the hell are you doing here? How did you—"

"I've just been over at Father Carrow's house down the block and . . ." He hesitated as his eyes skimmed over me. I followed his gaze and peered down at myself. Nothing but my T-shirt and panties. A blowtorch warmth spread up my neck, over my cheeks. "Father Carrow," he repeated, still not looking at my face, "pointed out which house was yours, so I drove over."

I stealthily attempted to tug down the hem of my T-shirt, but it barely covered my waist.

"Looks like you've stuck your finger in a light socket," he

observed, tearing his eyes away from my hips to stare at my hair. Damn Mrs. Marsh and that imp. And damn myself for kindling raw electricity without a caduceus.

"Well?" I prompted.

"You gonna invite me in, or you wanna talk out here?"

I moved from the doorway and gestured for him to come inside. Ten o'clock on a Friday night, and I was letting strange men into my house while I was half dressed. I reminded myself that he had, at one time, been studying to become a priest. That meant he took a vow of chastity, didn't it? I idly wondered if he stuck to it after he got kicked out, then decided that he didn't look all that chaste to me.

"Have a seat," I said, pointing toward the sofa in front of the television. At least the downstairs wasn't too messy. My bedroom looked like a bomb had gone off in it, and the master bath was disgusting. "I'll be right back. I need to . . . put something on," I murmured as he sat down.

The trek up the stairs was excruciating. *Why a thong— why today?* I guess it could have been worse. I mean, yes, the lower half of my rear was hanging out, but at least I wasn't wearing cheap multipack cotton panties, full of holes with the elastic worn out, like half of my others. When I got the nagging feeling that his eyes were on my backside, I wondered if it would look cowardly if I took two stairs at a time.

"Nice ass."

My bent leg hesitated on the step. I turned my head to glare, but found him staring intently at the screen of his cell phone—as if he'd never said a word. For a second, I wondered if I'd imagined it, but I hadn't. Thoroughly uncomfortable now, I continued my climb in silence without responding.

After I'd finished dressing, I started running a brush

through my frazzled hair, then stopped myself. *What the hell are you doing, primping?*

Mildly irritated at myself, I walked back downstairs and found Lon right where I'd left him. He was leaning down, face-to-face with Mr. Piggy. My curious hedgehog was standing on his hind legs and sniffing the air, trying to flirt his way into the man's lap.

"Mr. Piggy, get down," I scolded, reaching to pull him away.

"What *is* that?"

"It's a hedgehog."

"Is he your familiar?" he asked with a lopsided smile.

Funny. My "other car" was *not* a "broomstick," and if I saw that sticker on one more bumper in my neighborhood, I was going to ram somebody. I had nothing against Witches, Wiccans, Pagans, or anyone else on their own spiritual path, but my mother always taught me that "witch" was a slur; serious magicians were not witches. I didn't spend Beltane dancing around in the woods naked or calling up friends to hold a fucking drum circle: I do real magick with real results.

I glowered at Lon without answering the taunt. His eyes narrowed to slits in what I suspected was silent humor. Was he laughing at me? It was hard to tell. After a moment, he cleared his throat and glanced at the hedgehog.

"I didn't know they were so small," he admitted as I scooped up Mr. Piggy by his belly.

"He's a pygmy."

I shuffled over to a small gated pen set up in the corner of the adjoining dining room and placed him inside. He had a small bed, a couple of toys, a miniature litter box, and a water dish there. If I let him roam free all the time, he'd tear the place apart.

"Are you going to help me find my demon?" I asked. "Because if you are, I'll offer you something to drink. If you aren't, I'm not gonna bother."

He chuckled once and leaned back into the sofa. "Straight to the point, I like that."

"You didn't answer my question."

"I'll take coffee," he said.

Was that a yes? I wrinkled up my nose. "I'm out."

"What do you have, then?"

"Water or Coke."

"No liquor? And you're a bartender?"

"I don't drink liquor. I might have a beer, but—"

"I'll take it."

I stared him down for a few seconds, then retreated to the kitchen. I returned with two cans of PBR that were abandoned in my fridge by one of my hipster friends; the look of disdain on Lon's face was priceless. He set his beer on the coffee table like it might explode.

I stepped over his legs and alighted at the far end of the sofa, sitting with my back against the arm and my feet tucked under my legs. "So, you're going to help me."

"I talked to Father Carrow."

"Yes, you mentioned that."

"He seems to trust you, but he doesn't know exactly why you want the albino demon."

No, he sure didn't. I reached for my beer, cracked it open, and swigged. It tasted like dirty water and sweat.

"I decided that I would help you—"

"Great," I said with a fake smile, setting my beer back down.

"—if you are honest and tell me the real reason you want it."

"I can't do that."

"Then I can't help you."

Tired and angry, I began speaking louder. "You mean to tell me that you're some ex-priest, and you're not only refusing to be helpful, you're holding information hostage unless I give in to your demands?"

"I was never a priest."

"Oh, that's right. You were kicked out, weren't you? What could you have possibly done that was so bad, they sealed your records? That's like a dishonorable discharge, right?"

His eyebrows lowered as he scowled at me. After a short pause, he answered, "One of my teachers suspected I was a demon."

Oh.

"Are you?" I squinted at his strangely colored halo.

"Are *you*?" he countered, looking up at mine.

"Of course not."

"Well I *am*," he said. "So how come you can see my halo if you aren't?"

"I was . . . born different. That's all." You know, just your average magical breeding experiment.

"I asked around," he said after a long pause. "Lots of stories about bindings in your bar, but most Earthbounds seem to respect you."

Yeah, that was about right. "I'm a magician, and damn good at controlling demons—Earthbounds or Æthyric. Historically, our kinds have never been best buddies," I said, pointing back and forth between the two of us. "Once demons realize that I'm not a power-crazed mage forcing them to give up some divinatory vision or alchemical secret, they're usually cool with me. As long as they don't break shit in my bar, I'm cool with them."

He looked at me thoughtfully, then pulled out the same silver cigarette case he'd had earlier in the day. "Can we smoke inside?"

"Sure." Maybe it would get rid of the burnt-pig stench in my hair. I reached to open a nearby window, accepted his offer, and lit up with my own lighter before sliding it toward him.

"Your valrivia tastes fresh," I said after taking a couple of drags in silence.

"It is. I grow it."

Another long moment stretched as we both smoked and he looked around the room in curiosity.

"You've got magical wards over the doors and windows," he noted.

"Yep."

"What are you afraid of? Surely not demons."

"Hardly."

"Do you belong to an order? A magical organization?"

"No," I lied.

"But you were trained somewhere."

"I learned on my own."

He laughed. "Bullshit. No one learns summoning and binding demons on their own. That's an advanced skill and the goetias in publication are bogus."

"Most of them are. If you've got natural talent, you can teach yourself anything."

"Let's say that's true. How many Æthyric demons have you summoned?"

I shrugged, enjoying the euphoric effect of the cigarette. "More than ten, less than a hundred."

A flicker of surprise crossed his face. "For what purpose?"

"Mostly for practice in the beginning. Curiosity. Now I only do it if I need to trade information." Or skills. Just like

Earthbounds, most of the Æthyric demons have abilities. Only, theirs are *much* greater. Need to heal someone with stomach cancer? Find your grandmother's hidden stash of war bonds? If you know the right Æthyric with the right skill—and are willing to negotiate a trade—you might be able to get what you've wished for. Might. It is a tricky game. "I've had a few run-ins with some Æthyrics who weren't exactly thrilled to be summoned," I added. "Not all of them play nice."

"They're no different than humans in that respect," he agreed.

True.

"So, enough about me," I said. "Were you upset when you got kicked out of the seminary? How long ago was that, by the way?"

His face twisted up in mock surprise. "Are you trying to find out my age?"

"What? No." I glanced out the window. "But now that you mention it, how old are you?"

"Forty-two. How old are you?"

"Twenty-five."

"Twenty-five? Jesus, I was older than that when my son was born."

"You have a son? I guess that chastity vow didn't take, huh?"

He laughed, and for the first time, it was pleasant. All the meanness was gone. "I didn't take a chastity vow. I never really intended to become a priest," he explained. "And yes, I have a son. He's thirteen. Closer to your age than I am."

Thirteen? Christ.

"Is your wife an Earthbound?"

"I'm divorced, and yes."

"Oh . . . I'm sorry."

"Don't be." He looked at me intently, and I found my hand nervously moving up to cover the side of my neck, as if it were exposed. It took some effort to force my arm back down to my side.

"Do you see your son often?" I asked.

"He lives with me. I have full custody."

"Oh, good." *Good?* That was a silly response. My cheeks flushed as he absently scratched the hair behind one ear. He had really striking green eyes when they weren't narrowed into defensive slits.

"So why did you join the seminary if you didn't want to become a priest?"

"I wanted to get my hands on a few of their books."

"Aha! So you did steal those goetias that Father Carrow talked about! I can't say that I'm very religious myself, but even *I* think that's pretty low."

"Why don't most magicians believe in God?" he mused. "They witness more miracles than the average person."

I bristled. Most of the people in my order believe in some sort of creator. Maybe not a Abrahamic one, but they share many of the same ideals and moral codes: protect your family, accept responsibility for your actions—that sort of thing.

"I believe in a God," I argued. "Just not ghosts."

He chuckled, and after casually crossing his legs, ankle on knee, he slumped lower down into the cushions. "Just because I didn't intend to become a priest doesn't mean I don't believe in God. Maybe not with the conviction that Father Carrow has . . ." A gentle smile curled the corners of his mouth. "But you're right. Stealing from the church was stupid. I was only nineteen, if that counts for anything. Though, in the end, it was worth it. The books I took were . . . invaluable."

He took a long drag off his cigarette and observed me. I

was starting to feel lightheaded. Almost buzzed. I turned the cherry end of my cigarette toward my face and sniffed it suspiciously. "There's only valrivia in these, right?"

He draped his arm over the back cushion and leaned closer, ignoring my question. "Why do you want to find the albino demon?"

"Please don't ask me. I really can't tell you. You wouldn't understand anyway."

"You'd be surprised. Try me," he coaxed, his face softening. "Besides, I won't help unless you're honest. What other choice do you have?"

Not once in seven long years had I ever once told anyone the truth about my family. I'd never even been *tempted* to open the vault and spill my guts. Not even to Kar Yee, and she was the longest-running friend I'd had since this whole mess started. Sometimes I came close to telling Father Carrow. He was easy to open up to, and understood what it was like to be an outsider who didn't fit human or demon expectations. But no matter how convinced I was that he'd be somewhat understanding and keep my secrets, I just never allowed myself that luxury.

So why was I considering it now? I didn't even know this man.

I don't know if it was the stress of what was going on with my parents, or the physical exhaustion from staying up worried the night before, but suddenly I wanted to tell him everything. Not just because he was forcing my hand, and not just because I was desperate for him to help me—which I was. I think I just *wanted* to confess.

"Can you offer me absolution if I tell you?" I asked with a weak smile.

"No, I'm sorry. I'm the last person in the world to offer

that." His voice was soft and sympathetic, and when I met his gaze, the fortifying wall I'd carefully built around my stronghold crumbled. My heart hammered as an unexpected spike of exhilaration ran through me.

"My parents are Enola and Alexander Duval." The words raced out of my mouth, eager to be free after years of captivity.

His face drew up as if he was confused, or trying to place the names. Then his eyes widened. In shock? Terror? Certainly not pity.

"They didn't do it—the killings. They were f-framed," I stammered.

"You're . . . the teenage daughter?"

"Not anymore. It's been seven years."

"How—" he started, then hesitated. "Your parents are alive, too . . . on the news."

"Yes, they're back in hiding again, I guess, who knows where? They won't tell me," I admitted. "We separated after they were accused."

"And you've stayed hidden all these years? Alone?"

"Assumed identities. Changed my look. Protected myself with magick."

He blinked several times, then leaned forward, seeking a place to extinguish his cigarette.

"Here." I wiggled out a ceramic plate from beneath a potted plant on the coffee table.

After he stubbed his out, I did the same, then waited nervously for him to say something. The ramifications of what I'd just done hit me like a slap in the face. What was wrong with me? I was smarter than this. And why him? It's not like he was giving me warm and trusting vibes. There was a damn good possibility that I'd just made the biggest mistake of my life.

"Huh," he finally said, as my anxiety and regret rose to heart-attack levels. "I knew Arcadia Bell couldn't have been your real name."

I looked up to find him grinning ear to ear. *Oh, thank God.* My head lolled against the sofa as relief fell like a cool, cleansing rain.

"My order lifted the Arcadia identity from a homeless woman in Seattle," I explained.

"So you *do* belong to an organization? Your parents' order—Ekklesia Eleusia, right?"

"Yeah."

"I get them confused with that Luxe group."

"Our main rivals. A common mistake."

"Your parents were well respected before the killings," he noted.

When they were first accused of the murders, none of the orders believed it, even if the media and the police did. My parents were minor celebrities who wrote and published several occult philosophy books and were vocal advocates of a united magical community.

Before I was born, they famously campaigned for an umbrella committee to be created that would consist of leaders from each order. This was like herding cats. Esoteric orders are historically secretive and uninterested in sharing their secrets or banding together for a greater cause. However, my parents often acted as interorder liaisons with some degree of success.

"Wasn't it the Luxe group who blew the whistle on them?" Lon asked.

"Yep. After their leader was attacked, Luxe accused them. That's when they were brought in for questioning and the whole media circus started. A couple days later, the leader of the Luxe Order led the police to the murder weapon used in the Black Lodge slayings—I'm sure you've heard about that in the news as well."

He nodded, creasing his eyes as he studied me with greater intensity.

"When my parents' fingerprints were found on it, the warrant for their arrest was issued. At that point, they were facing serious charges from the law and even bigger threats from Luxe. There was no way out—they had to run."

"You too."

"Me too," I agreed, remembering the panic and fear, the sudden loss of my family. "I don't know how Luxe got their fingerprints, but it was rigged evidence. It was a demon, not a knife, that did the dirty work."

"The albino demon?"

I nodded.

"But they didn't summon it?"

"No. We think it was either someone from the Luxe group who was trying to sabotage our order, or some outside independent magician trying to take over all the orders. It might sound ridiculous to an outsider, but you really wouldn't believe the politics and power struggles that go on between the major occult organizations."

"Oh, I believe it. Whenever people organize, there's problems. That's why I'm not a joiner. I keep to myself and mind my own business."

That was true of most demons I knew. I smiled. "Except for the seminary stint?"

"That was self-serving." A trace of smile showed as he crossed his arms over his chest. "So, the albino demon . . ."

"If I can find it, I can force it to tell me who committed the murders. My parents will be exonerated."

"You need me to find it fast because the police are looking for your parents again?"

"Well, that doesn't help matters, but it's more because the Luxe Order has given my organization a mandate to turn over my parents—or me—in two weeks."

His eyebrows shot up. "What would they do if you turned yourself in to them?"

"Kill me," I said very seriously. "Eye for an eye, sins of the father, all that."

"Damn."

"Yeah."

A cool breeze blew in from outside the window and fluttered a few stray hairs around my face. I pushed them away, and noticed that our beers hadn't been touched in a while. Toying with a small tear in the knee of my jeans, I spoke again in a low voice.

"I bet you didn't expect all this, huh?"

"This? No. I thought you might be some angry kid with a vendetta. Not this."

"Well, I guess you can either help me, or you can rat me out to the feds and collect a handsome reward. It's up to you."

"Do you worry about people doing that? Turning you in?"

"No. There isn't anyone who knows who I am."

"No one?"

"A few people in my order, but they're willingly under magical oath to keep quiet. Otherwise, no one. I guess you think I'm pretty stupid, spilling my guts to a complete stranger. I'm not even sure why I told you. I could have made something up like I usually do."

We looked at each for a few moments, then he sat on the edge of the sofa and leaned forward, legs spread and forearms braced on his knees. "Two weeks, huh? That's a lot of pressure on me."

"Yeah, sorry."

"Mmm."

"Will you do it?"

"I think the bigger question is *can* I do it. I have some rare resources, and I can start there . . ."

He linked his fingers, staring at them, thinking. But all I heard was that he would help me, and I felt as if an enormous weight had been lifted. I had hope.

He stood up without warning, and I scrambled to follow.

"I'll start researching in the morning," he said. "I'll contact you again tomorrow night and give you an update. I'll be discreet. You have my word." He turned and walked toward the door, opening it and stepping out onto the concrete stairs. When he reached my driveway at the bottom, he turned and looked back up at me.

"What's your real name?"

"Seléne Duval."

"Seléne? Like the moon goddess?" He rolled his eyes.

"My parents are occultists, what do you expect? It's better than them being hippies and naming me River or Rain, right?"

He laughed. "Well, what do you want me to call you? I like Arcadia better."

"Me too," I admitted with a smile as I stood in the doorway. The cool night air sent a shiver through me. I folded my arms around my middle.

"Arcadia it is," he said definitively. "By the way, I apologize for lacing the cigarettes."

Goddammit. I *knew* it. Fucking hoodwinked by a demon—me! How many Earthbounds had I unwittingly dosed in my bar over the last couple of years? Maybe this was payback. Before I could protest, he tipped his finger in parting, then ambled away to his car.

7

Amanda set a large box down on the bar. It was half past three in the afternoon, and Tambuku opened in thirty minutes for happy hour. I came in to help with some deliveries and break it to Kar Yee that I wasn't working this weekend. She was mildly pissed, but that was tough. I just couldn't concentrate on babysitting a bunch of drunken idiots all night. I'd already spent the first half of the day jumping at every noise, freaked out that Lon had changed his mind and called the police. But no one came to arrest me. Hell, the media was barely even reporting about my parents' sudden appearance in Texas anymore. In a way, it almost felt like everything would just blow over and I could go back to my life like nothing ever happened.

But that was a pipe dream. As I'd told Lon last night, it was never the authorities that truly scared me; it was the Luxe Order. I called someone to cover my shift while I waited for Lon to contact me, hoping that he'd find some bit of information that I could use.

Amanda shook out her hands. "Wow. I'm amazed at how heavy a carton of straws can be."

"There should be fifteen new ashtrays in that box, not just straws," I pointed out.

"O-o-oh. That's why. Duh."

She got out a box cutter and went to work on unpacking the carton while I restocked the liquor and traded the tapered metal pouring spouts from empty bottles to full ones.

"Hey, why did you draw those new symbols over the door?"

They were drawn in clear ink. Only Earthbounds would be able to spot the soft white glow from the Heka charge, and Amanda wasn't Earthbound. Her father was Earthbound, her mother human. But all that made Amanda was nonsavage, aware of the existence of demons, but unable to see them. As far as I knew, all Earthbound-human couplings produced human children—no halos, no abilities, no preternatural eyesight—but they were embraced by the Earthbound community as family. Ugly ducklings, they were affectionately called.

"I saw you coming down off the stepladder after you scribbled something over the door," Amanda explained. "I figured it must've been magick."

Ah, okay. "They're nothing. Just symbols for extra protection."

"Why do we need extra protection?"

"You don't. I do."

She put the box cutter down and paused. "Why?"

"Not a big deal, I'm just being extra careful."

"Do you have another crazy stalker boy?"

Ugh. "Don't remind me," I said. A few months ago some punk kid starting hanging outside the bar after we closed, trying to follow me to my car. Turned out he was bipolar and off his meds; if I never saw him again, it would be too soon. "Hey, speaking of boys—well, men—I met someone from your neck of the woods. Have you ever heard of Lon Butler? He's a—"

"You met Lon Butler? Ohmygod, that's so cool! Was he nice? I heard he was kind of a jerk. I've seen him at the farmers' market a couple of times but I was too nervous to approach him."

I feigned casual interest, but I was dying to find out what she knew. "He wasn't warm and friendly. How do you know about him?"

"Everyone knows about him in La Sirena. He's got a cool piece of property at the edge of town on one of the cliffs overlooking the ocean. He inherited it from his father and built a house up there, but the only way to really see it is from a boat."

"Hmm." Boring. "What else?"

"Let's see, he travels around the world to exotic locations for photo shoots. Umm . . . Oh, yeah—you know his ex-wife, that model, Yvonne Giovanni?"

I shook my head. I had no idea who she was talking about.

"Where have you been living, Arcadia? Under a rock? She used to be a supermodel."

"Doesn't ring a bell."

"Back when I was a teenager, she was always in the gossip columns because she partied with tons of celebrities. I heard that's why they split up. His son goes to junior high with my cousin, Rosy. You remember her, right? I brought her by here a couple of months ago on my day off, that morning when you and Kar Yee were doing inventory?"

"Uh-huh, I remember." I didn't, but whatever.

"Well, *she* said the rumor going around school is that Yvonne is only allowed supervised visits with the son a couple of times a year."

I grabbed the box cutter off the bar counter and broke down the empty boxes that were accumulating at my feet. "That's a little weird. He mentioned that he had custody."

"Yeah, and you don't see a father getting that very often, do you? I think it's fishy. Anyway, how did you meet him?"

Kar Yee walked up to the bar and took a seat. "Who did you meet?"

"Lon Butler."

Kar Yee squinched up her face. "Who?"

"The famous photographer from La Sirena," Amanda said in exasperation. I should have known she'd be a wealth of gossipy tidbits; if you listened to her weekly reports from the home front, you'd think that La Sirena was populated with nothing but soap opera characters with elaborate backstories.

"Aren't there like a billion photographers in La Sirena?" Kar Yee stuck her hand inside the box of rice crackers that I'd just opened and scooped out a handful.

"That's not sanitary," I chastised. She shrugged and began munching.

Amanda made a frustrated noise, then proceeded to tell her about the model/ex-wife; Kar Yee hadn't heard of her either. "He's a local celebrity," she finished.

Kar Yee gave me a sidelong glance as Amanda's back was turned. "Whatever you say." She swiveled her chair around to face me. "Did you call Lisa?"

"Yeah, she's subbing for me tonight and tomorrow. I also called Heidi and asked if she'd help Amanda for a few hours tonight during peak hours since that concert will be letting out around midnight."

"Well, I guess you're off the hook, then."

I glared at her. "I'm half owner, you know. I don't need your permission."

Kar Yee formed her hand into the shape of a yapping mouth repeatedly opening and closing.

I picked up the stack of flattened boxes and set them down on the bar in front of her. "Get your hands dirty, why don't you?" I motioned toward the back door with my head.

She grumbled and begrudgingly peeled herself off the bar stool to haul them out to the alley.

"Speaking of tips," Amanda said, "we had a party of six last night and guess how much they gave me for a two-hundred-dollar tab?"

I put my hands on my hips and blew a stray hair off my forehead while checking the bar area to make sure I hadn't missed anything. "How much?"

"Sixty dollars, baby!"

Half the patrons didn't tip even twenty percent. "Good job," I praised, then partially tuned her out as she continued to tell me how one of them had invited her to some party across town.

A flutter went through my stomach as she talked, then a familiar voice filled my head.

May I show myself?

My guardian, Priya. It almost never came to me uninvited.

"No!" I whispered. "Hold on!"

Amanda stopped talking and gave me a strange look. "No? You don't think I should go?"

"Huh? What—I didn't mean that. Sure, you should go. Why not."

She relaxed and continued filling up the toothpick bin. "Yeah, I think I will. Like you said, why not. Have you ever dated a customer?"

"Excuse me, I'll be right back." I tried not to bolt from behind the bar. I headed toward Kar Yee's office, heard her on the phone, and switched directions toward the restroom. Once inside, I locked myself inside one of two stalls.

"Okay," I whispered. "You can appear now."

Priya emerged from the air, its image so transparent, I could barely see it.

We are being sought, it said plainly in my head.

"You and me? By whom?"

Searchers have been cast into the Æthyr. I am having difficulty hiding from them.

"What kind of searchers? You mean servitors?" Sometimes Priya's communication skills aren't the best.

No. Litchen, Priya insisted. *Small insect Æthyr beings. They are commanded by demon host in the Æthyr.*

Shit. My heart sped up.

"Are these searcher insects on earth too?"

No, only on my plane. They cannot be summoned to earth.

"It's got to be the Luxe Order. Can you avoid the insects? They can't injure you, right?"

I am doing my best to avoid them. If they kill me, I will be reborn in a new form and seek out a renewed link with you again, if you will wait for me.

Priya was nothing if not loyal. "Thank you, Priya. Is there any way I can help you? A spell I can do to fortify or hide you better?"

The spirit shook its birdlike head. The air undulated. *I merely wanted to warn you.*

"I appreciate that. Please keep me updat—"

Litchen are scouts for their host demons. If they find me, our link can be used to locate you, and their host can be summoned to earth in a physical body. The host can harm you.

Great. That's all I needed. "I'll put up a continuous ward around me somehow."

Priya faded. *I must go now. Guard yourself. I will do my best to stay hidden and keep our link safe.*

"You always do," I murmured as Priya disappeared, leaving me alone in the brightly lit restroom.

8

Not long after Priya left, Lon called at the bar, catching me right before I left. He didn't say much, just gruffly asked me to come out to his house. My first reaction was to insist that we meet at a restaurant or some other neutral location, but he refused, claiming that he had books to show me—rare books that couldn't be carted around. My curiosity got the better of me.

However, now that it was getting dark and I was lost in the woods, that curiosity was quickly dying. I pulled over to the side of the road and put my car in park so that I could study the GPS screen without running off the road.

"Turn left in two hundred feet," the computerized voice said in a cheery voice.

"There is no turn in two hundred feet, you bitch," I yelled toward the screen. "Zoom out." Nothing happened. "ZOOM. OUT," I said again, louder, before the screen responded to the voice-activated command. I studied the roads on the map; they didn't exist. I was stuck on the side of a small mountain, in the middle of the woods, at night. Beautiful.

I held down the button to turn off the GPS, then put the car in gear and began following the road up the mountain, hoping I could just find it on my own; I wished that I'd written down the verbal instructions Lon gave me over the phone. The road was narrow and made hairpin twists as it snaked back and forth up the rocky, heavily wooded landscape. After five or six of these sharp, steep turns, I found one road branching off, but it was headed down the mountain, not up, so I kept going.

Just when I thought I couldn't go any farther, the road suddenly ended and turned into gravel, then a few feet away, the iron gates to his house appeared, just as he'd described; I stopped in front of them. A small speaker box sat atop a bent pole. I rolled down the window and pressed the button.

"Umm, hello? It's Arcadia."

I waited for a response. Nothing. When I leaned out the window to press the button again, a buzz sounded and the gates began swinging open.

The gravel driveway was steep, but at least there weren't any more twists. Who the hell would choose to live way up here and navigate all those dangerous curves every day? *A mentally unstable person*, I thought, *that's who*. After a short time, my headlights fell on a break in the trees and his house came into view.

"Well, well, well," I muttered to myself. It certainly wasn't a mountain cabin. The modern house was constructed from dark gray stackstone with clean, horizontal lines and large plate-glass windows. Several of them were brightly lit from the inside, radiating a pleasant orange glow.

The driveway curved into a loop. Gravel crunched under my tires as I drove to the front of the house and parked.

A set of dark red double doors marked the entrance. No doorbell that I could see, so I knocked cautiously and tugged my purse higher up on my shoulder. With a force that suctioned wisps of my hair forward, both doors flung inward and orange light flooded the stone-paved entrance.

An adolescent boy stood inside the open doorway. Taller than me, he was lean and gangly, all arms and legs. Dark brown hair rose up in a mass of long, frizzy spiral curls that defied gravity and sprung out several inches from his head in all directions. His skin was the color of a chocolate milk shake.

"Hi," he said, unabashedly looking me over from head to foot, his eyes lighting up with curiosity when he spotted my halo.

"Hello."

He looked so much like his father—same green eyes, same long face and high cheekbones. A few things were different. His race, obviously. He was also skinnier and longer than Lon, which wasn't surprising, I supposed, his mother being a model. His halo was the normal demon green, not gold and green like Lon's.

"What's your name again?"

"Arcadia."

He scrunched up his nose and smiled. "Arcadia, that's right. What a weird name. It sounds like you should be a movie star or something, especially with that crazy silver halo of yours and that Bride of Frankenstein hair."

I laughed. That was better than the skunk comments I usually got. "Nope, just a lowly bartender."

"Do you like classic movies?"

"Sure."

"Ya know which one I'm talking about? *Bride of Frankenstein*? Elsa Lanchester had her hair kinda like that. She was really the Monster's bride—Frankenstein was the doctor. People always screw that up."

"Wow, I'm impressed. I dressed up as her last year for Halloween." I pulled up my hair to better show him the bleached-white strands that contrasted against the dark.

"Yeah, that's it! Cool," he said brightly. "You're human, right? My dad said you weren't demon, but you're not a savage either, so I should just treat you like another demon."

"Yep. I'm human, but I can see your halo. What's your name?"

"Jupiter."

"Jupiter?" I teased. "Talk about a weird name."

He grinned and leaned against the doorway, his arms crossed over his chest with a geeky sort of grace. "I know. Stupid, right? I was named after some poet—not the god. I hate poetry." He rolled his eyes and made a fake vomiting noise. "You can just call me Jupe. That's what my friends call me."

"And you can call me Cady if you want."

"Cady," he repeated, as if he were trying it out on his tongue. He was barefoot and dressed in jeans and a loose white T-shirt that fell at a crisp angle from his bony shoulders.

"Whoa, is that a charm?" He reached out to grab my necklace. I instinctually jerked back—I don't like people invading my private space, and I'm not a hugger—but he didn't seem to notice. He leaned closer and inspected the small metal pendant, holding it in his flattened palm.

After my worrisome visit from Priya, I realized I needed more continuous protection than my tattooed sigils offered. They were convenient, quick fixes, but because they wouldn't hold a permanent charge—allowing me the flexibility to turn them off and on at will—they required a constant influx of Heka to power; the longest I'd ever powered one was about an hour, and I passed out afterward. Seeking something more substantial, I dug out an oldie-but-goodie charm I'd created a few years back, at a point in my life when paranoia was getting the best of me. It was a basic deflector, which should keep me safe from hostile magical attack, and, with any luck, hidden from anything malicious originating from the Æthyr.

"Did you make this? Is it magick?" Jupe asked.

"Uh, what? Magick?" I said, as if he were crazy, pulling the pendant away from him and tucking it under the neck of my shirt.

"Yeah, magick. Dad told me you're a real magician. That's so cool!"

"He did, did he?" Shit, what the hell was I supposed to say? How much did he tell his son about me, anyway?

"I've read tons of books about famous magicians like Aleister Crowley. I have some questions for you—"

Lon's hands appeared on his son's shoulders and pulled him backward. "Don't talk her ear off yet. You'll scare her away before she even gets in the damn door."

"Hi," I said, smiling. He smiled back and an unexpected feeling of relief flooded through me. Call it instinct—or foolishness—but I was instantaneously confident that I could trust him; all my worries about his discretion over my true identity vanished on the spot.

"Come on Jupe," he said, "where are your manners?"

"Huh? Oh, come inside. You're letting flies in."

"Jupe," Lon chastised.

"What? That's what *you* always say." As his father wearily shook his head, Jupe grabbed my arm and pulled me inside; I guessed my no-touching rule was out the window too.

Their house was much larger than mine, but still comfortable. The foyer opened up into an expansive great room with a floor-to-ceiling stone fireplace at the far end and a wide, curving metal staircase to the right with gray, slab-stone steps.

The decor was minimalist and modern, lots of blond wood and stainless steel—like something out of an IKEA catalog, but higher-end. Very tidy and clean.

"Nice," I remarked.

"You want a tour?" Jupe suggested with great enthusiasm.

"She doesn't want a tour," Lon said. "This isn't the Louvre."

Jupe frowned, then his face brightened again. His pale green eyes were not as intensely colored as his father's, but they were bigger and enfolded by thick, downy lashes. Quite arresting. "We're having mashed potatoes for dinner. Do you like mashed potatoes?"

"Uh, yeah . . ."

"Then you'll like these. My dad's a real good cook."

"You're supposed to ask her if she's had dinner first, *then* ask if she'd like to eat with us."

Jupe rolled his eyes. "Blah, blah. What he said."

"Jupe."

"Sorry. Would you like to eat dinner with us, madam, please?" Jupe said with a terrible attempt at something close to a prim-and-proper accent, which apparently in his mind was a broad mix of British and Australian.

"There's more than mashed potatoes," Lon added.

"I haven't had dinner yet, so sure. Yeah."

"Sweet! I'm starved, let's eat, Dad." Jupe paused, then shouted at the top of his lungs—quite impressive, I can tell you—"Foxglove! Come here, girl!" He whistled with his hands cupped around his mouth, and headed off into the next room, leaving Lon and me standing alone.

"Sorry he's such a motormouth," he said. "He doesn't get it from me."

"Really? Color me shocked," I said dryly. He gave me a single grunt in return, which made me laugh. "He seems sweet. Cute, too. The girls are going to be all over him in a couple of years."

"You think?" He looked over his shoulder at Jupe, who was well out of earshot and continuing to whistle and call.

"God yes—he looks just like you." I realized, too late, what I'd just implied when one of Lon's eyebrows slowly raised and the corner of his mouth twitched in amusement.

"Who's Foxglove?" I quickly asked before it got too awkward.

"Our dog—a black Lab."

"Ah." Not a cat. Big points.

"She's outside, but don't tell Jupe. Looking for her will keep him occupied for a few minutes and give your ears a chance to rest."

He grinned and turned away, then starting walking out of the room. I guessed that meant that I was supposed to follow, so I did. We walked under a wide archway into a kitchen with gobs of white subway tile and stainless steel countertops. A long, curved island sat in the center, bordered with six stools. As he walked around the island, he motioned for me to sit.

"Whatever you're cooking smells terrific," I admitted.

It really did; my stomach was trying to eat itself.

"Thanks."

I waited for him to tell me exactly what if was, but he didn't.

"The food's not dosed like your cigarettes, right?"

"Like you've never dosed someone."

"How would you know?" If he'd been snooping, asking around about me, God only knew what he'd heard. A couple of my regulars at the bar suspected that I concocted medicinals; had they been gossiping?

He gave me a mysterious smile, then turned away and

changed the subject. "I've found ten albino demons so far," he said as a timer went off. He took the large stockpot off the range and turned his back to me to dump out the contents into a colander. The infamous potatoes. "When we get finished eating, I'll let you look at them and you can tell me what you think."

"That's great news."

"Hold off on getting too excited. I've only been through a handful of goetias."

"Oh?"

"It could take me days to finish with what I've got. If we can't find it, I might know someone we can call."

"Anything you can do to help is much appreciated. I know this is probably taking up a lot of your time, and you've got a job and your son—"

"I don't have a shoot scheduled right now. Don't worry about it."

Lon smashed the steaming potatoes in a large bowl as the sound of a slamming door echoed in the distance. Jupe's voice carried from somewhere in the house. "Goddamn dog, where the hell are you hiding?"

"Jupiter!" Lon yelled crossly.

"Oops, sorry," Jupe replied. His footsteps thundered across the wooden floor before he appeared in the kitchen.

"No swearing around company."

He flopped onto the stool next to me and spread his long arms across the counter. "I said sorry, jeez. I'm sure she's heard it before."

"I have . . . in the car earlier, when I was trying to find your house."

Jupe looked at me with a strange expression, then got it, and laughed, rearing back his head. "See. She cusses too."

Lon threw me a scolding look. "Not helping," he mumbled.

"Don't let him fool you," Jupe said, "he drops the F-bomb like a billion times a day, but he only pretends it's wrong in front of other people. H-Y-P-O-C-R-I—" he began spelling.

"Goddammit, Jupe."

"Language, Dad."

I covered my mouth with my knuckles to muffle a laugh.

We ate at a small table in a nook off the kitchen—braised short ribs that melted on the tongue, in a thick, dark wine sauce; a simple salad; and the hand-smashed potatoes, which were doctored with a sinful amount of cream and butter. After a long, dry spell of living off microwave dinners and cold cereal, anything homemade would've tasted good, but his cooking skills were surprisingly refined. I had to force myself to eat everything slowly so that I didn't appear desperate or greedy. Jupe had no such concerns and finished off two helpings with remarkable speed and gusto.

Throughout the meal, I was torn in two directions by two very different men. Jupe was bubbly and talkative, a fireball of innocent energy that contrasted with Lon and his understated way of thinking and speaking.

Strangely, though, I found a few subtle similarities between them as well. Jupe obviously considered himself a budding comedian and constantly tried to make me laugh—which he did, many times—but I also caught fleeting looks of amusement on Lon's face, and they lapsed into several bouts of gunfire-fast witty repartee. Yet, underneath all his manic energy, Jupe had his father's easy confidence, and occasionally made remarkably concise observations that caught me off-guard.

It was pleasant, being in a normal house with a normal

family. My mind wandered to the last few years I'd spent at home with my own family, when I was a teenager. My mom was never much of a cook, and making the meal that Lon had just served would have been beyond her expertise. Besides, my parents were vegans, so meat was never part of our meals at home—though I'd regularly sneak hamburgers and meat loaf in the school cafeteria and tell my parents I'd eaten salad instead. But there was an Indian restaurant close to our house in Florida that made awesome samosas. We used to get take-out from them every Friday and would eat it outside on our back patio. Afterward, my father would point out constellations and tell me stories about the myths behind them. Even though he repeated many stories, I never got tired of hearing any of them; Friday was always my favorite day of the week.

After clearing the table, Lon exiled Jupe to his room so that we could discuss business. I trailed him as he retreated to a door at the end of a small hall past the dining room. The door was locked electronically. He stuck a finger onto a small blue light over the handle of the door and a dead bolt slid open.

"Wow, serious security."

"There's dangerous information in some of these books," he explained as he flipped on the lights and let me inside. "Jupe's fascinated with magick right now. I don't want to risk his fooling around in here and getting himself in trouble."

Once inside the room, my mouth fell open. Hundreds and hundreds—maybe thousands—of rare occult books lined all four walls of the windowless room, and even more titles neatly filed around a large rectangular pillar in the center. On one side of the room was a chunky antique desk and a small fireplace with two stuffed armchairs in front of it anchored the other side. Six frosted art deco pendant lights hung from a high ceiling in two neat rows. A rolling wooden ladder attached to a track that extended around the room.

"Jesus, Lon." I studied the endless rows of cracked leather spines. "This is larger than the collection in the vault in our main lodge."

He walked alongside me with his hands behind his back. "I've spent twenty years collecting it. Almost got myself killed a couple of times in the process."

I didn't doubt it. He was right about there being dangerous information in some of those books. *Theurgia Mallecta Gotetica*, *Hellanicus Magica Infernal*, *Speculum Artis Bene Moriendi* . . . it was an occultist's wet dream. Plenty of people would go to less than ethical lengths to get their hands on these.

"Is this a first edition?" I asked, squatting down to inspect a tall, fat book with a green leather spine: *Liber Ceremonialle Magicke*.

"Yes, 1416. One of five known existing copies. Would you like to look at it?"

"Could I? I've only seen the later editions printed on paper."

"Sure. Let's wash up first." The mark of a serious, obsessive collector. He retreated to one of two small doors at the far end of the room, which contained a sink, hand soap, and paper towels. I washed and dried my hands, then returned. The book was sitting in the middle of his desk on a fresh white paper blotter. He motioned for me to sit down, then stood over my shoulder as I opened the book.

It smelled wonderful as I cracked open the cover—old leather mingled with the slightly musty scent of parchment. Lon smelled good as well, like the dinner he'd just cooked. It made me wish I'd ditched my pride and asked for seconds.

"Turn the pages by the corners," he instructed.

"Yes, I know." *Sheesh.* It wasn't like I'd never handled a valuable old book before. The pages were stiff and brittle, and I carefully turned each one, marveling at the old astrological calculations and tedious ritual instructions. "The illustrations are so bright."

"The previous owners took good care of it."

"Very well preserved," I agreed.

After a couple of minutes of browsing, I thanked him and gave it back. He shelved it, then brought a small stack of goetias over to the desk. The old tomes were each roughly the size of a coffee table art book; their cracking paper pages were swaddled in worn leather covers embossed with the names of the magicians who wrote them. Lon pulled up a wooden side chair next to me, sat down, and took a book off the stack.

"These are all the albino demons I've found so far." He scooted his chair closer until his shoulder brushed mine. A rush of chills spread over my arms at the accidental contact. I stole a quick sidelong glance at him, eyes roaming over his arms and the hint of defined muscle there, just visible through his long-sleeve T-shirt. *Christ*, I thought. How long had it been since I'd been on a date? I really needed to work less and get out more.

As I tamped these thoughts down, he opened the first book in front of me, gently turning past pages of scrawled arcane symbols, handwritten in ink centuries ago. Calculations for moon phases and detailed charts of summoning variables covered the entries: size of the summoning seal, what was used to draw it (red ochre chalk, soot, blood), where the ritual was performed. Crude drawings and engravings depicted the evoked beings. One had the head of a frog and the naked body of a boy. Another was covered in scales below the waist and had massive twisting horns; he was riding a flying crocodile.

Lon stopped at a pair of pages; tucked between was a small scrap of blue paper.

"This one is Lemansus," he said, removing the blue paper marker. "He fits all of your descriptions but two."

I leaned closer to study the small woodcut rendering. "No horns . . . oh, no eyes at all—blind," I said after a few seconds. "What else?"

"Not primordial. The text claims that the magician who first conjured him was told that this demon was born sometime in the fifth century."

He carefully flipped to the next marker in the book. "Eligostanzia. He mostly fits the description, but there's no mention of the rolling tongue that you're looking for, and it's hard to tell if those are talons or long fingers. The magician doesn't say."

"Hmm."

"He's also allegedly skilled at divinatory favors, not killing."

"Maybe I should copy down his name, just in case. Do you have something I can write with, or—"

He opened a desk drawer and pulled out a stack of papers; he'd already run off copies of the marked pages. "Let's make two stacks: Maybe and No. You can take the Maybe stack with you."

At that moment, it crossed my mind that I really shouldn't have needed to come all the way out there. He could easily have met me somewhere and handed over the copies.

"I thought you'd like to see the details on the original pages yourself," he explained, as if he'd read my thoughts.

Wait—my thoughts. A terrible realization struck me.

"Umm, Lon?"

"Yes?"

"You never told me what your knack is."

Knack. Earthbound slang for a demonic ability. Healing, telepathy, controlling weather . . . Most of the Earthbounds I knew had useless knacks that weren't even interesting enough to nab them a job in a carnival sideshow. But I had a sinking feeling that Lon's knack wasn't ordinary.

"I didn't?" He looked down at the desk, avoiding my eyes.

"No."

He shrugged. "I don't really have one."

"Liar."

Seconds ticked. "I'm an empath," he finally said, still gazing at the book in front of us.

"You sense other people's emotions?"

"Yes."

I instantly became anxious. I thought back to when we first met at the coffee shop, and how he must have known everything I was feeling. Crap. In my house, too. Could he tell when I was ogling him, then? What about a couple of minutes back, when I was getting all hot and bothered by our shoulders touching? Exactly how much could someone tell about you by reading your emotions?

He sighed.

"You can tell how I feel right now, huh?"

"Yes."

I tried to relax and clear my head. "I've heard of empaths, but I've never met one. How detailed is your skill? You can't read minds, can you?" *Please say no, please say no . . .*

"No."

Paranoia got the better of me. "Are you just saying that because I was thinking it?"

His smile was fatigued, like he'd been forced to explain this a billion times before; he probably had. "I really can't read your thoughts. Just emotions. Simple ones are the easiest. If there are too many at once, it gets garbled. But I can sense you're relieved that I'm not a mind reader, and that you're putting up a barrier to keep your emotions guarded right now."

"Sorry."

A long, awkward pause filled up the space between us.

"Can you block it, or do you just sense emotions from everyone you're around?"

"No, I can tune people out. If I couldn't, I'd never be able to leave the house."

"I suppose that would be . . . overwhelming."

"When other Earthbounds find out, they start avoiding me. Relationships are hard." One corner of his mouth puckered as gave me glance from the side. "The only person who doesn't mind my ability is Jupe. He's . . . well, an open book, so to speak." He closed the tome in front of us and smiled at me weakly before pulling the next one off the stack.

A low wave of pity rolled over me, and I let it, even with the knowledge that he could sense it. "Is that why your marriage broke up?"

"It didn't help. It's hard to stay together when you know someone's cheating on you and doesn't care that you know it."

"That sucks. I'm sorry."

He shrugged. "I married her after she got pregnant with Jupe. I thought it was the right thing to do, thought we were in love—or at least that we might be one day—but her demonic ability . . ." A scowl darkened his face for a few seconds. "Turned out, staying together was bad for us and bad for Jupe. So I divorced her eight years ago and took Jupe with me. He's a good kid."

"It's kinda admirable that you're raising him by yourself."

"I've had help. I employ an elderly couple who live on a small house on the property. They help take care of the house and watch out for him."

Housekeepers. Hmph. I knew a man like him couldn't possibly keep a house like that so clean by himself; I tried to erase that thought before he caught my smugness.

"Has Jupe's knack surfaced yet?" Abilities usually didn't until mid-teens, from what I'd heard.

"No, but as much as I hate my knack, I hope like hell he inherits mine and not hers."

He didn't offer any further information about her ability, so I didn't pry.

"Well, like you said, he's a good kid. You'll teach him to handle it fine." I smiled, and his tightly creased eyes relaxed.

"I'm glad you like him," he said. I wondered if that was just a casual observation, or if he sensed that I did. Before I could ask, he cracked open the second book.

"Here's the third demon I found," he said, going back to our shop talk as if his revelation was inconsequential. As if nothing had changed between us.

And maybe it hadn't.

9

I flipped on my high beams as I drove out of the gates and began the trek down Lon's rocky mountain. Despite the nice house, I really didn't see why Amanda had fussed over the piece of property. Maybe it looked different in the daytime, but right now it was pitch black, and the seaside cliff's steep road set my nerves on edge.

Lon had given me several decent leads. All told, I'd walked away with four possible albino demons, which was great. Problem was, to find out whether one of them was the particular demon I wanted, I'd have to summon and question each one. I *really* wasn't looking forward to that. Summoning Æthyric beings made me sick as a dog. Half of the ones I'd evoked in the past were utterly uncivilized, little more than wild beasts. Some only spoke Æthyric languages, maybe Latin or some Coptic dialect. The ones that spoke English had been summoned to earth frequently by other magicians, and were pretty savvy about weaseling their way out of negotiations. Some were even strong enough to attempt to break out of my binding triangles if I didn't charge them correctly.

Summoning was tricky business, and it took a lot of skill and smarts to do it without getting yourself killed.

As I rounded a sharp turn, a few raindrops splattered on the windshield and I hoped like hell that I could make it all the way down before a storm hit. I soon forgot about this, however, when the air around me bubbled.

"What the—"

A light flashed above the passenger seat, and half of my guardian's body became visible. Priya's birdlike face flashed and faded, then snapped back with static. I gasped in horror. Priya's body was cloaked in a swarm of small, ghostly entities with grotesque bodies—each had multiple, hairy, spidery legs and two sets of bulging eyes. Their mouths were firmly suctioned on Priya, and through their transparent bodies, a steady stream of energy was being leached.

They had to be the litchen insect creatures that Priya had said were pursuing her.

"Priya!" I screamed, slamming on the brakes.

My guardian's eyes, dazed with terror and pain, were fixed somewhere above my head. It only communicated one word to me before it vanished: *Run!*

The car came to a screeching stop, skidding sideways at the end of a hairpin turn.

My hands gripped the steering wheel harder. I tried to think, allowing the full weight of Priya's warning to settle. After several deep breaths, I shakily felt for my deflector charm beneath my shirt . . . gone! I tucked my chin and yanked my shirt down to be sure. It must have fallen off at some point. I strained to think how or when, but it really didn't matter.

A booming crack of thunder startled me, jerking my shoulders up. It was followed by a sudden downpour of rain that sheeted against my window.

"Keep calm," I said out loud as I tried to make sense of

my options. I couldn't go back to Lon's. The road wasn't wide enough to allow me room to turn around, and it was tightly bordered by trees and cut rock. Plus I didn't want to get him involved in this, especially not with his kid around. I had to go forward. If I could make it home, I'd erect a serious ward and hole up inside my bedroom.

For the time being, I needed to get the car back on the road, then charge one of the sigils on my arm once I could expend some attention for concentration. I needed something that would help hide me and give me a chance to escape.

I struggled to turn the steering wheel so that I could maneuver around the turn, then let my foot off the brake. Throwing the wipers on high, I had started around the curve when a heavy thump crashed down on the car roof.

For a second, I thought the storm had toppled a branch onto my car, then I looked up. Four dents the size of baseballs protruded through my inner roof.

That was no tree.

The car creaked and moaned. Whatever had landed on my car was now moving.

The cold realization of my guardian's warning exploded inside my head like a bottle rocket. The litchen insects had done their job and hijacked Priya's link to my Heka; their host demon had materialized from the Æthyr . . . and it had found me.

I rammed my foot down on the gas pedal. The car spun in place briefly, then shot across the pavement, full bore, propelling me across the brief straightaway segment of the mountain road. Whatever was on top of my car made a terrible noise, and the weight shifted to the back of the roof.

The next sharp turn came way too fast. I gritted my teeth and jammed the brakes with every bit of strength I had. As

I rounded the turn, tires squealing, the weight on the roof shifted again. The unbalanced load nearly caused the car to spin out around the curve.

I straightened the wheels out and floored it to take the next straightaway. Midway down the road, the driver's window exploded inward. I squeezed my eyes shut and turned away as a spray of rain and glass flew inside.

During that moment of distraction, the car slipped off the side of the road, plowing through bushes and several small trees. I yanked it back onto the pavement, unable to see clearly. The windshield was fogging over and something wet on my face was filming over my eyes; I couldn't tell if it was rain coming in from the busted window or my own blood.

Light darkened in the open window. I cut my eyes to the side and saw what had broken my window; it definitely wasn't a tree branch.

An upside-down face was descending from the roof.

The face was green and smooth as polished stone. A matching green halo misted around its head, neck, and shoulders. Red eyes blinked twice.

I could barely hear myself scream as a hand thrust itself into the open window and locked onto my arm. The car hydroplaned, and everything around me seemed to be moving in slow motion. My body jerked forward against the seat belt.

The sound of the crash was monumental. Deafening. Everything went white. Pain shot through my face—the air bag.

As it deflated, I sat in my seat, stunned. White, powdery dust released from the air bag clung to me and filled the car like smoke; I nearly choked trying to cough it out of my lungs. I glanced around, waving away the haze. The front end of the car was crumpled like an accordion around a tree trunk. The windshield wipers continued on high speed, as if nothing had happened, and the dashboard lights were still on.

I forced myself to test stiffened muscles, but nothing appeared to be broken. Every inch of my body throbbed as I unlatched my seat belt. Then a ghastly cry echoed around the woods from somewhere behind me. The demon. It must have been thrown off during the crash.

My hands fumbled for the door handle; it took me several tries to open it. I swung my leg out the door, then stumbled out, falling onto my hands and knees in the muddy ground beside the car.

Branches broke in the dark trees just past the wrecked car. I couldn't see it, but I could hear it crashing through the woods, coming for me. I scrambled to my feet, then sloppily ran around my car and took a sharp left to follow the road down the hill.

Soaked from head to foot within seconds, I pushed the rain and hair out of my eyes, pitched forward, and bolted down the steep incline.

The wooded road blurred as I ran; the sound of creaking metal resonated behind me. The demon was trying to find me inside my car. Maybe that would buy me some time. I whirled around the next sharp turn, then sped back up and busted ass.

Several seconds passed before I heard a new sound behind me. *Thump-thump. Thump-thump.* Dull smacks against the wet pavement . . . something loped in the distance; the demon had abandoned the car. Once he rounded the curve, he'd spot me on the road. Terrified, I veered sideways and tore into the bushes lining the pavement. I exploded through the underbrush and into the woods, attempting to plow a straight path down the mountain instead of sticking to the zigzagging road.

That might've been a mistake.

The woods were too thick, the ground below rocky and uneven. Branches lashed across my face like barbed whips. I might as well have been a buffalo galloping through the trees—he'd be able to easily hear me now. I tried to concentrate hard enough to activate one of the sigils on my arm, but I couldn't do it while running; it was just too hard.

I stumbled and recovered, and continued to race.

Don't fall, don't fall, I repeated to myself, as if that would help.

Up ahead, where the woods ended, I broke through and vaulted down onto the dark pavement. Though I'd bypassed one loop of the winding road, there were probably four or five more loops to go. I hustled down the road, listening to the sound of the demon in the woods behind me. I cleared one sharp turn, then went for the next patch of woods again. Either path was doomed; the woods slowed me down, but the road offered the demon a clear shot at me.

I stumbled through the dark underbrush again, crying out as I plunged through a thick spiderweb. My arms frantically brushed away the clinging web as irrational fear made me batshit-crazy for a moment. Scared of a damn spider when a bloodthirsty demon was chasing me down. Ridiculous. Just as I calmed down, the trees opened up again, and I floundered to hurdle myself out onto the road.

As I did, two bright lights lit up the rain in front of me and brakes squealed on the wet pavement. Before I could slow down, I ran smack into the front of a parked car like a linebacker doing drills. One leg slipped out from under me; I fell backward onto the pavement with a brutal thud.

I lay in the mud with my mouth open, unable to move for several seconds. Car doors opened and footsteps raced toward me. I lifted my head and glanced back to see the demon storming through the woods. With long arms and spindly, webbed fingers, he was swinging himself from tree to tree like an overgrown green monkey.

When he spotted me, he swung himself up higher into a tree at the edge of the road. Mad, crimson eyes glowed in the headlights. The scaly monster sniffed the air, then opened a mouthful of sharp, mangled teeth and bellowed out a bearlike roar.

He reared back in one final swing and propelled his body toward me, muscles straining and taut. My body stiffened, but I couldn't scream. All I could manage to do was roll to one side and cover my face.

10

A shotgun blast revived me.

The green demon landed at my feet, belly-flopping against the pavement with a boom that scattered a puddle of muddy water over me in a wave.

Frantic, I shuffled against the asphalt like I was trying to pedal a bike and backed up from the pile of quivering flesh. It groaned and moved. I stumbled to my feet and slammed against something warm and solid behind me.

"Lon!"

He wrapped one arm around my shoulders and pulled me back. His other arm held a Remington Model 870 shotgun.

"Get away from him, Jupe!" he shouted.

Jupe's wiry form darted in front of the headlights and headed for us.

"Take her," Lon commanded, thrusting me into Jupe's arms. Lon aimed at the demon and blasted him again in the back. The shot boomed in my ears and echoed through the woods. The beast jerked and let out a wail.

Jupe clung to me in fear, repeating "Oh shit, oh shit" several times before asking, "Is it dead, Dad?"

Lon took a step forward. Dark, brackish blood began pooling around the demon's torso; it groaned and attempted to get up. "Not yet." Lon's face was composed and focused as he racked the shotgun.

"No!" I yelled, breaking away from Jupe. "Don't kill it!"

Lon spun around with a snarl on his face. "What?"

"I can bind it—force it to talk."

"Are you fucking crazy?"

"It killed my guardian! I have no protection in the Æthyr anymore—if I can't get a lead on who did this, I'm a sitting duck."

Lon's initial angry expression momentarily changed to an alarmed one, then settled on emotionless deadpan. With his shotgun still aimed, he looked at the dying beast on the ground, then turned back to me, lowering his gun.

"What do you need?"

"I need something to draw a binding triangle." My eyes darted around the mountainous landscape. This was going to be nearly impossible. The rain was beginning to let up a little, but it wasn't as if I could use a pen to draw on the wet pavement—it would run and dissolve before I could even charge it. I needed something more permanent. "Oh! Do you have a pocketknife?"

He narrowed his eyes at me. "Pocketknife?"

"Don't men your age always have pocketknives?" I asked in a high-pitched voice.

"*My* age? I'm not a fucking grandfather," he snapped.

"There's a knife in the SUV!" Jupe yelled as he ran around the door to lean inside. He returned with a gardening knife, serrated on one side and slightly curved to double as a trowel. Twine was wrapped around the blue plastic handle.

"Perfect."

I snatched the knife and approached the demon; it lay facedown on its stomach. Keeping a wary distance, I leaned down and began scratching a rough triangle into the asphalt. The knife made a repulsive grating sound as it scraped the pavement. Jupe covered his ears with his hands.

The light gray trail that I made on the road dulled as the rain fell, but that didn't matter. I didn't have to see it gleaming in neon; the indentation I made was sufficient.

I finished drawing one side, then started on the next. Lon followed me as I went, training his gun on the dying demon. Second side done. When I started the third, my hand spasmed, weary from the scratching vibration, so I double-fisted the knife and pressed on until I'd closed the triangle. It was rough but workable.

"Hurry up," Lon demanded when the demon twitched.

"Hold on. I've got to do the symbols." I could draw them in my sleep . . . interconnecting circles and winding sigils with overlapping lines. The trapping magick is ancient and straightforward.

Before I could finish, however, the demon became cognizant of what was happening. He groaned and turned his head, eyes struggling to focus on his surroundings. As I scratched the last sigil outside the triangle's apex, the demon's eyes went wide in fear. He pushed himself up with a growl, fell down, then frantically reached out for the triangle's border in desperation.

"Arcadia!" Lon yelled.

I closed my eyes and sought out the nearest energy source, cursing the fact that the lightning from the storm was gone. Lightning is hard to control and certainly wasn't my first choice for electrical energy—I pity medieval magicians who were forced to use it out of necessity. However, I had to work with something; it took a good bit of Heka to close a binding.

The lightning may have passed us by, but Lon's SUV was there, and it was running, the engine generating a steady flow of energy. Good enough. Without a caduceus, the release was going to have to be raw again—twice in two days, and this needed more energy than the piddly imp portal.

The demon was using his webbed fingers to pull himself along the asphalt. He was inches away from escaping my crude trap.

I concentrated and pulled from the car engine. Hard. No time for it to accumulate. The headlights dimmed as the engine struggled and resisted, playing tug-of-war with me. I barked the binding words, whacked my palm on the triangle, and released the kindled energy. My stomach lurched: the demon gave one last push and touched the edge of the triangle . . .

The air crackled near his fingertips. He jerked his arm back and wailed.

Too late. I had him.

I stood up and wiped my hands on my wet jeans, then I spoke to him in a dry, cracking voice. "You are bound by me now, and must answer honestly. Who sent you to find me?"

The demon made a gargled sound.

"Answer me," I commanded. My stomach roiled from the raw magick; I hoped I wasn't going to throw up.

"Kill me," he replied in a rough voice.

Lon lifted his shotgun. "Gladly."

"Not yet." I put my hand on Lon's arm, then stared down at the dying creature. "Demon, answer me. You are bound, those are the rules."

He sputtered out a cough, then a low laugh. "Yes, those

are the rules. All right, Mother of Ahriman." A backhanded slur that meant demon queen; I'd been called that before by other summoned Æthyric demons. "The name you seek is Riley Cooper. She looks a lot tougher and meaner than you, Mother. I doubt that she will accept my failure and move on. She's prepared to bring you to her people."

Lon shot me an inquisitive glance.

"Is there anything else you can tell me?" I asked the demon.

"I can tell you how you're going to die . . . would you like to know?"

Without hesitation, Lon lifted his shotgun and blasted the demon in the head. Black blood sprayed across the bottoms of our jeans and over the wet pavement, only to be washed away by the rain seconds later.

The demon was dead.

"You could have asked me if I was finished," I complained, staring down at the oozing green lump of grotesque flesh.

"You were."

"Can I look now?" Jupe peered from behind the open car door. When his father didn't answer, Jupe took that as a yes and sprang to our side. "Gross! Oh my God!"

"Maybe you shouldn't be looking at this," I said.

"You've *got* to be joking. This is the coolest thing that's ever happened to me!"

"Jupe—" Lon said in an exhausted voice.

"I mean, I'm glad you're okay, Cady. You are okay, aren't you?" He reached out to touch my cheek. I winced and drew back, then gingerly patted my face. When I brought my fingers back down, they were red with blood.

"Did you fall?" Lon asked, gently turning me toward the headlights for a better look.

"No. Glass from my side window. Or the air bag. I'm not sure."

He tilted my chin and inspected my face. "Just a few cuts. Nothing major."

"How did you find me?"

He pulled out my deflector charm from his jacket pocket and held it out to me. "Jupe found this in the dining room—looks like the clasp is broken. We were going to try to catch you before you got too far, then we heard the wreck. Sound carries up here."

I took the charm from him, fisting it with a sigh and cursing my bad luck. "But how did you get in front of me?"

"There's a side road that's faster than the main one. Not so many twists."

"I wish you had told me that when I came up here," I grumbled.

"So, who is this Riley Cooper? She sent a Pareba demon after you. That's nothing to ignore."

"Someone from the Luxe Order, I'm assuming. You've read about this kind of demon?"

"Sure. See all those lesions on his back?" Lon broke the triangle and nudged the green corpse with the toe of his low-top sneaker. "He's a host demon. He carries insect babies on his back that he sends out—"

"As scouts, yes. My guardian told me. I saw an image of them attacking before the Pareba appeared."

"You have a guardian angel?" Jupe asked, pushing his wet spiral curls out of his eyes. He looked like a drowned rat with his hair all flattened out on top.

"More like a guardian spirit. Priya. We'd been linked together since I was sixteen." Not only had I lost Priya, but I'd lost my only connection to my parents. Raw emotion caught me by surprise. I blinked several times and shook it off.

"We need to move the body," Lon said. "His Æthyr energy could be tracked. Not likely, but we shouldn't take chances. How bad is your car?"

"Huh? I dunno, pretty bad, I think. Wrapped around a tree a couple of loops up the road."

"Why don't you stay with us tonight? We'll call a tow in the morning."

"No. I've got to work on . . ." I tossed a wary look toward Jupe. He'd seen more than I would've preferred already. ". . . what you gave me earlier and I've got to feed Mr. Piggy."

"You're being hunted. It's not safe," he argued.

"My house is heavily warded. I'm safer there than here."

Jupe snorted. "I doubt that. My dad put up a gigantic protective circle around the house last spring," he said proudly. "We used to have imp problems, but not anymore."

Lon closed his eyes and flexed his jaw.

"You put up a ward? You . . . practice?" I asked, taken aback.

"Nothing major. I dabble."

A strange tightness took root in my chest. Though he was the first demon I'd come across to do so, I could understand his wanting to study demons; for him it was like studying history. But a demon practicing magick? It just didn't happen. Humans practiced magick, demons succumbed to it. At least, that's what I'd always been taught. Granted, that rule was meant to apply to Æthyric demons, not Earthbounds. But I'd never once run across an Earthbound who practiced magick. Never. I don't know why this shocked me so much, but it did.

And why didn't he tell me earlier? If I was going to be honest with him, then he damn well better be with me. His face tightened, then I remembered his empathic abilities. "I'll explain more later, okay?" he said in a low voice. I knew what he meant: not in front of Jupe. I swallowed and nodded.

"Let's get this body in the back of the SUV. We can dump it in the ocean. There's a private road on my property we can take—"

"I need to get my purse out of my car and call a cab—"

"—then after we dump the body, we'll take you home," he insisted.

I was too exhausted to protest.

11

I glanced at the clock on Lon's dash. Almost 2 a.m. We were only a few blocks away from my house. Lon was quiet and thoughtful, eyes on the road and one hand draped over the top of the steering wheel. His hair and jacket were smudged with dried black blood; the two of us had weighted down the green Pareba demon with rocks and dumped him off a low cliff into the Pacific a few miles from Lon's house. That was a new one for me; I'd never had to kill anything, nor get rid of a body. When I apologized to Lon for dragging him into this mess, all he said was, "Shit happens."

Jupe sat in back of us with his head stuck between the front seats, talking nonstop the entire trip to Morella. "Hey," he said as we made the final turn onto my street, "do you think that's what our ancestors looked like before they were stuffed into human bodies?"

"Invoked into human bodies," I corrected. "Not stuffed."

"We're not descended from Parebas. We're Kerub. They aren't green," Lon added.

Jupe blew out a hard breath. "That's a relief. I was imagining myself with scales and red eyes. That's kinda cool in a way, but kinda gross too. He looked like an alien. How old do you think he was?"

"I don't know." Lon gave me a sidelong glance in the dark car before pulling into my driveway. I'd been sort of numb during the drive, but now that I was home, my stress level was rising again. From the inquisitive look on Lon's face, I guess he must have sensed the change in me with his empathic ability.

He instructed Jupe to stay inside the SUV while he walked me to my side door. I was glad to have a few seconds alone with him. "What about Jupe?" I asked.

"He'll be fine," he answered.

"No, I mean . . . don't take this the wrong way, but he's pretty chatty. Will he go back to school after the weekend and tell all his friends that he watched his dad shoot an Æthyric demon who was chasing a magician from Morella?"

His lips curled up into a muted smile. "He's a loudmouth, that's for sure. But he's good at keeping quiet about things that count. You're not the only one living a lie, you know. Earthbounds hide their abilities and identities around humans every day."

"Oh. Yeah, I guess you're right."

"Don't worry, I'll talk to him," he assured me. We stopped at the bottom of my steps. "Are you planning on summoning the albino demons I found for you tonight?"

I licked dry lips. "I had been, but I'm feeling pretty drained from that binding."

"Maybe you should wait and try them tomorrow. If this Riley Cooper person was able to bargain with that Pareba to track you down, you might be in more danger than you thought. Maybe you should take the time to ward yourself first. If you're dead, who's going to help your parents?"

He was right, of course.

"And if you don't mind," he added, "I'd like to watch you summon them. I've never seen it done before."

"Sure. But only if you tell me what you have seen and done as far as magic goes."

He nodded once. "Deal. Get some rest. I'll continue looking through goetias tomorrow and let you know what else I find."

"Thanks, Lon."

He sniffled and glanced back at the SUV. "Better get him home and into bed. Talk to you tomorrow."

I watched him retreat down my driveway and get in the car. Jupe's lanky form slipped through the seats as he took my place up front while Lon drove away. As the red taillights disappeared, a final reminder of the Pareba demon's red eyes, I felt an unwelcome hollowness settle in my chest.

Though I wasn't comfortable accepting help from other people, I wasn't too proud to listen to good advice, and Lon was right about protecting myself. But that was easier said than done, since I didn't even know what or who the enemy was. The Pareba demon had given me a name: Riley Cooper. That was a good place to start.

An hour of internet searches gave me squat on any Riley Cooper with occult affiliations. But a lot of magicians used alternate names; Bob Smith the VP might not want his corporate colleagues to know about his occult leanings on the weekends, so he'll be known as Frater Wolverine in his order. Some occult organizations even issued new names to members who achieved higher grades. And in the E∴E∴, only the highest-ranking officers had access to members' actual surnames.

After assessing my options, I figured if Riley Cooper had

used magick to track me down, then I would do the same in return. And now that I had her name, I decided that a servitor was the easiest way to find her.

Servitors are Heka boomerangs: roving balls of focused magical energy that I can shoot out into the world. They're able to perform simple but mindless tasks, like remote viewing and spying, information gathering.

Creating servitors is an advanced skill that most magicians never master. My parents thought they were too risky and hard to control, so they discouraged me from learning about them; despite this, after I was on my own, I taught myself the basics through trail and error.

First, I needed a physical vessel to anchor the Heka. I stockpiled a supply of crudely sculpted clay dolls for this purpose; only a few inches tall, they looked like miniature versions of the First Emperor of Qin's Terracotta Army. Whenever I needed to send out a servitor, I'd draw an appropriate sigil related to its task on the body of one of the dolls. Then it was just a matter of conducting a simple life-giving spell. The servitor itself didn't look like much, just a loosely humanoid shape made of light. Once charged, it would emerge from the clay doll like a tiny fairy and be on its merry way to do my bidding.

To ensure that the servitor returned to me, I had to keep the clay doll safe. After creating and sending out a servitor to locate Riley Cooper, I stashed the doll in my pocket and put it out of my mind; it might take a day or so for it to return from its mission.

After I faked my death with my parents, I was terrified that Luxe or another order would use servitors to track me down, but it never happened. The caliph thought it might be whatever my parents had bred into me during my conception—that my energy was hard to track. Or maybe it was all the magick I did to keep myself hidden. There were dozens of minor wards that would protect someone from being found by another magician's servitors, and if Riley Cooper was able to control that Pareba, I should expect resistance. But I had to at least try; maybe I'd get lucky.

Creating a servitor to track down Riley Cooper exhausted me, so I slept for a few hours, thinking I'd eventually call Lon and find out if he still wanted to watch me summon the albino demons he'd found. However, I woke up early the next morning with a left-field idea that made me change my plans.

Shortly after my parents and I went into hiding, the Black Lodge slayings were the subject of several talk shows featuring guests who were loosely connected to the killings—mostly former police officers who profiled serial killers and occult "experts." But two people caused a minor uproar: Mr. and Mrs. Tamlin, former members of the Luxe Order.

On a popular talk show, the Tamlins claimed that the killings were done by a big, bad horned demon. In the human public's mind, this was the equivalent of saying that they'd been committed by Sasquatch or the Loch Ness monster. Their claim was ignored, but they were so insistent and quirky that their five minutes of fame became a popular internet clip for several months. A few parodies even popped up, along with creatively edited versions featuring comical music.

The Tamlins might have been ridiculed by the public and dismissed by the authorities, but they'd also been booted from the Luxe organization. This fact was only mildly interesting to me back when my only concern was staying hidden; but now that my family's lives were on the line, I was willing to exhaust every thread of possibility that might get me one step closer to finding the albino demon. And just *maybe* the Tamlins lost their membership because they had actual information that Luxe wanted to cover up.

I did some quick research and discovered that the Tamlins were now living in San Francisco, only a couple of hours north of Morella. I gave them a call in the morning, posing as a reporter covering the recent appearance of the Duvals on the security tape in Texas. I said that I believed their story from years ago and wanted to speak with them in person. Surprisingly, Mrs. Tamlin agreed immediately and asked me to come before dinner . . . which was at four. Some days I hadn't even eaten breakfast by that time. But I consented and made the trip north in a rental car.

I arrived in San Francisco around three and threaded through a couple of beautiful old neighborhoods until I found their address at the bottom of a long hill in Noe Valley. Even though I loved the Bay Area, I detested parallel parking on steep inclines; in my new rental car that had a spiffy park-assist feature, though, I felt a little invincible. And with my deflector charm on a new chain and the large ward that I'd drawn on the hood of the rental car in clear ink, I also felt safe. Well, somewhat.

I staked out a parking space up the hill, then made my way back to the Tamlins' address on foot. It was a small, blue Victorian row house with bay windows and crackled white trim. The front stoop was in disrepair and the windows were dirty.

After knocking, I stepped back as locks clicked. A tiny elderly woman peered from behind a cracked door, then smiled when she saw me and opened it. With white hair pinned in a bun, she was dressed in a pink sweater and had a painful-looking hump on her upper back. She squinted up at me in the afternoon sun.

"Hello," I said with a smile. "Are you Mrs. Tamlin?"

"I am. Are you the reporter?"

"Yes, Amy Smith."

"Oh, that's right. Come in, won't you?" Mrs. Tamlin led me through a narrow entry into a formal living room and called out to her husband. "Frank! The girl on the phone is here."

A tired grunt came from another room, and shortly after, Mr. Tamlin emerged. Not much taller than his wife, Mr. Tamlin was a bald man with thick white eyebrows. He sported a red polka-dot bow tie.

"Frank, this is . . ." She looked up at me apologetically.

"Amy," I finished, and held out my hand.

"Oh." He looked me over, then said with profound disappointment, "A blonde."

I'd worn a long wig and glasses to complement my new role as reporter. Better safe than sorry.

"She's not here for your entertainment, Frank," Mrs. Tamlin said angrily. "Angie, please sit. Would you like tea?"

Angie, Amy. It didn't really matter. I declined her offer of tea and sat in the worn armchair she offered as they slowly sank into a pink love seat across from me.

"Where did you say you were from?" she asked once they got settled.

"Sacramento."

"Oh, yes. We've never been there. More familiar with the southern part of the state."

"That's right; you haven't lived in San Francisco all your life, have you?"

"No, we're from San Diego. After we left the Luxe Order, though, there was no reason to stick around there. Our grandchildren live up here and in Portland."

"Speaking of the Luxe Order, can you tell me exactly why you left?" This seemed as good a place to start as any.

"Oh, we were dismissed," Mrs. Tamlin said.

"Kicked out was more like it," Mr. Tamlin corrected. "Over forty years in the order, and the bastards refused to stand by us after we appeared on that talk show."

"Because you told the truth?"

"What? No. Because we"—his fingers curled to make air quotes—"embarrassed the organization and broke our vows of silence. That's what our discharge letter said."

I crossed my legs and tried to breathe in through my mouth instead of my nose; the room smelled musty. "On the talk show, you said that a demon killed the three victims of the Black Lodge slayings."

"That's right," Mrs. Tamlin agreed, her eyes fixing on mine challengingly. "Do you believe in demons, Anna?"

"I believe anything is possible."

Together they gave me identical, slow smiles. *Really* creepy smiles. These people were part of the reason that occult practitioners had a bad public image.

"You never said exactly how you knew that a demon did it," I noted. That was primarily because they spent all their on-air time yelling back and forth with the studio audience, trying to convince them that demons really existed. UFOs and demons were equal in the minds of savages—just conspiratorial BS. Anyone who cried demon or claimed to be abducted by spaceships was gullible or uneducated at best.

Mr. Tamlin leaned forward to pick through a small crystal bowl of colorful hard candy that stuck together in clumps; I wondered how old it was. "We knew it was a demon because we were there when Magus Dempsey was killed."

Magus Dempsey was the third murder victim, the head of

a small Portland organization called Societas Mysterium An-
glia. I'd counted on the Tamlins to relay bits of gossip about
the fourth botched murder attempt at the Luxe temple—their
own order's temple in San Diego—but I hadn't expected them
to be witnesses to the third murder. What in the world were
they doing in a rival order's temple?

"Was that known publicly?" I asked. "Because I thought
you were witnesses to the Luxe attempt—the fourth incident."

"That damned talk show," Mr. Tamlin said. "Their pro-
ducers got the information wrong. We weren't there during
the fourth attempt."

"But the talk show aired after the Duvals were killed in
the car accident," I pointed out. "Why did it take you so long
to come forward?"

Mrs. Tamlin sighed heavily. "The killer cast some sort of
confusion spell on us after Magus Dempsey was murdered.
We found a sigil drawn in sand on our doorstep when we got
back home from the crime scene. Not soon enough, though.
We both stepped through it before we noticed it. As soon as
we did, wham! All the events got muddled."

"We didn't even remember the murder for weeks. Once
memories started trickling in and we realized we'd been
crossed, it took us more than a month to shake off the spell,"
Mr. Tamlin explained. "We tried everything to clear the fog.
All that magical talent in Luxe, and would you believe that
not *one* of the officers could remove that damned spell? In the
end, we finally got an old hoodoo priestess to do a successful
uncrossing."

"After she removed the spell, all our memories came back
sharp as a tack. That's when we told the Luxe leader everything that happened a few days before he was attacked."

Uh-huh. I was beginning to doubt my bright idea to

interview this couple. "So you told him at that time that you'd witnessed the third murder?"

"Not the murder itself," Mr. Tamlin admitted. "But we did walk in shortly after."

"Can you explain in detail what you saw and who was present?"

Still poking around the bowl of hard candy, Mr. Tamlin finally found the piece he wanted and struggled to pry it away from another. "Sure. I'll tell you exactly what we told Luxe. We drove up to Magus Dempsey's house early in the evening—"

"But Magus Dempsey was head of a rival organization, not the Luxe Order," I argued. "Why were you at his house?"

"Yes, he was the head of the Portland order. His daughter married our second son. We were good friends."

Interesting. If anyone from the E∴E∴ married someone from another occult order, it would be scandalous. It surprised me that Luxe wasn't the same way. I knew our order was definitely more of an old-world organization, and that others were more liberal, but still, who knows? Maybe all that crap my parents wanted to do with their United Occult Order plan would have been more universally accepted than I'd imagined.

"Like I was saying, we had flown in to meet him for our quarterly ghost-banishing ritual. He had terrible problems with ghosts, you see—"

Oh, Mother of God. Them too? Come on, folks; it's just imps. Say it with me: *There are no such things as ghosts*. Sometimes I really wished other people besides Earthbounds could see what I could.

"—and when we rang the doorbell, Magus Dempsey didn't answer, so we walked inside. Saw him split in two on the living room floor. His body was lying in front of a demon that was being forced back into the Æthyr inside a binding triangle. Enola and Alexander Duval were standing beside it, and another fellow."

What? My parents were there? My heart began racing. There were too many questions I wanted to ask them at once. I tried to stay calm and work through them. "I wasn't aware that the Duval couple was present at any of the killings—only the attempted fourth murder of the Luxe head in San Diego. Are you sure it was them?"

"Oh yes, we were quite sure," Mrs. Tamlin said. "Everyone in the magical community knew who they were. They had several occult books published in the 1980s and '90s. Let's see, *The New Aeon and You*, that was an early one. *Why Magick Matters*, that was popular."

"Yes, I'm aware of their publishing career," I said impatiently, cutting her off before she recited every title they'd written.

"Well, that's how we recognized them—their photo was on the back of all their books."

That was true. I knew that during that time, my parents were representing our lodge in a series of annual occult meetups around the country. Plus, they were on friendly terms with Magus Dempsey. So maybe they really *were* present during the third murder; it still didn't mean that they were guilty.

"So, you walked in and recognized the Duvals, but who was the third person?"

"Wish we knew," Mrs. Tamlin said wistfully.

"We only saw him for a second or two," Mr. Tamlin confirmed. "He was turning to run out the door."

"And probably headed straight to our house to lay down that confusion spell," Mrs. Tamlin added.

"Did you have any contact with the Duvals after this? Do

you know if they'd been crossed by the same confusion spell?" I wasn't even sure if I believed them, but spells like that did exist, and it would certainly explain why my parents never mentioned being present during the Dempsey murder: Maybe they didn't remember it.

Her husband shrugged. "We never talked to them again. It's not like they're in the phone book." Hardly. Even when we weren't on the run from the law, my parents kept a low profile. My mom used to be a marketing manager; back then she publicly used her maiden name, Artaud. After my parents were accused of the murders, dozens of her former coworkers came forward to bitch about how they were now scarred for life that they'd been working with a serial killer. Never mind that she'd been one of their favorite colleagues.

Mr. Tamlin continued. "But I wouldn't be surprised if that strange man had cast the same spell on the Duvals. They didn't know who he was either. They were just there to meet with Magus Dempsey and had walked in a few seconds before we did."

"We were all shocked and trying to figure out what to do," Mrs. Tamlin said. "There's something called the Code of Silence among magical orders—"

"Yes, I'm aware of that," I said.

"Well, it applies not only to the work we do in our order, but it also prevents us from talking to outsiders about order business."

I scratched the edge of my wig; it was starting to get itchy. "But surely that doesn't apply when it comes to murder."

Mr. Tamlin shook his head. "We discussed it with the Duvals and agreed to share what we'd seen with heads of our orders—let them decide how they wanted to proceed. We called the police anonymously and parted ways."

Unbelievable. I knew all orders operated outside the law, but this was insane.

"What did the third man look like?" I asked. "Can you describe him?"

"He was a young gentleman with white hair—"

"Blond hair," Mr. Tamlin corrected.

"Was it blond?" his wife replied, poking a finger inside her bun to scratch her head. "Yes, maybe you're right. Anyway, he was much younger than us, dressed in his ritual robes."

"Oh? Ritual robes? What color?"

"Blue, I think," Mr. Tamlin replied as he enthusiastically sucked on his candy.

"No, the robes were definitely black," Mrs. Tamlin said impatiently.

"It was dark," her husband said. "There were candles lit. The room was prepared for our ghost-cleansing ritual. All the furniture was moved back as it usually was."

"What were the Duvals wearing?"

He shrugged. "Everyday clothes. Enola was wearing a short skirt, I remember that much. What a looker that gal was. Dark brown hair, long sexy legs—"

"Frank, keep it in your pants, why don't you?" Mrs. Tamlin scolded, much to my satisfaction. *That's my mom you're talking about, you dirty old man.*

He muttered to himself and leaned back against the love seat.

At least I knew that my parents weren't in their robes at the time, which only solidified my belief that they didn't summon the demon. Along with many other people their age, they were strictly old-school magicians who always donned robes before any rituals. The kind of impromptu magick that I often performed was frowned upon by the order. If my parents knew that I bound demons inside my bar, I'd get a long lecture about the difference between public and sacred spaces and the importance of the Code of Silence among magicians. Hell, if I wasn't the stupid "Moonchild," I'd probably get booted out just like the Tamlins.

"Okay," I said, "So, one man was fleeing the house while the Duvals stayed, but you also saw the demon, right? What did it look like?"

"It was really dark," Mrs. Tamlin started. *Oh, for the love of Pete*, I thought. Maybe coming out here was a colossal waste of my time after all. "And the demon was beginning to dematerialize, like I said, but it was white as snow and tall. Big, spiraling horns. Red eyes."

"More pink than red," Mr. Tamlin corrected. "Had a weird tongue too."

"But there *was* one thing we remembered years later."

"I thought you said the hoodoo priestess uncrossed you and that your memories came back 'sharp as a tack.'"

Mr. Tamlin gave me a sheepish look. "Well, almost all of them. A few things didn't come back for years . . . one being the demon's talons. I'd never seen anything like them in my life."

"Frank's right," his wife agreed. "The beast had four arms—two long ones below, and a short set of arms above those. The short ones on top had a single talon on the right arm, but the left arm was missing its mate."

"Really? That's interesting." That sure wasn't part of the caliph's description.

"Isn't it? There was a hole in its stumpy hand where a talon once was. It had been extracted like a tooth. But that's not all—the remaining talon on the other arm was about the size of a banana, made of crystal," Mrs. Tamlin.

"Crystal?" I replied incredulously.

"That's right, crystal. Or maybe glass. Have you ever heard of such a thing?"

"No, I haven't," I admitted.

"I think it might have been made of diamond," Mr. Tamlin amended. "Either way, it was clear and shined like glass in the candlelight before the demon disappeared."

Then a sudden realization hit me; my heart rate instantly doubled.

One of the unusual aspects of the Black Lodge slayings was the murder weapon: a glass knife. Along with two other pieces of testimonial evidence, the glass knife was the foundation of the police case and led to the warrant being issued for my parents' arrest. Along with my parents' fingerprints—which were planted by Luxe—was another unidentified print. Maybe that print belonged to the real killer, maybe even the Tamlins' robed mystery man?

"Are you saying that the glass knife mentioned in the case file was really a glass talon?"

"Yes," they confirmed in unison.

Okay, this was crazy, if it was true, but there were still too many strange things that didn't fit. "If your Code of Silence prevented you from going to the police about the Portland murder, then why did you break it for the talk show?" I asked.

Mr. Tamlin snorted in disgust. "After the Duvals were accused, we were shocked. We'd managed to clear most of the confusion spell by this point, you see, enough to know they weren't guilty. Like we said earlier, we talked to the Luxe leader and told him what we'd remembered. He advised us to keep quiet and promised to look into it. Then he was attacked and our temple went into lockdown. No classes, no services, and we weren't allowed communication with any of the upper officers. Then the media went crazy."

"Since our own leader wasn't talking to us," Mrs. Tamlin explained, "we tried to contact the E∴E∴ on our own, to help clear their names, but we could never get past their Bodymaster. She thought we were some sort of spies for Luxe. Then the Duvals died in that accident. Our son suggested we tell our story on the talk show, but that didn't work out very well either, as you know."

"We tried," Mr. Tamlin said with a sigh, "but no one wanted to hear the truth. The Black Lodge slayings were committed by a demon. And I'd swear on the sacred name of Hecate herself that the person who summoned it was the robed man who ran out the door of Magus Dempsey's house that day."

Hecate herself, huh? I still wasn't completely convinced that their memories were a hundred percent correct. But it was clear that, wacko or not, they certainly believed what they were saying. And if this mysterious robed man who fled the scene really *was* the person who summoned the albino demon, how was I going to find out who the hell he was?

Then we had the enigmatic glass talon. Let's just say the Tamlins *were* telling the truth, and this really was the murder weapon. And maybe my parents had been crossed by the same confusion spell and never remembered the third murder. They were still present during the fourth attempt and saw the albino demon there; surely they noticed something as strange as talons made of glass. So why hadn't the caliph mentioned it in his description?

12

I returned from San Francisco to find my driveway occupied by a large, backed-in truck. I parked the rental behind it, my rear bumper nearly sticking out into the street. A dense row of cedar trees created a natural screen along the front of my yard, ending at the driveway, so prying eyes couldn't see the front of my house. Most times, that was exactly what I wanted; it gave me privacy, and privacy was the only reason I owned a home instead of rented an apartment. That day, however, it was a nuisance.

I pushed up my sleeve to activate a sigil that rendered me nearly invisible. Not *literally*. It just encouraged people to disregard my presence by tricking their senses. Like the other sigils on my arm, this magick is temporary. It also requires a lot more Heka than some of others; keeping it charged was physically draining, so I'd have to make it quick.

My servitor hadn't returned to me yet, so I hoped to God Riley Cooper hadn't already found me. Just in case, I prepared myself by retrieving a small ceremonial dagger from my purse. It wasn't all that sharp, but it was better than nothing.

I peeked inside the cab of the unknown vehicle. Nothing. Then I stood on my tiptoes and surveyed the bed of the truck.

The tailgate was down. There were several enormous bags of pebbles and some other red landscaping material. I certainly hadn't scheduled any kind of professional yard work; my idea of lawn maintenance was paying the twelve-year-old kid down the street twenty bucks once a month to mow.

A loud thump came from the backyard. Maintaining the invisibility spell, I strode past my side door until I rounded the corner of my house. Bent over a wheelbarrow was someone in a pair of dirty jeans. I sidestepped the wheelbarrow in a slow circle, then jumped when the person stood up and turned around.

"Dammit, Lon," I said as I dropped my ward.

Upon seeing me, he let out a low yelp and nearly fell over backward.

"Jesus fucking Christ, you scared the shit out of me!"

"Excuse me for being wary about a stranger in my yard," I snapped.

"I'm not a stranger, and how the hell did you sneak up on me like that? You appeared out of thin air."

"It's a spell."

"That's one hell of a spell," he remarked.

I nonchalantly motioned toward my white tattoo like it wasn't a big deal, but I was pretty damn proud of the spell. Like my imp portal, it was something unique I created after I got out on my own. The basic sigil was Armenian in origin, and I had to tweak it and experiment before I finally hit on the right results.

"Why haven't you answered my calls?" I asked.

He wiped his hands on his T-shirt. The man was covered with red clay. It was on his shirt, the front of his jeans, and both hands. "You called? When? I got your message about going up to San Francisco. How'd that go?"

"Not that. I called you again several times over the last couple of hours on the ride back." I stepped forward to wipe a small streak of clay off his chin that was staining one side of his mustache. He flinched; guess I wasn't the only one who didn't like people touching me. "Hold still," I reprimanded. My motherly attention didn't help the streak, it only transferred some of the clay to my fingers. "What the hell are you doing with all this? Wait, this isn't normal clay—it's red ochre."

"I must have had the ringer turned off, and yes, it's red ochre. Slightly hydrated hematite powder, if you want to get technical. Don't breathe it in. It'll irritate your lungs."

"Holy shit! I've never seen it in this kind of quantity. There must be a small fortune here!"

He shrugged. "I get it from a local mineral supplier who mines it in Russia."

"Lon?"

"What?"

"What do you mean, 'what'? What the hell are you doing with all of this?"

His face relaxed as a grin spread across it. "I'm putting up a moat around your castle."

I arched a brow and waited for the rest.

"A ward," he clarified. "The same one I put up around my house last spring. The one motor-mouth spilled the beans about yesterday."

"Ah, that one." I tapped the flat of my blade against my thigh. "Jupe is at home, I take it?"

"Yep." He turned away to continue dumping the damp hematite powder into the wheelbarrow.

"And?"

"And what? You want me to cite the source I got the ward from?"

"Maybe for starters. Then you can tell me how you managed to charge it."

He finished emptying the hematite and folded up the empty plastic bag before stuffing it inside a trash can. Correction, my trash can. He'd taken it hostage. "Don't just put that in there like that," I complained. "The city won't take it away unless it's inside a garbage bag. Anything loose in there, they leave behind."

"Well, then, can you please put that knife down and bring me a garbage bag?"

"Fine." I pocketed the dagger and hiked through the yard.

"While you're at it," he called out behind me, "you might want to change into something grubby. This shit is messy as hell."

"I never volunteered to help."

"Then I guess I'm going to have to charge you."

"I didn't request your landscaping services—I'm not paying for something I didn't order."

"Bring an old spoon too," he added as I rounded the corner to unlock my door.

After changing clothes, I returned to find Lon using a dolly to tote a large white plastic bucket toward his wheelbarrow. When he lowered the dolly, with some effort, the contents of the bucket made a sloshing sound. I opened up one of the black garbage bags I'd brought with me and fished out the loose bags from the trash can.

"So, how did you charge this ward the first time you did it, and how long have you been practicing magick . . . and what else can you do?"

"You look cute with your hair up," he said in response. "Jupe's right—Bride of Frankenstein."

I couldn't tell if he was making fun of me or giving me a compliment. Either way, I resisted the urge to straighten my ponytail, which sat high on my head. "You're a strange man," I muttered as I squatted down to pick up one of the shovels he'd brought. "How far away does your empathic ability work?"

"Why? You plannin' to whack me on the head with that shovel?"

"Don't give me any ideas."

"Only a couple of feet away. Maybe five feet max, if the emotion is clear and strong. It's much easier for me to read a person if I'm touching them."

"Note to self, always maintain a five-foot distance," I said with a smile.

"Only if you have something to hide."

"I don't."

"You sure about that?" he asked with a suggestive smile that sent an unexpected ripple through my chest. Christ, could he sense that?

"*So* sure," I answered, forcing away the unwanted feeling. "How does this ward work?"

He studied me for a moment longer, the corners of his mouth twitching once, then dropped his eyes. "It emits a strong suggestive vibration. Anything that comes within a couple of feet of it with the intent to do you harm will be dissuaded. Most will just give up and leave."

"And if they don't?"

"If they cross the barrier completely, first you'll see that the ward's been breached. A network of blue lines will appear. Then a high-frequency sound will drop them to their knees. It's like a dog whistle—you won't hear it, but they will. If they persist, the sound will incapacitate them."

"Hmm, sounds good. Now tell me how you charged a ward this big."

He bent down over the white bucket and made repetitive digs around the lid with a small metal object to slowly pry the lid off. "I hooked myself up to a small electrical generator."

"What? You shocked yourself with a generator? Are you joking?"

"Nope."

"That's . . . insane. You could have been killed, you know?"

"Yep."

"You can't pull electricity on your own?"

"Not well enough to kindle the amount of Heka I needed to charge the ward sufficiently."

"I'm speechless."

"I didn't bring a generator this time. After seeing how well you pulled from my car last night, I was kinda counting on you being able to kindle enough Heka by yourself."

He finally got the lid of the bucket open far enough to leverage it off. I took a few steps closer, I peeked inside, smelling it before I saw it—pig's blood. It had already started coagulating.

I puffed up my cheeks and held my nose while backing away. "Good God almighty."

"You've never worked with pig's blood?" Lon said.

"Not that much of it. I buy it by the pint!"

"It's not so bad when you get used to—" He turned his head to the side and winced. His eyes began watering. "Fuck, I forgot how bad this reeks in big batches."

"Is it rotten?"

"No. I got it straight from the slaughterhouse this morning."

"Are we going to need all of it?"

"Maybe. If you've got any circles you need to make with

the leftovers, feel free." He coughed once, then backed up another step toward me.

I eyed it with greater interest. "Now that you mention it, I could use a couple of new imp portals. I burned up my last one at Mrs. Marsh's house the other night."

"Come on. Let's finish this first before it gets too dark." He held his hand out, requesting the shovel, then dipped a large metal can inside the bucket and began scooping blood into the wheelbarrow with the hematite powder.

"What do you want me to do?"

"See that jar over there?" He nudged his elbow at the grass behind me. "Be careful when you're opening it. Sprinkle two or three spoonfuls into the wheelbarrow. Don't get it on your skin or let it blow in your face. There are gloves and a surgical mask inside my truck if you want them."

I cautiously picked up the large mason jar. The contents were black. "What's this?"

"Ashes."

"What kind of ashes?"

"Don't ask."

"You didn't kill someone, did you?"

"Not so far, no."

I donned the gloves and mask and followed his instructions as he mixed up the nefarious concoction with the tip of the shovel. It churned together into a thick, dark paste.

"Tell me what you found out in San Francisco," he asked while he worked.

I related the story of my visit to the Tamlins in great detail until he started shooting me impatient scowls; after that, I sped up my narration. I followed behind him while he began shoveling the dark red paste around the base of my house, making a foot-wide border.

"Do you have to put it right up next to my house?" I complained.

"I'm going to cover it up with pebbles. Would you rather have an unexplainable ring of pebbles a few feet away from your house, or right next to it?"

I sighed. "Go ahead."

It seemed unfair to let him do all the labor, so I picked up the second shovel and offered to help. He instructed me to scoop up the nasty paste and sling it on the ground a few feet ahead of him; he followed and packed it down. As we worked, I continued my story until I got to the part about the glass talon.

He dug the shovel into the ground, leaned on it, and furrowed his brow. "No shit?"

"I know." I pulled the surgical mask down to hang around my neck. "If they're right and not crazy, then the bad news is that the albino demons you already found—"

"Probably aren't the right ones."

"That's *if* the Tamlins aren't insane," I reminded him.

"I wonder if there's any way to find a photo of the glass knife anywhere, to see if it looks like it could've been a talon."

"I've never seen a photo, but I was thinking about *Devil's Friends* on the way back from San Francisco."

He bent his head to wipe his chin against his shoulder. "Huh?"

"Some cheap exploitation paperback written about the Black Lodge slayings. I only thumbed through it, but I remember a drawing of the glass knife. The writer said it was based on a police officer's description. The handle was round and the blade slightly curved. I remember thinking that it looked more like . . . never mind."

Lon cocked a brow.

"Anyway," I quickly said, "what I mean is that the Tam-lins could be right about the talon. Maybe it wouldn't hurt to start looking for Æthyric demons with glass claws."

"I found four more albinos today. None with glass body parts of any kind." Something close to a smirk briefly crossed his mouth, then faded. "I don't know. Maybe you should hold off on summoning anything right now and let me refine my search for a day or two. If I can identify some with glass tal-ons, you could start with those. What do you think?"

"Maybe you're right. I guess I still have time." Honestly, the thought of summoning a host of unknown Æthyric de-mons for a lineup made me bone-weary. "Well, the good news is that it will be easier to identify, right?"

He pushed the half-empty wheelbarrow forward a few paces, then continued shoveling. "A hell of a lot easier to identify, but no easier to find. Still the same number of books to go through."

I hadn't thought about that. "I guess you're right," I said glumly as he patted down the section he was working on with the back of the shovel. I snapped my mask back over my mouth and returned to my work in silence.

We finished with the first batch, then he hauled two more bags of hematite from his truck and we started the pro-cess all over again. After three batches, we were halfway done. The sun was beginning to set, but we were both sweaty and aching, so we allowed ourselves a short break. We washed off our hands with the garden hose as best we could, then I went inside to get water. When I came back out, he was sitting in the backyard on an old rusted lawn chair lighting a valrivia cigarette. Shirtless.

In the last of the day's light, his skin was golden—in

contrast to my own complexion, which was either pasty or milky white, depending on your point of view. He was also lean and muscular. Not in an I-work-out-at-the-gym way, but more natural and honest. My eyes followed a thin line of honey-colored hair that bisected his torso from a small patch in the center of his chest down past his belly button. My clothes suddenly felt too tight.

I stopped in my tracks and pretended like I'd forgotten something, then turned back and rounded the corner of the house until he was out of sight. A few cleansing breaths gave me some control over my feelings. No way was I going to let him catch me mooning over him like some teenage girl.

The second time I approached him, I kept my head down and tossed him a bottle of water, then dragged another lawn chair over. Not too close. How far had he said his ability extended? I made a quick calculation and placed my chair several feet away.

"Do I smell that bad?" he asked before offering me a valrivia cigarette.

Dammit.

I leaned forward out of my chair to reach for it, then quickly sat back down, only to realize that I had no lighter. So I held out my hands, coaxing him to toss his over. Instead, he flicked the lighter and puckishly beckoned for me to come to him.

Double damn. I begrudgingly got out of my chair.

"Yeah, you kinda stink," I said after my cigarette was lit.

"So do you," he answered with a grin. Before I could make it back to my seat, he scooted down, stuck his leg out between mine, and hooked his foot around the leg of my chair, dragging it closer. Well within range of his ability. I plopped down in defeat.

"When's your servitor supposed to return?" he asked.

"I allowed it one day, so by tomorrow night, give or take. That kind of magick sometimes has problems adhering to strict schedules, so it could be a couple days."

He nodded, then we smoked in silence for a long moment. I tried not to look at him, but I couldn't help it. Fine lines creased the outer corners of his eyes. As he ran a hand through his hair, stray strands of ash blond and platinum floated in the wind at the crown while deeper shades of caramel brown flittered over the tops his shoulders. My eyes stubbornly wandered down his bare skin. He had a thick, pale scar, several inches long, that ran diagonally across his lower left ribs.

"What did that?" I asked.

He looked down, tucking his chin against his chest, then slumped back in his chair, his legs lazily falling open. "My ex-wife, Yvonne."

"Uh . . . wow. I thought she was a model, not a grizzly bear."

His knee rocked sideways once, almost touching mine. He studied me through slitted eyes. A smile threatened to lift up one side of his mouth as he took a long drag off his cigarette. "You've been studying up on me, I see."

"One of my waitresses lives in La Sirena. She thought I should be impressed that you were once married to a supermodel."

"Were you?"

"I'd never heard of her, so not really." I did, however, look up images of her online. She was lovely, all right. Medium brown complexion, full lips. Her face was long and regal—a feature she'd passed along to Jupe—and the lower half of her was just as stunning. Though, petty or not, I personally thought her hips were a little skinny. She was also flat-chested.

"From what I could tell, she seems quite attractive." And in some of the photos, Yvonne bore the same green-gold halo that Lon had. I started to ask about this, but he spoke before I could.

"She is. She's also high-strung and gets off on danger. If she's not getting coked up and gambling, she's participating in orgies or wrecking her car."

My mouth twisted as I remembered the image of my own car wrapped around a tree.

"Your wreck was different," he acknowledged with a smile. He flicked ashes and ticked off a short list of complaints. "Yvonne hated La Sirena—hated the beaches up here. Too full of sea lions and driftwood instead of sexy sunbathers. Hated my job. Hated being a mother; said it slowed her down, and she had no patience for Jupe's energy and questions. In her defense, though, he was kind of a handful when he was a toddler."

"I can only imagine." I chuckled, pushing hair out of my face. "What does Jupe think about her?"

"When he was younger, he thought she was glamorous. She'd bring him expensive presents when she visited. A couple of years ago he started to see her for what she was. Now he just feels sorry for her."

That made me a little sad, but I didn't say anything.

"He's close to Yvonne's sister, though—Adella—and his grandmother. The two of them live in Oregon. Adella's a university professor. She and her mom drive down here every few months to visit us, or we go up there. They've been real supportive. Love Jupe to pieces."

"At least he has that," I said. "Not everyone does." I gave

him a closed-lipped smile and his face softened. "My mom's parents died when I was about Jupe's age. I never knew my dad's parents."

"My parents are both dead," he said. "I inherited my money and property from them."

"Siblings?"

"Only child."

"Me too, but I guess you know that from watching the news." I squinted at his scar. "So how did she do that?"

He traced his finger along it and exhaled. "She cut me with a kitchen knife on my way into the divorce courtroom."

"Holy shit." I was shocked and slightly horrified.

"In the end, it was worth it. My request for full custody of Jupe was granted without question. The judge said she should be locked up in a mental institution, but I didn't have her arrested."

"Why not?"

"Because . . . my dabbling with magick is the reason she's the way she is," he said without emotion, stubbing his cigarette into the grass. He looked away, as if that were the end of the conversation.

"What? Don't think you can just drop a bomb like that and not explain it."

He shrugged, but didn't respond. Clearly he thought he'd said too much and was clamming up again.

"I've shared secrets with you," I reminded him, "so it's only polite that you return the favor."

The barest hint of a smile, but he wasn't budging.

"Fine," I said, brushing my hand on my jeans. "If you aren't ready to tell me now, I can wait."

He looked at me for a moment, then nodded. I interpreted that to mean that he'd tell me eventually. "Ready to get back to work?" he asked. "We need to get this finished. You've still got to charge the damn thing with Heka once we're done."

I sighed and pushed myself out of my chair with a groan, carefully scanning Lon's face for clues to his feelings. Funny that after all my years living in hiding, I was struck by the realization that someone else's secrets might be just as interesting as mine.

13

A day had passed since Lon and I erected the ward around my house, and my servitor still hadn't returned. I was beginning to worry, and contemplated pulling it back prematurely.

Apart from my house or Lon's, or my now heavily warded rental car, one of the safest places I could be was probably the bar. Being around people coming and going would help to disguise my energy from any lurking spies. So, regrettably, I resumed my shifts at Tambuku until Lon had had a chance to research our new glass talon lead. Most of our regulars acted glad to see me back behind the bar. I only had to break up one fight yesterday, and it didn't involve binding anyone, so not too bad.

Tambuku was busy today, and the work kept my mind off matters. During a short break early on in my shift, I tried to email Caliph Superior in Florida. I wanted to tell him about the glass talon and the visit to the Tamlins, but I didn't think it was a good idea to phone him, just in case his calls were being monitored. However, my email bounced back, saying that his in-box was full.

While I debated whether to risk a call to the caliph, my phone rang. Lon's number.

"Hey there," I answered. I'd been getting antsy waiting to hear from him today, so it was a relief that he'd called.

But it wasn't Lon's voice that answered in reply; it was Jupe's.

"Heya, Cady, whatcha doing?"

"Umm, working. What are *you* doing calling me on your dad's phone?"

"You're not mad, are you?"

"No—"

"Whew! You scared me there for a second. I didn't know your number and he checks all the calls I make on my cell phone, I mean, uh, not that it matters . . . anyway, are you at your bar? I looked it up online. How come you don't have a website?"

"We do have one, it just isn't very big."

"Pfft. A tiny photo with your address and phone number—that's not a website, that's a web *page*. You should let me build you a better one."

A thirteen-year-old kid can build a website these days? Holy shit. "Umm . . . we'll see."

"Hey, you wanna go on a date?"

"Huh? With who?"

"With me."

"Uh, Jupe, I'm flattered, but I'm a little old for you."

He laughed. "My dad said the same thing—he said you're too old for me and too young for him and told me not to get any ideas."

"Well, he's probably right." Though it stung to know that Lon thought I was too young.

"Look," he said, lowering his voice. "It's not *really* a date. There's this movie playing at the drive-in that I wanna see real bad. It's only playing for two more nights. My friend Jack was supposed to come with me tonight, but his parents won't take us. They say he's not allowed to stay out after ten on a school night."

"When I was your age, I couldn't either."

"Well, that's dumb. I can stay up till midnight."

"Impressive. Why can't your dad take you?"

"He says he's too busy."

Amanda walked up to the bar and gave me a three-drink order for a booth.

"Who are you talking to?" Jupe asked.

"I'm working, remember. I'm talking to a waitress."

"Oh, cool," he said, unfazed. "Anyway, so I was thinking, you could come pick me up and we could go see the movie together in your rental. I asked my dad what kind of car you rented and—"

"I can't tonight, Jupe. Working, remember?" God, the kid was hardheaded.

"What about tomorrow? Please. I'm begging! It's the last night. I'll *die* if I can't see it."

"Jeez, you'll die? What movie is it?" I finished mixing one drink and started a tray for Amanda.

"*Creature from the Black Lagoon.*"

"The one from the sixties?"

He snorted derisively. "The sixties? Man, I thought you knew about classic movies—1954. It never gets screened anywhere around here. Please, Cady. Please, please, *please*—"

"I have to work a half-shift tomorrow, so I won't get off work until eight-thirty."

"It starts at nine-thirty. How long would it take you to get here?"

"Uh, thirty minutes. Maybe less now that I know the shortcut up your cliff."

"COOL! We have time!"

"I don't know, Jupe . . ."

"Hey, you kinda owe me. My dad's been locked up in his stupid library for the last two days doing research for you and ignoring me. Besides, he says I'm driving him nuts anyway. If we leave him alone, he'll do your research faster."

I laughed. "Hell's bells, where did you learn to negotiate?"

"Will you do it? Huh?"

"All right," I said, caving in. "I'll pick you up at nine. Does your dad know?"

"No, but he won't care. He likes you. Wait, hold—"

I finished mixing the drinks just in time for Amanda to return with more orders; as I lined up four new tiki mugs, muffled conversation on the other end of the line turned into muffled yelling.

"Arcadia," Lon's voice said from my phone.

"Who is this?" I teased.

"You can't take my son on a date."

"I didn't ask him. He asked me."

"He stole my cell and called without permission."

"Sounds like a personal problem to me." A low growling noise came out of the phone. "It's just for a couple of hours. I'm not going to let him make moves on me, sheesh."

"You better not. He's still a virgin and I'd like to keep it that way."

My jaw dropped. "Are you joking? I can never tell if you're serious."

"Mhmph."

Okay, he was joking; the sad thing was that I was starting to be able to read his grunts better than his words.

"I'll try to control myself," I said. "Come on, it's just baby-sitting. Don't you trust me with your kid?"

"Says you, the person attacked by a Pareba demon a few days ago."

Ugh. He had a point. What if something happened while Jupe was with me? Lon would never forgive me. I sure as hell wouldn't if it were my kid. "You're right, maybe I shouldn't—"

"I know you've got your charm and have warded the rental car, I'm sure it's fine. To be honest, it's not you I don't trust, it's him. He once sneaked off from the drive-in."

"Oh, really? Well, I've never had a date bail on me before."

"I bet."

"You bet what?" What the hell was that supposed to mean? I accidently overpoured the Mai Tai I was making and started cussing under my breath as I grabbed a bar towel.

"Look, he's kind of a pain in the ass, so if you're just telling him yes because he put you on the spot, don't worry about it. I'm sure you've got bigger boys waiting in line for dates on your nights off."

I held the phone away from my ear and looked at it momentarily before speaking. Oh, too young for him, was I? "Lon Butler, are you trying to find out if I'm dating someone?"

Amanda leaned over the bar to grab napkins and gawked at me. "You're talking to Lon Butler on the phone?" she whispered excitedly. I made a face at her and put my finger up to my mouth to get her to shut up.

"No, I was just saying—" Lon began. Low grunt, long sigh. "Don't feel obligated to entertain Jupe."

Wide-eyed, Amanda giddily puckered up her mouth before I pushed her away from the bar. Great. Now I was going to have to concoct some lie about why I was talking to him.

"Well, it's not a big deal," I told Lon. "I like Jupe and I'm happy to get him out of the house and give you some quiet time. Besides, if I had 'bigger boys' lined up right now . . .

well, more interesting ones than the two losers who've asked me out tonight already—"

One of said losers, Tambuku's favorite Earthbound healer, Bob, looked up from his drink with a wounded look. Oh, brother . . . "Sorry, Bob. You know I didn't mean that," I whispered before turning away to finish with Lon.

"Anyway, I probably wouldn't be settling for movie-night with a teenage boy if I did."

He paused, then replied, "It's your funeral."

"All right, well, I'll pick him up at nine tomorrow. I take it you haven't found anything today, research-wise?"

"No."

I sighed. "Well, I gotta get back to work."

"See you tomorrow," he replied. "I'll make sure he's ready on time."

"Sounds good, have a go—" But the line went dead before I could finish. "So rude," I mumbled to myself. Maybe dating the younger Butler was preferable after all. He didn't grunt.

14

The next day, I stopped by Father Carrow's on my way to work. He was in his front yard watering plants. He glanced up to watch me step out of the car and smiled as I approached.

"Good afternoon, Father."

"Cadybell, what a nice surprise. On your way to work?" He rested the garden hose trigger on the porch steps and took a red bandana out his back pocket to wipe his brow. He was wearing a large floppy straw hat and dark blue pants.

"Yep. Watering your special shrub? What's it called? Yesterday . . ."

"Yesterday, today, and tomorrow. See, it still has all three flower colors on the side. The dark purple are the youngest, lilac middle-aged, and white are the oldest."

I leaned forward to breathe it in. The shrub stood the same height as me. "It smells so good. I can't believe it's still blooming."

"Lots of fertilizer and love, my dear. How's it going with Lon?" If I didn't know better, I would've said there was a little mischievous sparkle in his eye when he asked. I ignored it and answered casually, "Not bad. I was going to give you the latest update on the demon."

"Has he found it already? I told you he was good."

"He's been working tirelessly, but no luck yet."

Father Carrow picked up his hose and continued spraying around the base of the flower bed. "Oh, I'm sorry. What's the update?"

"Well, I found out that the description of the talons was wrong. Remember how I told you that it had two sets of arms?"

"Yes, and long talons on all of them."

"Turns out the talons might be glass."

"Glass?" He raised his floppy hat and scrunched up his face at me.

"Or a glasslike substance."

"That's a new one for me, dear. I've never come across anything like that before in my studies."

Rats. He finished working on the flowering shrub, then moved up a couple of steps to water three hanging baskets on his porch. They were in a precarious position, and he was having trouble reaching them. "Here, let me do it," I offered, setting my purse down. He relented and perched on the steps while I watered. I began telling him how one of the talons might be missing.

"Extracted like a tooth, supposedly. What Lon and I have been puzzling over is why. I mean, if the demon was just injured, then the talon would be broken, right? It seems like if someone or something pulled it out from the root, then they might have wanted it for some reason."

What I refrained from saying was that Lon and I really couldn't figure out why someone would remove the talon and use it to kill when they could just command the demon to kill for them. The good Father hadn't yet asked exactly why I needed to find the albino demon, so it was probably best that I omit any gory details regarding murder.

He thought about my question while he removed his hat and fanned it to cool his face. "I've never heard of a demon talon being a sought-after object. Still, it does remind me of the old fairy tales in children's books. Have you ever heard of *Struwwelpeter*? It's a famous German children's book."

"No. What's it about?"

"It's a group of nasty stories with descriptive pictures meant to frighten children into behaving. Kids who play with matches burn and die, kids who suck their thumbs get them cut off by a wicked tailor."

"Yikes."

"It was a Victorian-era book, and there were several copy-cat versions that followed once it gained popularity. One of those had several stories about demons. I had a rare copy of it as a child—it was my grandfather's. I've told you my mother's family was German."

"Oh, yes, that's right." I finished watering the last of the hanging baskets and began winding up the hose to put it away.

"Anyway, the book was written in German, so I couldn't read it, but the pictures were very descriptive. In one of the stories, a wicked witch gets angry at a girl who goes traipsing through her flowers on her way home from school every day. So the witch summons a demon to attack a little girl in her bed every night, biting off one finger before he disappears. On the fifth night, she only has her thumb remaining on her left hand. To stop the demon from taking it, she cuts off one of his horns and hides it in the woods. The next night, the demon doesn't come, because he can only be summoned by the person possessing the horn."

I turned the squeaky faucet handle to shut off the water, then sat down next to Father Carrow on the steps.

"Do you think that could be true? That my demon can't be summoned, even if we find the name and classification, because we need the talon to complete the summoning?"

"I really don't know, but it's an interesting notion, don't you think? Fairy tales sometimes contain small gems of truth, no matter how outlandish they might seem. Remember that children's book about the Lost Colony of Roanoke that was published in the early 1900s? It said that all the colonists who disappeared were really elves who moved west along with the Indians."

I gathered up my purse and car keys. "Pretty crazy that something as silly as a kids' book would be so on the nose."

"Exactly. If people only knew that it was really Earthbound *demons* and not elves . . ."

"Or that some of their next-door neighbors were really Earthbounds and not humans," I added with a wink. "By the way, speaking of demonic neighbors, Mrs. Marsh was asking about you yesterday. Let me know and I'll hook you guys up . . . I'm just sayin'."

He patted my shoulder. "My dear, if the good Lord has helped me to resist temptation this long, I assure you that your Mrs. Marsh would not be the thing to send me over the edge."

15

I knocked on Lon's door at five till nine, still contemplating Father Carrow's fairy tale; it worried me.

"Hi," Lon said upon opening the door.

"Hello yourself. Is my date ready?"

"He's getting his jacket. It's supposed to get cooler tonight."

"You're awfully spiffed up." Not really, but he was wearing a short-sleeved button-up shirt that wasn't covered in stains. Nice jeans, chunky silver belt buckle. His wavy brown hair was neatly tucked behind his ears, and a couple of seconds after I noted all this, the front of his neck darkened. Then I observed that he was blocking the doorway.

When he didn't answer, I glanced behind me toward the gravel driveway. There were two cars parked, one of them being the black truck he'd used to haul the hematite powder over to my house. The other was a small blue sports car, but I just figured it was his. I had no idea how many cars he owned. But now . . .

"I'm sorry," I said, stepping back a foot. I was pretty certain I was out of his empathic range. "I didn't realize you had company."

"Tell her I'm coming, Dad! I can't find my jacket." Jupe's voice carried like the west wind from the upstairs balcony inside the house. When Lon turned to answer him, I caught a glimpse behind him into the house. At the far end of the living room was a tall blond woman wearing a curvy, dark green sleeveless dress and heels. She was holding a wineglass and looking at a picture on the wall. Lon noticed that I'd seen her and moved to block the door again.

"Oh." I took one more step back. Our eyes met, and I knew immediately that he knew I was trying to get out of range. I didn't care, as long as I got there. "Gosh, Lon," I said. "A little free time on your hands, and you've already got a model lined up, huh?"

"She's not a model." His voice was deliberately hushed, almost a whisper.

I shrugged. "Long legs, pretty face. Might as well be."

"She's a photography rep."

"Regardless, I'll try to keep Jupe out as long as I can to give you guys time to . . . whatever." I tugged my purse higher up on my arm and crossed my arms over my chest as I gave him a sugary smile.

Stupid, stupid girl. There I was thinking that just maybe, possibly, he might have been showing a spark of interest on the phone the day before, but I was obviously wrong. Though I was accustomed to being the rejector, not the rejectee, I reprimanded myself for even entertaining the notion that any silly attraction I had for him might be mutual. Like Jupe had told me, Lon probably didn't think of me that way. Too young.

"I'm not dating anyone. It's not a date," Lon argued in a low voice. By now, the redness in his neck had darkened and was creeping upward in splotches. Wasn't a date, my ass.

"None of my business." I spoke as nonchalantly as I

could manage, keeping my eyes low as Jupe ducked under his father's arm and burst through the door.

"I'm ready!" he announced gleefully. "Let's go so we can hit the snack bar before the movie starts—come on!" He grabbed my hand to tug me across the graveled driveway.

"Enjoy yourself," I said to Lon before succumbing to Jupe's pull and turning away. It wasn't until we were halfway down the cliff that I realized I'd completely forgotten to tell Lon about Father Carrow's theory.

I was still stewing about Lon's date when Jupe and I found a parking space at the drive-in a few minutes before the movie was supposed to start; we'd already made a quick trip to the concession stand and had loaded up with popcorn, Cokes, and three kinds of candy. Revenge is sweet, right? Well, I was going to have the damn kid bouncing off the walls with a stomachache when I took him back home later.

Jupe showed me how everyone else had backed into the parking spaces with their trunks facing the screen so that they could sit outside the car with the radio tuned to a station that played the soundtrack to the movie. A few people had even set up portable lawn chairs and small hibachis. Since we didn't have chairs, we popped the back door to the rental and stowed the rear seats in the floorboard to make some room, then sat in the back with our feet dangling against the bumper.

"So, who was that chick your dad was seeing tonight?" I asked, unable to stop myself from prying.

"Huh? Who knows. Someone from work. I tried to check her out but she was kinda snotty and talked down to me."

"I bet he has a ton of women from work come over." I hoped he wasn't realizing what I was doing.

"Not really. He says models are nothing but trouble and that he'd never date another one again. Crap, I almost spilled my Coke. That was close."

Best not to keep prying. The kid was smarter than I thought. "So . . . do all the other people in your class like these old movies?" I asked, not really knowing what kids his age were into these days.

"Are you kidding? Me and my friend Jack are the only people with taste. Everyone else is into those dumb Hollywood action flicks they play at the newer cineplex down in the Village. They only show those kind of movies here on the weekends. All the good stuff like this is during the week."

"Is Jack your best friend or something?" I settled the popcorn between us and scooped up a handful.

Jupe shrugged. "I guess. Jack's Japanese. The rest of the kids in my class are either white, black, or Latino. Jack and me are the only ones that don't fit in."

"Jack and I."

"Whatever, Jack and I—God, you sound like my dad."

"Why does it matter what race the other kids are?"

Jupe tore into the popcorn, spilling more than he grabbed. "You wouldn't understand."

"Why?"

"Because you're white."

"So? My oldest friend is Chinese and she's demon. My coworkers and friends are all different races and cultures. Nobody cares anymore."

"Maybe it's different in Morella," Jupe said in a preachy voice, "but in *my* town, once you get to junior high, everything changes. People that used to be friends . . . well, they just aren't anymore. Everyone's got their own groups, and I don't fit into any of them."

"Because of your race?"

He shrugged. "When I figure it out, I'll let you know. It's not like they hate me or anything. It's just, well, it's easier for Jack and me to understand each other because we're both different. He's the only Asian kid in my class. Most of the Asian kids in La Sirena go to private school. Jack and I have been friends forever—like two years. He taught me all about Toho movies."

"Huh?"

"Toho. They made the Godzilla pictures—please tell me you know about Godzilla," he said in an impatient voice that told me if I didn't say yes, I was the most uncool person on the planet.

"Godzilla's some kind of flying squirrel, right?"

"What?" His jaw flapped open.

"Joking! I know who Godzilla is."

"Whoa," he said, crunching a mouthful of popcorn. "Foa secon there ithaw I—"

"Wait until you finish eating. I can't understand a word you're saying."

He tried to laugh, but popcorn stuck in his throat and he choked instead. I patted his back to help him out. "Okay there, kid?"

Finally getting the food down the right tube, he said, "I haven't had popcorn in forever. My dad never lets me get it because I always eat it too fast."

"Oops."

"Don't worry. I won't tell him you bought it for me. Or the candy. I'm not allowed to have sugar, like, ever. Only on special occasions." His big, green eyes glittered with restrained humor.

"Double oops."

He reconsidered with a mischievous grin. "Actually, if you maybe want to take me to another movie next week, I'll be *extra* careful not to accidentally let any of it slip out."

"Well, Jupiter, movie or no movie next week, *I'll* be sure not to tell him that *you* said 'fuck' back at the concession stand in front of the cashier," I countered.

He laughed and held out a buttery hand for me to shake. "You win, deal. Oh, the movie's starting. Can I turn up the radio now?"

While Jupe gave me a running commentary, which included telling me everything before it happened, we ate all the popcorn and half the candy during the first half of the movie. I let him have the rest of my Coke after he slurped down all of his. When the creature got captured, we booed at the screen, along with all the other moviegoers parked on our row. Then I got a text message from Lon; we texted back and forth a couple of times.

From Lon, 10:12 PM: IS J BEHAVING?

ALL IS WELL. HOWS YR DATE?

From Lon, 10:14 PM: GONE. NOT A DATE.

BOOTY CALL. WHATEV.

From Lon, 10:14 PM: SHES A COWORKER, NOT A HO.

I snorted a soft laugh after that one. Jupe tried to see what I was typing, but I held the phone out of his reach and thrust the rest of the box of Raisinets in his hand. *Eat up, my soon-to-be-diabetic friend.*

HO OR NO, NONE OF MY BEESWAX.

From Lon, 10:15 PM: REALLY NOT A DATE. SERIOUSLY.

NEITHER IS MINE. GUESS WE'RE EVEN.

I didn't get a response to that, but at least my jealousy had calmed. He may not have been attracted to me, but at least he cared what I thought about his extracurricular activities. I interpreted that to mean that he had a certain amount of respect for me. Even so, I figured that I better reel in my feelings—and fast—or I was just going to get hurt, and I didn't have time for that.

A few minutes later, during the climax of the movie, a small flaw appeared on the film, obscuring the face of the creature. "Crap!" Jupe said. "This blows. How did a pink spot get on a black-and-white print? This is the best part of the whole stupid—"

We both yelped. The film wasn't pink; the air in front of the car was. Jupe scooted backward into the SUV, kicking the empty popcorn tub onto the pavement. "Holy shit!" he whispered in fright, just as I realized what it was.

"Whoa, whoa, whoa," I said, putting my hand on his feet. "It's okay, buddy. It's nothing bad. Just my servitor."

He looked at me with crazy eyes. "Your what-a-tor?"

"My servitor." I quickly dug around my coat pocket and retrieved the clay doll that anchored the spell. "It's not an imp or anything." I held the doll in my open palm and we watched as the tiny pink figure bobbed and floated through the air, then slowly filtered into the doll while the spell was absorbed back into its anchor; within seconds it had completely disappeared.

"What's a servitor? Is it a fairy?" Jupe looked from me to the doll in amazement.

"There are no such things as fairies. I created it, with Heka."

"Does it have a name?"

"No."

"But it's good, not bad?"

"It's not good or bad. It's just an energy spell. I need to do another spell to retrieve some information from it. You wanna scoot up to the bumper and watch the rest of the movie? I'll just do the spell inside the car so no one can see me."

"No way, I've seen this movie a thousand times. Will the pink fairy thing come back out when you do your spell? I want to watch. Can I? Please?"

"I thought you said you'd 'die' if you couldn't see this movie."

He gave me a sheepish grin.

"Are you even allowed to see magick without your dad's permission? Or am I going to get in trouble for that too?"

"I don't think there's a rule about that," he said, cutting his eyes to the side. What a punk.

I debated for a second, wondering if I should let him watch or not. My deflector charm was still around my neck; the wards on the rental car were intact. It wasn't a dangerous spell. I reached down to grab the popcorn bucket off the ground and shut the back door.

"There's not much to see," I said. "It just dumps images into my mind. You can watch, though, if you stay quiet. Reach over the front seat and grab my purse, will ya? Turn the radio down while you're at it."

For on-the-go magick, I always carry a small notebook to jot written spell components. I also used to carry a sigil cheat-sheet until I forgot my purse in a restaurant a few years ago; I got the purse returned to me intact, but it made me realize that if it had fallen into the wrong hands, it might cause all sorts of problems.

Scribbling a squared circle on a sheet of notebook paper, I began to draw the symbols inside it that would trigger the information upload from my servitor. Jupe questioned my every stroke, and I explained as best I could until I lost my patience. "Zip it, kid, or I'm going to put you outside."

"Zipped! Keep going, I'll be quiet—I swear!"

I had a sneaking feeling it wasn't the first time he'd been told to shut up.

When I finished my drawing, I warned him one last time to be quiet—no matter what—and made him watch from the front seat. With intent, I spit on the sigil, charging it as Jupe whispered, "Gross." The retrieval spell was now ready to be used, so I loosely grasped the head of the clay doll and smashed it against the charged paper sigil. It cracked in several pieces, releasing both the servitor's energy and the information it had collected.

The images it showed me weren't happening in real time, but they were most likely gathered within the last few minutes; once the servitor located its objective, it returned pretty fast. They rushed into my head and began flipping slideshow-style. A bedroom—no, hotel room. A girl sat on the bed. Riley Cooper, I presumed. Early twenties? Long black hair, dark eyes. Petite.

She was dressed like she was headed to fetish night at some goth club: skintight black leather pants, purple vinyl top that was cut low to show off cleavage and high to show midriff. That, and the sides of a really bad tramp-stamp tattoo with batwings and paw prints that circled around from her lower back to her sides. Leather boots laced up the front with ridiculous heels, big silver hoop earrings. Lots of dark makeup and matching black nail polish. A pair of handcuffs sat on the bed beside her, along with a handgun and a large grimoire.

The image stuttered, then focused on a matchbook next to her bed. It read PALMS CASINO, LAS VEGAS.

Perfect. I had a location, and I now knew what she looked like. Better than nothing, and at least she wasn't in the area.

I expected that to be the end of the servitor's magick-fueled transmission, but I couldn't disengage from the spell. The last image blurred, crackled, then . . . changed. I wasn't looking at stills anymore. It was the same hotel room, but now it was like a video playing in my head. The girl had moved off the bed. She was looking me square in the face. She walked forward. Toward me. Or toward my servitor? She reached above her head, lips moving, and a green dot appeared in the middle of my vision before darkness ate it all away.

The transmission dropped and my head hit the floor of the SUV as I fell backward. Jupe's face was wedged between the front seat, a look of thrilled wonder glazing over his pale green eyes. As he stared at me, an unexpectedly strong wave of postmagick nausea hit me.

I barely had time to grab the empty popcorn bucket before I threw up.

16

Apart from making me sick as a dog and giving Jupe his second biggest magical thrill ("The Pareba demon binding was cooler," he'd remarked), the servitor, I decided later, was a bust. Sure, it was a relief to know that Riley Cooper wasn't in Morella. But unless I planned to chase her down in Las Vegas—no thanks—all I had was a face to go with a name that didn't match up with any known magicians. I had nothing to tie her directly to Luxe or to any other order. Disappointing.

With her identity still up in the air and the glass talon being researched, I really needed to talk to the caliph in Florida. I tried to email him again; it bounced a second time. I tried calling multiple times from public phones and just got his voice mail. That left me one option: the local E∴E∴ lodge.

The morning after my date with Jupe, I headed to the lodge after checking on my car in the body shop. When I arrived, Soror Yolanda was speaking to a member on the far side of the main temple. Trying not to pace, I looked around at all the sigils painted on the walls and waited for her to finish. Just when I thought I couldn't be more miserable, her blond assistant, the over-friendly Frater Kantor, appeared.

"Soror Seléne."

"Keep it down," I cautioned, quickly glancing across the room. "If the FBI comes knocking at my door because of your indiscretion, I'll hex you before the oath spell even has time to shut your mouth."

An idle threat. I really didn't know much about hex spells, but whatever.

"Frater Hadler couldn't hear me if he was a foot away. He refuses to wear the hearing aide that his doctor prescribed," Kantor replied. "Anyway, back so soon? Does this mean you've reconsidered my offer? I'm quite skilled in the art of tantric sexual rites, you know."

"Okay, seriously. Let's pretend we're normal people, not magicians. If you saw me in a coffee shop, would you really think that you had a chance with me? I'm not trying to be mean, just realistic."

He gave me a confused look. "Ritual sex does not require a mutual attraction between partners, you know."

"Are you deaf, or can you really not imagine a life without magick?"

"Why should I? You're here, I'm here, we're both talented magicians." He ran his fingernails through the blond, cropped hair over his ears. His nails were too long. Disgusting. I wanted to find a nail clipper and chop them off.

The Grandmaster interrupted us before I had to endure him any longer.

"Sorry, temple business," she said wearily.

For a second, I wondered if she and Frater Kantor had ever engaged in ritual sex; maybe they got it on with her husband right here in the temple. Nothing would surprise me.

"Can we talk alone?" I asked, shaking that thought away.

"Of course. Frater Kantor?"

He bowed his head obediently and turned to leave, but not before winking at me as he exited. I might not be able to hex him, but I could brew up something that would knock his ass on the floor for the better part of the day. If only.

"I've been trying to get in touch with the caliph," I said once we were alone.

"Look, Seléne. I'm going to be frank. No one in the Florida lodge knows where Caliph Superior is. Not his children, his assistant, no one. He disappeared three days ago."

"What?"

"I've sent my guardian to find his, but he's warded and refusing communication. The elite mages at the main lodge have sent out servitors. Only one has returned, and the transmission was too weak to decipher much of anything. All we can gather is that Caliph Superior is in San Diego."

"The Luxe Order?"

"We believe."

I clicked my jaw. "Kidnapped?"

"Not exactly. He was stubborn about trying to find a solution to your problem, and I personally think he went there willingly to try to negotiate in secret. No one in the order would have allowed him to go if he had told someone beforehand."

"They won't hurt him, will they?"

"No, no. Not yet, anyway. The council they offered us was binding. They'll stick to their word until the final date. Which is seven days away, by the—"

"Yes!" I snapped. "I know damn well how far away it is. Do you think I'm not trying? That my parents' lives being at stake—my own life—isn't motivation enough?"

She ignored my rising anger. "Do you have anything to report?"

Total attitude.

Suddenly furious, I realized that I didn't trust her or Frater Kantor or anyone in that damn lodge one bit. I had planned to ask her advice about Riley Cooper, and the strange green dot that had appeared in my servitor transmission . . . I had even planned to tell her about the glass talon. Not now. No way in hell.

"Nothing that I can tell you," I said coldly. "When you get an update on the caliph, you call me immediately instead of waiting around for me to come to you. Otherwise, I'll speak with you before the final date for the council."

"Of course," she said with forced politeness, inclining her head.

It probably wasn't the brightest idea for me to piss off my last possible link to the caliph, but I didn't care anymore; I was tired of being nice to people I didn't like.

17

I was still fuming and stressed over the Grandmaster's news when I pulled into Lon's driveway after lunch. He greeted me at the door in his typical stained T-shirt and faded jeans that had holes in both knees. Not fake deconstructed holes made in some factory, but the real kind. I wondered how many years of wear it took to get them. He was on his cell, so he waved me inside and pointed me to a set of sliding glass doors at the far end of the living room that led out to a patio.

I made my way across the room and dumped my purse on an olive-colored sectional sofa. A plush area rug was here, along with a couple of leather chairs that looked comfortable and inviting. I glanced around looking for examples of Lon's photography; I hadn't noticed any the first night I'd been here. Just a couple of large paintings and a colorful 1920s print advertising a circus. I spotted a few small photos hanging high above the sliding glass door, but before I could examine them closely, I became distracted by what lay on the other side of the glass. Amanda had been so excited about Lon's property; now that I was witnessing it in the daytime, I understood why.

I slid the door open and stepped outside onto a deep patio covered by matching modern cement ceiling that sheltered it from the weather. Where the patio stopped, a large, wraparound redwood deck started, with three tiers of long steps that led down to a narrow yard filled with native California plants: small palms, lavender, coastal sagebrush, and several stunning Monterey cypress trees with their unusual wind-sculpted trunks that curved beneath the flattened evergreen tops. The verdant patch was well tended inside curving stone borders that wrapped around the side of the house.

Beyond the small garden of Eden lay a long, wide strip of bright green lawn; past that, the land became rocky. The house stood on the edge of a steep cliff that dropped, leveled off, then dropped again and fell into the ocean. Miles and miles of the blue Pacific. The tree line had been cut to reveal a spectacular unobstructed view, but became dense at the edges of the property so that you couldn't see another house, building—not another living soul. It was as if civilization didn't exist. I stood at the top of the tiered steps and looked out over it in amazement as the coastal wind whipped my hair around my face.

A couple minutes later, a glossy black dog with a purple collar emerged from the garden and bounded up the steps to greet me.

"You must be Foxglove," I said as I bent down to offer her my hand. She sniffed twice, then nuzzled her nose against my arm. Two powerful paws lurched up on my knees as she shot toward my face and began licking my chin. "Whoa, down, girl!" I said with a laugh, turning my face away. "You're definitely Jupe's dog—no boundaries, huh?"

I stood and wiped my face as she looked up at me, panting happily, tail wagging. I scratched her neck as she sniffed my legs; maybe she smelled Mr. Piggy on me. Then her ears cocked at the sound of a bird, and she darted away as quickly as she'd arrived, disappearing through a small cypress grove at the side of the property.

"Do you like it?"

I turned to find Lon sauntering up behind me. "The view? Unbelievable."

"See that bit of land jutting out down there? The sea stack?" He pointed to the coast below where the waves were breaking furiously against several rocky columns of graduated cliffs that extended into the sea. "That's Mermaid Point. Ever heard of it?"

"No."

"It's what La Sirena was named after. The local Pomo Indians say that their ancestors believed a strange spirit lived in the water there. They'd offer it gifts for good luck—floated planks of wood with food and flowers in the water."

"Interesting. I wonder if there really was something there? Sometimes there's truth in old myths."

"I don't know, but Jupe swears he's seen a ghost out there a few times. Foxglove sometimes howls out there."

"Mmm . . . sure it's not an imp?"

He chuckled. "Probably."

We stood together in happy silence, and for a long moment, I forgot about everything. My mind just went blank. It was so peaceful. Morella seemed so far away . . . Then it all came back in a jarring rush—my parents, the albino demon, Riley Cooper, the caliph. I wanted to kick something.

Lon must have sensed my mood change; he gave me a sidelong glance and tapped my elbow. "Come and sit with me on the patio."

I followed him up the wooden deck stairs and back

under the cement ceiling to a small metal table with four chairs. A pot of steaming tea sat there along with a book and his silver cigarette case.

"You want the heat on? It's kind of chilly out here today. Overcast."

"Uh, sure."

He punched something into a panel on the stone wall near the sliding door, then sat down next to me and poured us each a cup of tea without asking if I wanted any.

"Jupe at school?" I asked.

"Yeah. Mrs. Holiday picks him up."

"Who's Mrs. Holiday?"

"Housekeeper . . . half of the elderly couple I told you about that works for me."

"Oh, that's right."

"They live in a small house down the cliff over there." He pointed toward the side of the house where the trees thickened. "Check this out," he said, doling out cigarettes. "I've been poking around since you dropped Jupe off last night and mentioned Father Carrow's fairy tale. He might have been right." He slid a small book toward me. *Liber Demonica III.* Paper pages. It mustn't have been too valuable for him to have brought it out from the confines of his library. I allowed him to light my valrivia while I turned to the page marked with one of his little blue pieces of paper.

The entry was titled "Rules of Possession." I began reading, then skipped ahead when Lon guided me forward several paragraphs. I read out loud.

"*If the summoner desires Prime Possession of the Entity, and all the privileges of its special talents, He must secure a Kieyda by using the following formula to calculate a Secondary Circle that should connect to the apex of the binding triangle, as shown in figure*

171. The Entity should be tricked to cross over into the Secondary Circle using the one of the methods listed within table 54—"

"Some of those methods are barbaric," Lon mumbled.

"—then the desired Kieyda should be removed quickly. Banish immediately after removal with the full Greater Banishing Ritual. The Primary desirable Kieydas are as follows: Horn, Tooth, Bone, Talon, Tip of Tail, Boney Crest. Please keep in mind that neither Skin nor Scale holds sufficient power for Kieydas."

I held my cigarette away from the table and looked at Lon. "Kieyda?"

"A kind of amulet derived from the body of an Æthyric demon.

"It goes on to say here"—he pointed at text on the following page—"that the summoner needs to have possession of the Kieyda when the demon's seal and name are used for summoning. If the Kieyda is lost, the demon can't be summoned to earth again until it's found. Drink your tea. It's jasmine."

I glanced down at it with feigned suspicion. "*Just* jasmine?"

"Cross my heart," he said with a sly smile.

I inhaled the tea and sipped it cautiously. It was wonderful.

"Give me a second," I said, collecting my thoughts.

He looked at me curiously but stayed silent, which I appreciated. After a minute or so, I sighed and put the tea down. "Why are my feet warm?" I ducked to peer under the table.

"Heated floor. I asked you if you wanted it on."

"Ah. Fancy."

"Convenient," he corrected. "It gets brutal out here at night in the winter. I like to be able to use the patio year-round. Hate being trapped indoors." He plucked a stray valrivia leaf from the tip of his tongue, transferred from the open end of the hand-rolled cigarette.

I nodded, then dropped my head and spoke into my half-empty teacup. "If the Tamlins are right about the albino demon . . . we have to find the summoning name, the demon class, *and* the damn talon. That's impossible. It's all over. Done. Doomed."

"Why?"

"Because the talon—or glass knife, or whatever they're calling it—is in police evidence in Portland."

"Portland? I thought they recovered it in San Diego?"

"The local FBI in Portland was working on Magus Dempsey's murder. I guess they sent it up there for the investigation. Besides, it doesn't matter where it is. We can't just walk in and ask to check it out like a library book."

Several seconds ticked by. "Are you sure about that?" he asked, a glint in his eye.

"I'm pretty fucking sure, Lon."

He sat back in his chair with his leg crossed over the opposite knee in a lazy figure-four shape. "And I'm pretty fucking sure I know someone who owes me a big favor."

"What kind of favor?" I asked as my heart rate shifted from resigned to intrigued.

"Big enough. His son works for the Morella PD."

Correct that, intrigued to excited.

"I can't promise anything, but I'll call him tonight. In theory, you might be able to use the talon with a servitor. Program the servitor to find the summoning name of the demon it belongs to. Like a bloodhound following a scent. I'm not positive, but it stands to reason."

He was right. I'd used other objects as tracers for servitors in the past. Theoretically, there was no reason I couldn't program one to find the book with the albino demon's information if I had the talon.

"So let's stay calm but hopeful, okay?" He lowered his eyes and gave me a serious look.

I pressed the warm sole of my shoe against the edge of his chair and tried to push him away. "Calm but hopeful, huh? No fair using your empathic hoodoo on me, you jerk. Move back." I strained to push with my leg, but broke into a laugh when his chair wouldn't budge. "Dammit!" He grabbed my ankle and threw me off, laughing with me as we engaged in a brief hand-and-foot wrestling match.

While we finished our tea and cigarettes, he asked me what I was going to do about Riley Cooper; I had no idea. I'd spent hours trying to find her on the internet and had called every magician I knew even tangentially whom I could trust, but no one had heard of her.

Then I told him about Caliph Superior disappearing off to San Diego.

"He must be dedicated to your parents to go through so much trouble to protect them all these years and put himself in danger now. That's above and beyond."

"My family has been in the E∴E∴ for generations, at least on my mom's side, back when the order used to be head-quartered in France."

Lon sipped his tea. "You look a little French. Something in your mouth."

"I look just like my mom. Only, she's taller and more . . . elegant. Less hip-y."

His eyes dropped to my hips in evaluation; I couldn't tell by his expression whether he liked what he saw or not. My mind floated back to last night's embarrassment over his date—or colleague, or whatever he claimed she was. Tall and slender. I wondered if that's what Lon preferred; his ex-wife was built the same way.

This was not the time to conjure up unwanted emotions, not when he could sense them. Best to keep talking and distract both of us. "My mother spent her childhood in Paris before moving to the States. My father was American, but his family was from Marseilles. It was one of the things that originally drew my parents together, *la connexion française*. That's what my mom always said."

"*Parles-tu français?*" Lon asked brightly.

I shook my head, slightly embarrassed that I didn't. "A few words here and there. You speak it?"

"I pick up languages pretty easily."

"My parents used to speak French when they were arguing or discussing something private." And by private, that usually meant it involved sex. My parents weren't shy about their affection for each other. They were always sharing intimate glances, kissing, holding hands. I used to joke that they were like Morticia and Gomez from *The Addams Family*.

We didn't speak for several moments, then Lon's brow furrowed. "Did your parents ever tell you about the albino demon when they were charged with the murders?"

"A little. They'd flown to San Diego to meet with the head of Luxe and a few officers from the orders whose leaders had been murdered. By that point, the media had already latched onto the whole 'Black Lodge' angle, and everyone was concerned about the organizations coming under fire, getting a bad rap. My parents went to represent the E∴E∴ and mediate talks. They flew back a day early and told me all hell had broken loose, and that the meeting was a trap—that Luxe was trying to pin the murders on them."

"And they told you about the albino demon?"

"They said someone had summoned an Æthyric demon for the killings, but they never gave me details. I was too young and they were overprotective. I never knew what the demon looked like until Caliph Superior told me last week."

"Don't you think it's strange that he helped your parents look for this demon for seven years, and he'd forget a detail like that?"

"Maybe my parents were under the same confusion spell that the Tamlins claimed."

"Definitely a possibility. But your parents saw the demon a month later, when the Luxe leader was attacked in San Diego. That's what they told you before you faked your deaths."

"Yes. What are you trying to get at?"

"Well, on one hand, if that mysterious man the Tamlins saw running away from the third scene was the murderer, and he cast confusion spells on everyone at that time . . . What was to stop him from casting the same spell again on the witnesses of the fourth attack? Maybe that's why your parents didn't tell the Caliph about the glass talon detail. Maybe they didn't remember it."

"It's possible. But you said 'on one hand.' What's the other possibility?"

He paused. "How much do you trust Caliph Superior?"

We looked at each other. I bit my lip. "He's my godfather," I said slowly. "I grew up seeing him almost every day."

"But?"

"But I hadn't seen him in seven years until last week. I don't know. I—"

Lon held his hand up. "I don't want to jump to conclusions. But maybe it's good that you can't contact him right now."

Crap. Lon was just confirming something that had been eating at me since I'd talked to the Tamlins. I'd known the caliph all my life. He was a good person. A peaceful man. He couldn't be connected with the murders. Why would he? And what was the motive? He was leader of a prestigious occult order and had everything he wanted—money, power, a loving family. It just didn't make sense. And yet, something wasn't quite right.

I let out a slow breath and put my elbow on the table, leaning my head in my hand. "I've had this nagging memory of my parents talking to him privately before the fourth murder attempt on the Luxe head. My mom was upset and scared. Something I heard, but I can't quite . . . They were all speaking in French—the caliph is fluent. I don't know. Maybe I just didn't understand what he was saying. I've tried to remember it for years, but I think the trauma of going into hiding blocked some of my memories during that time."

"If so, that's understandable. You were just a kid. You don't go through something like that without a few battle scars. Ever gone to counseling?"

"Um, no."

He shrugged. "Hypnosis sometimes restores memories."

"Again, no. I have no guarantee that the person doing the hypnosis wouldn't turn me into the cops."

"You trusted me."

"You drugged me!"

He grinned. "Yeah, I did."

"Do you know how to hypnotize someone?"

"No, but I have a book of memory spells. Some remove memories, some restore them."

I sat up straight. "Really? Have you tried any of them?"

"On myself, no. They're tandem spells. Most memory spells are."

"Huh? Tandem spells?"

"You have to perform it on someone else. You can't perform them on yourself—you can't erase your own memories."

"I've never heard of such a thing."

He smiled triumphantly. "Interesting . . . the novice knows something that the master doesn't." He hooked his finger around the handles of our cups and gathered the teapot in his other hand. "Bring that book. I think we should take a peek at the memory spells in my library."

"I need to leave in about forty-five minutes to get to work," I warned.

"We're just looking."

Just looking, but I was very, very curious.

18

I perused the bookshelves behind Lon while he sat with his feet propped up on the desk and thumbed through his tandem memory spells, reading the descriptions aloud to me.

"*Memory Erase by Time Period: designate a length of time to eradicate thoughts.*"

"Nope."

"*Memory Erase by Subject: designate a subject to remove from subject's memory.*"

"No, but you should keep that one marked. That could come in handy."

He plopped a blue marker in the crease, then flipped to the next entry. "*Complete Memory Erase: wipe out all memories of events, places, names, times.* Jesus, that's dangerous. Remind me to put this book in the locked cabinet. If Jupe got a hold of this . . . Okay, hold on. *Memory Restoring.*" He flipped through several pages then started reading to himself in low mumble, taking his feet off the desk.

"What? Did you find one? Memory Restore by Time Period?"

"I found it."

"So? What's the spell? Does it need kindled Heka?" I leaned over his shoulder and read. "*Memory Restore, otherwise known as 'The Wheel.' Push and pull magical energies to ignite slow memory restoration gently.* That sounds like an overnight laxative." I grinned at him.

"Ha, ha," he said dourly, getting up from his seat to stand.

"Lighten up." I elbowed him in the shoulder, then continued reading. "'*Magick for The Wheel must be charged with fluids from sexual arousal . . .*'" My voice tapered off. "Oh."

"Mmm-hmm."

I read the rest of the entry to myself. The person doing the tandem spell—that would be Lon—had to receive Heka-rich sexual fluids from the recipient of the spell, me, to jump-start a series of lost memories. A magical sigil and incantation were provided.

It wasn't the first time I'd run across sex spells: they were just as common as electricity-kindled spells. They just aren't convenient for your average on-the-go magical needs.

"Do all the memory spells require that?" I asked.

"I don't think so. I just noticed it on the last couple of retrieval ones."

"Uh, maybe I could just get myself, you know, privately . . . ?" I suggested. I regretted it immediately, and felt my face flush with warmth. What the hell was I going to do? Ask Lon if he had any porn I could borrow and hole up in his library's washroom?

"Did you read this part?" He pointed. I read.

The spell instructions claimed that "shared sexual arousal" between the participants was required so that a tight "energy link" is formed. Otherwise, the process would be too jarring and "memory leak, further loss, or permanent damage" could occur.

"Oh, well," I said, "it was worth a try."

He looked at me challengingly with his arms crossed over his chest. "Don't think I can arouse you?" I froze. Maybe he was joking. "Or is it that you're afraid you can't arouse me?"

"Uh . . ." The word *arouse* coming out of his mouth made my nostrils widen. I took a long step backward. Must get out of range ASAP.

"Too late," he said with a dark smile.

I gritted my teeth and made a face. "Goddammit," I mumbled under my breath.

"It's not a sex spell that requires . . . completion," he said. "We don't need to have sex, just stimulation." At that moment, I truthfully wasn't opposed to either, but I didn't want him to know that. I stepped back again. "And we just need your fluids, not mine." He moved forward again, thwarting my attempt at retreat. "It's up to you."

"Why is it up to me?"

"Because . . . your memories, not mine."

"Oh, that's right."

"Your sexual fluids, not mine."

For the love of God, would he please stop saying that?

"Don't find me attractive?" he challenged playfully. "Not young and hip enough for you?"

"I . . . uh . . ." My heart hammered. "Jupe told me that you thought I was too young for *you*."

He stepped forward again, dragging the open book along the edge of the desk. "Hmm . . . I don't recall saying that."

"Memory loss is the first sign of aging." .

"I'm not the one with memory problems, am I?"

I laughed nervously.

"Come here."

"No."

"Come here . . . please?" he asked, raising his eyebrows.

I took a hesitant step toward him.

"Closer."

Again.

"Closer," he commanded in a low voice.

Screw it, I thought, and complied, this time boldly positioning myself so close, a piece of paper couldn't slide between us. I lifted my face toward him, daring. He put two fingers on the side of my chin and gently tilted my face sideways and down to the desk.

"Here's the spell. It's in Latin," he said in an even, professional tone.

I glanced down at the book, eyes scanning over the page but not reading. His hand came into view as he pointed to the incantation words, tapping on the page.

"Yep," I said, discreetly licking my lips.

"You need to be thinking about that memory you're missing when I say the spell."

"All right."

"As for the mutual arousal, a kiss would be easiest," he suggested. "Have you ever kissed a demon?"

"Yeah . . ." A couple, actually. Same as kissing a human, in my experience. Humans dated and married Earthbounds every day, with or without the human half of the pair realizing exactly whom they were dating. As I said before, Human-Earthbound unions produced human children, so unless their demon mate had an exceptional knack that was impossible to ignore, they could live out their entire lives thinking that they were in love with another human. Myself, I dated an Earthbound once; before anything juicy happened between us, I found out that his knack was the ability to seduce. Umm, no thanks. At least the guy had been honest about it.

I remembered this, then told Lon the first honest thing that came to mind, "I've kissed an Earthbound, but I've never kissed a man with a mustache."

Lon found this extremely amusing, and we both fought back laughter. A quick joy spread over me. It was so pleasant to be enjoying his mood, no grunting or growling or trying to guess what his motives were. And it was exhilarating, being so close to him; my heart kicked wildly inside my chest.

Then he stopped smiling, and his eyes slowly blinked and drooped lower. He gingerly brushed my hair away from my face with the tips of his fingers.

I craned my neck to meet him halfway. Warmth flooded between my thighs before our mouths even made contact.

His lips were much softer than I expected, and he tasted like valrivia smoke. I don't remember closing my eyes, but I must have. His mustache grazed my skin, but I quickly became accustomed to it; either that, or I was distracted by the way his tongue filled my mouth and rolled with mine in slow waves. Or the way goose bumps rushed over my arms. Or maybe even how warm his skin felt under my fingers as they mysteriously found their way under his T-shirt to trace the line of golden hair that ran down his stomach.

Somewhere in the back of my head I knew we'd long ago accomplished our goal, but I was genuinely surprised when my knees gave out, and a small moan escaped my mouth as I slipped away from him. He made a quick grab and steadied me, hands circling my waist. That had never happened to me before, and I sure as hell didn't want him to know that, but he probably sensed my surprise so it didn't really matter.

By that point, I'd forgotten all about the memory spell. He began kissing me again, then forced himself back with a groan and spun me around to face away from him. He pinned me between his chest and the desk, slinging an arm around my shoulders to hold me tight as his erection pressed against my lower back.

He pushed my hair away from my shoulders and settled his chin in the crook of my neck.

"So . . ." he whispered huskily in my ear, "we've discovered that you can arouse me." He demonstrated this fact by pressing harder against me, just in case I'd forgotten. "However, we don't know about you. And there is the small matter of Heka."

His free hand moved to the button of my jeans, which he deftly maneuvered open with a quick flick. My zipper followed. Then his hand slid into my jeans, under my panties, and kept going until his fingers slid unexpectedly and we both breathed in sharply. When he found the right spot, I moaned, and he made a small noise of happy discovery. He flattened two stroking fingers against my sensitive flesh. My hips couldn't make up their mind whether they wanted to move forward on his fingers or backward to arch against him, so they alternated repetitively between the two.

Then he unexpectedly broke away, deserting his efforts between my legs and withdrawing his hand. I moaned again, this time in disappointment.

He cleared his throat. "All right. Ready?"

"Oh, yes," I chirped with great enthusiasm, temporarily mistaken about what I was agreeing to. My brain was having trouble adjusting.

His fingers glistened as they swept over the sigil, leaving behind the Heka needed to charge the spell; so much for the pristine edition of his rare grimoire. When he spoke the incantation, his voice cracked, then settled. His Latin was flawless—as good as mine, if not better. I scrambled to focus on the lost memory that I was trying to recapture, and when the last of his Latin tumbled out, I realized why the spell was called The Wheel.

His energy poured into me in a steady torrent. I felt it, recognized it as his. Such a strange feeling, almost as intimate as sex, and something I'd never experienced. It mixed with my Heka, then left me in a rush, just as if I'd pushed it out intentionally. The energy link. That was what the instructions for the spell had meant. Our combined energy moved in a circle, gathering strength and speed as magick circulated between us. His arms wrapped around me, and mine around them, and we held on to each other like we were in the middle of a tornado, trying to ride out the spinning storm.

A flood of jagged, partial memories surfaced and faded, each one vying for attention. Flashes of faces. Fragments of sentences. My old life returning after years of sitting idle under a layer of dust. Streams of hot, silent tears spilled over my cheeks, but I wasn't sure why.

Then it became painful. Wrenching. The magical wheel was off-track. Colors blurred into blackness and my mind felt as if it were being bulldozed from the inside out. I strained to break away and heard Lon groaning to do the same. Without warning, the spell derailed completely, and the shock of it threw us backward together. The room reappeared in my bleary vision as I slammed against him. We hit the shelves behind us so hard, a row of books flew out and rained down on our heads as we tumbled to the floor.

I gasped for air and struggled to untangle myself from Lon as someone called in the distance. Three loud knocks pounded on the locked library door. Apparently now home from school, Jupe spoke in a muffled voice from the other side.

"Dad? What was that loud noise? Is Cady here? Her rental car is outside." He pounded on the door again. "Are you guys okay? What just happened?"

I wondered the same thing as I zipped up my jeans with shaking hands.

19

"Well, Mr. Piggy, it looks like I'm going to be your second mommy for a few days." Kar Yee bent down to open the door to my hedgie's crate and reached inside to pull him out. The two long locks of hair on either side of her face were a little messy. It was early; she hadn't tweaked them into points yet.

"You sure you don't mind?" I asked, plopping down on the white couch in her living room. Everything in her apartment was white, cream, or gold. Not my taste, but her stuff was way nicer and cleaner than mine, so I couldn't really complain.

She held Mr. Piggy up to her face and inspected him critically, one eye squinting. I was a little worried that he would take a nip at her for doing that, but he behaved. He obviously knew he needed to make a good impression.

"He can stay in his crate while I'm at work. I'll put up his pen in the kitchen and let him get some exercise while I'm at home." She tucked him under her arm and lazily plodded over to an armchair. "If he pisses on anything, he's getting locked up in the bathroom."

It wasn't the piss she had to worry about; he was a poop

machine, but I didn't want to remind her about this or she might change her mind. "There's plenty of dry food in that clear container, and he can go without crickets for a week, so you don't have to feed him those."

"Good, because I wouldn't."

"But give him a little fruit once a day. I already cut it up into cubes for you."

"Yes, yes. Quit being a worrywart. He's a hedgehog, not a baby. I'll manage."

I sat cross-legged on the couch but unfolded my legs when she gave me a disapproving look. "My shoes aren't dirty, you know."

She clearly disagreed. "So you need a week off from work. Go ahead and tell me what to expect."

"Huh?"

"The trouble you're in. Is it boy trouble or family? Or did you steal something?"

I laughed. "No stealing. I guess it's . . . family trouble."

"How can a woman whose parents are dead have so much family trouble?"

When I first met Kar Yee, I told her my parents had died in a plane crash, a hard lie to maintain when you're continually worried about two people whom you should have buried and mourned years before; but as the years went by, it became second nature.

"It's trouble with my godfather," I said. Not completely a lie. "And trouble involving magick."

Lon had gotten us a meeting with an evidence tech who worked for the Portland police department. When Lon had called earlier that morning to tell me this, he'd carefully avoided discussing the sex magick we'd done in his library yesterday afternoon, just asked me if everything was "okay" on my end. I took that to mean that he was curious if the spell had awakened any buried memories (which it hadn't). After telling him this, he bluntly informed me what time he'd pick me up to drive to the airport, then hung up.

It was a quick flight to Portland—just a couple of hours—so we were going up and back today. But there were now only five days left before the Luxe deadline, and I didn't feel I could spare anything for work. I wanted to use every bit of my time to help Lon research the albino demon. Even if we were somehow able to persuade the evidence technician to let us borrow the glass talon, we still couldn't do anything without the demon's summoning name.

Kar Yee drew up her mouth as she stroked Mr. Piggy. "You are the most guarded person I've ever met, Cady. I think you have some black luck following you around."

"You have no idea," I muttered.

"You might be unlucky, but I don't think you're a bad seed, or I wouldn't be in business with you, no matter how long we've known each other."

That was true. Money was a very serious matter to her.

"But I think you need to get rid of what's dragging you down," she said. "Tear it out by the roots and be done with it. You should be happy, enjoying life." She held up her hand and began holding up fingers. "One, you have a good job—"

"I don't know if I'd call it good, exactly."

"It's good, trust me. And two, you are a smart and fair sorcerer—"

"Sometimes."

"—and three, you are very pretty, for a white American."

"Gee, thanks."

"Your life should be better than it is."

Kar Yee always had a way of cutting something down to

its simplest form. She was right: my life should be better. And I was unlucky. It wasn't my fault, but it wouldn't get cleared up by itself.

"Kar Yee," I argued.

"Don't 'Kar Yee' me. Just listen and make the right changes. When you come back to get Mr. Piggy and return to work, I expect to see you smiling."

I sighed and watched her run her nails through Mr. Piggy's spiny coat. "I hope I come back smiling too." I mainly just hoped I came back.

"Only one week away from the bar, yes?"

"Give or take a couple of days."

"One week," she said firmly.

Reaching for Mr. Piggy, I made a short clucking noise near the side of his face while trying to dampen the small but insistent worry that it might be the last time I would see him.

20

When the light turned green, Lon sped through the intersection and put some quick distance between our rental and the car behind us.

"Nobody's trailing us," I grumbled.

"Hmph."

It was overcast and dreary in Portland, which I normally found rather pleasant. People complain about the lack of sun in the Pacific Northwest, but I never really minded it when I lived in Seattle with Kar Yee during college. Today, however, it put a damper on an already grim situation.

I was worried about meeting the evidence guy and trying to persuade him to give us the talon. On top of that, I was nervous around Lon. Because the flight was overbooked, he ended up sitting in coach while I was in first class. I wasn't used to sitting up front; he was, so I offered to trade with him, but he refused. So we weren't able to talk on the flight.

We were, however, able to talk on the ride to the airport, and we were certainly able to now, but he was back to his tight-lipped communication style. Eyes on the road, short answers, nothing unnecessary. We still hadn't breathed a word about what happened between us the day before; I was left wondering if he regretted it, and now it was awkward. It made me more miserable than it should have, but I was too proud to do anything about it. So we sat in silence. No small talk about Jupe, no generic comments about the weather, nothing.

And that's exactly how we spent the drive to the evidence warehouse.

After handing over our IDs to a man behind a thick glass window—I used an ID from an alternate fake identity unconnected with Arcadia Bell, just to be extra careful—we sat on metal benches inside a white waiting room. A few minutes later, a supervisor came and we were escorted down a sad, gray hallway. We passed by a door that opened into an enormous warehouse, as big as a football field and lined with long rows of shelves. Confiscated and stolen property, the officer explained. Things that people could reclaim after they were no longer needed in a case; if left unclaimed, the goods were eventually sold off in a state auction.

The officer led us to a much smaller warehouse for sensitive evidence. A row of plastic seats sat against the wall by the door. In front of us was a ceiling-to-floor cage with a yellow sign that read AUTHORIZED PERSONNEL ONLY. Inside the cage were several evidence-processing desks; beyond them stood rows of tall warehouse shelving filled with white boxes of multiple shapes and sizes, all labeled with green and yellow stickers.

We took a seat while the officer called out to someone sitting at one of the desks. "You got visitors, Wesley."

A short, middle-aged demon emerged from a door in the locked cage. Lon's contact. We stood to greet him.

"Danny Wesley?" Lon asked.

"You must be Mr. Butler."

They shook hands, and Lon introduced me as my sign-in name, Cindy. He rolled his eyes a little as he said it. I tried to give him a sharp look in return, but had to quickly change over to a smile as the evidence technician looked me over. My skunk-streaked hair was tucked under a short brown wig.

"There's a place where we can talk," the technician said, looking back at the other people mulling about inside the cage.

We followed him into a small room with two break tables and an old vending machine that dispensed coffee and cocoa. Sitting down at one of the tables, we all looked at each other warily.

"So, Officer Wesley," I began.

"I'm a civilian. Just Danny is fine." He interlaced his fingers on the table in front of him, sitting up stiffly. "The captain said you guys need a favor, and I'm to do anything in my power to help you. So, what is it that you need to know?"

"We need to borrow a piece of evidence," Lon said.

"Borrow? I'm afraid that's impossible. We don't loan out evidence. Not from this room."

I tapped Lon's foot under the table. "Well, before we talk about that, maybe we should make sure we're in the right place first. Could you check to see if a certain piece of evidence is on file here?"

Fluorescent light from the ceiling glinted off the skin that showed through the thinning spots in Danny's graying hair. He smiled at me again. "Now *that* I can definitely do. I need some information first. Do you have the case number and the date it entered evidence?"

"Uh, no. It's kind of a well-known case though. Perhaps you can look it up."

"Depends. I've worked here for ten years, so anything before that I'd have to ask around or research. Got an approximate time frame?"

"Seven years ago. The Duval murder case."

"Duval?" he said, wrinkling up his forehead. Something changed in his eyes, though. He blinked faster and began rubbing the knuckle of his right thumb.

"The Black Lodge slayings," I offered.

"Oh! Of course. Yes, I know it."

"We were hoping to take a look at the murder weapon. It was a glass knife. I'm sure you remember."

Drops of sweat began beading on his forehead. "Yeah, I know it, but I don't have access to that case. It's . . . protected."

"Oh, come on now. Surely after ten years, you have access to anything," I said.

"Not really. I'm sorry."

Lon leaned back in his seat. "Why are you lying?"

"Lying? I'm not—"

"He's right, you are. Why won't you let us see the glass knife?" I asked.

Danny swallowed and quickly wiped his forehead.

"Look, Mr. Wesley," Lon said, "cut the shit. We're here for you to sneak that glass knife out of evidence for us and you damn well know it."

"Uh . . ."

Lon leaned forward and spoke in a hushed voice. "Don't pretend to be some upstanding, moral guy. I know you've accidently 'lost' several thousand dollars in cash and more in guns from that room this year."

Danny closed his eyes tightly for a second, then leaned down over the table and spoke in a low voice. "Look, I'd really like to help you, but I can't. The knife isn't here."

"But you just said it was," I argued.

"It was here. It's not now."

"Where is it exactly, then?"

He sighed. "We've had people asking for that knife for

years. True-crime aficionados, weirdos, people offering all kinds of money. I didn't want to touch it because it was too high profile. But a collector came in about six months ago and offered me twenty grand for it. My wife needed a new car. I'm not a bad person."

"No one thinks you are," I assured him. "Who'd you sell it to?"

"I can't remember the name. It's probably on the log. Ron Casler? Ron Castor? Ron . . . Castle, maybe. Anyway, I think it was an alias. Who'd come in here and sign in under their real name?"

He had a point; we certainly hadn't.

"He was a professional collector. Paid me under the table. The records still say it's there, so until we're audited, no one knows it's missing."

"Describe him. Tell me where he was from."

"Demon," Danny said, looking at my halo suspiciously. "Tall. Light orange hair and eyebrows. Lots of freckles. Like a giant leprechaun." He gave us a weak smile.

I glanced at Lon. His faced was flushed and his mouth was hanging open.

Danny continued. "He said he was from Detroit, but he sounded like a California boy to me. He obviously had money. His clothes were expensive. One of the officers up front said he drove up in a flashy red convertible."

Lon got up out of his seat and offered his hand to Danny. "Thanks. We'll let you get back to work."

"Wait, what—"

Lon shot me a hard look. I read it perfectly: Keep your mouth shut. Which I did . . . all the way back to the sign-in window up front, through the parking lot, and until we closed our car doors and sat in the front seat.

"Explain. Now."

Lon stuck the key in the ignition and paused.

"I know exactly who he sold it to. He lives in La Sirena."

"Lon!" I said excitedly and slapped his arm. "Who? How? What?"

"That's the first time you've smiled the whole damn day," he noted.

"And that's more words than you've spoken to me all day."

He started up the ignition and began putting his seat belt on. "The man who bought the knife is a member of a club I'm in. He's . . . slippery."

"I thought you weren't a 'joiner.'"

"I'm not anymore. But once you join this club, you're in it for life."

I clicked my seat belt and moved my purse to the floorboard as he pulled out of the parking lot, turning on his windshield wipers to clear the late-afternoon drizzle. "That sounds spooky and ominous."

"It is. I'll make some calls and see if we can meet him."

"Fantastic! You are chock-full of networking goodness," I said, eagerly pulling the pins out of my wig as we pulled out onto the main road. I couldn't wait to get it off. It was itching something fierce.

"Truth is, it would have been way easier to get the talon from evidence than from this guy. But what are we going to do? We don't have a choice anymore."

And we didn't have much time.

21

Our flight home wasn't overbooked, so we both got to sit in first class together. I refused the complimentary champagne this go-around, because I was already sleepy from my schedule being thrown off. It was hard to shift from bartender days to normal days.

When we'd been up in the air for about fifteen minutes, I asked him a few questions about his mysterious ginger-haired friend, but he wouldn't say much. Only that he would make some calls and let me know something later that night if he could manage it. After more drinks and snacks were served, I gave up on trying to pry information out of him.

The sun had set, so the pilot turned off the cabin lights. A few reading lamps switched on above the seats around us. I closed my eyes and turned toward the window, hoping that if I fell asleep, I wouldn't snore.

"Did it at least work?"

"Huh?" I lifted my head to look at Lon. He was flipping though the in-flight magazine without looking at the pages; it was too dim to see anything.

"If you regret what we did, I understand, but did it at least work?"

Now I was wide awake. I pushed myself up in my seat.

"Not so far, no. But why would you think I regretted it? You're the one acting all weird. Can't you just"—I lowered my voice—"read me?"

"I'm not acting weird. I've been trying to read you all day. I can't. You're chaotic."

"Umm, you are *too* acting weird. You've gone back to being all clammy and Neanderthal. I mean, I didn't expect for you to start calling me 'baby,' but I thought you'd at least be cool about it. I'm not going to latch onto you like some love-sick brat, or cry and beg you for a date or anything, sheesh. I didn't regret it, but I'm starting to now."

I crossed my legs and arms at the same time, settling back and staring at the seat in front of me. Until I got riled up again.

"P.S.," I added angrily, trying to keep my voice down, "When you first told me about your ability, I thought that trying to keep my feelings hidden was going to be the worst part about being around you. Guess what, it's not." I turned in my seat to look at him, pointing my finger into the center of his chest. "I couldn't give a good goddamn if you know what I'm feeling anymore. The worst part is not being able to read you back. Being around you is so damn frustrating sometimes. The only way anyone could ever figure out your intentions is if they had some kind of special ability like you've got."

For several long moments, we were actors in an old Western, standing alone in the middle of a dirt road. We stared each other down until he finally dropped his eyes. I won. Yippee.

"I thought I was being plain," he said after a few seconds. His voice was low and even.

"What are you talking about now?" I griped.

"I paid you compliments."

What in the world was he referring to? Compliments? "You mean when you told me that I had a nice ass?" I asked, sarcastic.

"You do. I also told you your hair looked pretty."

"No you didn't. You said it was cute."

"Same difference. I invited you to my house that first time—"

"You insisted that I come over because the books couldn't leave your library."

"—and made you dinner, which you could have refused. Introduced you to my son."

"He actually introduced himself," I mumbled.

"And trusted you to take care of him, even though you're a magnet for trouble right now. What else? I told you personal things about my life that I don't normally share with other people." I started to protest, but he bulldozed me over. "I've tried to make sure you're safe, even though you'll probably just say that you didn't need my help—and you probably don't, because you're a better magician than me. On top of all that, I told you that I was available."

"What? You certainly did not."

"Keep your voice down," he said, looking behind him toward the couple across the aisle.

"Don't shush me," I whispered.

"And, yes, I did. I told you I wasn't dating anyone."

"You were drinking wine with some dishy woman when you—"

He narrowed his eyes. "I'm not even answering that again. It was work, and I couldn't possibly be less interested in Sarah."

I huffed and looked away. Then I thought about what he was saying, and what he really meant by it. I normally considered myself pretty sharp, but it took me several moments to get it. When I did, a strange tightness filled my chest, and I immediately tried to stomp it out.

"Garbled, chaotic," he complained, covering his eyes with his hand in frustration. "Can't you just stop all that and be decisive one way or another?"

I bit the inside of my lip and silenced a random song that was repeating in my head. After a little while, everything began sliding into place in my mind, and I tried to stand outside myself and look at it objectively.

He was attracted to me? Well, hell. I guess I could admit to myself that I was attracted to him too. That's what this boiled down to, right? Attraction? A simple thing, really. A thing that happens every day to random people everywhere. It was just poor timing on our part, because of what was going on in my life. And because of our age difference. Well, as much as we joked about it, maybe that didn't really matter so much after all.

It was still too fresh to know what it would amount to down the road, and I sure as hell didn't know what or where my life was going to be in a few days, but . . . there it was. Huh. I picked at the fabric of the armrest between us. I didn't guard what I was thinking, and I didn't try to confuse it.

"That's better," he whispered. "Thank you." I looked up to find him smiling at me. His strange halo looked more gold than green. He lifted the armrest between us and pushed it up into the seats. "Now then, will you please kiss me again? You might not be willing to beg, but that doesn't mean I'm above it."

He gave me the most beautiful grin, and I replied with

a short, happy laugh. Then I scooted closer, tentatively, and complied with his request.

Our second attempt at kissing was even better than the first. No nervousness, no pretense that it was for any other reason than the fact that we both wanted it. It was slow and deliberate and lingering, and it created a heat within me that spread like wildfire, lighting up every cell in my body.

It ended as slowly as it started, and I couldn't bring myself to pull too far away. He must have felt the same way, because he rested his forehead against mine as my body continued to hum for him. The scent of his skin was intoxicating; he smelled safe and dangerous, comforting and alien, all at the same time. I breathed him in greedily. Then we slunk down sideways in our seats facing each other, hunched over together. He picked up my hands in his and held them as if they were made of the antique paper in one of his books—like they might crumble in his fingers.

I leaned forward and whispered in his ear, a little giddy, "What the hell are we doing?"

"I don't have any fucking idea," he answered. "But I wish we weren't on an airplane full of people because I'd really, *really* like to stick my hand down your pants again."

I muffled a giggle into his shoulder, which quaked a couple times with silent laughter in reply. Then I pushed his hair away from his ear. "Honestly, I'd really, *really* like to do the same to you," I whispered, lips grazing his earlobe, "for starters."

"Jesus fucking Christ," he whispered back. "Don't say that."

"Why not?"

"Because I'm very close to dragging you off to that tiny restroom over there like the Neanderthal I apparently am, and you're only making it worse."

"Those restrooms aren't big enough for one person, much less two. Unless the first-class restrooms are bigger?"

"They're not."

Still, I considered it. We gave each other loopy grins just as the cabin lights came back on, blinding me, and the pilot began making the announcement for the final descent.

"Ugh," I complained, squinting. "This is *so* not fair."

Sitting back up, we reluctantly faced forward again. For the remaining minutes of the flight we sat close, knees touching. After we landed and began a short taxi to the gate, as I leaned forward to fish out my purse from underneath the seat in front of me, Lon's cell buzzed.

He pulled his phone out of his pocket and looked down at the screen. "Not even at the gate and the little bastard's already bugging me," he murmured before answering the phone with an impatient "What?"

I chuckled to myself, then felt him stiffen next to me.

"Slow down. Where are you exactly?"

My heart began racing in alarm.

"You're not going to run out of air. Calm down." He stopped to listen to whatever Jupe was saying. "We won't call the police, I promise. I'm getting off the plane now. We'll be there in half an hour. Don't open the door, you hear me? Jupe? Jupe?"

He pulled the phone away and looked at the screen in shock, then shoved it in his pocket and stood up.

"Sir, please sit down. It will be a couple of minutes before the Jetway is in place."

Yanking me up out of my seat, he pushed forward and got in the flight attendant's face. "My son has been kidnapped. Let me off this damn plane right now."

Her eyes widened as a low rumble rippled through the

passengers around us, then she turned and ran to the phone on the wall next to the pilot's door.

"Lon?" I yelled, shaking his arm.

His eyes were blank as he turned to face me. "It's Riley Cooper," he said. "She's got Jupe cornered in a closet at school."

22

It was after 10 p.m. when we finally made it to La Sirena Junior High. Riley Cooper knew we were coming, so Lon didn't bother to be stealthy. He skidded into the parking lot with the same abandon that he had just used while speeding from the city to the coast in well under a half hour.

"Goddammit, I wish I had a gun," he complained as he flung open his car door in unchecked anger. "I'm never leaving home without one again."

I wished that he did too, though at that point I was a little worried that he was contemplating shooting me along with Riley Cooper; he was furious with me, and I was sick to my stomach.

He hiked up the front steps, but I raced to stop him.

"Hold on! My invisibility spell," I said as I pushed up my sleeve to reveal my white tattoo. His expression changed from angry to hostile. "I just need blood to make it strong enough to cover you . . ." I trailed off into silence.

"You've *got* to be joking," he snarled. "Haven't you done enough magick? Because unless I'm missing something, the only reason my son is being held hostage in there is because you didn't have the sense to stop for a second and think that maybe it wasn't a good idea to upload your fucking servitor in front of him."

I suppose I deserved that. He'd been stewing the entire trip here, after I'd suggested the only obvious reason behind all this: the strange ending to my servitor's transmitted images, when I could see her looking at me. I thought she'd somehow sensed my servitor in the room with her, or it set off a ward. But the green dot I saw must've been some sort of tracking spell. Maybe she couldn't trace my energy because of my deflector charm, but Jupe was there with me, unprotected.

Lon was right. This was my fault. I tried to hold my head up, but I couldn't maintain eye contact. He shook his head and stormed off, acting like he was going to break down the doors to the school, then changed his mind at the last second. The door was open when he tested it, so he entered and I followed.

The school was dark, silent, and eerily empty; each footstep we made was conspicuous. Rows of turquoise metal lockers lined either side of the hallway, broken up by the occasional classroom door. We crept along, frantically eying each door as we went, until I couldn't take it anymore. While Lon was looking the other way, I bit down on a sore hangnail, wriggling it in my teeth until it bled. It hurt like hell, and it didn't produce much blood, but it was enough. I smeared it on my invisibility ward and mouthed the incantation for the spell, momentarily losing my balance after it took hold. His neck stiffened. I was certain he felt the spell—he had to. At the very least, he could surely sense that I was being sneaky? Perhaps his immediate concern for Jupe overrode his instincts, because he continued on without comment.

After we passed under a faded paper football banner strung overhead—GO BLUE DEVILS!—he stopped and looked back and forth down two branching hallways. Jupe had tried to tell him what classroom he was in, but Lon didn't know where he was going. His hand twitched as he debated, then he made the decision to go left.

As we approached the first pair of doors, one on each side of the hall, he slowed and crouched low. I peered into the room on the right while he looked to the left. Nothing. We both turned to each other and shook our heads, then continued.

I'd never tried to maintain a substantial temporary ward for two people. It made me dizzy, and it was taking everything I had to walk a straight line. Lon gave me a suspicious sidelong glance, but kept going.

When we came to the second set of doors, we crouched again and followed the same routine . . . until a dull cracking noise startled us. We peered farther down the hall, then took off.

Running is difficult when all of your energy is being drained by a ward you're attempting to keep up on the fly; when we got within a few feet of the cracking sound, my ankle gave out and I tripped. Right as my fingertips stubbed against the cool tile floor, Lon jerked me back up. I swayed. The gold from his halo seemed to move in horizontal trails as my vision doubled.

We moved to the side of the door, and Lon peered inside. I waited for several seconds, but he showed no reaction. I pushed him aside to get a look. The light in the room was on, but that had been the case in several other rooms we'd passed. Then I noticed the desks. Three near the far windowed wall were crooked and out of place; all the other desks conformed to tight, neat rows. The askew desks sat in front of a closet door at the back of the room . . . a door marked by the slightest tinge of blue light.

Riley Cooper wasn't in there, but some sort of ward glowed around that door.

"Closet," I whispered.

Lon wasted no time. He pushed me out of the way to get inside the room. I hurried to follow, closing the door behind me as he ran around the desks and bolted for the closet. I was still trying to hold the ward, but he was no longer part of it. What was the point? I dropped it with a silent gasp as I spotted him reaching for the closet door.

"Lon, no! There's magick around the door!" I hissed, trying to keep my voice low. He hesitated, then drew back.

A weak voice floated from the bottom of the door. "Dad?"

"Jupe! I'm here, it's okay."

"Dad!"

Jupe began sobbing behind the door, trying to talk, but failing. It broke my heart. I raced behind Lon and stopped him just in time from renewing his attempt to open the door, slapping his hand away.

"It's a spell! Stop! Can't you see it?"

"Cady?"

"Jupe, can you open the door from the inside?" I asked.

"She said I'd die if I did," he cried.

"What kind of spell is it?" Lon asked, his face tense and wired.

I leaned closer to study it. Some sort of blue energy field. An active ward of some kind.

"I don't know," I admitted. "Jupe, did you hear any of the words she said when she did the spell?"

"N-no. It was some weird language."

"Where is she now?" Lon asked.

"I don't know. Patrolling or something. She said she'd be right back. Dad, I can't breathe in here much longer."

I looked down at the wide crack below the door. He had plenty of air. Lon noticed the same thing. "He's claustrophobic," he muttered.

I nodded, then began trying to work out a solution. "I've never read about any kind of ward that would kill a body that crossed it. Especially not one that was put up fast like this. No blood or anything."

"Me either," Lon admitted. At least he was being civil enough to get through this.

"The worst I've seen is one that drained the energy out of the person who crossed the barrier."

"No, the worst I've seen is the ward around both our houses," he replied. "The sound it makes causes enough pain to make someone black out."

A dull thump came from inside the closet. Jupe was moving around. "Please, please get me out of here," he pleaded between sobs. "My arm hurts so bad. It's making me cold."

Riley Cooper was going to be back any second. Indecision might be our downfall.

"We're going to have to take the risk."

"No!" Lon barked, completely panicked, but before he could stop me, I got my hand on the door knob and turned it. The blue air flickered and made a loud popping noise, then disappeared as I flung the door open.

Just a warning ward. A simple warning ward, nothing more.

A muffled cry came from the back of the dark supply closet, then Jupe struggled to get up. Light flooded in from the classroom and we saw his long legs scrambling. Lon lunged forward to get him out, but jumped back when Jupe hollered at the top of his lungs.

I winced. We'd already tripped her ward and were now

making enough noise to wake the dead; Riley Cooper would be here soon enough.

Lon yanked Jupe out by the legs, scooting him across the floor until he was halfway out of the closet and in the light. Hot tears left tracks on his cheeks. His eyes were shut, trying to adjust to the fluorescent classroom lighting after being in the dark for God knows how long; it was after ten, and school let out at three.

But that wasn't the worst part.

His hand was swollen, fingers crusted with dark blood, his thumb was black and blue, and he was holding his arm at an awkward angle.

"Oh, God," Lon whispered. "What happened?"

Jupe just continued sobbing with his eyes shut, holding his arm out and shuddering.

"She broke his arm," I said, fury rising fast. "She did this, didn't she?"

He nodded his head, blinking back tears.

"Get him out of here *now*," I said. "She'll be back and she might be armed or—"

Lon halted. "Does she have a gun, Jupe?"

"I-I don't think so," he cried.

"Sure I do," a raspy voice said from behind us. We swung around to find a petite young woman standing in the doorway, patting the front pocket of her leather pants. "I just don't need to use it," she finished with a dark smile. "Yet."

There she was, exactly as she looked in my servitor's transmission, dressed like a slutty road warrior with too much makeup.

"So, this is the big bad Moonchild," she observed as she slowly walked around the teacher's desk at the front of the room. "Now that I see you, I'm not sure what all the fuss is about."

Jupe's sobbing stopped immediately. He retreated back into the closet before Lon could stop him. Not good. Best to be calm about it, and lure her away from them so that Lon could get Jupe out of there.

"Luxe sent you?" I asked, moving away from the closet.

"Luxe made me, baby. Despite what they say about you, I think they might have made me a little better than Eleusia Ekklesia made you—or maybe all that running away that you did made you miss out on some important training."

I took several more steps forward as she paused in front of the desk and fiddled around with some of the papers stacked there.

"Why do you say that?" I asked.

"Let's see, first off, it took me like one day to kill your guardian."

"Yeah, thanks for that."

"You're welcome. Second, your servitor magick stinks. I was able to put a tracer on it with no effort."

"The green dot." I knew it.

"Very good. You spy on me, I spy on you. I'd been warned that you're hard to trace, but that little boy over there was quite easy. Nice and earthy." She punctuated her words by scraping a couple of long fingernails across the chalk-board.

"Yeah, well, you kinda fucked up when you decided to mess with him." I stole a quick glance behind me. Lon had managed to get Jupe back out of the closet and on his feet.

"Look," she reasoned, "if you had just come quietly when I sent that Pareba after you, we could have avoided all this. All I wanted was for you to come with me so that you could stand trial for your psycho parents. But now you got these people involved. So all three of you are coming with me now." She looked behind me and called out, "I see you trying to leave back there."

She patted her gun again, still looking at them, then smiled at me.

"That seems like a lot of trouble," I said, pressing the tips of my fingers together to reopen the wounded hangnail. "Why don't you just take me and save yourself the hassle?"

She laughed, tapping one of the heels of her boots on the floor. "This isn't up for negotiation."

All right, then. No chance of a peaceable outcome now.

I couldn't escape, because she'd only hunt me down again. She might have been an overconfident bitch about my magical training at the E∴E∴, but she was right about one thing: She knew how to detect servitor magick and tag it well enough to find Jupe. I didn't. Maybe if my parents hadn't been so overprotective and had taken the time to teach me, I might've known better; as it was, I did the best I could on my own.

But even if she *could* track me down, I sure as hell wasn't going to give myself up to her, either. I hadn't stayed alive all this time just to kowtow at the last minute to someone like her.

Still, fight or flight, after years of considering only my own survival, it really came down to one crucial thing that had nothing to do with me: she had hurt Jupe. And she was going to pay for that.

"Oh, well," I lamented as I smeared the tiniest drop of blood on my invisibility ward and erected it one more time. The air wavered in front of me, and for a second, the nausea almost dropped me to the floor. Drained from the first time I put it up, I was afraid it wouldn't work. But in the middle of trying to keep my balance, the bewildered look on Riley Cooper's face said it all—she couldn't see me.

Better act fast, before she wised up and realized what I'd done.

You hear about adrenaline giving people access to super-human strength during moments of crisis. I'd experienced this twice—once when my parents and I faked our deaths, and the other time about a year later, when a cop almost blew my alias.

I probably didn't have enough adrenaline in me now to lift a car or anything quite that spectacular. I did, however, have enough to unhinge the wooden top off the school desk next to me. Bracing my foot on the seat, that's exactly what I did.

The desk creaked and protested as I twisted it, then the screws popped out. I flew back a step with the flat weapon in my hand. It must have looked as if it were floating in air, be-cause Riley Cooper's eyes went wide. Jupe whimpered behind me after my name died on his lips.

I raced forward several steps with the desktop and as Riley stepped back, her spiked heel caught on the sunken grout between two cracked floor tiles. She faltered as I dropped my ward and materialized a couple of feet away from her out of thin air. As Lon had noted in my backyard, it was, indeed, one hell of a spell. Guess this untrained girl knew a few tricks after all.

When Riley saw me, her hands automatically went to her gun. I'll admit, her reflexes were pretty fast, but I was faster.

With both hands, I gripped the desktop and reared it back over my left shoulder, swung with all my strength, and nailed her right in the side of her face. Hard. The hollow *crack!* of wood hitting bone reverberated around the room. Her body slammed against the teacher's desk, knocking a flurry of papers and books into the air.

A slow trickle of red blood began seeping from her hair-line above her ear. Her arms flailed as she struggled to get a grip on the corner of desk and pull herself up. Not gonna happen. I brought the board down on top of her head. The wood fractured in two and fell apart on impact, sending a sickening jolt of pain through my arms. She went down face-forward. Her chin hit the tile and one of her teeth popped out and skipped across the floor in five quick hops.

Lon and Jupe said, "Fuck!" in unison from the back of the room.

Chest heaving, I tossed the split desk and dropped to my knees, tugging the edge of a pair of shiny handcuffs from her back pocket. She lay still on the floor as I straddled her legs, twisted her limp arms back, and cuffed her as tight as I could. It was the first time I'd ever gotten to do that; it felt a little satisfying.

As I stood up, she still didn't move. I worried for a second that I'd killed her.

Lon sprang toward us as I bent down to flip her over and check her pulse. The side of her face was splotched with crimson. Blood was also leaking out of her mouth.

"She's alive," I reported with relief.

"Jesus Christ," he mumbled. Then he repeated it. Twice.

"Cady!" Jupe yelled as he shuffled over to us. "You saved us!"

Lon did not echo his son's sentiments.

"This ends right here," he said bitterly, surging with re-strained rage.

"Lon, I'm sorry that—"

"No," he said, shaking his head. "That girl hurt Jupe because she was trying to track you down. This is your fault. *You* put my kid in danger by doing magick in front of him. *You* turned him into bait."

Jupe's words streamed out in a long, flat note as he tugged on his father's shirt with his good hand. "I asked her to, Dad. I made her do it. She didn't want to but I begged her. You know how I am—you always say that I could wear anybody down and—"

"She's the adult here, Jupe." He glared at me. "At least I thought she was."

Jupe's mouth fell open. I wasn't the only one in shock. "Shut up, Dad—she rescued us. You're being an idiot."

"Stay out of this, Jupe," Lon warned, then barked at me, "This is just business as usual for you, isn't it? Danger? Violence?"

He shook his head, covered his eyes with his hand, then he resumed speaking in a distracted voice, as if to himself, "I can't raise my son around that. What was I thinking? This is happening all over again. I'm a horrible father."

"Lon!" I said, tears threatening to spill from anger and confusion. "I said I was sorry about the servitor. I wouldn't put Jupe in danger on purpose, and as far as violence goes, you probably would've shot and killed Riley if you'd had a gun."

"Maybe. It doesn't matter." He sounded weak and defeated.

"I didn't have a choice," I protested, my confidence shattering as I said the words. "She would have killed me or taken me in. She hurt Jupe."

"You might not have had a choice, but I do. Right now I'm taking my kid to the hospital, and you're going to stay away from him." He put his hand on Jupe's back and tried to push him forward.

"Dad!" Jupe cried. "Cady, I'm not mad, don't listen to him." He was still crying a little. I wasn't sure if it was from pain or shock, but he was trying so hard to be grown up. "I know you didn't mean for this to happen. It's not your fault."

"I said stay out of this, Jupiter!" Lon yelled.

"I'm so sorry," I whispered.

Lon gave me a blank look then herded Jupe toward the classroom door. When he got there, he paused. "What are you going to do with her now?"

"I don't know," I admitted. My hands started shaking.

"Maybe you should have thought of that before you gave her a fucking concussion."

"Maybe." My voice barely carried.

"Find your own way home," he said, laying a protective palm around his son's neck.

Jupe sobbed, screaming at his father, "I hate you," as they walked out the door.

23

My basement looked like a mobile field hospital. I didn't want Riley Cooper to be able to use spells to escape, so I painted four old sheets with sigils that blocked magick and hung them around a small area of my basement that the previous owners had intended to convert into a bathroom. An old toilet and a drain for a shower were as far as they'd gotten.

Adding grand theft auto to my list of crimes that night, I'd managed to get Riley back to my house blindfolded in a hot-wired Ford from the school's back parking lot; I had to plaster the backseat in old newspapers so she wouldn't bleed all over it. Once we got home, it took me fifteen minutes and several tries to remember the counterspell that would allow her to breach Lon's house ward. Then I had to contend with all my other minor wards; every time I tried to get her through the door, a series of irritating warnings ballooned in my head and she started moaning and shaking, but I finally managed a successful cloaking spell.

I found the key to the handcuffs on a small key chain in her pocket. After digging out a length of rusted chain from the shed in my backyard, I shifted her hands to the front of her body and cuffed her wrists to one of four metal support posts that were bolted into the cement floor. Nothing within her reach but the toilet and a musty couch I'd dragged to the metal post. I brought down a satellite radio and switched it on, then left her there and locked the basement door.

It was nearly six in the morning by the time I crawled into bed.

I slept a few hours, woke around noon, then fired up the courage to call Lon. He didn't answer. I sent him a text and told him that I hoped Jupe was okay, and waited for a response, but it never came. If he was serious about my not seeing Jupe again, then he was serious about my not seeing him either. All the work we'd done was for nothing, and I was back at square one.

Not only was the possibility of helping my parents look like the biggest long shot in the world at this point, but I couldn't even focus on the futility of it, because Lon's words were competing for attention: *This is your fault.* The accusation repeated in my head ad nauseam, along with the blank look he'd given me. My heart felt like it'd been buried under a pile of rocks.

Dazed and drained, I plated some fruit and crackers and carried it down to my kidnapping victim. She was asleep on the couch behind the makeshift antimagick curtains. I woke her.

"Do you want to eat?" I asked.

She stuck out her handcuffed hands and raised both middle fingers.

"Look, I don't have any problem leaving this food on the floor, but you're going to drink the water before I leave."

She initially resisted but gave in without too much prodding. It took her two tries to empty it.

"How old are you?" I asked after she'd finished.

Water ran down her chin. "None of your business." She threw the empty plastic bottle in my direction.

"Eighteen?" I guessed. "Seventeen?"

"Twenty-one. Where are we? Are we still in La Sirena?"

She didn't know where I lived. That was good.

"We're in Fresno," I lied.

"Fresno? What are we doing here?"

I ignored her. "What were your instructions from Luxe?"

She shifted her legs to curl up on the couch, facing away from me. She looked uncomfortable. "Bring you back to San Diego . . . alive, unfortunately."

"Why me and not my parents?"

She laughed. "My brother's hunting your parents in Mexico, don't worry."

"I doubt he's having better luck than you are, then. I'm sure they're already farther away than that."

"But you don't know? Interesting."

"Whatever. The less we know about each other's where-abouts, the easier it is to stay hidden. So it's kinda useless, you see, trying to bring me in to get info on them. Because I don't have it."

"Hmph."

"Why did your order kidnap our caliph?"

She wrinkled her nose. "What are you talking about?"

"The head of Ekklesia Eleusia. Why did you kidnap him?"

"I have no idea what you're talking about. Nobody's kid-napped anyone except you, and you're going to regret that when my order finds out."

Perhaps they hadn't told her about the caliph, or she wasn't high up enough in the hierarchy to know—just a bounty hunter instructed to do a job.

I'd removed her leather pants and boots so that she couldn't use them as projectiles to knock down the sheets, and now she had on only underwear and a sheer black spiderweb print shirt. The dirty soles of her feet faced me as her toes curled; the black polish on her toenails was chipping. "Are you cold?" I asked. "There's a space heater I can turn on."

"Are you mad that they left you?" she asked, ignoring my question.

"My parents? No. They were protecting me."

"By deserting you? If you were so fucking special, why wouldn't they guard you with their own lives?"

"The three of us being seen together would draw suspicion. It was safer to separate."

"Or maybe they just told you that. Maybe they realized that you weren't the savior to Ekklesia Eleusia that they'd thought you'd be. Maybe they thought you weren't worth the troub—"

"Look, this isn't going to work. My parents love me. They just did what they had to."

She shook her head. "Still protecting them after all these years, huh? One of our mages has a theory that you helped them with the killings."

"They didn't kill anyone," I snapped.

"I know for a fact that they did." When she tried to smile, all I could see was the gaping hole in her teeth. The incisor that once held that spot was now in my pocket.

"Let's see, you were fourteen or fifteen during the Black Lodge slayings? I seriously doubt you knew much more than your math homework back then."

She relaxed her shoulders and stared at me for a moment. "Huh," she said thoughtfully.

"What?"

"You really don't think they killed all those people, do you?"

I gave her a weak smile. "They were framed by the head of your order."

"Wow, you're dense."

"Alrighty, then. This is going nowhere." I moved the fruit and crackers toward her with the tip of my shoe. "Have fun eating like a dog off the floor." I left her a small length of toilet paper on the arm of the couch and parted the hanging sheets to exit.

"I know your parents killed the other heads of the orders," she said behind me, "because they tried to kill my dad."

Her dad? I froze in place.

"That's right, Moonchild. I'm Phil Zorn's daughter."

An uneasy chill ran down my back. Magus Zorn? Holy shit. I had just kidnapped the Luxe leader's daughter. This was either the worst mistake I'd ever made, or a once-in-a-lifetime piece of leverage; I wasn't sure which.

24

By late afternoon I'd checked on Riley twice and brought her more water. At least she'd eaten. She was refusing to talk anymore, which was fine by me, merely requesting that I change the satellite radio station, which I did. Then I dug through an old toolbox that the previous owners of the house had left behind and found an old sliding lock, which I installed on the door to the basement. Having some extra security made me feel less anxious. More than that, it gave me something to do.

After finishing, I plopped down on my living room sofa, gloomy and miserable, weighing my options. Only four days left until my time ran out.

I laid out in a neat row on my coffee table the contents of Riley Cooper's pockets. Her gun, a driver's license, a key card for a motel room in La Sirena, about a thousand dollars in cash, a piece of red ochre chalk, her key ring, a cell phone. I scrolled through her contacts several times. Read all her text messages. Most of them were just brief I-love-you's to her father and another man—boyfriend, brother? She hadn't made or received any calls in two days; at least no one would be suspicious about calls suddenly stopping. Hopefully I could just continue texting in her place to keep up appearances.

I was haunted by her implication that my parents had ditched me. It wasn't like I hadn't thought about it before or confronted them with the same charge, especially during my first year in hiding. I'd tried to persuade them to take me with them, even after a couple of years had passed. One especially dreary winter in Seattle, when Kar Yee was busy marrying her fake husband to get her citizenship, my mental health went south. I'd already linked myself to Priya at that point, and sent the guardian to ask my parents to call me.

It took them three days to respond. The longest three days of my life. I locked myself in my room and did every spell I could find to draw them to me. After two days, I dosed myself with a medicinal elixir and slept on my closet floor. By the time they called, I was weak from hunger and hallucinating from the medicinal. I remember sobbing on the phone, begging them to come to get me. My mom spent a couple of hours talking me down, flew from France that night and stayed with me for several wonderful days. I missed all my classes and had to repeat one of them the following semester, but it was worth it.

That was the last really bad time for me. Apart from the occasional bout of self-pity, I had moved past all that long ago. It made me mad that Riley Cooper was able to dig it back up, so I did my best to squelch any lingering feelings of abandonment.

My thoughts floated back to another subject I was trying to avoid, and I wondered how Jupe was doing. It crossed my mind that I could send a servitor to check on him, but if Lon ever found out . . . *ugh*. No thanks. I glanced at my cell. No calls. I stupidly dialed Tambuku to double-check that I had service, then chastised myself for being desperate and put it back down. I lay down on the sofa on my side, staring at it, trying to will it to ring.

I guess that's why I never heard the door open and close.

"Hey."

I yelped. Lon was standing by the coffee table.

"God . . ." I put my hand over my jackhammering heart and quickly sat up.

As the surprise wore off, I realized I had no idea what to say, so I remained quiet. His gaze dropped to the row of Riley's items on the table. He set down a book he'd brought and picked up her keys. "You still have the girl?" he asked.

"In the basement."

One brow rose in question.

"I'm treating her humanely."

He didn't reply. Just tossed the keys back on the table and crossed his arms over his chest.

"How is he?" I asked, embarrassed that I couldn't bring myself to say Jupe's name.

"A friend healed his hand. The breaks in his arm were too big, so he's in a cast."

"Is he in a lot of pain?" I couldn't look at him, so I just stared at the floor. My hands gripped the edge of the sofa.

Lon snorted, sounding just like Jupe. "He's high as a kite on pain pills and glad to be missing school for the rest of the week."

I tried to laugh, but it got distorted by a sudden surge of emotion. *Don't you dare cry*, I thought.

Lon pushed Riley's things to the side and sat down on the coffee table facing me, his legs surrounding mine. He leaned forward until his face was only a few inches away. He smelled like valrivia smoke. "Listen up," he said, "because I don't say this often."

I stiffened, drawing back, unsure of his intentions. He put his hand on my forearm to stop me. I shook it off. "What?"

"I overreacted," he said.

It took several moments for his words to register.

"Look—" he started.

"I understand." I raised my voice to drown out his explanation. "I understand you being scared and upset about Jupe—"

"No, you don't."

"Yes, I do. I may not be a parent—"

"Yeah, you're not a parent, that's right."

Anger flared inside my chest. "Don't give me some bullshit about how I can't understand because I didn't give birth to him, because even I know that you don't have to do that to care about someone."

"Will you calm down and let me talk for a second?" Lon said in exasperation. "I'm trying to apologize."

I pressed my lips together.

"Thank you," he said crossly.

I waited for several moments while he collected his thoughts.

"When I said that you don't understand, I meant that you don't understand why I reacted like I did. Hell, I didn't understand it." He dropped his eyes. "It was Jupe who pointed out some things. How I was getting you confused with Yvonne."

I raised an eyebrow.

"You aren't like his mother," he clarified, "but I was reacting to you the same way. It's just that . . ." He squinted his eyes and creased his brow, engaged in some inner battle to find the right words. "Yvonne put Jupe in danger a couple of times when I was away on shoots. When he was four, she left him at someone's house, some guy she was screwing. A stranger. She took Jupe with her, and that's one thing, but then she forgot him—her own child."

Well, shit. I really didn't know what to say to that. He was close enough to sense my feelings, which was probably helpful for once; let him figure it out.

"That was neglect," he continued, "and it was her fault. What you did wasn't the same. You didn't know that girl could track you that way. I didn't either, frankly, and that led me to my second realization."

"Which was?"

"I guess I was mad at myself and taking it out on you. Like I told you before, I can't totally blame Yvonne for all her actions. She was a wild child before I got her initiated, but after I did, she got worse. So that's my fault."

"What do you mean, 'initiated'?" I asked. "You still haven't told me what you did to her."

He closed his eyes briefly and inhaled. "I let her talk me into having a spell done on her to increase her demon powers."

I ran through all the spells I'd come across that could be applicable but came up short. "I don't understand. Was this some spell you found, or . . . ?"

"It's a spell that one of my father's friends learned back in the sixties. My father and a few others cast it on each other. Like I said, it amplifies latent demonic traits."

"Makes you more demon?"

He nodded. "That's why my halo looks like this. Both my parents underwent the spell before I was born. I had it cast on me when I turned eighteen. After I started dating Yvonne, she found out about it and wanted it done too. I should have said no, but I didn't."

"What exactly does it do? I mean, was your empathic power not as sharp as it is now, or . . . ?"

"It allows Earthbounds to transmutate."

"Huh?"

"To shift. To become less human, more demon. Your powers are ramped up, and not . . . tempered by your human nature like they normally are."

I stared at him, dumbfounded. I'd never heard of such a thing. "So you can do this? Transmutate?"

"Yes."

"What happens when you do?"

"I can read emotions really strongly, and pick up a few conscious thoughts too."

"Oh."

He cleared his throat. "I can also manipulate emotions. Temporarily change the way people feel."

Wow. That didn't sound good. "Have you done that to me?"

"Huh?" He squinched up his eyes like I was crazy, then shook his head. "No. You'd *definitely* know if I transmutated. It's not something I can sneak by you."

"Oh, okay." I thought about it, then my mind turned back to his ex-wife. "What is Yvonne's ability? Why do you hate it so much?"

Silence.

"Don't ask me that right now," he pleaded in a soft voice. "I'm not trying to hide anything from you, and I will tell you eventually."

He reached for me, and I flinched.

"Please," he whispered, and picked up my hands in his. He looked down at them, stroking my fingers. We were silent for a moment, not looking at each other.

"I didn't mean to get started on all that, but I suppose

you'd find out soon enough any way. What I meant to say about my behavior last night is that I was mad at myself for being indirectly responsible for putting my own child in danger in the past. Granted, I'm not happy that he got hurt, and I'm not saying I think it's no big deal." He leaned his head to the side to catch my eye. "But I don't blame you for what happened."

"Okay," I said lamely.

"Honestly, Jupe's seen me do magick before, so if you did something wrong, well, I have too. Jesus, you're shaking like a leaf."

"Too much magick," I conceded with a wry smile. "I get drained, and . . . it doesn't matter."

He gave me a tender look, then squeezed my hands firmly, as if that would help.

"Maybe you haven't thought this all the way through," I said after a few moments. "I mean, I would never do anything to hurt Jupe on purpose. But you were right the first time—it *is* my fault. Like you said, I'm a magnet for trouble. I'm not a good person to be in Jupe's life. He deserves someone more stable. I mean, look at me. I'm holding a kidnapped girl in my basement. What would Father Carrow say about me now if he knew that, huh?"

"Well," Lon said in a diplomatic voice, "I can't think that he would approve of kidnapping, or of injuring her, but I'll bet he would give you a little slack for the situation you're in. And like Jupe told me, the girl *did* have a gun, and she didn't seem all that sorry about slamming my kid's arm in a door. You might have saved our lives, like Jupe thinks you did."

"Hmm."

"Besides, no offense to Father Carrow, but I'm more concerned about what opinion my son has of you right now."

"Why?"

"Because you might be the first woman Jupe and I have both agreed on."

My heart vaulted. A cautious hope threaded through me. Did he mean that?

After a short silence he dropped my hands and asked, "So how did you get her back here last night?"

"Uh . . . taxi?" Umm, yeah. He wasn't buying that. I reckoned if he was being honest, I should too. "All right. I kinda stole a car."

He closed his eyes in resigned annoyance.

"But it's been returned, good as new. The door was unlocked, so I didn't have to break the window or anything. Bob even put gas in it."

"Bob?" he said, narrowing his eyes.

I sighed. "He's this guy at the bar. A regular. He's a pretty good healer—Earthbound, of course—so I asked him to come over and help her out." I tilted my head toward the basement. "Told Bob that she was my cousin, and that she's the one who stole the car. Him and his buddy drove it back to La Sirena. Bob's got a crush on me, so he was happy to do it."

He made a low, disapproving noise. "Are you and this Bob . . . ?"

"What? God no! Bob is a supernice guy, but he's kinda like a stinky stray dog with one leg—you feel sorry for him, but not enough to bring him home."

"Hmph."

"If you met him, you'd understand."

"I don't handle jealousy well," Lon said. "I'm warning you."

"Well, I'm a bartender, so I get hit on a *lot*. I'm just warning *you*."

"I don't like to share." I could tell by the way he said it that he meant it.

"Me neither," I agreed.

I smiled at him, and he smiled back, and I guess that was that. In what I was just beginning to realize was typical for him, he didn't dwell on matters once they were settled in his mind. When he was finished with something, he was truly finished. It was a tidy way of living, and I envied him for being able to do it so effortlessly.

So I guessed we were back on again, though exactly what that entailed, I had no idea, and I doubted Lon did either.

"We didn't read the last page of the spell," he said out of the blue.

"Huh?"

"The memory spell. The Wheel. We missed a short paragraph on another page. I guess we were too distracted at the time." He gave me a soft smile, then continued. "You don't get the memories straight back. The person who casts the spell does."

"Explain, please."

"I had a dream last night that made me go back and check the spell." He reached behind him and picked up the book he'd brought—the tandem memory spells. He sat down next to me on the couch.

"The Wheel spell moved the memory fragments to me," he said. "The reasoning is that a fresh pair of eyes looking at old memories will give a different perspective and see things you might have missed or buried."

His fingers flipped open the book to a blue marker; he showed me the page we'd missed. The memories could surface in the spell caster as visions or dreams. I closed the book and looked up at him, suddenly self-conscious. It was one thing to share my emotions with him, but my memories were another thing entirely. "What was your dream?"

"I was seeing things from your point of view. You were young, a child, sitting at a small table playing with wooden puzzle pieces. They had astrological symbols and names on them."

"Yes!" I said in astonishment. "My dad gave that to me. A round puzzle of the zodiac."

Lon nodded. "Your mother was standing in front of the table. Dark hair, very pretty. Tall. You were right about favoring her. Spitting image. Not her eyes, though."

"No, I have my dad's."

He smiled softly, then continued relating the dream. "Your mother was speaking with a transparent being with feathers and tufted ears. She called the being Scivina."

"Yes, that's right." My pulse quickened as excitement rose inside me. "Scivina is my mom's guardian. Like mine, Priya—the one Riley Cooper had killed."

Lon brightened with curiosity. "Both are Hermeneus spirits, right? I've seen them mentioned occasionally in grimoires."

"Yep. Messenger entities. They're finicky, and their knowledge and skills vary, but they can be an invaluable resource in the Æthyr. I'm surprised you haven't tried to call one yourself."

He smiled. "I wonder if they'd agree to link with an Earthbound?"

"I don't see why not. Earthbounds are descended from Kerub demons. Priya always told me that the Hermeneus spirits in its tribe were generally on friendly terms with the local Kerubs."

Lon acted surprised. "You would get that kind of information?"

"Sometimes. You have to dig for it. Priya would never just offer up information unless it directly related to me."

"Do you think a Hermeneus could locate my ancestors?"

I shrugged. "Maybe. That would be kinda cool though, huh? You should try to call one and see if you can link up. I'd help you with the ritual if you needed it."

He thought about this for a moment, eyes gleaming with possibility.

"Anyway, the dream?"

"Oh, sorry." He shook away his thoughts and continued. "Your mother was saying that magicians normally can't see each other's guardians, but you could see hers."

"Yep, I can see everyone's guardians. Just like I can see Earthbound halos or imps or anything supernatural in origin."

"That's what your mother was saying. She was asking Scivina to confirm if she saw anything unusual about you, and the spirit told your mother that you were beginning to show traces of a silver halo. Your mother was very pleased. Then the dream ended and I woke up. That was it."

Huh. That wasn't as exciting as I hoped. "Why would that memory surface?"

"I don't know. Is your silver halo the reason Riley called you Moonchild?"

The details surrounding my conception and title never came out in all the media coverage of the killings. Though several of the higher-ups in the other magical orders knew about me, they remained quiet about it during the scandal. Some honor still remained among thieves, I guess you could say.

"Magicians have always tried to conceive children during rituals," I explained. "It's mostly a ceremonial act, just symbolic. The Moonchild ritual is the granddaddy of all fertility rites. Magicians in the past mentioned it in their journals, like an urban legend. Many people have tried it and failed. Symbolically, it's supposed to draw down lunar power inside me—imbue me with stronger Heka—which I guess it did."

"But it also gave you the halo. And your preternatural sight."

I grinned. "The sight thing has been mighty handy."

"I can't imagine how other humans live without it," he admitted. "But regarding the ritual, I've never run across any mention of it in my books. Do you know what they did exactly?"

I stared at him. "Umm . . . they had sex? My mom got pregnant?"

"The spell," he clarified.

I shrugged. "While some old mage from our order officiated, they had ritual sex inside a silver circle outside in the woods during some special lunar phase."

Lon looked at me like I was crazy.

"Dude, you're preaching to the choir. I know it sounds nutball. My parents aren't exactly apple pie and *Leave It to Beaver*. To hear them talk about the conception ritual, you'd think it was the greatest achievement in the history of the universe. My mom claimed my conception was a holy experience, and that she wore white the entire time she was pregnant with me to ensure that I was 'blessed by the moon.'"

"So everyone in your order thought it was an urban myth until your parents proved them wrong?"

I shrugged. "I guess? I kinda tuned it all out. Who wants to think about their parents having sex? Not me. The only thing I know is that every year I used to get a shitload of expensive birthday presents from all the bigwigs in my order. Not anymore. Now I'm just a bartender who can see halos and kindle Heka."

Lon was reserved and thoughtful. I hoped I hadn't weirded him out; this wasn't something I shared with people, ever. But I guess I didn't need to worry, because a few seconds later, he stood up and stretched, as if we'd just been discussing the weather. "Now then, why don't you take me down and show me your prisoner." He scooped up the grimoire and thumped it with a knuckle. "I'm thinking since The Wheel spell works, then the other spells in here might too."

25

"Who the hell are you?" Riley Cooper asked again, glaring at Lon as he pulled down the last of the antimagick bedsheets. I slid out a copy of the Memory Erase by Time Period spell from his book.

Brushing off his hands, he continued to ignore her and spoke to me as if she weren't there. "I'm thinking we should wipe out all her memories since the day your parents were spotted in Texas two weeks ago."

I nodded. "That should cover things. She won't remember what we look like or where she's been." Most importantly, she wouldn't remember Jupe; he'd be safe.

Riley scooted backward on the couch into the corner farthest from us. "What do you mean, 'wipe out' my memories? What kind of spell book is that?"

"Then we can try the Memory Twist spell to convince her that you're someone else . . . so you won't have to keep her chained up."

"That will be a relief. You'll need blood," I noted, reading the text for the second time, just to make sure we didn't skip anything. "Sure glad it doesn't require what The Wheel spell did."

He cocked one eyebrow at me, then removed something small and metallic from his jeans pocket. I realized what it was and laughed. "A pocketknife?"

"You said men my age should carry one. This was my father's. I got it sharpened. Do I need my blood, or will hers do?"

I skimmed the text again, a little happier than I probably should have been in a dank basement with my kidnapped enemy. "Any blood will do. The spell just needs a bit of Heka to set it in motion, and she should have plenty—she's got Magus Zorn's Heka-rich genes."

He flicked open his knife and eyed Riley. "All right, let's do this."

"You sure you don't want me to do the spell? It's my problem, you know. I'm willing to be responsible for it."

He shook his head without looking at me. "Nope. It's my problem too. I won't sleep if I think she might come back after Jupe. Key to the handcuffs?" he requested.

I slipped it off her key ring and handed it to him.

Riley Cooper pulled her hands out of Lon's reach. "Who the hell is Jupe? That mixed boy?"

"That mixed boy is my kid," Lon clarified as he hovered over her. "Does the Luxe Order condone hurting children, or is that your own personal thing?"

Her eyes were dark and defensive. "He ran from me. If he'd just followed inst—"

"You broke his arm in two places."

"He kicked me in the stomach!"

"He's thirteen and built like a green bean." Lon grabbed her by the ankles. In one quick tug, he yanked her down on the couch until she lay flat on her back.

"Fuck you!" she shouted, trying to kick Lon while he

straddled her legs and did his best to hold her still. She was a fighter, I had to give her that. I helped him secure her as he removed the cuffs.

"Sigil, please," Lon said, gritting his teeth.

I set the paper down. "Just use my blood." I ran my finger along his pocketknife. The pain was sharp but brief, and a line of blood welled immediately. "Ready?"

"My father is going to kill you," she threatened. Her eyes were wild and menacing.

"Ready," Lon confirmed in an angry voice. He switched his grip to put a hand over her forehead, his palm covering her eyes. I held my finger over the sigil and squeezed while he spoke the incantation.

Mouth open, she belted out a scream that lost its luster after a few seconds and morphed into panting. All the hairs on my arms stiffened. Energy surged around her as Lon's words ended. Her body went still beneath me, so I released her.

Lon stood and wiped both sides of his pocketknife several times on his jeans. We watched her, waiting. For a long moment she continued to lie there, but eventually she shook her head and sat up. Her gaze skittered around the room and fell on us. "Where am I?"

"You don't know who I am?" I asked.

She squinted. "You look familiar . . . did we go to high school together?"

Lon glanced at me and shrugged. "That'll work. Let's go ahead with the second spell and get it over with."

This time, when she freaked and struggled, she didn't fight us as hard. Lon spoke to her calmly, repeating that she knew me from high school and could trust me. Meanwhile, I charged up the second sigil and recited the spell. When it was done, her eyes fluttered shut. Just when I thought we might've screwed up or taken it too far, she inhaled deeply and sobered up.

"Jane?" she asked.

"From high school," I confirmed. *Please let this work . . .*

"God, I remember now," she said, pushing herself up to sit on the couch. "You went to school in Rancho Bernardo! I haven't seen you in, what? Three years? Where are we?" She rubbed her temples and cracked her neck. "I feel fuzzy."

Lon nodded at me in confirmation; she wasn't lying. Excellent. Finally, a good use for his stupid empathic ability.

"Don't you remember? We, uh . . ." I tried to think up something.

"You came to visit Jane for the week," Lon said quickly. "The two of you had a car accident. You have a minor concussion and the doctor said your memory might take a few days to adjust."

Her face tightened. "Damn. That must be why my head's killing me."

"I'll take care of you," I said. "You're going to stay here with me—"

"Your old buddy, Jane," Lon repeated.

All right, already. Sheesh. I shot him a cross look. "And take it easy until you feel better. I've got some medicine to help with the headaches."

Some really strong medicine. Successful memory spell or not, I was going to dose her ass to hell and back, just to make sure.

By all appearances, the Memory Twist spell had worked brilliantly. Even without my narcotic medicinal, Riley seemed pretty damn convinced that we were old friends. She asked a few questions about the fake wreck, then nodded off in front of the TV on the bed in my guest room upstairs. I had to admit, without her ruthless edge, she wasn't so bad. Pleasant, even.

It took us over an hour, but Lon helped me lock up anything lying around that would give her a clue as to where she was, anything that might make her question our story. We added extra wards on the doors and windows to discourage her from leaving; even if someone knocked on the door, she wouldn't answer it. I locked up the landline and told her that her cell had been lost in the accident—convinced her that she'd already spoken to her family and that she didn't need to contact them again for the time being.

"Well, until I decide what to do about her, she's clueless," I said in my living room once we'd finished securing everything.

"And she's not chained up. I think Father Carrow would be much happier with this arrangement." He gave me a soft smile. "Right now I've got to get back and make dinner for Jupe."

"Of course."

I walked him to the front door. He paused as he reached for the handle. "Do you have anything nicer than jeans and T-shirts?"

I wondered if that was an insult. "Why?"

"I made some calls. Remember that club I was telling you about, the one where I met the man who bought the glass talon?"

"Yes?" I looked at him intently.

"They meet monthly. Their next meeting happens to be tomorrow night."

For the last twenty-four hours, I'd convinced myself that I was going to have to use Riley Cooper for leverage at the

Luxe council, and that any hope I'd ever had of finding the talon or the albino demon's summoning name was forever lost.

Lon watched me, waiting patiently for his words to register. "You still want to get the talon, right?"

"Yeah," I said. "God, yeah."

"Okay, then. This club is strictly for demons, and I was just going to go there and do this myself, but . . . I think I'm on a roll with you, being open about things."

"I feel honored."

"You should." He grinned, tucking his hair behind one ear. "Anyway, I think even though you're human, you're novel enough to pique their curiosity. They'll let you in, and your being there might help our cause."

I wrinkled my nose. "Just what kind of club is this?"

"We-e-ell . . ." he drawled, "have you ever heard of a Hellfire Club?"

"Like in England, back in the eighteen hundreds?"

"Seventeen hundreds, but yes. Exclusive high-society clubs—"

"Where rich men went to whore around and drink?"

"Pretty much."

In the midst of all the chaotic thoughts in my head, an unsettling pang jumped to the forefront. He laughed softly, identifying it before I even could. "Mmm . . . someone is jealous. Guess I'm not the only one."

"I'm not jealous," I protested.

"The one in La Sirena is not strictly a men's club," he explained. "Women are members too. That's not to say that there's any lack of immoral behavior at these things. Depends on how easily you shock."

"Not easily."

"Excellent. We're just going to go in there, talk to our guy, and get the talon. In and out."

"Why am I novel enough to get in?"

"Your halo."

"Oh." Duh. I smiled. "Am I going to have to lie and say I'm demon?"

He squinted out of one eye, contemplating. "Just don't admit to being human."

"What time tomorrow?" I asked, hopeful again.

"It's not going to be a fun night out, so don't expect to enjoy it. If I ever get a chance to take you on a proper date, it won't be to this damn thing." He turned to leave. "I'll pick you up at nine."

26

The ties of my black wrap dress fastened into a tidy bow. It was the most adult thing I owned. Maybe the most expensive thing, too. The thin fabric hugged the curves of my hips and made my breasts look bigger. My ass too, and it didn't need any help, but there wasn't much I could do about it. The only jewelry I wore was a wide silver bracelet and the small silver moon pendant that my mother had given me on my sixteenth birthday.

"You look fantastic." Dressed in my pajamas, Riley Cooper stood in the doorway, holding a bag of chips. I'd scaled back to a milder medicinal that kept her calm. Unfortunately, it also made her chatty. And hungry. I'd already had to go to the grocery store and bring back food. It was pretty weird to be playing house with the person who'd recently been chained in my basement. It set my teeth on edge, but I did my best to keep up the charade.

"Hey," she said. "Remember when Joey took you to prom at my school, and you wore that crazy strapless dress?" Her eyes were bright and cheerful as she recalled some memory with Jane. "God, we got wasted that night."

"We sure did," I agreed. "I really need to hurry now, though. Can we talk about this later?"

"Oh, yeah, no prob. I've already picked out two DVDs to watch while you're gone. It's been so long since I just sat around and chilled. I'm looking forward to it."

"Enjoy yourself, but don't overdo it with"—*that concussion I gave you*—"your injuries from the car accident."

"Oh, Jane. You were always such a worrier." She shook her head slowly, then stuffed a chip in her mouth. "Have a great time, and if I'm asleep when you get back, wake me up and tell me how your date went."

"I might be out late. Don't wait up."

"In that case, I'll see you tomorrow, then," she said brightly.

I patted her on the arm. "Alrighty."

As she tromped off to the guest room, I turned off the bathroom light, then flipped it back on. In an inexplicable moment of audaciousness, I decided to take out my brown contacts. The change it made startled me. Just when I began considering putting them back in, I heard a loud knock at the door downstairs.

On my way to answer it, I grabbed a small clutch, then unlocked the door and gawked at the debonair demon standing in the porch light. "Holy shit, is that you?" I asked with a grin. Lon was dressed in a tailored black suit over a white shirt. The jacket was unbuttoned, no tie.

His eyes wandered over me in all directions: up, down, across, and back. Quickly, then leisurely. Many times. At first I was flattered, but when he didn't say anything and his expression was blank, doubts rose.

"Okay, if this isn't appropriate then you need to tell me, like, right now, because it's going to take me a few minutes to dig up something else."

No response.

"Dammit, Lon."

His eyes connected with mine, and he finally spoke. "Christ, they're blue."

I relaxed when I realized what he meant. "I took my colored contacts out. You are the first person in seven years to see the real deal."

Yet again, no response.

"Appropriate or not? I'm starting to get irritated now, in case you can't sense it."

He nodded several times in quick succession. "Appropriate."

I made a face at him, then locked the door to my house. "Let's get this over with."

We drove in silence from Morella to the coast in a silver Audi coupe. The chrome-and-leather interior was spotless, in noticeable contrast to his truck and SUV, both of which were matted with dog hair, the backseat floorboards hidden under a pile of comic books. The owner of those comic books was apparently feeling better today, Lon told me when I asked, but that was the only conversation we engaged in for half an hour.

When we got to La Sirena, Lon pulled onto Ocean Avenue, which runs the length of the town's beaches. We headed away from the Village into neighborhoods that were a mix of small businesses, restaurants, and homes. The rocky cliffs that bordered the edge of town loomed dark in the distance, standing out against a sky hung with a bright, waxing moon. I hadn't really spent a lot of time out here near the beach, especially at night; it was rather pretty and romantic.

"I didn't expect you to look so nice," Lon said abruptly. "It caught me off-guard earlier."

I stared at the glove compartment, weighing his clumsy words, then said, "Thanks?"

He nodded once, clearly relieved to have that out of the way. "I'm going to be transmutated the entire time we're in the club. Remember what we discussed, that I'll be able to hear you in my head. So you can talk to me without speaking."

Yeah, I still wasn't all that sure how I felt about this enhanced ability of his. I'd only just become comfortable with the old ability. "How many others besides you are going to be transmutated?"

He slowed the car to turn into a small, unmarked road that I never would've spotted on my own. Bordered by beach cottages on one side, it wound along the side of the cliffs toward the ocean. "There are only thirteen of us in the club who can shift."

"Does that make you one of the higher-ups?" I asked with a nervous smile.

An elongated strip of light from an oncoming car briefly lit up his face. His shoulders lifted slowly, then fell. "My father and his best friend started the Hellfire Club before I was born. Club rules strictly limit the number of members who can join the higher ranks and undergo the transmutation spell. Only thirteen knights at their Round Table, I guess you could say. They keep those thirteen seats filled, so the only way to get a seat is when a member either dies or is kicked out. That's how I got mine—someone died."

"What about Yvonne?"

"Same thing. The seats are highly prized, and there's a long waiting list for them. Being the son of one of the founders moved me to the top of the list, and I pulled rank to get Yvonne inducted. On hindsight, that was a mistake."

From the little he'd shared about her, I'd have to agree.

The road split. To the left were more beach cottages. To the right, a Dead End sign posted above a larger No

Trespassing/Private Property sign. We turned right. The road dipped down and opened up into a large parking lot filled with cars. Lon drove to the front and parked in a space marked with the number 9; except for spaces 1 and 3, the remainder of the thirteen numbered parking spaces were already occupied.

Lon turned off the engine and sighed, slouching forward.

"Are you okay?"

He took the keys out of the engine and handed them to me. "Take these. If something happens, and you want to leave . . . I just don't want you to be stuck. There's only one taxi company in La Sirena and they won't come out here."

"Okay, now you're starting to scare me."

He curved his hand around the parking brake. "Let's just talk to Spooner about the talon and get out of there."

I couldn't agree more. I stashed my clutch in the glove compartment and exited the car. After setting the alarm, I stuck his keys in a small, hidden pocket in the side seam of my dress.

It was after 9:30 when we walked out of the parking lot through an arch cut into a sculpted wall of shrubbery, and down a stone sidewalk bordered with gas torches. The wind whipped off the ocean and cut right through my dress. It had to be ten degrees warmer inland in Morella than out here by the water. I shivered and wrapped my arms around myself to stave off the chill.

The beach narrowed and we continued walking through another archway, this time carved into a stone wall, and emerged into a circular patch of beach. A large bonfire burned in the middle. The sidewalk looped around in back of the bonfire and led to a grand set of dilapidated stairs that headed straight into the rocky cliff.

"A cave?" I murmured.

"A network of caves."

At the top of the short set of stairs, I tapped my shoes to knock off sand that was clinging to my heels. We stood in front of a large set of thick wooden doors, each with a small round window covered by crosshatched iron bars.

Lon's hands covered my shoulders. He rotated me around to face him and, without warning, kissed me. It was close-mouthed and insistent, much different from the way he'd kissed me before, and during the last second, it got strange.

Something had changed. His lips were on mine, but he wasn't really kissing me anymore. I wanted to pull away, but I just . . . couldn't. The air shuddered and a rush of crazy energy rushed around me like an army of a thousand soldiers galloping past. Then he released me with a disarming groan. I inhaled sharply.

When I opened my eyes, words left me. I stumbled backward in shock, mouth gaping open. He had transmutated.

It was still Lon. He'd hadn't grown extra arms or a tail. But he'd changed. Drastically.

His eyes were different. They were more intense. Harder.

His halo had altered from a solid, steady glow around his head into a crown of dancing flames. The green was nearly gone, and the speckled gold moved and flickered, growing and shrinking. It formed an aureole of fiery light that flamed higher in the center and draped around his shoulders. The golden fire was almond shaped, like the halos of Tibetan and Persian deities that I'd seen in dozens of paintings and sculptures.

As dazzling as this was, it paled in comparison to the most radical alteration in his appearance. Just above his hairline, two thick, spiraling horns jutted out from his head and looped backward over his ears. They were auburn brown, with the satiny finish of a fingernail, and ringed with ridges. Each horn was nearly a foot in diameter.

Transfixed, I blinked, both awed and frightened at the same time. I'd summoned demons from the Æthyr that looked similar to him—with the addition of a few scales or wings or hairy body parts—but they were always safely enclosed inside a binding triangle. To see something like that standing in front of me . . . to see *Lon* like that . . . It was intimidating, and, at the same time, astounding. I didn't realize that I was clutching my hands together in front of my chest until he gently pried them away. My fingers were cramped, knuckles white.

"It's still me." Though gentle, his voice was deeper—so rich, it sent chills up my arms.

He held one of my hands while I tentatively stepped forward and reached for his spiraling horns with my other. My fingertips danced over the surface, inspecting the texture. The horn was surprisingly warm. Living. Not an illusion, but real.

Fascinated, I continued to touch both horns gingerly, as if he were a goat in a petting zoo. When he made a small noise, I became self-conscious. "Sorry," I mumbled and drew my hand away. Nostrils wide, he gave me a mischievous smile that sent a flutter through my chest.

My face and neck flushed as I laughed nervously, suddenly realizing that the horns and gilded halo were only physical. How could I have forgotten? He could *hear* me now. Not just my emotions but my thoughts. *Everything.*

I froze, trying not to think about anything at all. That plan shattered almost immediately; the more I tried to empty my mind, the worse it got. A vortex of random images and thoughts swirled in my brain. *Don't think about the time you slept with that skanky delivery guy who worked at Thai Garden, or when you threw up on the middle couch cushion and just wiped it off and flipped it over, or . . .*

My eye twitched as panic fired through my chest. Was he seeing all this roiling around in my head, like Dorothy watching her family being swept up in the tornado?

"Slow down," he said. "I can only read surface thoughts."

"If that's true, then why did you just tell me to slow down?"

"I can still hear your emotions, remember?"

Oh. That's right. Crud. Was nothing safe? I was going to be sick.

"You're not going to be sick," he insisted.

"Oh, *God.*"

"Please, Arcadia. I really need to you to be okay with this. I know it's hard to accept, but I won't betray anything I might hear in your head."

"I know that," I grumbled, "it's just . . . I'm a private person. I'm not used to sharing anything with anyone. Emotions are one thing, but this is different. I don't want you to see something that might embarrass me."

"I've seen all kinds of shit in people's heads. Believe me, there's nothing you could think that I haven't already heard somewhere else."

I cringed. "Seen it all, huh? You're like an OB-GYN of the mind-reading world?"

He snorted a laugh. And, surprisingly, that made me smile. I took a few breaths and tried to come to terms with this more invasive side of his knack. As long as he couldn't poke around in my memories—

"We've already done a spell for that."

I stomped my foot. "Goddammit!"

"Well, we *have.*"

Ugh. This was more difficult than I expected. I grappled with the magnitude of his ability for a long moment while he waited in silence, watching me. Finally, I said, "Okay, I'll get used to it eventually. Just try not to pry, and don't judge me. Be nice." I folded my arms and looked him over once more. Damn. He was a demon. I mean, I knew that, obviously, but no getting around it now. "Do you have a tail or scales under your clothes?" I asked.

He chuckled softly and shook his head. "Would that make a difference? Is there something you draw the line at?"

Okay, I felt silly now. He was still Lon. Just with horns, that's all. Right?

Oh, crap. I was dating a demon. Me—a magician. What would my parents say? They wouldn't be all that thrilled about it, I knew that much. But maybe I didn't care. Was that bad?

I really liked Lon. He'd saved my life when that Pareba demon was attacking me, and he was helping me save my parents. He'd used up his police favor and was getting my memories back for me. He put up the ward around my house and helped me deal with Riley. Who does all that for someone they've known only a couple of weeks? Demon or not, he was a good person. And on top of it all, he was smart and thoughtful. Funny, even, especially for a curmudgeon. We had a lot in common. Okay, and he was damn fine to look at, even now, like this. His halo was oddly beautiful, and in a weird way that I couldn't really justify, the horns were kinda sexy.

"Well, shit," he said softly, shaking me out of my thoughts. "Now I don't know why I was so worried."

"Let's not get cocky." I twisted up my mouth to hold back a smile.

His big hand enveloped mine as he grinned back at me. Then he tilted his head toward the door. His halo left a trail of flames in the night air as he moved. "Ready?" he asked. And I guessed that I was.

He knocked twice at the cave entrance. One of the windows darkened, then a door swung inward. A burst of sound and smoky red light illuminated the doorway as a tall man stuck his head out; his neck was wider than my waist.

"Mr. Butler, nice to see you. It's been a while." He opened the door wider in invitation; my eyes dropped to the gun strapped to his side.

"I'm sure you've managed without me." Lon herded me inside, past the beefy doorman, who shut the door behind us without saying another word.

We meandered through a narrow tunnel strung with white lights. After a few sharp turns, it ended and opened into an enormous cavern. The low, rounded ceiling was populated with stalactites hanging only a few feet above our heads, but the room extended in all directions, as big as a gymnasium. Strings of grapefruit-sized globe lights illuminated everything with a crimson glow while casting deep, ominous shadows in dark corners.

Rock walls, eroded with holes and crevices, divided the room into smaller sections; each of these areas was covered in throw rugs and dotted with intimate groupings of antique armchairs and sofas. And between these lounging zones, the jagged stone skeleton of the cave wove around small pools of water.

It smelled of damp stone, stale cigarettes, and alcohol. Another low-note scent mingled below those, spicy and herbal, and it rose like incense in a soft haze from metal braziers that swung from the ceiling.

A long, uplit bar carved from stone stood against one wall, a couple dozen stone and leather seats lining the front of it. Heavy red velvet curtains hung toward the back of the cavern, blocking two dim passageways. Three long, wooden banquet tables surrounded by red tufted Louis XIV dining chairs sat in front of a medieval tapestry woven with Bosch-worthy scenes of debauchery and near-comical torture.

An opera reverberated softly around the space, competing with the hundred or more Earthbounds who were laughing and talking throughout the cavern. Dressed to the nines, they were drinking and smoking, clustering among life-size stone statues of Æthyric demons with curling horns and tails, massive wings, and muscular torsos; some were quite beautiful and seductive, others were menacing.

My eyes trailed around the room. Trays of beautiful bites of food and flutes of sparkling wine circulated through the crowds, carried by voluptuous women and men wearing togas or pleated Egyptian shendyt kilts. The fabrics were white and sheer; they might as well have been wearing nothing at all. I did my best not to stare.

I was used to seeing halos in the bar, but not nearly as many as I saw now. Earthbounds, all of them. And in the mass of green and blue, it was easy to spot the transmutated ones. Golden flames sprang from the horned heads of a middle-aged man at the bar, an elderly man on a couch, and a tall, young woman who was fondling a much younger, possibly teenage, boy sitting on her lap.

"This is the ballroom," Lon said in my ear, as I caught a glimpse of several transparent imps milling under the stools around the bar. "Things get worse in the back rooms and the grotto." I lifted an eyebrow and he added, "Don't use your full name. I don't want these people bothering you later." I glanced at a long-haired man pissing in a dark corner against one of the cave walls; I was pretty sure I didn't want them bothering me later either.

Another fiery-haloed man approached us with outstretched arms. In his seventies, perhaps, he had short, gray hair and drooping wrinkles below his eyes. He was dressed in a black three-piece suit with a red tie. His horns were short, knobby, and ashy-looking, not half as lovely as Lon's imposing spirals.

"Lon," the elderly man purred as he enthusiastically shook his hand. "Two years is too long. Your father, rest his soul, would be glad to know you've returned to the fold."

Lon acknowledged these comments with a brief nod. "David."

David's gaze lit on me. He was stoned out of his mind. Through slitted eyes, he looked me over from bottom to top, then jerked his head in surprise when he spied my halo. "Well, now. Who is this, son?"

"This is . . . Cady. Cady, David. He's one of the original members of the Hellfire Club."

"Cady? Charmed. Delighted . . . and quite surprised." Bringing my hand to his lips, he flipped it over, smelled my wrist, and planted a lingering kiss that radiated a strange heat up my arm. "Lon always had excellent taste in women."

Lon wrangled my hand away from David and slid a shoulder in front of mine, blocking David's access to me. "No," he commanded. By the tone of his voice, I could tell that he really meant to say "Mine." Frankly, I wasn't offended. Especially under the circumstances.

David pursed his lips and frowned, then moved his head to look around Lon. "My apologies," he told me. "We're not used to seeing Lon with anyone significant since Yvonne. How is she, by the way? Still in Miami?"

Lon grunted an affirmation.

"She was a little much to handle, even for my tastes. Passion without joy is *so* draining. Shame we didn't recognize that before, well, you know." He shrugged and looked up at my halo again. "May I ask about you? I've never seen anything like it. Have you undergone some sort of initiation elsewhere? Where are you from?" He squinted his eyes at me in curiosity.

"No, it's natural," I said with a light smile. "I'm from the city. Morella, I mean."

"Natural, eh? What kind of demon are you, chickadee?"

As he spoke, I began to feel lightheaded. Why? I glanced around us. Everyone was either drunk or high. Manic laughter, roaming hands, comatose stares, stumbling gaits. If they were in Tambuku, I'd be worried about a fight breaking out any minute. Well, what did I expect? Hellfire Club, duh.

"Something regal and quite special, I'd guess," David continued babbling. "Higher echelon. Can you trace your bloodline back to the Roanoke colonists? Or maybe descended from one of the strays that popped up during the Middle Ages?"

"Not Roanoke, no. My family is originally from Europe," I said. That was true enough, but I certainly wasn't going to offer up anything more.

"Fascinating," he said before waving his hand toward the bar. "Would you like anything? Wine? Food? Drugs? Please, come meet the others and tell me more about your ancestry." He tried to move around Lon, but he wasn't budging.

People were starting to stare and murmur, mostly at me. I was used to being the only human in a room. Days often elapsed in Tambuku without another human in sight. I was also accustomed to Earthbounds staring at my halo, so I wasn't sure why it made me so uncomfortable all the sudden. Perhaps because they were all eyeing me like a piece of meat . . .

KINDLING THE MOON   243

"We need to speak with Spooner," Lon said. "Is he here yet?"

"Oh, yes. He's here. A little indisposed at the moment back in one of the gypsum rooms. I'm sure he'd love company, if you two would care to join him."

"It can wait," Lon said.

David shrugged as if it were our loss, then turned to me. "What's your knack, dear?"

I smiled. "You first. What's yours?"

"Temperature control." The air around my legs warmed considerably. That explained the earlier heat from the wrist kiss. It felt pretty good, admittedly. The cave was cool and damp and I regretted not bringing a sweater.

"David," Lon scolded.

"Pooh." The gray-haired man frowned in disappointment and the heat faded. "Let me get you both drinks and find the others. I'll be right back."

He sauntered off, swaying a little as he walked. I took a step and swayed myself. Then I eyed the braziers. "What the hell am I inhaling?" I whispered.

"Ketynal."

He gave me a questioning look, but I knew exactly what he was talking about. Ketynal is a mixture of two powdered roots, one of which grows only on a couple of islands in the Philippines. That particular root is expensive and hard to come by, but I use it in one of my medicinals as a calming agent. However, when combined with the second root, it synergizes to create a compound that gets you buzzed and lowers inhibitions.

"Try not to get too close to the braziers," he warned.

Too fucking late for that.

27

We spent almost an hour in the smoky ballroom rubbing elbows with various members of the inner circle, The Thirteen as they called themselves. To my dismay, I was left unattended for a small chunk of time and fell prey to David again, along with a couple of city councilmen who tried to grab my ass, and an heiress in her fifties who did. I had to get out of this place before things got worse.

After all the freaking out I'd done earlier about Lon's enhanced abilities, I genuinely hoped that he was monitoring me now. *Distress signal!* I thought. *Mobbed by smarmy demons trying to cop a feel . . . where the hell are you?* I had no idea how well he could hear my thoughts in a crowd like this, but it was worth a try. In the meantime, I wasn't going to sit around waiting for him to rescue me. I made an excuse and shuffled off into the melee, navigating my way between chattering cliques and underdressed servers. The occasional transparent imp ran underfoot, making me itch for my portable imp portal.

As I made my way toward the back of the room, I slipped out of the crowd and edged around a stone wall. Without warning, an arm grabbed me around my waist. I squealed as

I was yanked behind the wall into the shadows. Panicked and furious, I rammed a clenched fist back over my shoulder and struck a hard blow on my assailant's face.

"Oww!"

Released, I twirled around, ready to fight . . . only to find Lon holding his hand over his eye.

"Goddamn!"

"Oh, Lon—I'm so-o-o sorry. I didn't know it was you."

"Jesus, that hurt."

I shook out my hand. It hurt me too. "Why'd you grab me like that? I thought it was one of the drunk perverts."

He rubbed his eye. "You asked for a rescue. Next time, I won't bother."

"You heard me?" I moved his hand away from his face to inspect it. His left eye was shut. After a couple of squints, he finally relaxed it.

"I told you I could. Are you ready to talk to Spooner?"

"What?"

Lon leaned down, his horns nearly touching my forehead. He lifted my chin with his fingers and studied my face. "Are you already so high from the ketynal that you forgot our mission?"

I slapped his hand away. "Not too high to injure a man twice my size."

He chuckled, then leaned closer and spoke in a low voice near my ear, "Come on, then . . . Cady. Clock's ticking."

We made our way through the noisy cavern, his hand warming the back of my neck as he guided me forward. For a moment, my mood improved. But when I figured out where we were headed, I wasn't all that keen on going to the back rooms, where Lon said things "got worse." Awesome.

An armed guard nodded at Lon and parted thick red curtains that obscured a dim passageway beyond. We stepped through, and the red ballroom lights changed to blue. Water-etched lines ran the length of the narrow stone tunnel. Below our feet, the flooring was gouged and uneven. The sounds of the party faded behind us, replaced by a variety of grunts, groans, and moans that echoed from small chambers lining the corridor.

"Jesus, it smells like a brothel back here," I whispered.

"No money exchanges hands."

"That's a shame. Someone could be making a fortune."

"Don't get any ideas. Turn left up here."

We yielded to an even narrower passage guarded by a chubby college-age Earthbound who was too busy browsing the Web on his cell phone to pay us any attention. We continued past him, and after three small chambers, we turned into a larger one curtained off with a threadbare piece of green fabric.

Inside was a spacious, round room lined with gray rock walls; the ceiling was so low at the entrance that Lon was forced to duck his head to clear it. Dull, opaque veins of crystallized gypsum hung from the ceiling and trellised down the walls like crystal rosebushes.

Toward the back of the room, a single showerhead hung straight down over a round pit carved into the floor; water steadily dripped down and drained into a hole at the base of the cavern wall. The left side of the room was occupied by three thick mattresses pushed together on the floor. Tumbling off the mattresses were dozens of pillows, most that had seen better days. Dozing among them were two nude bodies, a male and a female.

A wide stone bench was carved into the wall opposite

the mattresses. A padded cushion sat atop it, and sitting on it was—I surmised—Spooner, smoking a cigarette.

He was hard to see in the shadows until he shifted to face us, allowing the blue light to illuminate the side of his face. Middle-aged and awkwardly tall, he had pale skin, stark orange hair, and matching freckles. Only a plain green halo, so not one of The Thirteen, then.

He studied me with an unsettling smile. Freshly showered, his pumpkin hair was slicked back, his cheeks pink. He wore an odd, crumpled suit; the jacket was brown and the vest beneath it cheetah-spotted, and topped with a green ascot instead of a tie. The man at the evidence room in Portland was right on the money; this guy really *did* look like a giant leprechaun. A badly dressed one.

"Hello, Lon . . . and friend." He took a long drag off his cigarette, lazily crossed his long legs, and leaned back against the stone wall.

"Spooner."

"And friend?" he prompted again.

"Cady, this is Spooner. He doesn't have a real job, but he's wealthy, if that impresses you."

It didn't. Lon must have been reading my thoughts, because he lightly pressed his thumb against my neck in acknowledgment.

My eyes settled on Spooner's socked feet. They were mismatched, brown and black; the black one had a hole in the toe. His shoes rested on the cushion beside him. He moved them to the floor and patted the fabric. "Please, Cady. I wish you had come back here sooner." He waved a pointy finger toward the couple on the mattresses. "They're momentarily exhausted, but they'll recover fast. If not, there are others."

The dozing nude male rolled to his side, eyes closed.

That's when I noticed the gray scales on his shoulders and the tiny blunt horns on his head. No fiery halo, so he wasn't transmutated. Then I spotted the purple patch of skin at the top of his sternum.

"Incubus," I said in an even voice.

"And succubus." Spooner exhaled smoke in my face. *Rude.* I waved it away. It wasn't valrivia. It smelled like a stimulant, which was the last thing in the world anyone in these caves should be using.

"How do you have . . ." My words trailed off when I spotted the narrow channel that ran along the floor. A binding triangle inside a larger circle. The channels were lined with thin glass pipes containing a thick, dark substance. "Not red ochre," I said, inspecting the glass. It was hard to tell much of anything in the dim lighting. "It looks like oil paint . . . a mineral bound in oil. Cinnabar?"

Spooner gave me another unsettling smile. "Close. Vermilion. You can enter freely without breaking the binding."

Huh. I thought it was used mainly when you wanted to ensure that nothing could inadvertently break the binding, not to allow the magician free passage in and out of the binding area. Most magicians go to great lengths to protect themselves from contact with summoned Æthyric demons, and with good reason. A lot of demons don't like being summoned out of their plane. Would you like being ripped away from your life unexpectedly by some wheezing, power-hungry magician who only wanted to get information out of you or use you for your knack? Probably not.

Like humans, Æthyric demons vary in intelligence and physical prowess. There are plenty of docile demon classes, but just as many wild ones. And if you summon a demon who's pissed off and ready to rip your head off, given half the chance? Well, that *might* not be someone you want to lock yourself up with inside a small, contained space. Honestly, the Pareba demon that Riley had summoned was only the second Æthyric demon I'd ever witnessed who'd been allowed to roam free without containment.

Granted, succubi and incubi aren't really dangerous; in fact, they readily enter pacts with magicians, willingly exchanging sexual favors for bits of earthly information or temporary use of a magician's guardian. But considering the elaborate binding in front of me, it was pretty clear that these two were being held here against their will.

This setup is kind of repulsive, just FYI, I thought to Lon. He squeezed my neck lightly.

Spooner cut his eyes toward Lon. "Don't tell me you've brought her here to skip ahead in the initiation queue."

"No one's taking your place in line. Don't be paranoid."

"Good. Because I think one crazy wife is enough for this club."

"Don't test me, Spooner," Lon replied.

"I'm not here to join," I confirmed.

He studied my halo but made no comment about it. "What *are* you here for, then?"

"We want to buy something you've recently acquired," Lon replied. "The glass talon."

Something dark crossed Spooner's face, but he remained composed and relaxed.

"Why would you want that?"

"Why would *you*?" I asked.

"I'm a collector."

"And an opportunist. How much?" Lon asked.

Holding the cigarette in his mouth, Spooner settled the shoes in front of him and tugged at the laces to loosen them, slipping one on. As he tied it, he said, "I don't have the talon."

Lon toed the second shoe and kicked it aside. "Yes, you do. I talked to the person who sold it to you in Portland. I know how much you paid for it."

Spooner leaned forward to hook the heel of the shoe with his fingertip. Scooting it back into place, he stuck his hole-y toe inside. "I sold it already."

"When? To whom?"

"A week ago, and none of your business."

Lon sat down next to Spooner and clapped his hand on his shoulder. Spooner cried out and tried to move back, then robotically stopped. A confused look flittered across his face. Then he smiled and laughed. "I always liked you, Lon."

"Then do me this small favor. Tell me who you sold it to. Come on." Lon grinned at him, and I realized that I was watching a show: Lon was manipulating Spooner's emotions. Holy Night, that ability had some scary potential. He swore he'd never use it on me; I hoped like hell my trust wasn't misplaced.

Spooner sighed and began tying his shoe. "Craig Bailey."

"The retired cannery owner in the Village?"

"That human's got more cash than people realize." Spooner made a neat, tight bow and moved on to the second shoe. "He's obsessed with magick. To be honest, I told him the talon had powers that could . . . *grant immortality*." He waggled his fingers in the air in a faux-spooky manner and chuckled.

Craig Bailey. We had a name, and it was local. I knew it was too much to hope that we could just walk away with the talon that night, but maybe now we could go visit this Bailey guy and be done with it. If Lon could manipulate someone like Spooner, who obviously hated his guts, then surely someone with no strong feelings one way or another toward him would be easy as pie, right?

"How much did you sell it for?" Lon asked.

"Come on, Lon. I love ya, but a man has to have his secrets."

Lon pressed him, and they went back and forth, laughing and joking. I started to feel a little sick, and for a second thought it might be all that phony brotherly love. Then a humming sound filled my head, low and steady; distant but moving closer. I bit the insides of my cheeks trying to stave off nausea and turned away from the men.

A movement across the room caught my attention. The eyes of the incubus opened and his head popped up. He crawled to the edge of the mattress, looking down at the vermilion-designs on the floor. His eyes brightened with hope when he saw me.

Send me back, please.

His mouth didn't move, but I heard the words in my head, clear as glass, just like I'd hear my guardian Priya. I didn't realize incubi could communicate this way. I shot a look over at Lon and Spooner. They were still talking.

Mother! Send me back to the Æthyr. I'm weary of being trapped here. I'll do anything. What do you require? Information from the Æthyr? A task? Pleasure? Just get me out of here.

Another wave of nausea rose and broke. I tried to reply to the incubus without speaking. *Are you talking to me?*

Lon stopped talking and turned his head to give me a puzzled look.

Yes! Mother of Ahriman! Please!

That damn slur again. You'd think someone in his position would try to be a little nicer. *I'd like to help, but I didn't summon you so I can't—*

The air shimmered around the mattresses. I blinked, and everything went black. I could still see the two sex demons, and Lon, Spooner . . . but they were all transparent. Like imps. The vermilion binding in the floor was black and shiny like a glistening oil slick. Everything else was swallowed in a void. No cave, no creepy shower, no bench. Just darkness.

In the air above the two demons, a bright blue light appeared. About the size of a coin, it began expanding and changing. It grew until it was a round, blue disk of light. Pieces of the inside began falling away, like dough being removed with a cookie cutter; negative spaces revealed the blackness behind them. My head pounded. I held out my hands to the side to keep myself from falling.

The blue circle of light began forming an intricate design, like a laser etching the air. Then I recognized the pattern. It was a distinct combination of symbols . . . it was mine. My magical creation that I'd worked so hard developing for months: my imp portal. As far as I knew, it was completely unique. I'd damn sure never heard of another magician using one, nor had I seen one exactly like it in any grimoire.

The portal glowed in the void, a flat sheet of light. Then it flipped to its side and floated above the incubus. Heka began flowing from me, strong energy that I hadn't kindled. It poured into the blue portal, and in a bright flash, turned to silver, solidified in the air.

Thank you! The incubus's voice in my head was fading quickly. *My name is Voxhele of Amon. I owe you a favor.*

The portal snapped and disappeared, the incubus and succubus along with it.

Blackness lingered for a moment, then rushed away as the room and everything in it became solid and normal again and the humming stopped.

It was just the three of us now: me, Lon, and Spooner. They were still talking; had they not seen what just happened? Couldn't Lon hear me talking to the incubus? As I was thinking this, Lon's head turned, and he shot me a questioning look; he could certainly hear me now.

Spooner glanced across the room, then cried out in alarm. "They're gone! They've escaped!" He scrambled out of his seat, grabbed Lon's arm, and pointed to where the sex demons once were. "How—?"

"What the hell?" Lon muttered.

We all stared at the empty beds in silence.

"Shit!" Spooner said. "Do you think they're loose in the club? Did one of the vermilion pipes burst?"

A tiny puff of smoke trailed away from the mattresses. Spooner ran forward to inspect it.

I did it, Lon. I don't know how, but I sent them back, I said in my head.

"They're gone!" Spooner said again. "Not loose, they're—" He turned around and gave us a suspicious look. Then he pointed at me. "You. What *are* you? Did you do this? Why is your halo that way? Lon, what is she?"

Eyes creased hard, Lon let go of me and took two quick strides to grasp Spooner. "Hey, it wasn't her. She doesn't even have a proper knack. She's nothing. It must have been something else. Maybe the binding beds in the other rooms are affected too. I'm sure someone can fix them. No big deal."

Lon smiled at Spooner, who calmed down immediately. "You're probably right. It's no big deal."

"Glad you finished up before it happened, right?" Lon said.

Spooner laughed. "Yeah, yeah. You're so right. Night's still young. Plenty to do."

"All right, buddy. We're going to step out now. Take care."

"Right, yep. Well, it was good talking to you, Lon."

Lon clapped him once on the shoulder, then turned to me, green eyes wide with panic.

Herding me out the curtained doorway, he whispered in my ear, "We need to get out of here, now. Move."

I was too shocked to do anything but comply. Clearly there were more succubi trapped in other rooms, and for a brief moment, I wondered if I'd be able to repeat the unexpected banishment I'd just performed.

"Unh-unh," Lon whispered, reading my thoughts. "These people are *not* going to take this lightly. We've got to get out of here before they realize what you've done."

Or what? He didn't answer, just forced me to walk as fast as I could without breaking into a full-on run. We breezed through the narrow passageways, back through the red velvet curtains, and into the din of the ballroom, where Lon wove us in and out among the people, a few protests and murmurs rising as he barged through.

We'd almost made it out when David stepped in front of us. "Hey kids! Where ya headed? It's not even midnight yet. Aren't you going to stay for the entertainment?"

"Just getting some air," Lon said. "Be right back."

His head turned and I followed his gaze to the back of the ballroom. Spooner was emerging from the velvet curtains. He didn't look happy; just how long did Lon's suggestive influence last? Flagging down a bald man with horns and a flaming golden halo, Spooner began speaking to him in a whisper, then he pointed right at us.

28

"Where have you taken Lon?" I demanded, glaring at David as two demons held me by my forearms. They'd separated us, guiding me one way down the blue corridor, Lon down the other, dragged away by three large demons who pulled him by a long length of rope tied around his hands. One of them kept a gun trained on him. They stayed several feet ahead, I assumed to avoid Lon's emotional manipulation.

David smiled as he paced in front of me. "We've been experimenting with some interesting summonings. Succubi and incubi are our bread-and-butter, but it's good to change things up to avoid boredom. Lon is going to be our volunteer for tonight's entertainment. Our last volunteer isn't ready to get in the ring again just yet."

"Ring? What ring? What the hell are you doing with him?"

A man stepped in the door and nodded at David before retreating.

"Wonderful!" David said while clapping his hands once. "Let's go see, shall we? Maybe you'll be more inclined to tell us how you pulled that little stunt in front of Spooner. I'm bored with trying to guess your origins. Oh, wait . . . what's this?" He fingered the deflector charm around my neck, then snatched it, breaking the chain. "I don't know what kind of ward this is, but I don't think you'll be needing it tonight."

Protesting, I stumbled as they dragged me back down the passage. Several half-dressed people stood as witnesses in the doorways of the small caves that lined the blue corridor. Quite drunk, they cheered us on, laughing and making crude remarks as I passed.

The men at my side shoved me into a larger cave where dozens of demons congregated around something in the center of the room. The crowd was boisterous and more than a little excited. Small red spotlights flooded the wet stone walls around them. Water dripped from the ceiling into small pools on the rocky floor.

A clicking sound ticked from within the throng. The buzzing spectators murmured in response before breaking out into sloppy applause.

"Step aside," David said to the people around the edge. He plowed his way through, my chaperones and I trailing him until we made it to the center. I bleated a small cry when I discovered what was inciting the horde.

Another glass vermilion circle was embedded in the floor, maybe twenty feet in diameter. Captured inside, a willowy gray demon defended one side of the containment space. Its skin was darker around the elbows, neck, and navel. Genitals on the outside of its body initially led me to believe it might be male, until I got a closer look at several additional unrecognizable fleshy components. Sex . . . indeterminable.

The gray demon lacked horns or wings, but possessed something much nastier: shiny black nails with narrow fishhook endings that doubled back at the tips. The source of the clicking noise. It clacked them together in anticipation.

Crouched on the opposite side of the circle, Lon moved clockwise around the inner edge as the gray demon stalked him. A red mark was painted on Lon's forehead; upon closer inspection, I recognized it to be a sigil that allowed him to enter the circle without breaking it, but prevented him from leaving.

My stomach balled up into a knot.

This was the ring that David was talking about; instead of pit bulls, it was Æthyric demon versus Earthbound. I had no idea what had happened to the first volunteer that David mentioned, but a sneaking suspicion told me it wasn't good.

The men held me tighter at the edge of the circle, so tightly my circulation was cut off and my arms tingled. I didn't want to call out Lon's name; it might create a distraction that the gray demon could use to its advantage. But I had to do something.

"Mmm . . . exciting," David murmured to my side. He looked out over the fighting ring and spoke louder. "So kind of you to volunteer, Lon. Good sport. After all, you're already carrying around that nasty scar courtesy of your ex-wife, I'm sure you won't mind a few more."

Lon didn't respond. He was concentrating. Blank. Centered. The only betrayal of his rising panic was the splotchy redness accumulating on his neck; seeing it made my stomach queasy.

But as I listened to the talk around us, I noticed that not everyone in the audience was ecstatic. "David is really pushing it," one person remarked. "Mr. Dare wouldn't approve of this if he knew what was going on." I didn't know who this Mr. Dare was, but most of the thirteen parking spaces outside were filled, so I hoped like hell that he was somewhere inside the caves. I turned to one of the dissenting couples nearby.

"Please, go tell Mr. Dare—get help," I whispered.

They looked at me, shocked that I'd spoken.

David put a hand over my mouth and chastised the couple. "Now, now—don't go running to Daddy or I'll get you kicked out. We're just having some fun, nothing more. If you don't like it, leave."

Refusing to look at me, they turned and left the room, along with a few other people.

"I mean it!" David called after them. "If there's a rat in here, I'll find out. Don't cross me." A manic laugh bubbled from his lips. The people around us went back to cheering the fight on. David then turned to me and spoke quietly near my face. "Now, then, love, no more tricks like that. Since neither one of you wants to tell me exactly what kind of Earthbound you are and how you banished our sex demons—or why we can't seem to summon them back, for that matter—then we'll just leave Lon here to battle it out with the Salixen. You and I can retire to another succubus chamber and have some fun."

Oh, *hell* no.

Before I could respond, a high-pitched snarl stole our attention. The gray demon made a swipe at Lon. Lon made a clumsy duck but not fast enough. A line of blood welled on his cheek.

As the crowd cheered, David clapped ecstatically, then turned back to me. Pawing my chin, he whispered in my ear, "Exciting, no? Just like you did with me earlier, we'll make a new game of all this and see who breaks first, you or Lon. I'm betting on Lon. He has a bad history with women, but I think he's learned his lesson with Yvonne. I doubt he really wants to put himself on the line, even for a pretty young chickadee like you."

I stared back at him as he smiled at me, hearing him but not listening. My mind scrambled to piece together a solution. I couldn't reach the sigils on my arm; they were being squeezed dry by my guards, so that was out. What else? I hadn't summoned the gray demon, so I couldn't banish it . . . except that I was somehow able to banish the incubus and succubus. Maybe it was due to something elemental in the caves? Something that enhanced my Heka? I concentrated and tried to will the floating blue imp portal into existence. All that did was give me a headache. Nope, not happening.

If I couldn't banish the gray demon, and Lon couldn't leave the charged circle because of the red mark on his head, then the only option remaining was to break the circle. But how? I couldn't even reach it. We were several feet away.

David twisted my face to his and planted a brutal kiss on my lips. I tried to jerk away, but he clamped his hand on the back of my head. His mouth tasted of top-shelf liquor, cracked lips scraping against mine. He stank of sweat.

Furious, I shut my eyes to concentrate and pulled from the electricity wired through the caves, as hard as I could. The lights in the cavern wavered and flashed. A murmur spread through the crowd. I pulled harder, kindling Heka until it made my body quake. I held it for a moment, then slowly released it through every pore in my body.

David pulled away from me, crying out and covering his mouth with his hand at the same moment that the body-guards dropped my arms. Heka kindled with electricity creates a nasty shock without a caduceus to pinpoint the release. They fucking deserved it.

The shock would disorient them, but it wouldn't last.

My eyes flew to the edge of the circle near the gray demon. I shoved the person in front of me, then dove with outstretched arms. My fingertips barely grazed the glass circle. Close enough.

The remaining kindled Heka poured through my fingertips into the embedded piping, heated the glass instantly, and scalded my fingers. I lurched away from the glass and crashed into the legs of the bodyguards, bowling them over like tenpins.

Vermilion bubbled and surged through the pipes. Like a lit fuse, it spewed inside the glass until it found my willed mark near the demon.

"Get down!" I yelled to Lon. He covered his head as the sound of shattering glass filled the chamber.

The gray demon wailed and emitted a dog-whistle-worthy cry that set off a chain reaction of pain-filled screams throughout the crowd. Glass glittered on the stone floor around the broken circle. Some of it was also lodged in the calf of the gray demon, who was now limping. I'd only blown a small section of the glass pipe, just a few inches. In the break, liquid vermilion was oozing out and running in rivulets through shallow crevices on the surface of the rock. Toxic rivulets, to be exact, because vermilion is a mercury compound. It burned with a whispery, delicate blue flame that spread up the pants and dress hems of a handful of club members. They screamed in horror, frantically slapping at the creeping blue fire. *Hello, mercury poisoning.*

"Lon!" I called out, vaulting onto my feet as the lights in the room dimmed again. It wasn't me that time. Unless someone else was pulling, I must have fucked up the electrical current; in my defense, the whole place was probably shoddily wired to begin with.

The circle now broken, I stormed forward and grabbed Lon's arm. *Let's get out of here!* I thought. He shook his head to clear the shock, then hustled alongside me before taking the lead and ramming the crowd out of the way. They weren't concerned with us.

The gray demon was recovering from its injury. Any second it would realize that it wasn't bound. As Lon and I dashed out of the doorway, I glimpsed David scrambling to hide behind his bodyguards as the mob backed up and the lights popped and sputtered.

Without much enthusiasm, I hoped the electricity held; someone had an unpleasant containment job on their hands, and it would be a hell of a lot harder with the lights off.

29

The stone sidewalk that led from the Hellfire caverns to the parking lot was clogged with people mingling near the bonfire, people who had no idea what was going on inside. Lon yanked me behind some shrubbery off the path. The door to the caves opened and slammed behind us and someone shouted, "Stop them!"

"We'll have to sneak around the beach," Lon whispered. He tugged me along behind him. We headed into the shadows.

"Wait!" I squeaked, leaning down to pry open the metal buckles on the straps of my shoes. I got them off in record time, grasped them by the straps, and sprinted in my bare feet. The sand was cold and damp beneath my toes.

We stuck to the shadows and trailed a line of beach shrubs that curved around the back of a large dune stretching away from the base of the cliffs. Voices faded behind us. From this distance, I could barely see the crowd outlined against the distant light of the bonfire. But I was still able to identify one person: the bald guy Spooner had sicced on us earlier. His flaming gold halo stood out in the darkness. At least we had a considerable head start on him. No way could he catch up. I hoped.

"How—are we going—to get to the car?" I asked haltingly between breaths as I ran.

"Forget it. We can't go back that way. Sengal is a hyperosmiac. Preternatural sense of smell. He can hunt us."

"What? The bald guy following us?"

"Yes. We'll get the car later. Keep running."

Away from the caves, we headed deeper into the dark coast, trudging through sand until we cleared the massive dune and were forced to slow our pace along the edge of the incoming tide. Chilly water broke around my feet.

We continued running along the water's edge until I thought I was going to die from exhaustion. I peered over my shoulder for the millionth time, but couldn't see anyone behind us. "Stop, please," I begged. My sides were cramping. We slowed to a brisk walk. "These are your people . . . What will they do to you? Don't they know where you live?"

"Tomorrow they'll have sobered up. And David will be reprimanded by the head of the Hellfire Club." He paused, then murmured, "I'll make sure of that."

"I heard some people talking about Mr. Dare."

He looked down at me and nodded. His chest rose and fell as he caught his breath. "That's right. He started the club with my father. Practically runs this town. So I'll be fine." He gestured toward the caves in the distance. "They just need to cool off. Especially David. Right now they are all drunk and unreasonable."

"Fucking insane is more like it."

"Contained insanity," he corrected. "That's the whole purpose of the Hellfire Club. Most of these people are okay in the real world, but at these parties . . ."

I nodded. He was right. I'd seen perfectly normal, upstanding demons walk into my bar and after several drinks turn ornery and out of control. I wondered what Lon would be like if he ever got that crazy.

"Look," Lon said immediately, in response to my roving thoughts, "I used to go to these things religiously until Yvonne got out of control, then I quit. Except for a brief backsliding period a few years ago when I got depressed, I don't go anymore. I've seen and done my share of immoral things inside that place, but that whole demon-fight-club thing is new."

He touched the stripe of coagulated blood on his cheek and winced. "First you clocked me in the eye . . . now this. It's not my night."

I couldn't see him smiling, but humor lightened his voice, and this softened my panic. His spiraling horns were dark against the golden light of his halo. Just when I thought I'd gotten used to them . . . but there I was, staring like a fool. I pushed away the urge to touch them again, just to be certain that they were still real.

"I don't mind," he murmured.

Mildly embarrassed, I twined my fingers around his and we resumed our walk, shoulder pressed against shoulder. The farther away from the Hellfire caves we got, the better I felt. Inside, at least. Though his hand was warm in mine, my feet were Popsicles. Occasionally I stepped on a piece of shell or rock that broke the numbness. I'd never hated the beach so much.

After we'd walked for a good fifteen minutes, Lon stopped.

"Shit."

"What?" I asked, turning back to look. I didn't see anything.

"I can hear Sengal again. He's not going to give up."

I scanned the shoreline and spotted a tiny speck of gold

up on a low hill in the distance. It floated down the hill and toward the water, following our tracks. Hovering, it turned and began moving toward us.

"I can't run anymore!" I complained. "We can't just keep plowing down the length of the whole damn beach. How are we going to get away from him? Isn't there anything out this way?"

Lon scanned the beach ahead of us. "Over there. See those?"

My eyes followed his finger, but I saw nothing but night and the shifting glisten of the moon on the surface of the ocean. Darker cliffs towered in the distance. Then I spotted blocky shapes up the beach. They stood in a long row, farther away from the water.

"We're headed away from the Village. Those are rental cottages," Lon explained. "That inlet area out there will be a popular surfing spot next month when the waves get better. Right now it's dead." He then pointed toward the cliffs in the distance, several miles away. "And see those? My house is up there on the other side."

The thought of walking miles on a cold beach was disheartening at best. Impossible was more like it.

"Too bad there's not a way around the cliffs," he added. "We'd have to swim a mile out around Mermaid Point to get to a place we could climb."

"Nuh-uh. No way, José," I said, shaking my head, just in case he was considering it.

He grunted in amusement. "Let's just try to make it to the cottages."

Fifteen minutes later, the first of the small houses came into full sight. No lights inside. That could have been because it was off-season, or maybe because it was after midnight.

"For fuck's sake!" Lon mumbled.

"He's still back there?" I studied the dark beach behind us. "Shouldn't you shift back down to your human form? Can't he see your halo? I can see his."

"His eyesight and hearing are shit when he's trans-mutated. It's our scent—we're going to have to get rid of it."

"What? How?"

He looked toward the ocean.

"You've got to be joking! We've already been walking in the water. Isn't that enough?"

"Up to our ankles."

"Lon—"

"You see any people out here who can give us a lift? Any cars you can hot-wire?"

I squinted and desperately searched the row of seem-ingly empty cottages. "No, no, no," I whined. "We'll freeze to death."

Lon glanced back at Sengal. "I'd rather freeze to death than go back."

"Can't we take him?" I suggested. "He can't be that strong."

"Strong enough, especially with the two armed men ac-companying him."

I cursed under my breath.

We stumbled across the wet sand until the tide hit our shins. I was already shivering. We walked farther in. The water came up to my knees and lapped at the hem of my dress. Lon sighed dramatically, machismo quickly draining away. "Come on," he said without fervor. "Count of three."

"One," I said, faking a sob.

Without warning, he pulled me forward and plunged me underwater. My protest drowned beneath the icy waves. Salt stung my eyes as my mouth and nose filled with water.

As quickly as we went under, we emerged. As I gasped for air, Lon gurgled, "Quiet!" He was holding one hand up in surrender. I panicked, then realized that he was just holding his cell phone above his head. Smart man.

My entire body shook as we sloshed out of the tide. I pushed dripping hair out of my face. My dress clung to my body like a wet suit as water streamed down over my legs. I held my arms to my chest in a futile attempt to regain warmth.

Was it worth it? Where the hell was Sengal? A fiery halo danced in the distance. I wanted to cry, but I was too cold.

"C-come on." Lon's suit squished as he walked, but I could barely hear it over the sound of my teeth knocking together faster and faster. It took all of my willpower to force my cramped muscles to move; I halfheartedly jogged alongside Lon until we got to the first cottage.

"Around back," Lon instructed.

We trotted around the side of the tiny house, where packed sand substituted for a green lawn, all of it surrounded by beach shrubs and a low picket fence. An empty paved driveway led up a steep hill to the small street. I became hopeful until I realized that there was nothing there. No streetlights, no cars, no sounds but the ocean. Nothing at all, really. Just cliffs beyond the road, and darkness.

We exited the sandy yard and continued on to the next cottage, only a hundred or so feet away. No car there either. As we plodded past the fourth house, I saw several more ahead of us.

The near-full moon that gave us a small amount of dusky light darkened with cloud cover. A rumble of thunder sounded in the distance. We were already cold and wet; a storm on the beach was the last thing I wanted. A streak of lightning cracked near the cliffs ahead.

"Good." Lon picked up speed to head to the next cottage.

"Good? What's good about it? If it rains, then we just dove into the ocean for no good reason."

"That masked our body scent. The rain will wipe our trail."

Whoop-dee-fucking-doo. I wanted to strangle him, and I hoped like hell he "heard" me; if he did, he didn't show it. After a few feet, he slowed and headed toward the back of the cottage. A small cypress tree grew in the side of the yard near the driveway. The small beach rental mimicked the old-world storybook architecture back in the Village: wood shingles, gingerbread trim, cheerily painted shutters framing each window. Almost large enough to accommodate a small family of gnomes.

Lon reached over the wiry brush that grew around the house and tried to jimmy the back window open as it thundered again. No luck.

"What if there's an alarm?" I asked.

"There's not." He pounded on the window in demonstration as lightning lit up the night sky. The storm was getting closer. I was betting that Sengal was too.

I shadowed Lon around the side of the cottage, beneath a tiny carport. The door was locked, so he tested the window next to it. The frame protested with a harsh creak, then the window gave way and slid open.

"Hell yeah," he said with smug grin, pushing the window up as far as it would go. "Come on, I'll help you." He held out a hand to me as the sky opened wide and an angry surge of rain fell.

30

"He's out of range," Lon said as we stared from behind the curtained window of the cottage. He lowered the blinds and pulled the curtain tight.

Finally. Half an hour had passed while we stood in the dark living room, watching Sengal and his men snake up and down the beach in the thunderstorm. I never would have imagined that shivering from cold and anxiety could be so physically exhausting.

I'd already given the cottage a cursory inspection while we waited. Nothing more than a sparsely furnished living room, open kitchen, one bedroom and bath. And no electricity. Either the storm had killed it, or the rental agency had temporarily shut it off. The house had running water, though it was warm, not hot. "Gas water heater," Lon had guessed. "Probably on a vacation setting." The closet door to the water heater was locked, so we couldn't change it.

Gas water heater, and gas fireplace with tacky fake logs. Now that Lon was certain that Sengal and his goons were long gone, he made a beeline for the fireplace and told me to keep my fingers crossed. I did. It worked.

"Woo hoo!" Instant heat. I'd never been so thankful. We

hovered in front of it, trying to get warm. "Is it up as high as it will go?"

"Mmm-hmm."

I ditched the knitted afghan that I'd stripped from an orange-striped couch. Now that my clothes had soaked through the scratchy yarn, it wasn't helping my shivering.

"Why don't you take a shower?" Lon suggested. "It'll warm you up. We can't sit around here in sopping wet clothes all night. Are there more towels?"

We'd already used up two of them drying our hair. "Still four more under the sink," I reported.

"Put your wet clothes outside the bathroom door and I'll try to rig up something by the fireplace and hang them up to dry," he said, rubbing his hands together.

"Hey, Lon? What are we going to do?"

He cracked his neck, then started taking off his shoes. "I've been thinking about that. There's a road that leads around the cliffs, but we're a few miles from one that gets any real traffic. Hitchhiking is a long shot, and we can't just wander around out there in the storm."

"Please, no. Your phone?" I asked, remembering that he'd held it out of the water.

"No service." He glanced down at the coffee table. "We're at least a couple of miles from the Hellfire caves. The club members usually stay through the night—most people end up passing out around sunrise and leave at noon. If we head back over there after the sun comes up, we can probably sneak our way over to my car while they're sleeping."

"What about Jupe?"

"Mr. and Mrs. Holiday are staying in the guest room tonight. I told them I'd be out late. Maybe a little later than I planned, but . . . what about *your* charge?"

"Riley? She knows how to use the microwave."

He nodded, exhaling through his nose. "As far as the talon goes, I figure we can't just show up at Craig Bailey's house at this hour anyway. If we can ride this out until morning and get my car, we can go straight over there."

Thinking that was as good a plan as any, I headed to the bathroom after grabbing a small candle in a glass jar from the kitchen. We had to light it in the fireplace; Lon's trusty cigarette lighter was sea-logged.

Small hotel soaps and shampoo were stocked inside the bathroom, so I helped myself. The shower halted my shivering until it went cold; I promptly got out at that point. I towel-dried my hair again. No comb or brush. At least I'd warmed up. I wrapped myself in a second towel and gathered up the candle

The rain pattered on the roof of the small cottage as I made my way down the cramped hall to the living room. Lon had removed two sofa cushions; he sat on one in front of the fireplace, huddled to the neck inside the blanket he'd stripped off the bed. He was nothing but a mass of damp golden brown waves poking out from the top.

Our shoes sat together on the hearth beside his pocketknife, my silver bangle bracelet, and the car keys from my pocket. Wet clothes dangled down from the mantel, held in place by small stacks of books. My bra and panties hung from two nails like Christmas stockings. *Lovely*, I thought with a ripple of embarrassment.

Lon had washed the Hellfire Club's red mark from his forehead. He'd also reverted to his normal form. No more horns, no fiery halo . . . no more reading my thoughts. I set the candle down on the hearth and smiled as he looked up at me.

"What?" he asked.

"I used up all the hot water, sorry."

He grunted. "What else?"

"Is that the real reason you were kicked out of the seminary? You said one of the teachers suspected you were a demon—did someone see you in your transmutated form? Humans can see your horns, right?"

His cheeks were ruddy from the fire. He gave me a devilish grin.

"Uh-huh. No wonder you got booted. That makes more sense now."

He motioned toward the floor beside him. "I found another blanket."

Not a scratchy one, much to my relief. I draped it over my shoulders. He politely kept his eyes down, so I shimmied out of the wet towel beneath it. Much better. I kicked away the towel and plopped down on the cushion next to him.

"They took my deflector charm," I said.

"I'm sorry. I might be able to get it back for you later."

I nodded, but we both knew it meant that I was now open to magical attack. At least Jupe was far away from me right now, safe at home; I wondered if Lon was thinking the same thing.

"So," I said. "Are you mad at me again?"

He narrowed his eyes at me suspiciously. "Should I be?"

"I thought you might be because of what started all this. The incubus incident."

His face relaxed. "That sounds like a bad movie, and no. But what happened?"

I drew my knees up to my chest under the blanket. "I have no idea." I explained the strange event as best I could and he was equally puzzled.

"Maybe something in that particular room?" he suggested.

"Like a vein of alien metal running through the walls? Some sort of antikryptonite?"

He shrugged. "Vermilion? Or maybe gypsum?"

"No, that wouldn't be it."

"Some other kind, a magical moon rock for the Moon-girl?"

"Moonchild, not Moongirl." I propped my forearms on my knees and rested my chin on them. "I definitely think I *should* be concerned, but at this point, I don't have the strength to care anymore. My life is in total disarray. I don't know whether I'm coming or going." I lazily watched the gas flames lick at the ceramic logs. "I'm just glad you're not angry."

"If anyone's to blame for tonight, it's me, for hauling you over to that damn place. I should've just gone by myself like I originally planned."

I sniffled and wiped my nose as the fire loosened my sinuses. "Why *did* you bring me?"

It took him a while to answer, but I didn't rush him. "I wanted to know how you'd react to me transmutating. And, more selfishly, I wanted to experience you from that perspective."

Embarrassment flared through me as I remembered all the random thoughts he overheard.

"Stop. It was . . . nice."

I scrunched up my face and turned to look at him. "Nice, huh?" It was his favorite word.

"I liked the way you saw me." His eyes darted toward mine as he stretched out his legs until his toes peeked out from the edge of the blanket. "Yvonne never saw me that way."

"I'm sorry."

He grunted and shook his head once, as if it was of little consequence. "As much as she keeps coming up, I want you to know that I *am* over her. If it weren't for Jupe—well, it's just harder to work through issues with him in the picture." His toes curled and flexed several times in succession.

"But, you know what?" he said. "Every shitty thing she ever put me through, all the grief . . . I would endure it all over again just to have him. He's the most important thing in my life and I wouldn't give him up for anything."

I smiled at him. "Don't blame you one bit."

"Hmm."

"Hmm, what?" I asked.

"You really aren't bothered at all that I have a kid."

"Why would I be?"

"Most women try to be gracious about it, but they see Jupe as baggage. You don't."

A crack of blue-white lightning illuminated the windows outside, followed seconds later by a roaring boom that rattled the windowpanes. We both started, then relaxed. "I'll admit that I was kinda freaked out by the notion of you having a kid that *old* at first. When I met him, though . . . well, he's pretty easy to love, isn't he?"

Lon smiled. "Is he? I don't think anyone's ever said that about him. He'd be pleased."

"Don't you dare tell him I said it or he'll use it against me. What a manipulator! Maybe he got that from you, huh?" I grinned, elbowing him, and we both laughed.

I propped my chin back on my forearms. I was finally thawed out. My face was even starting to get a little warm.

"What about me?" he asked.

"What do you mean?"

"Am I . . . easy?"

A bold question, considering the amount of time we'd known each other. I laid my cheek on my arm to look at him. I thought he might be teasing me, but I wasn't sure, so I answered honestly. "Not exactly."

Considering my answer with the barest suggestion of amusement on his lips, he drew his legs up to his chest, mimicking my posture. The flames from our less-than-romantic fire cavorted across his face, deepening the long hollows of his cheeks and darkening his tight eyes. He made a small noise, then spoke again. "When I've said that I 'sense' someone's feelings with my ability, that's not really accurate."

"Oh?"

"Especially when I'm touching someone. It's more like I *feel* what they feel. I experience their emotions as if they were my own. But when I'm not transmutated, I can't read their thoughts, so it's like solving a puzzle; I have to figure out what caused the emotion."

"Like a blindfold taste test," I suggested.

"In a way, yes. It's like someone has blindfolded me, stuck a piece of raw fish in my mouth, and I have to figure out whether it's salmon or toro."

"I think I could tell. Toro is way better." I grinned at him, and he extended his foot to gently kick me.

A few moments of silence passed before he spoke again. "Remember when I shook your hand? When Father Carrow introduced us?"

I nodded in affirmation.

"When I meet someone, I feel their first impressions of me. I call it listening, but I suppose we could call it tasting, like you said. And everyone tastes different." He poked a finger through his blanket to scratch his cheek. "When I met you, well, I knew there could be something between us."

"Hmph. That's probably just because you saw me in my underwear that first night," I teased.

"That was just a bonus." He grinned. "What I meant is that there could be something more between us than just me wanting to jump in bed with you."

Huh. Okay. Not exactly poetic, but his words made me smile.

"Have you been serious about anyone in the past?" he asked.

"Not until recently. It's always been difficult. Last year, I saw someone for several months, but I broke it off because it got to the point where it either had to go forward or stop. I couldn't tell him who I really was, and I couldn't keep lying."

He shifted under his blanket. "But you don't have to lie to me."

"No . . . no, I don't." Not much of a choice in that; but I guess I really didn't mind too much, and he probably knew that.

A long moment stretched as we sat together in silence, staring at the fire. His eyes fell on me now and then, but he didn't say anything. Then a detail of what he'd said shifted around in my head. It wouldn't go away, and I became self-conscious that we were both sitting there naked, with nothing between us but a couple of ratty blankets.

His lips curled into a slow smile.

I groaned in annoyance, then gave up trying to hide anything. What was the point?

"So you *don't* think I'm too young?" I challenged.

"That depends. Do you think I'm too old?"

"Like you told me before, you're not a 'fucking grandfather' or anything."

He chuckled.

My blanket had dipped down my back, so I rocked forward onto my knees to pull up the slack and tug it over my shoulders.

"Are you on birth control?"

I froze, kneeling in front of the hearth. Several seconds ticked by before I answered.

"I am. Is that your idea of seduction? Because if it is . . ." I turned in place to face him.

He rose up on his knees and waited for me to finish, a merry glint in his eye.

"Because if it is," I repeated in a softer voice, "you kinda suck."

His head bobbed up and down in resignation. Clearly he agreed with my summation, but felt powerless to do anything about it.

"Do you trust me?" he murmured.

"Should I?"

He nodded. "And I trust you. Are you still cold?"

"No . . ."

"Then drop your blanket. I want to see you."

I squinted, heart on a roller coaster headed up an incline. "Nope. You first."

Frankly, I didn't expect him to consent so fast. The blanket fell around him, and there he was, on his knees, proudly on display in front of me without a stitch of clothing.

I looked him over as slowly as I could manage, appreciating the beautiful intricacies of bones and muscles, the angle of the scar over his ribs . . . using every ounce of willpower I could muster not to follow the golden line of hair on his chest all the way down. But, half a second later, when my eyes disobeyed me, my lips parted. I began breathing hard through my mouth. My belly tightened.

"Hmm?" he inquired, one brow arched.

"Mmm-hmm."

Then I let my own blanket puddle around me.

Damp, uncombed hair . . . no makeup, no flattering lingerie. For the tiniest fraction of a second, insecurity raced through my brain carrying a small sign that read *Supermodel ex-wife—what are you thinking?* But the sign began fading as he gaped at me . . . and when I became plainly aware of the physical effect I had on him, the sign disappeared in a poof.

"Jesusfuckingchrist," he said huskily. His half-lidded eyes roamed without inhibition.

A soft chuckle buzzed in the back of my throat. "Jesus-fuckingchrist yourself."

We locked gazes, and in one sweeping movement, we both lunged forward.

31

His mouth was hot and welcoming. A flood of chills ran down my arms and bloomed through my chest. I wrapped my arms around him and tasted salt water on his skin, while his open palms skimmed over my neck and shoulders, down the length of my back. Slowly, with adoration. His hands lingered over the curves of my hips, then grabbed my ass with great enthusiasm, pulling me against him. He felt fantastic.

We broke apart just enough for a rush of cool air to glide over my now-exposed skin. His hands competed with mine for occupation of the slender space between us. We managed a compromise: his on my breasts . . . mine lower. He groaned when my fingers circled him. He was heavy and thick, and I wasn't sure whether his age was a factor, but he felt more like a man to me than anyone else I'd touched. My body turned cartwheels in anticipation.

Liquid and on fire, I placed my hands on his chest and forced him back against the cushion. He leaned back on his elbows, half lying, half sitting. As I crawled across his hips, he reached forward with one hand to slip several searching fingers between my legs.

I impatiently pushed his hand away and continued on to my goal. He aided my cause by unabashedly holding himself rigid as I reached for an anchor, clasping both hands around the back of his neck. Heads bowed together, his pirate mustache tickling my cheek, silver halo mingling with gold, we both watched as I slowly slid down upon him.

Neither of us drew a breath during the first shallow stroke. But as my body accommodated him, I broke the silence with a gasp. He pulled his head back, and grass-green eyes peered at me through narrowed slits. "Goddamn," he murmured reverently.

As we settled into a rhythm, he continued speaking to me in a hushed, urgent voice. A stream of whispered sentiments, instructions, and praise spilled from his lips—some tender, others downright crude and filthy. He'd never been so chatty. Surprised by the unexpected intimacy, I listened carefully to each word, answering his questions between metered breaths as he thrummed his fingers across every inch of my skin within his reach.

Halfway through, he staged a coup and pried me off. I protested weakly until I found myself on my back, him above, his weight resting on his forearms. My legs fell open around his hips as he plunged into me, over and over, with ardent zeal.

Drunk with lust, mouth open, my teeth gripped the side of his neck. Lightly at first. But the harder I bit, the faster he labored. When I tasted copper, I eased up, but he begged in a rough whisper, "Don't stop." I repeated the plea to him in turn with an urgent arching of my hips; we both got what we wanted.

"Arcadia . . ." He groaned in desperation as he slipped a hand between us to ensure victory. I knew he couldn't last much longer; it didn't matter, because I was already there.

Straining against him, I shook uncontrollably, crying out. His head reared back, then he joined me, releasing into my body with abandon while I spasmed beneath him.

As my tremors calmed, he slumped in exhaustion, then rolled us to our sides and clung to me like death. "Jesus," he said between breaths, "*Je*-sus."

Amen to that.

After a long moment, he made a low, satiated noise in the back of his throat, then kissed my forehead. "*Et in Arcadia ego*," he murmured with a crooked grin.

I laughed in surprise. "I don't think that's what that phrase means."

He grunted, cracking one eye open. "It does now."

Though spent, I suddenly thought of a hundred things I wanted to tell him all at once. "Lon—"

"Shh, hush now." He ran a tender hand over my hair, holding me firmly against him. "I'm trying to listen to you."

I buried my face in his neck and didn't say another word.

I was groggy; Lon's twitching woke me. It took me three panicked heartbeats to realize where I was. Head nestled on his shoulder, I'd dozed off in the small cottage bed, with one leg slung over his hips, staking a stubborn claim on my newly won territory. He was still asleep. Droplets of sweat hung on his forehead and matted his hair.

I tried not to wake him as I lifted my head to glance at the hands of the tiny battery-run alarm clock on the bedside table. Six thirty. *We should be leaving soon*, I thought with a reluctant, silent whimper. Leaving, as in trudging several miles back down the beach to get his car, after only bits and pieces of sleep. Worse, leaving behind the safety and comfort of the tiny cottage that had provided me hours of pleasure and joy . . . maybe more than I'd ever allowed myself. Certainly more than I'd ever been offered.

Lon inhaled sharply through his nose and lifted his head. I waited for reality to register for him. He tucked his chin to his chest and looked down at me, grunted, then smiled and let his head loll on the pillow as he stretched his legs.

"I had another dream." His deep voice was graveled with exhaustion as he shifted his arm around my shoulder to draw me closer.

"My memories?"

"Mmm-hmm. Maybe sex helps the spell along. We should make a note of that in the Memory grimoire," he said with amusement.

"Go on, tell me." I quickly cleared cobwebs from my sleepy brain.

"You were older this time. You were sneaking inside a large, dark room. A temple. A large silver hexagram hung in the front of the room on a wall above a raised sanctuary with two ornate thrones. There were four doors leading into it from the back. They had roses carved in them."

"The main lodge in Florida!" I lifted my head to prop my chin on his chest.

"You sneaked in through one of the doors and hid behind a column." He looked down at me. "Do you remember this?"

"No."

"Your mother was having an argument with someone. I could only see his back, but they were all in purple ceremonial robes. The man had long white hair, halfway down his back—"

"Caliph Superior," I confirmed without reservation.

"Oh? He looked like an old wizard from a fairy tale."

"He used to. His hair is short now. Go on." My hand

trailed lightly across his ribs, down the slight concave of his stomach, back up again.

"Well, he was saying that you—his words—'should have already manifested qualities that would indicate deification.' He kept insisting that his guardian told him that you should be able to pull energy from the moon by now. That you could use Heka inside you to kindle moon energy and harvest it for more powerful magick. That some ancient text claimed that you should be able to do this after you started menstruating."

"Wait, what?" My roaming hand stopped, taut on his ribs.

"Just the messenger," he reminded me.

"Well, that means I was at least twelve when this happened, because that's when I had my first period, but kindling the moon? The Moonchild spell doesn't just strengthen Heka? I'm supposed to be able to generate magical power from the moon? What the hell?"

"Just repeating what your caliph said. That he'd personally tried to get you to kindle moon energy for several months but nothing was happening."

"Weird. I don't remember him trying to teach me moon magick. Christ, I wouldn't even know how to start. Anyway, keep going."

"He said that he had no doubt that you were special, because his guardian had examined you. He mentioned your halo. His guardian told him about it. Then he was trying to get your mother to show him the ritual they used for your conception. She insisted it was the proper one, from the order's private library."

My cheek moved against his chest as I nodded. "That's where I read about it."

"He was also asking for the name of the man who presided over the ritual. She gave a name, Frater Oben?"

"Yes. That's the old mage I was telling you about. The one they had sex in front of." I grimaced, shucking away the thought. "He died before I was born. Kind of a relief that I never had to look the man in the eye."

Lon grunted in agreement. "After that, they argued back and forth. He insisted that he was only concerned for her and had her best interest at heart. She got upset and walked out crying. Then the dream ended."

"Huh," I said, puzzled. Was it possible that my parents had failed or screwed something up with the Moonchild spell? It pissed me off to know that the caliph had made my mom cry. I had to remind myself that this had happened years ago. Still . . . I thought about Lon's earlier suspicion of the caliph. I hated to think he was right. It made me a little sick to consider it, even. But what if the caliph was only concerned about the order's reputation? Only concerned that they had a real Moonchild in their ranks? In the dream, was he accusing my mother of having failed at the spell?

Then I allowed myself to think about something worse. "Hey Lon? What if the caliph wasn't really kidnapped by Luxe this past week? What if . . ."

"He was working with Luxe? It crossed my mind, but some things don't fit. You said the caliph was the only person, apart from your parents, who knows where you live. If he was working with Luxe, why would they send Riley Cooper to track you down with a Pareba demon?"

"They wouldn't. If he wanted to turn me over to Luxe, he could just come and get me himself."

"Exactly." He thought for a moment, then asked, "Right now I'm more curious about the moon kindling. Do you think that's what happened back in the caves with the incubus?"

"I doubt it. I think I would have known if I was kindling

moon energy. I wasn't even trying, it just happened. Plus, why would an ability like this appear out of the blue if it was supposed to have happened during puberty? It doesn't make sense."

"If we can get our hands on the damn glass talon, maybe you can just ask your parents," Lon suggested. "Seems like they have all the answers about the caliph and the moon spell."

My heart fluttered. He was right. If I could just finish this and prove their innocence, then I could have them back. They could help me figure out what had happened with the incubus. We'd sort it out together. If they failed with the Moonchild spell, who cared? I sure didn't.

I laid my head back on Lon's shoulder and thought for a while, trying to make sense of the dream until he yawned and stretched again. "We should probably get going," he remarked.

"Boo." I gave him a thumbs-down sign, peeling myself away and flipping onto my back to lie beside him.

"Are you sore?"

I laughed. "Why, you want an award or something?"

"Maybe."

I burrowed my fingers into his ribs. He recoiled with an involuntary, pained grunt. He was ticklish, I'd discovered by accident over the last few hours—a gold mine of an Achilles' heel.

"That's it. Now you've done it." He grabbed my fingers.

"Oww!" I yelled, laughing.

"I was trying to be considerate, but screw that. We're going one more round before we leave, whether you like it or not."

"Oh, *really*? You're awfully spry for a man *your age*."

"Honestly, my back's fucking killing me."

"So are my legs," I admitted, laughing.

He peered at me critically. "Looks like you fell into a vat of cherry Kool-Aid."

I tentatively touched the swollen skin around my lips. They stung like hell. "That's your fault! You gave me mustache burn. There, and other places . . ."

"Mmm." He chuckled, eyes narrowing in humor. "Come here, girl." Sweaty and sticky, he pulled me back up onto his chest and wound his fingers into my hair, now the consistency of a bale of dried hay. "I want you to shock me with Heka like you did last time," he added in a husky, seductive voice, "right at the end."

"'Bite me, Cady. Shock me, Cady.' Christ, you're demanding, aren't you?"

He grinned against my cheek. "Are you complaining?"

I wasn't. Not one bit.

32

Craig Bailey lived on the outskirts of the Village. His narrow, three-story brownstone was modeled to look like an English country estate, complete with trellised vines and plenty of stained glass. I watched from a distance, waiting nervously in Lon's coupe. The driver's-side window had a radiating crack in the glass and the hood was dented in two places, but he didn't say a word when we found it like that outside the Hellfire caves.

Watching him stroll out of Craig Bailey's driveway, I couldn't decipher his body language. Like me, his wrinkled clothes were stiff with sea water, and we were both sporting rat's-nest hairdos; we looked like homeless people who had stumbled upon evening wear in a trash bin. He opened the driver's door, got in, and closed it without looking at me.

"Well?" I asked, barely able to contain my curiosity. "Did he have the talon?"

"He's dead."

I closed my eyes. Not out of reverence—I didn't know the man from Adam—but in mind-numbing frustration. "What?"

"Died of a heart attack yesterday morning," Lon elaborated. "I talked to his son. He was pissed as hell that Craig spent the family money on worthless occult collectibles. Would have been more than happy to sell the talon to me, but it wasn't there."

"Wasn't there? Are you sure?"

"I'm sure. That fucking piece of shit sold Bailey the talon, then stole it back."

"Who? Spooner? Why would he do that?"

"Because then he could make money without losing the talon. He's pulled stunts like this before—at least, that's what I've heard."

"So he sent us out here on this wild-goose chase, and he had it all along?"

"I'd bet my life that he does."

Desperate for a hot shower, I scratched the back of my head; my scalp was dry and itchy. "How do we get it from Spooner?"

"We've tried asking nicely," Lon said with a bitter smile.

I nodded. "We're going to have to take it by force."

"Yep."

"You think you can remember the incantation for that memory spell we used on Riley?"

He tapped his temple. "Mind like a steel trap."

"I think I can remember the sigil, if you can do that part."

"Hmm . . . I might have something better in mind. It's in the trunk." Carefully considering whatever scheme he was cooking up, he idly stroked his mustache with his thumb and index finger. I pulled aside his collar and winced at the nasty indigo tooth marks I'd left on his neck. He lifted his eyebrows, inspected the bite in the rearview mirror, then gave me a smug smile as I covered it back up.

"You got a lighter in that tiny purse you stashed in my glove compartment?"

"I do."

"Good. There's some valrivia hidden in a box under the car manual. It's not fresh, but I don't care at this point, if you don't mind rolling it up for us. We'll stop somewhere and get food along the way."

"And some coffee, please."

"And some coffee," he agreed as he started the car.

It was just before one in the afternoon when we arrived at Spooner's place of business, an art deco building in a commercial district on the outskirts of Morella, just ten minutes away from my house. Lon identified Spooner's car parked in the alley by the back entrance, so we pulled behind it and marched up a short flight of steps bounded by a painted metal railing.

"I thought you said Spooner didn't work."

"He doesn't. He's a collector. This is where he cons people out of money." Lon battered the metal door with his fist, cigarette dangling between his lips. He leaned forward, ear to the door, and listened for a response inside. Seconds ticked by, ten stretching to twenty . . . a minute.

"I hear movement," Lon reported before banging on the door again and yelling, "Delivery!"

I heard it too, then a series of approaching steps. Locks began clicking open from the other side of the door. When the door swung inside, Spooner stood a few feet away in the same garish suit he'd worn the night before. With shocks of orange hair shooting out at all angles from his head and bloodshot eyes, he looked even worse than we did.

He was also very, very surprised to see us.

Lightning fast, he shoved at the door to shut it, but Lon wedged his foot against the kickplate before it closed. He stuck his Remington inside the humble opening and racked it once. Slowly, the door opened again. Spooner stood in the doorway, hands apathetically raised in submission.

"Hello again," I said brightly.

"Let's talk," Lon added, prodding Spooner's chest with the gun's barrel.

We dogged Spooner down a sterile hallway until he halted in front of a frosted glass door. He opened it and entered.

All four walls of the intimate room were lined with locked glass display cabinets. In the center, a low, square metal table was surrounded by four green armchairs and a swing-arm lamp.

Lon was wrong; this wasn't the room of a collector. It wasn't carefully arranged and tended like his library, and the items weren't cherished or admired. They were displayed with the care of a pawnshop owner. Spooner was a fence, not a lover of rare mysteries.

That didn't mean there wasn't a jackpot in here. A multicolored supernatural fog swirled around the haphazard arrangements. Pink, green, yellow, blue—nearly every item in the cabinets was Æthyric in origin. Hundreds of them.

I looked closer. Horns, bones, teeth, and talons cluttered one crowded shelf. They gave off the strongest visual marker, but they weren't the only occult treasures. He also had a staggering selection of metal and clay pendants and charms . . . dozens of books and scrolls. The earthly items were nearly as interesting and varied as the Æthyric ones: a small animal skull covered in precious gems, a leaf-shaped Aztec sacrificial blade, a golden Middle Eastern puzzle box with Jinn markings.

"Shut the fuck up," I whispered, in awe at the breadth of the collection.

"Your collection has grown since I last saw it," Lon

commented. "You used to specialize in earthly amulets, now half of this shit is glowing with Æthyric dust."

"I've expanded."

Lon glanced at the shelf I was inspecting. "The Æthyric demon body parts are new."

"To be fair, some of them are angel. One Banshee tooth, or at least that's what the former owner claimed."

"Go big or go home, huh?" Lon observed.

Spooner shrugged and straightened his green ascot. "I only discovered their existence a few years ago. Most collectors aren't willing to sell what they've acquired. It's a tough but profitable market."

"Tough enough that you had to steal back the glass talon from Craig Bailey?"

A cruel smile boosted Spooner's freckled cheeks. "He knew he didn't have much time left on this plane. He wanted to . . . give it back to a fellow collector."

I investigated the shelf of talons and bones. Nothing remotely glass. However, one empty display stand cowered alone in a back corner, a wire clamp attached to an indented metal base. The right size to hold a talon?

"Where is it now?" I asked.

Spooner squinted his eyes. "Hmm, I'm not sure if I remember. Cady, isn't it?"

Lon looked at me and nodded. "You're up to bat."

Right. I surveyed the amount of space I'd need. The chairs would have to go. I began moving them aside.

"What are you doing?" Spooner asked.

I left one chair in front of the table and motioned to Lon.

"Have a seat," Lon said, raising his gun. Spooner complied.

From the small pocket in my wrap dress, I removed a fat

stick of red ochre chalk that we'd purchased from a local occult shop on the way over—the only one in La Sirena: more
of a catch-all New Age-slash-Pagan supply shop, really, but it
was convenient and they had what I needed so no sense in
being too snobby about it.

The chalk marked the cement floor beautifully. A dark
red, dusty line trailed behind my sketching hand as I bent at
the waist to sketch the binding triangle, nice and big, to en-
close Spooner right where he sat.

"What are you doing?" Spooner asked.

"What does it look like?"

His eyes followed me, head swiveling. I began hashing
out the binding symbols surrounding the borders. Ancient
symbols, arcane fortifications. It flowered at my feet like a
beautiful, complex math equation scribbled on a scientist's
blackboard.

"It looks like one of the Hellfire's vermilion seals,"
Spooner noted, his voice betraying the tiniest bit of panic.
"Which, by the way, is going to cost us thousands of dollars
to repair."

"Bill me." I finished my work with a flourish, snapping
my wrist, then stepped back to admire my work. Flawless.
Retreating to scour the glass cases behind Spooner, I found
what I needed without much effort. "Aha!" My eyes focused on
a small caduceus lying next to some Nordic broadswords. "Do
you have a key to this?"

Spooner eyed Lon's shotgun, then reluctantly snapped his
fingers in the direction of the cabinet. The door swung open.

"Spooner's demonic talent is opening locks," Lon explained. "Manual ones, at least. That's one of the reasons I've got
electronic locks. Ten years ago he stole a couple of books from
me, before I built my house. But I got those back, didn't I?"

"You did. I also fucked your ex-wife."

"No, I believe *she* fucked *you*, along with everyone else in the Hellfire Club. Don't flatter yourself."

After examining the core of the caduceus—it was graphite, thankfully, not a dud—I walked over to the point of the triangle and exhaled.

"What's she doing?"

"Looks to me like she's putting you in a magical pigpen," Lon said.

I pulled from the electrical current. The lights dimmed.

"How can you . . . ?" Spooner was now alert and more than a little alarmed. "You're a magician?" He stood up. Lon racked the pump shotgun again and aimed until he sat back down.

With a gentle push, I released kindled Heka into the carved staff, charging the triangle in a brilliant display of white light as I recited the binding spell. I teetered on my feet when the nausea came, but recovered quickly and gave Lon a dizzy smile. Ta-da.

Spooner squealed like a fifties housewife who'd just spotted a mouse on the floor, folding himself up in his chair, legs drawn up tight. He covered his ears with his hands. "Stop it! What have you done? My head—" He ground his teeth together. "Too much pressure. My head!"

He'd never been bound. Most Earthbounds haven't. It's always a shock the first time.

"Where's the talon?" Lon asked.

The orange-haired man ignored him. "Oh, God, my head. Please make it stop."

If I had a dime for every time I'd heard that during a binding in my bar . . .

"Spooner, you are now bound by me, and I command

you. Those are the rules. Now answer me. Where is the god-damn glass talon?"

"In the table," he intoned, voice low and obedient. His eyes shot open and he covered his mouth with both hands, shocked that he'd said it. "You could have just put the gun to my head and I would have told you. Please unbind me—please!"

"Do you know the name of the demon it belongs to?" I asked.

A confused look crossed his face. "Name? No."

A long shot, but I had to ask.

I took a step, then rubbed my foot over a corner of the triangle, breaking the spell. Spooner fell over in his chair, a floppy puppet with slackened strings. He whimpered as I approached and set the caduceus down.

Each side of the thick tabletop bore a small indentation flanked by horizontal lines. Deceptively decorative. I pressed my finger into the indentation on one side. Nothing. Second side. Nothing. Third . . . a small drawer creaked open. Inside were two wads of dog-eared hundred-dollar bills bundled with wide rubber bands, a small ladies' pistol, and in the back, a swirl of pink fog surrounding what could only be the glass talon.

I gathered it up with shaking hands. It was cool, and heavy. Not smooth, as I'd expected, but marred with long, rough ridges. The base was ragged and opaque ivory, the remainder clear.

After all the worry and frustration, there it was.

Could I use it to find the summoning spell for the albino demon?

I nestled it in the center of my palm and closed my hand around it, situating the talon between my index and middle fingers. Gripping it tight, it felt like a weapon in my hand. I slashed at the air once, wielding its power, testing. I relaxed my fingers and transferred it into my other hand, dropping it to my side.

Spooner continued to whimper. I glanced at Lon and nodded. He lowered his gun and spoke to him in a low, rational voice. "I wanted you to know what she could do. Don't look for her, don't ask about her. Don't even think about her. If I find out that you have, I'll come back, and I damn well won't be happy. That goes for my kid too." He gaze captured Spooner's. "We're not afraid of you, but *you* should be afraid of us."

Lon turned his back and began walking away, then paused. He looked at the ground as he spoke. "Later today I'll wire you the money you paid for it. I'm not a thief." In a barely audible murmur he added, "Not anymore."

33

"Amazing," Lon said. "It really *does* look like a fairy. Jupe was right."

I gripped a freshly charged clay doll and watched my servitor's small pink figure float above our heads in his library, hoping against hope that the glass talon would generate enough live energy to link it to a book containing the albino demon's summoning name. Hoping also that the book was here. Only one day remained until the Luxe deadline, and if it turned out that the servitor *could* find the right book, but it was in someone else's library across the globe, I was screwed.

It was early afternoon. Jupe was watching a movie in his room, but Lon had made him promise to stay in bed; he didn't even know I was here. We stopped by my house after the confrontation with Spooner, to check in on Riley and pick up the supplies I needed to do the servitor spell, then I followed him in my rental.

The servitor hung at the ceiling. Not unusual. It sometimes took a few moments for it to get a fix on its objective and begin hunting. The pink light would either go through the ceiling, or float back down. Through . . . or down, through—

It floated back down.

My heart pounded.

Hovering near the tops of the bookcases, it glided in front of the fireplace, past Lon's small sealed cabinet of stolen rarities, behind the desk, bobbed in place for a few seconds, and like a birthday balloon with a slow leak, it lazily dropped and floated to me, filtering back into the clay doll.

I had the servitor retrieval spell neatly prepared on one of Lon's blue paper markers. Spitting on the drawing, I whispered the incantation and smashed the clay doll against it.

It was off-putting to be in the same room as the transmission image. I could see myself and Lon through its vision, the shelf of books it had spotted, and the particular book it singled out. A fat, red leather binding. "There!" I said, pointing as the image disintegrated.

The transmission acted like a magical decongestant; loosened Heka seethed inside me. Head swimming, I swayed, dropped to my knees, and fell onto my back with a loud thump. Closing my eyes momentarily, I waited until the nausea subsided. Lon's knees hit the rug beside me. I squinted one eye open as a red leather-bound tome was dangled in front of my face.

"Is this it?"

Goetia Demonica Muliebris, read the worn gilded title on the front cover.

I laughed. "Yep."

"Goddammit," he murmured, sitting back on his heels. "I never would've thought to look in here." Cracking it open on my extended legs, he hunched over and began hurriedly skimming the entries.

"Why not?" I pushed myself up into a sitting position.

"Because," Lon explained, fanning carefully through

crackling vellum pages, "I just assumed from what you said that the demon was male."

"That's what the caliph told me."

"This is an encyclopedia of female demons."

Well, damn. I watched him flip through the goetia, carefully turning each page. Then he stopped. I moved closer to read the text along with him.

Next to the simple relief of a woodcut demon, the border of which was illuminated in flaking silver, was the name of the primordial being: Nivella Krustallos Daemonia.

"Not male, and not an albino either," Lon said with wonder. "A White Ice Demon."

I'd never heard of this class, but now that I knew it, I could look up the correct summoning seal.

Lon read the text out loud:

"*NIVELLA THE WHITE. The sixty-fourth spirit is called Nivella Kurstallos Daemonia, or Nivella the White. She is a Grand Duchess, and appeareth in the Form of a Beautiful White Beast with pink eyes, horns, and four arms bearing four crystalline talons. Her Office is to teach the Mysteries of the Occult Arts perfectly within the Æthyric tribes. Her wisdom was sought in Olde Ægypt and Ancient Greece. She can be forced to answer those questions regarding the Harvesting of Æthyric energy, which the querent may wish to put to her, if desired. She is partly of the Order of Thrones, and partly that of the Seraphim Angels. She ruleth 10 Legions of Spirits.*"

I silently reread the entry twice before Lon spoke in a soft voice. "Well, there it is."

"Yes."

"'Harvesting of Æthyric energy?' Maybe she teaches how to kindle Heka. Doesn't sound like much of a bloodthirsty hunter, but I guess a demon can be forced into doing whatever they've been commanded to do by the magician."

I nodded my head and swallowed. "Pretty much."

"Well, do you want to summon her and ask?"

"Not yet."

"Why?"

"Before, when we didn't know if we had the right one, I was going to summon any of the demons you researched to find out if they were present during the killings. Now I know it was Nivella, and to ask who originally summoned her, well, some Æthyric demons, especially the primordial ones—"

"They're only obligated to answer truthfully one time."

I nodded. "I don't want to waste my only shot if I don't have an audience. The Luxe Order isn't just gonna take my word for it. I need them to witness it."

He studied me quietly. "When are you going?"

"Tomorrow. Midday, I guess. It's a seven-hour drive to San Diego."

"I'll make arrangements for Mr. and Mrs. Holiday to watch Jupe."

I shook my head. "I've got to do this by myself. If something goes wrong, you can't be in the middle of it—Jupe depends on you."

His protest was interrupted by a soft crackling noise. A fine network of blue lines formed along the floor, walls, bookshelves . . .

"What's going on?"

Lon sprang to his feet. "The house ward."

The air distorted in front of us. Bits of smashed shards from the servitor's clay doll crunched under my feet as Lon hauled me off the floor.

A soft white light appeared before us, one that quickly manifested into a wispy, floating figure. For the shortest moment, my heart leapt when I thought it was Priya, somehow miraculously reborn. Before disappointment fell, though, I realized that the being *was* familiar to me, even if I hadn't seen it for a few years . . . my mother's guardian.

"Scivina!" I cried out. "It's okay, Lon. It's just a projection from the Æthyr."

Fragile, closed wings skimmed the shoulder tops of the Hermeneus spirit. Like Priya, Scivina was birdlike in the face, and vaguely human below. But where Priya had carried the face of a young owl with pointed ears and big eyes, Scivina's was a hawk, fierce and proud. As projected images that never fully materialized on earth, they were both a translucent milky color, lacking color and definition.

Scivina's halo appeared as a soft puff of cloud. She was calm, the epitome of service and decorum, as most guardians are. No emotion registered on her face at the sight of me. She blinked once, canting her head in greeting, then spoke in my head, like Priya used to.

Seléne, your mother requests your presence.

"When? Where?"

Anno IVXIX, Sol twenty-two degrees in Libra, Luna twenty-nine degrees in Aries.

"Gregorian calendar, please."

Tomorrow night at ten thirty. The Luxe Order's Sapphire Temple in San Diego. Do not be late. This is important.

"Yes, I'm headed there already. My parents will be there? Do they know about the council?"

I will tell them you have accepted the appointment and will prepare myself to locate you when you arrive. Do not enter the temple or approach anyone. It is not safe. Wait for me to find you, Scivina said before bowing her head.

"Wait! Tell them that I can prove their innoc—"

It was too late. Scivina dissipated without acknowledging

my final words. The air wobbled and bent, then became still again.

A chilly dread began eating away at my chest. *It is not safe*. That warning had come from my mom. My parents were probably worried sick about me; they always were. But they didn't know what I'd found. Didn't know I could save them. Once they realized this, we could go up against the council together.

"Hmph," Lon said. "I guess they *do* know about the Luxe mandate, huh?"

"You heard Scivina?"

He nodded. "Like I can hear people's thoughts when I'm transmutated."

"Maybe they're planning to turn themselves in. I better get there a little early to make sure that doesn't happen."

Seconds ticked by while neither one of us said anything.

"Nerves getting the best of ya?" Lon asked with a weak smile.

"I just want it to be over."

"Stay here tonight," he murmured.

"I need to take care of some things at my house." I also needed a hot shower and a good, long nap.

"Then come back later tonight and stay here. Leave in the morning." He intertwined his fingers with mine. "Please?" he amended.

There was no need to answer, I supposed, because he could probably sense that his proposal not only pleased me, but also ignited an unexpected tenderness that echoed deeper. Too bad it was all being drowned out by the worry coiling in my stomach.

34

Morning sun blinded me as I sneaked out of Lon's bedroom. He was taking a shower, and I didn't have the guts to drag out our good-byes. Dodgy feelings about the trip to San Diego trailed after me like an annoying child underfoot. He said when we woke that he didn't have a dream flashback of my memories. I took it from his abrupt manner that he was either anxious about not having had one, or he was lying. I preferred to believe it was the former. If the caliph really wasn't on my side, Lon wouldn't dare let me walk into a bad situation unaware; I knew that much for sure, and it gave me some amount of solace.

Last night before I came back here, I left Riley with the instruction to be ready to leave when I returned. She acted genuinely sad to be going home to San Diego, but was overjoyed to be leaving the house. It was just after ten now, so I wanted to speak to Jupe before I left. When I'd come back here last night, he was asleep, so we hadn't seen each other since that horrible night at his school.

With my tattered navy hoodie zipped to the neck, I shoved my hands in the pockets and shuffled silently along the hardwood floors of the second-story hallway. I tossed a look over the railing at the open living room below and desperately wished I could just chuck the whole trip and stay there.

Lon had told me Jupe's room was three doors down. I'd been worried about Jupe hearing us the night before, but he assured me that the place was built like a fortress. I counted doorways, navigating my way past a bathroom and a guest room, then I found a closed door. A sign hung on it that displayed a still of Gene Wilder wearing a white lab coat. The sign read, DO *NOT* OPEN THIS DOOR!

Pressing my ear against the blond wood, I listened for a second and heard rumbling chatter from a TV, so I knocked softly.

"Yep," came the reply from within.

I cracked open the door a couple of inches. "Are you decent?"

After a short pause, Jupe answered, a little unsure. "Cady?"

I took that as a yes, so I pushed the door farther and leaned my head inside. Jupe was sitting up in his bed with wide eyes. He was wearing a faded Funkadelic *Maggot Brain* T-shirt and red pajama bottoms. He lit up like a Christmas tree when he saw me. I'd never felt so admired, but I tried not get too gooey about it.

"Hey, kid."

"Cady! I tried to get my dad to let me call you on your cell but he said you were too busy so I called up your bar a couple of days ago but some bitchy woman answered so I hung up."

He didn't even take a breath when he spit all that out. My head was already spinning. "Uh, you probably got Kar Yee, then. She doesn't have very good phone manners. Kinda like your dad," I said with a smile.

His bed sat in the center of the room, a queen-size mattress resting on a low, modern platform a few inches off the floor. A corner of the bed was lit by a long slice of sunlight that streamed in from the large window above. I sidestepped over a hefty pile of books and magazines while evading another mound of dirty clothes to get there.

"How's the arm?"

"It aches real bad when I don't take the pain pills, but if I *do* take the pain pills then I forget that it's broken and I do stupid stuff. I bumped it yesterday—on accident—and it hurt like hell." Sitting cross-legged, he scooted back on the bed to make room for me. I plopped down while he muted the volume on a large TV hanging on the wall across from us that was twice as big as mine at home.

"The cast is huge, Jesus," I said.

"It's heavy too—feel." He tugged my hand so he could rest the elbow in my palm. "See."

"Yeah, that's pretty heavy. When do you get to take it off?"

"The human doctor at the emergency room said six weeks, but my real doctor's Earthbound, and he said I can probably take it off in two, and he can heal it up the rest of the way himself then."

"Being a demon sometimes has advantages."

"I guess."

I surveyed Jupe's domain. Pretty big for a kid's bedroom, but hard to tell from all the clutter. A door opened to a private bathroom on one side of the room. On the other, old movie lobby cards lined the walls, along with a signed poster of some Brazilian soccer star and another of Pam Grier as Foxy Brown. The wall in front of us supported floating shelves from floor to ceiling, each packed with neatly arranged vintage horror movie toys. A vertical series of three large black-and-white framed photographs hung nearby.

"Who are they?" I asked, pointing to the photos.

"Oh, that's Aunt Adella."

"Your mom's sister?" I guessed.

"Yeah, and that's my gramma. My dad took those this summer."

Adella had a darker complexion than her sister, and a softer, rounder face. Strikingly pretty with a kind smile. My age, maybe a little older. Her hair was a mass of spiral, electric curls that stuck out just like Jupe's, barely tamed by a wide polka-dot headscarf tied just above her forehead. A gray wisp of a halo was just visible. "Christ, you look like her." More than his mother, even, just going from photos.

"Yeah, my hair, huh? Nose too. She's *so-o-o* cool. You would love her. She's supersmart and really funny. She emails me almost every day and I talk to her on Sunday nights," he bragged, then added, "and I already told her all about you."

An odd feeling tightened my chest. Something between embarrassment and pleasure. "You did?"

"Uh-huh." He didn't offer anything more, so I didn't pry. "She asked me what I wanted for my birthday yesterday."

He was totally fishing, but I took the bait. "When's your birthday?"

"Next month. Halloween."

"That's pretty cool."

He gave me a smug look. "I know, right? When's yours?"

"Febru . . ." I paused. No, that was the *actual* Arcadia Bell's birthday—the one I was used to spouting off on cue. I struggled for a moment to remember the real date. I hadn't celebrated it in years. "Wow, I guess it's tomorrow."

"What? Tomorrow? Happy birthday! The big twenty-six, huh?"

"Twenty-five," I corrected without thinking.

"I thought you were already twenty-five? That's what my dad told me when I asked him."

According to my fake driver's license, I was. "Nope. Tomorrow."

He cocked an eyebrow at me like he'd just discovered some salacious secret, then mumbled, "Talk about cradle robbing . . ."

I gave him a soft punch on his shoulder, then glanced back at the photos on the wall again. The last one was a shot of Adella and Jupe pretending to balance on a surfboard, their arms held out. They were both grinning.

"Those are the first photos I've seen of your dad's—well, in person, anyway. At first I thought he only shot women in bikinis, but then I found his website and saw the other stuff, *National Geographic* covers and the local photos of the coast."

"Yeah, he sells a ton of those in a shop down in the Village. You know how much people pay for some of them? The signed prints? Guess."

"Uh . . ."

"A thousand dollars! Can you believe that? Who would pay that much for a photo of the stupid beach? All they have to do is walk outside and see it for free. Man, people are dumb." Jupe shook his head and kicked several open video game cases off the side of the bed. God only knew where the games were or what shape they were in. "Wait a minute, why are you here so early?" He looked askance at me.

Busted. I had no idea what to say. On one hand, he might be angry or uncomfortable. Then again, he probably deserved honesty, and he wasn't a child. But maybe it wasn't my place to say anything at all. "Uh . . ." I hedged, trying to make up my mind.

Jupe's pale green eyes widened. He looked away for a second, forehead wrinkled, then asked me straight up, "Did you stay here last night?"

"Kinda."

"In the guest room?"

"Yes," I answered quickly. I think it was the forceful-ness of it that gave it away. All my well-cultivated lying skills seemed to be just out of reach.

"You stayed . . . *with my dad*?" He sounded like a gossip columnist uncovering the scandal of the year, shocked but titillated.

I squeezed my eyelids shut. "Maybe," I said, then warily cracked one eye back open.

"Huh." He sat back, wheels turning. "No one's ever stayed over here before. Well, there was one lady, but my dad tried to sneak her out in the morning before I woke up. That was a couple of years ago. I guess he thought I was too young to see that. She never came back."

"Hmm, well, you're not weirded out about *me* staying here, are you?"

He contemplated this, then asked, "Do you like him?"

I nodded.

"I mean, do you *like*-like him?"

Lon's whispered morning words still swirled in my head like a drug. Goose bumps blossomed over my arms and my neck became warm. I sighed, utterly defeated. "Yeah, Jupe. I *like*-like him. A lot, I think."

A long pause stretched between us.

"Cool," he finally said, grinning.

Whew.

"I'm just glad you gave him a second chance. He can be *really* dumb sometimes. I told him that if he didn't apologize for acting like a dick that night at my school, he was the stupidest person in the world."

"He kinda *was* a dick, wasn't he?"

Jupe laughed, then gave me a confident look. "I set him straight. Don't worry."

I held up my hand. "Thanks for looking out for me."

He smacked it with more force than I expected. "Anytime. Hey, wanna sign my cast?"

"Sure. Where's a pen?"

He scrambled to snatch up a Sharpie that was sticking out from beneath his pillow and slapped it into my hand. I squirmed around to get into a better position and nearly knocked over a half-eaten bowl of Cheerios, wobbling in the covers at the foot of the bed. He was even more of a pig than I was.

On his cast were Mr. and Mrs. Holiday's signatures, JACK in big, bold letters with a deformed Godzilla head drawing, and then in small, tidy print, a string of sentences that wound around the plaster near his wrist. "What's all this?" I asked.

"Pfft. My dad thinks he's funny."

I leaned in and read it aloud. "*IMPORTANT REMINDERS. One: I will not jump on the bed pretending to be a rock star and break my other arm.* Sound advice," I agreed with a smile. "*Two: I will not leave dirty dishes in my room.*" I looked at the cereal bowl. "Well, that one sure didn't stick, did it?"

"That bowl's only been in here a few minutes. It doesn't count," he argued with a grin. "Especially if I get it back down to the kitchen before he sees it."

I shook my head and continued reading. "*Three: I will only ask one question at a time. Four: I will not leave the freezer* *door open overnight and force my dad to throw away all the food inside and mop up the floor while I'm at school. Five: I will not call the dog a f**ktard.*" Two bright red stars censored the word.

Jupe snorted loudly in amusement, and giddy peals of laughter incapacitated me for a few moments. He joined in halfway through, giggling like a fool. I had to force myself to stop.

"All right, all right, all right," I said between breaths, fanning my face. After a brief string of hiccups, Jupe finally calmed enough for me to sign his cast.

I drew a circular, flat open rose with three tiers of petals and a crescent moon cradling it below. Jude watched in fascination and—miraculously—waited until I was finished to speak.

"What in the world is *that*?"

"It's my personal symbol . . . as a magician."

"You have a symbol?"

"Yep."

"What does it mean?"

"It means Moon Rose. That's my middle name, Aysul. It's Turkish."

"Whoa. Is that a Turkish symbol above the wheel thingy?"

"No, that's my sigil. And it's not a wheel, it's a rose. See, these three inner petals in the inside represent alchemical elements. The seven petals around those represent the classical planets, and the outer petals contain the twelve signs of the zodiac. Twenty-two petals total."

"Twenty-two," he repeated, tracing the rose with his finger.

"It's an important magical number. It's the number of paths on the Tree of Life in Qabalah, the number of letters in the Hebrew alphabet, and the number of cards in the Tarot's major arcana."

"Cool."

"So, now you have my symbol, and that means you have my protection."

"*Whoa*," Jupe murmured.

"I'm real sorry about the mess that put you in that cast," I said. "Your dad wasn't being a dick about wanting to keep you safe. He had a right to be angry at me. It was my fault."

"Don't worry. I was never mad about that. You're pretty strong. That was like an old-school wrestling move—you should be a *luchadora*!" An honest smile softened his face and lifted a huge weight from my shoulders.

I grinned back at him, suddenly much happier. "You, my friend, are insane." Without thinking, I ran a quick hand through his springy curls. He leaned into my hand with the enthusiasm of a dog being scratched behind the ear.

"Will you teach me how you did that invisible spell? Because that was the best part of the whole night. I told Jack about it but he didn't believe me. He thinks magick isn't real."

I tightened the cap on the marker and handed it back. The dread that I'd kept at bay in the hideout of Jupe's room returned, bringing with it an aching sense of sadness. "To tell you the truth, Jupe, sometimes I almost wish it weren't."

35

The Big Sur region of California that borders Morella and La Sirena to the south is one of the most beautiful parts of the entire country. Rolling green mountains stretch across one side of Highway One, and the Pacific's waves crash on the other at the bottom of craggy, lush cliffs.

Going this way, instead of taking Five—the faster route—added an extra hour or more to my drive, as Lon tried to point out to me, but I didn't care. The mental serenity it provided was well worth it. It wasn't a weekend, so there weren't *too* many people slowing down traffic by constantly pulling over at scenic spots. I'd hit L.A. after rush hour and would still get to San Diego well before 11 p.m.

"Hard to believe it's real, huh?" I said to Riley Cooper as I drove. "The view, I mean."

She sat in the passenger seat smacking gum. "Fantastic. I'm kinda sorry you're taking me home. I've never felt so calm and relaxed in my life."

"Vacation can't last forever." And neither would my supply of the opiate elixir I'd been using to dose her.

She sighed. "True, true."

"I'm sorry about the accident, Riley."

She shrugged. "I feel much better now, no harm done. To tell you the truth, Jane, I'm really glad I came. It was nice to catch up after all these years." The smile she gave me was so authentic that I almost believed we *were* old friends. Then I reminded myself that the *real* Riley had hurt Jupe.

A couple hours into our drive, I stopped at a gas station and called her father, Magus Zorn, in private on her cell phone, using up the last of her battery. He was alarmed and demanded to speak to her. I refused, but told him that she was okay and wasn't hurt, except for the missing tooth. Like Riley, Magus Zorn denied knowledge of Caliph Superior's whereabouts, but it was hard to tell if he was lying over the phone. Regardless, I told him to make sure his council was ready for me to prove my parents' innocence at midnight. I figured that gave me time enough to talk to them beforehand.

I tried to keep my eyes on the road, but I had a terrible headache and was fighting constant nausea. A couple of times I almost blacked out, but it passed quickly. Of course I would manage to get sick during all this, probably from that stupid midnight dip in the ocean.

Early that morning, before I left Lon's house, I scribbled a quick note to him and asked Jupe to deliver it. I made him swear not to read it, but I doubt those kinds of promises mean to much to a stubborn thirteen-year-old.

Dear Neanderthal,
There is no way I could possibly thank you for everything
you've done for me, even if you only did it to get me in the
sack. No matter what happens, I will pay you back the
money you wired to Spooner. My order has it. You may
not be a thief, but I don't like being in debt to people. I

*was going to tell you some mushy private stuff, but I don't
really trust Jupe not to read this. Plus you already know
it all anyway, maybe better than I do.*

—*Cady*

It was just after ten when I pulled into a deserted parking
lot on the edge of Old Town. I paused to inspect the building across the street. Hard to believe, but there it was, the
infamous Luxe Sapphire Temple. The place where the final—
attempted—Black Lodge slaying had failed seven years ago.
And the place my parents had been framed, when all they'd
wanted to do was mediate peaceful talks between the other
occult organizations.

As a rule, I usually avoid any of our rival orders' temples
and lodges, on the off chance that someone might recognize
me; however, one time out of curiosity, I'd driven by this
particular building when Kar Yee and I were loping around
California after college. The largest occult temple in the world,
their website claimed. It was intimidatingly big and contem-
porary in design, topped with a three-sided triangular blue
glass window on the roof; the blue pyramid was lit from the
inside and illuminated the night sky like a beacon, easily seen
from blocks away. It was so grand and distracting that I almost failed to notice the series of Heka-charged wards around
the main parking lot. I had no doubts that if I crossed those
wards, I'd be attacked, so I kept my distance.

According to their propaganda, the inner temple held over
a thousand people. So crazy. Like one of those megachurches
that brings in flocks of attendees every Sunday. Quality, not
quantity, as the caliph always said. I wondered if he would be
here tonight, and if so, on whose side would he be standing?

I pulled my rental into a dark parking space under a tree

at the edge of the empty lot and rolled down my window. The night air was brisk but energizing. I'd been stuck in the car far too long. Such a shame we didn't arrive in the daytime. After navigating around the brown, smog-filled skyline of L.A., San Diego was the promised land, with warm, clear blue skies and even bluer water.

Dull yellow lights glowed from the smaller windows around the sides of the temple. A handful of cars were parked near an entrance, but I didn't see any people or movement. I patted my jacket, double-checking that the crystal talon was still tucked away safely in the inner pocket. A copy of the White Ice Demon class seal was rolled around the talon for easy access, but I'd also memorized it, and hidden a spare piece of red ochre chalk in the side of my sock, just in case.

Riley was snoring loudly in the seat beside me; I'd dosed her one last time when we stopped outside of L.A. for gas. I'm sure my parents weren't going to be thrilled about the kidnapping. Nothing I could do about it now but own up to it.

Oddly enough, I was nervous to see them. It had been years, after all, since that last time my mom flew from France to see me in college. I'd changed a lot; I was sure they had too. I didn't worry about it for too long, because the air bubbled outside the open driver's window and Scivina materialized.

You are here, she said stoically.

"Hello to you too. Where are my parents?"

She didn't answer me. Before I could say another word, she faded away.

"Hey!" I cried to the distorted air she left in her wake.

Pissed off, I stepped out of the rental, leaving the door open. A long black limo pulled into the lot. I stuck one foot back inside the car, wary, but the limo door opened and a familiar figure emerged.

"Mom?"

She was wearing a well-cut navy business suit and had her dark hair pinned up, the crown of it now gray. Not only that, but her face was harder; the lines around her mouth were more deeply etched and she'd lost weight. The long, straight nose and deep-set eyes were still the same, but her complexion was sallow. She looked as if she'd aged ten years or more. It broke my heart a little.

My feet didn't want to move. I felt unexplainably shy, like a child. Older or not, she still commanded a great deal of respect. People always said that about her. She could just step into a room and everyone would stop what they were doing to look at her.

She strode to me with outstretched arms. "Darling," she said, a sliver of her once heavy French accent slipping in.

Her arms folded around me, and I stiffened. Then I smelled her perfume and her hair, and I fell into her. It was like being drawn into a soft, warm cocoon. Everything just went away, all the worry and stress and bad feelings. My persistent headache pulsed a little softer, and I almost forgot why I'd come. None of it mattered. Only that she was there.

The shoulder of her jacket was wet when I pulled away, but I didn't realize I'd been crying.

She held my face in her hands. "Hello, my beautiful girl. It's all okay now, yes?"

I nodded rapidly, sniffling. There was so much I wanted to say, but my tongue was numb. It was all I could do to breathe and stand up straight.

"Seléne." A low voice sounded from behind her.

I looked over her shoulder to glimpse my father standing there.

"Dad."

His short walnut brown hair was going gray like my mom's. Especially over his ears. Even his eyebrows were gray. *Jesus, they're old.* My mind recalled all the recent U.S. presidents, the stress of the office rapidly aging them over four years' time—how you could look at before and after photos and be shocked by the difference.

He made a one-word comment to my mom under his breath that I didn't quite catch as she moved out of the way. He was wearing black dress pants and a white shirt with the sleeves folded up to the elbows. He smiled, offering me a gleaming white mouthful of teeth. It was his used-car-salesman smile. I always used to tease him about that. It was worse in photos.

We hugged, briefly, and he pushed me back to look at me before I was ready to end it. Brown eyes darted over my face. "I'm sorry, but we don't have much time, and I need to know a few things."

"Okay, but I have some good news . . ."

He gripped my shoulders. "Have you experienced any change in your magical ability?"

Oh, thank God. They knew about the moon kindling. "Two nights ago, I was able to banish an incubus and his mate back to the Æthyr. I didn't summon them."

"Tell me exactly what happened," my father instructed. "It is important."

I told them about the room darkening to black, about the blue light that drew the symbols in the air. My mother cried out, then covered her face with her hands and tilted her head to the night sky.

"What's wrong? Is that bad? Is something wrong with me?" I asked.

She raised both arms up and said something in French,

while my dad grinned his funny grin and patted my back with enthusiasm. "No, no. It's wonderful. Perfect. It is exactly as the old books said it should be. On your twenty-fifth birthday, your powers will manifest." He grabbed my mother and embraced her as her eyes teared with joy. "We did it, my love. They doubted us, but we did it!" He laughed into her hair and kissed her head several times.

I suddenly felt left out. Hello? Haven't seen me in years? And weren't there more pressing concerns? Annoyance flared up inside me. "So what is this power? And how could it be more important than the Luxe council? You *do* know that they're planning to kill you, right? They tried to kidnap me." I pointed at Riley's snoozing figure in the car. "That's Magus Zorn's girl—the Luxe leader sent his own daughter after me."

My mother squinted into the car. "Mmm. She might be useful later."

"No time for that, Enola." My dad tapped his watch. "We need to get going."

"Wait!" I protested. "I have big news. I found the white demon. We can call it to prove your innocence." My irritation faded, replaced by a surge of excitement as I waited for their reaction.

My dad smiled, and I for a moment I was ten again, being praised for acing a test. But while he was grinning, something slipped out under his breath. "*Merde.*" His mouth barely moved when he said it. My mother poked him on his hip with one finger, admonishing him. His grin got bigger. "That's wonderful. Good job. Well-done. Come here."

I shook away my confusion and stepped forward to hug him. As my arms went around his neck, a gleam of metal moved in his hand. I barely felt the warmth of his palm against my back when something jabbed the side of my neck.

I cried out, drawing away and reaching over my shoulder. As I did, he pulled back a syringe.

"What—what are you doing?" My fingers found the tiny stinging wound. I shuffled away from them in horror as my vision blurred and doubled. "Dad?" My feet stumbled. A rush of pinpricks slid down my arms. I reached for the open car door to brace myself. Just as I did, my knees quivered.

Numb. Frozen. I was able to see and hear when my face hit the pavement, I just couldn't feel anything. Not my legs or my arms. I wasn't sure I was breathing anymore. That worried me, but I couldn't do a damn thing about it. Confusion clouded my thoughts.

The ground spun and glimmered with light. In the distance, dark shapes bounded out of the Luxe temple, running toward us. Animals, maybe. No, people.

I was surrounded by strong hands. My parents. Another man. They picked me up off the ground and carried me to the limo. The dark figures kept running toward me, but I was inside a tornado and they'd never breach it in time. *If I can't breathe, will I die?* I thought in a druggy haze.

As hands pushed my head down into the limo, I tried to call back to people running toward us, but I just couldn't. I had no voice.

It didn't matter. It was too late anyway.

The swirling, black vortex drew me up and away.

36

A slow bead of sweat trickled down the nape of my neck. When it ran down my back, I realized that my nose was cold. Actually, cold on one side, hot on the other. That was strange. Strange enough to speed my ascent into consciousness. My eyes opened.

I was outdoors. A clearing in the woods that was bare of grass. A rocky hill lay in front of me, several dozen yards in the distance. A single man clothed in ritual robes stood at the base. His head was bowed, as if in prayer or meditation.

My vision was tinted red. Blurry. Obstructed, perhaps?

A ring of luminaries circled the surrounding area, but they weren't projecting as much light as the Æthyric glow that brightened three points around me like compass markings. Small binding triangles were carved into the ground. One was directly in front of me, some distance away—ten yards, maybe. Two on either side of me. When I realized what was inside the triangles, I felt certain one lay behind me as well.

All were pulsing with light and flickered with movement; translucent entities were trapped within each one. Metaphysical holograms, just like my guardian Priya. But these weren't friendly messenger spirits, they were Æthyric demons.

The first, ensnared in the circle straight ahead of me, was built like a rock, twice the size of a human, with massive legs and feet. His skin was the texture of tree bark.

To my left was a human-size woman with round features and long, wavy hair. She wore a loose shift, the hem of which was tattered and dripping with water.

In the circle on my right was a winged, male, sylphlike demon. His wings opened and closed anxiously as he paced the inside of his circle, searching for a way out.

And just behind me, elongated flame-shaped shadows flickered on the ground.

Earth, Water, Air, Fire.

I was inside an enormous circle, the cardinal points of which were stationed by four metaphysical projections of Æthyric demons who represented four elements. The projections were also unstable; they occasionally disappeared altogether, only to remanifest a second later.

"She's awake."

My vision left a blurry trail as I moved my head toward the voice.

It came from my father, now dressed in an elaborately decorated ritual robe; my mother stood next to him wearing much the same. Handwritten symbols streaked across their necks. They were smiling, and their faces looked red and blurry. I shook my head, attempting to get rid of the obstruction in front of my eyes. It clung to my face like a spiderweb.

"What are you doing?" I asked. My voice echoed weakly, going nowhere and traveling for miles at the same time. "Why did you dose me? Who were those people chasing us?"

"Probably the caliph. He's been tracking us through our guardians for the last week." My father smiled, then added, "As if we wouldn't notice. Don't worry, though. We warded you on our way over here and temporarily banished our guardians—no bread crumbs for him to follow now."

And no deflector charm to protect me, either, thanks to the events at the Hellfire caves. I did my best to sober myself up, but whatever they'd used to drug me was laced with magick. "Why am I here?"

My mother floated in front of me like a dream. "Seléne . . . you're here to fulfill your destiny. You have returned to us like Malkuth returns to Kether."

"We didn't realize the role you would eventually play all those years ago when we conceived you," my dad explained, "but Frater Blue enlightened us."

"What the hell are you talking about? Who's Frater Blue?"

My father's hand gestured to the praying man outside the circle. "Does he not look familiar to you? He was present when you were conceived."

The mage who presided over the Moonchild ritual? That name didn't sound right. "I thought that was Frater Oben? Who is Frater Blue? Is that another magical name, or another member of the E∴E∴?"

"A rogue magician," my mother said. "We met him in Dallas a couple of years before you were born."

"You lied to the caliph? Why did you tell him it was another mage?"

My dad laughed. "Work with someone outside the order? We'd have been expelled."

I didn't think that was true; the caliph had been okay with the fact that I'd worked with other magicians over the last few years. Or was that a lie? Confusion clouded my thoughts. I strained to see the robed man, this Frater Blue. He had light-colored hair. Maybe white. I couldn't tell. Wait . . .

the Tamlins, the crazy couple in San Francisco who told me about the glass talon and the mystery man they saw running from the crime scene in Portland . . . was Frater Blue the man who committed the murders? The man who conjured the white demon? I laughed out loud. Surely it was the drug talking. I was making connections that weren't there.

"Why is he here, Frater Blue? Why are we all here? What are you doing?"

A soft night breeze fluttered my mother's graying hair. "Magick requires patience and time. Rituals take too long. All the summonings and spells require manual work." She spoke dramatically, with an intensity behind her eyes. Like she was giving a speech to an audience at some occult gathering. I'd sat through more of those speeches than I could remember when I was a teenager. "Technology improves and science continually advances," she continued. "But we use the same crude techniques that were used a thousand years ago. We've made no progress. Humans no longer use typewriters, they use computers—magicians use the same crushed minerals. We labor to draw the same old symbols to conjure and control the Æthryic spirits one at a time."

My father chimed in, cheeks flush with excitement and the warmth of the fire spirit behind us. "We tried to get people to think outside the box, but no one wanted to change. Everyone was happy with the status quo."

"They won't be now," my mother said. "Because we can finally prove to them that progress is possible. With your powers inside of us, we will have an army of demons at our disposal, instantly. There is no need for any of *this*." She gestured toward the hand-carved ritual circle surrounding us. "The old ways can stay in the past. We will tear down the tower and build a new aeon. We will change the world."

They sounded like crazy people. I fell into their semantic trap, though, unable to see past the words.

"You always said ritual was important. You made me learn all the old ways . . . *I'm* the one who thought outside the box. I experimented with spells and mixed traditions—not you." The red spiderweb was tickling my nose. I tried to blow an upward breath to push it away.

My father leaned in close. "We wanted you to have all the knowledge within you, but it's your birthright that makes you think differently."

"That stupid Moonchild bullshit?" I said, as fury rose up in me.

"Do not curse, Seléne," my mother scolded. "It is unfitting for a messiah."

"I'm not a messiah."

"Of course you are. Everyone believed in the beginning, when you were a child, but their faith wavered when they became impatient for results. They doubted us. Talked behind our backs."

My father nodded. "They made us doubt it too. When your powers didn't manifest at puberty, we were all confused. We waited and hoped for several years, but nothing happened. You wore the silver crown of the messiah, but did not wield her power."

"Who cares? Why are you talking about all this crazy stuff? What about the council? I came to prove your innocence—the Luxe Order will start a war if we don't."

My father laughed. "Let them! Once the ritual is complete tonight, there won't be a single magician in the world who will doubt us or wield enough power to stop us."

"Besides," my mother added in a practical voice, "we aren't innocent."

I looked back and forth between them, my altered vision making it hard for me to differentiate who was who.

"We killed the three," my mother said . . . or maybe my father. "Our plan was to kill all five heads of the major orders, but we were sloppy."

"You—"

"When you didn't manifest the Moonchild powers, it hurt our reputation as magicians. No one believed in our abilities anymore. People stopped inviting us to conferences to speak. Our book sales declined. Your father lost his job."

"We realized that we had to do something big to shake things up," my dad explained. "You don't build a new city without razing the old one. And we tore it all down."

My world began shattering. As pieces broke off, I tried my best to catch them before they were lost forever, but it was happening too fast. "Tore what down?"

"The entire occult community!" My father swept his hand across his throat. "We tried to get the orders to unite under a larger umbrella—"

"What?" I said in disbelief. "You killed those people because they wouldn't back your stupid United Occult Order? You can't be serious."

"No, this is much bigger. It stands to reason if you take out the leaders, the order weakens. So in that regard, we succeeded. But we were also experimenting with an old, rare spell. One that Frater Blue helped us find. It enabled us to siphon the Heka from dying magicians and absorb it into ourselves."

I recalled the white demon's goetia entry: *She can be forced to answer those questions regarding the Harvesting of Æthyric energy.* Dear God, they were using her to harvest Heka from the murder victims?

"This increased our Heka reserves and created chaos

among the orders at the same time—killed two birds with one stone, so to speak." My father gave me his used-car-salesman smile; I thought I might be sick. "And it worked beautifully. We are *so* much stronger from conducting those rituals. We'd be even stronger if the Luxe Order hadn't meddled. That ruined everything."

My mother nodded with a pained expression, remembering. "It was a terrible time for your father and me. We felt as if we'd failed twice. Once in conceiving you, and then the Black Lodge scandal . . ."

"I was a mistake?"

My father shook his head. "That's what we thought, but we were wrong. You, little butterfly, were not a failure at all, but our greatest success. Once we left you in the States, we found a cache of old grimoires in France. And that's where we discovered a journal kept by a magician and his wife in the twelfth century. They completed the Moonchild ritual, and like us, thought it failed. But they had expected results too soon. The power wasn't supposed to manifest at puberty. It came later."

My mother pressed her hands together. "You are a modified human, able to evoke beings from the Æthyr at will. Able to control them without drawing the messy seals. Inside, you have the ability to summon not *one* demon, but an entire army! Imagine that—an entire legion of servants ready to do your bidding. A god's power inside a human body. You, my love, are progress."

"The new Aeon," my father announced proudly. "Your power will allow us to usher in a new age. An Aeon ruled not by the laws of earth and man, but by the laws of the cosmos and the strength of the Æthyr! Your birth was engineered to save this world. Transform it. *Cleanse* it."

"Oh my God, you're both out of your fucking minds!"

I said, laughing hysterically. "I'm not progress—your stupid Moonchild ritual didn't work! I've got a halo and can see Earthbounds. Big deal. I still have to do the spells the same old way anyone else does them—by hand. And . . ." I instantly realized my error. "The incubus in the Hellfire caves. I was using Heka to kindle moon power . . ."

My mother straightened her robes, smoothing out the lines around her waist. "You've had only a taste of it. As we learned from that twelfth-century grimoire, your powers don't fully manifest until you're mature. The age of your magical maturity, twenty-five, will occur in . . . fifteen minutes."

Twenty-five. Traditionally, there is a public ritual marking a magical adept's twenty-fifth birthday. The symbolic coming-of-age, like a quinceañera or bar mitzvah.

"We realized a way to bring everything together. Learned from our mistakes." My mother's brows darted up in smug excitement. "Siphoning Heka from other mundane magicians wasn't enough. But we could apply the same technique to siphon something much more important."

My father lowered his head to look me in the eyes. "We've watched you over the years, you know. Through our guardians. You had a chance to make something of yourself. You didn't have your full powers, but you had an advantage in your gift of preternatural sight. Instead of using this, you wasted it. A bar, Seléne? Really?"

"You're soft. It's our fault. We coddled you."

"We did warn you many times that emotional bonds create weakness," my father said. "Yet all you've done is settle into a normal life, surrounding yourself with people. And then, not even people, but *Earthbounds*? Demons are tools to be used and controlled. They are not our equals." He shook his head. "We realized when your mother visited you in Seattle a few years ago that no amount of power would matter if you were that empathetic and soft."

My mother nodded her head emphatically. "The world doesn't need another benevolent goddess. It needs a fierce gardener to rip out the weeds. You were no longer our messiah, and we couldn't play the roles of Mary and Joseph publicly with everyone shouting 'killers.'"

"But it all happened for a reason. We learned from our errors. And that's why we're here. Everything will turn out just fine after all. Patience and time were all we needed." My father grasped my mother's face in his hands and kissed her.

The drug was wearing off. I could feel my heart squeezing, and it beat faster than a hummingbird's. My pulse throbbed at my wrists. I tried to blow away the red obstruction again, then looked down. The spiderweb was a thin, red transparent shroud. I was naked underneath. The shroud covered my head and fell to the ground, weighted down at the bottom by a series of metal beads sewn into the hem.

I was standing inside a strange metal object. Several feet in diameter, it looked like a giant communion bowl with a flat lip around the outside that was etched with symbols. I tried to read them. Rebirth, sacred, transference . . . sacrifice. It was an oracular bowl.

It was used to catch sacrificial blood.

Panicking, I tried to move, but my arms were bound. I was tied to a metal pole affixed to the bowl below me.

"You're going to kill me?" I demanded in a shaky voice.

My father looked over at me, breaking away from the kiss, taking my mother's hand in his. "We're going to transfer your power to us through a short ritual. I'm sorry, but there is no other way. You are too weak to wield that kind of power. We have no choice but to take it from you."

"It would be irresponsible to let it decay," my mother agreed. "This is bigger than all of us."

"And the only way we can siphon your ability is to harvest it when it's captured in the blood, right as the soul lifts from the body."

"There is no shame in sacrifice," my mother added. "Just because you couldn't fulfill your destiny as our messiah doesn't mean your life is wasted. Don't you see? Once we realized that you weren't suited to keep the Moonchild power, and once we realized that the siphoning spell could harvest more than Heka, it all fit together neatly. We are all redeemed. Your power will live on in us, giving back to us . . . just as we lived on in your body, like we gave you life. It's a fair exchange, and please know it's done in love."

"Love?" I repeated.

I began shaking uncontrollably, sobbing, screaming. My life, my family, it was all a sham. They thought of me as a possession right from the beginning? Something they created that failed? And now they were nothing but pathological killers, and I'd wasted my adult life in hiding, believing that they were innocent . . . that they loved me.

How could I have been so blind? My head felt like it was splitting open as dark recollections began surfacing, piling on top of one another, spinning. The memories that Lon saw in his visions solidified in my head.

The caliph hadn't been the enemy. Half-remembrances tangled in my brain, quiet moments of him talking to me when I was a teenager, after my parents were wallowing in self-created shame, thinking that their reputation was ruined because they'd failed to bring a real Moonchild into the world. The caliph told me many times that it didn't matter, and that he loved me anyway. The dream Lon had . . . My mother had been arguing with the caliph because he must have suspected something was wrong. Maybe he knew they were hiding something. Maybe he suspected that they were sick in the head.

"Did the caliph know you killed the other leaders of the orders?" I asked.

My mother smiled. "He was suspicious, so we did a little spellwork on him. Something to confuse the mind."

"You performed that spell on me, too, didn't you?"

"On you?" She shook her head. "No need. Your loyalty to us kept you blind. The caliph, however, we had to control by force."

My mother then explained that they didn't know what to do with me after they were accused of the murders. They knew that they had to run, and I was baggage, weighing them down. Useless baggage, because they hadn't yet come across the twelfth-century Moonchild journal. It was easiest for the caliph to watch over me. He always doted on me, they said, so it was simple to persuade him to accept the responsibility once they'd cast the confusion spell on him to eliminate any lingering suspicion or doubts he might have had concerning their motives.

"Unfortunately," my mom lamented, "that particular spell was not permanent. It fades with time. We are not sure whether the caliph's spell began waning, or if he underwent a counterspell to remove it, but something changed recently. Anyway, it doesn't matter now."

Whatever happened must have occurred before they were spotted in Dallas, because now it struck me that the caliph hadn't sent me after the albino demon to prove their *innocence*—he wanted me to find it to *prove they were guilty*. "The albino demon. Nivella," I whispered.

"Oh, *oui*. We found the talon and seal in your clothes,"

my mother said. "How did you find out about Nivella? We didn't tell anyone about her."

"You lied to Caliph Superior—gave him a bad description of the demon," I realized.

"Of course," my father replied. "We couldn't have him snooping around and digging her up. She helped us with all the siphonings."

"Siphonings? You mean *murders*."

"Well, that's why we removed the talon, so no one else could conjure her and find out what we were doing. It also served as a beautiful ritual dagger. When it was confiscated, we had to search for another demon with the same power. It took us years, but we found one, and were prepared to summon her tonight, but now that you've brought us Nivella's talon, we can just use her. Better the devil you know, yes?"

"How did you piece together that we'd originally used Nivella?" my mother asked.

"The Tamlins."

My parents looked at each other in disbelief. "The confusion spell—"

"They had it removed," I said. "Mostly."

My father nodded in understanding. "Not a particularly bright couple. We thought about killing the Tamlins when they caught us in Portland during the third siphoning, but they weren't worth the effort. Not enough Heka to even consider harvesting."

"They still think you're innocent."

"Regardless, we might need to pay them a little visit soon to keep them quiet." My father shrugged. "Almost time now." He smiled and turned to Frater Blue and gave him a silent signal. The man stepped inside the circle and lifted the hood of his robe.

Panic sobered me. I screamed at the top of my lungs.

"Calm down, don't wear yourself out," my father said. "We're deep inside Balboa Park, off a private hiking trail. There's no one for miles. The ritual will go smoother if you remain calm and centered."

"How could you do this?" I sobbed, tears blinding me, stinging my eyes. "I'm your daughter. You loved me—I know you did. Why did you stop?"

"Darling," my mother said, moving her hand near my cheek but not touching me, "how many times have we told you that strong emotions are weakness? That's not to say we don't care. We planned your conception. Meticulous, careful planning. You weren't just an accident or a result of some unplanned erotic passion, like most savages are."

"I was the result of some stupid, loveless ritual—that's worse!"

"No, you are very mistaken, it was not loveless, and we were so happy when you were born. We treated you like a goddess. Gave you every tool you could need to be successful and enjoy the life that you were given. We were good parents."

"Good parents don't kill their children after raising them!"

"It's an honorable death," my father argued. "Not a wasted one. People die honorably for their country in war every day. How could dying for this be any less?"

He said this like it was the most reasonable thing in the world. And instead of being repulsed by the motive behind the words, all I could think about was trying to get back what I'd lost. Raw, painful sobbing hobbled my reasoning. And I snapped, racked by memories of better times.

"I can change," I pleaded. "I can be what you need me to be. Whatever you envisioned, you can teach me. I can learn." A shadow crossed my mother's eyes. Emotion. I know I saw it. "You can take me overseas with you. I can stay hidden. I've never been caught, not in seven years. I'm smart. I can . . ." What? What would I do? "I can help you start your new Aeon. I'll summon whatever you want. Please. Give me a chance to show you."

For a moment, just a moment, I thought I might have reached her. Thought I spotted some spark of motherly instinct inside her that would override her insanity. But then my father touched her shoulder, whispering something low in French that I couldn't hear. And her face hardened along with her will.

"There is no shame in this," my father said gently. "It is a beautiful gift, what you are giving us today, and we are grateful for it."

My head spun as madness overtook me, and I screamed again. It reverberated off the rocky hill and echoed around the dark trees, the only witnesses to the my last breaths.

"Shh, now. Calm and centered," my father repeated.

Calm and centered? Ironically, it was good advice. Begging them to spare me had been weak and pathetic. A mistake made in desperation. I had to pull myself together. Focus. This was no time to fall apart. If I could survive, I'd have time for that later.

I compartmentalized my panic and surveyed my escape options.

The bonds around my hands and ankles were too tight to break. Maybe my wards? I tried to spit on my arm to activate one of them—*any* of them—but my mouth was dry from the drugs they gave me; what little saliva I could muster just stuck to the red shroud or trickled down my upper arm, stopping far above my elbow.

There was no electricity nearby. I reached out, straining

to pull anything at all, but came up empty; we were too deep in the woods. And Priya was dead, so I had no guardian to call for help. My mind flashed back to the incubus in the caves. He gave me his name, Voxhele of Amon. I could summon him. But why? How could he help? Offer to have sex with my parents to distract them? Useless.

Think, think. What else?

The caliph was trailing my parents, they'd said. Could he have been one of the people running out of the Luxe temple? It probably didn't matter; we were hidden and warded.

Then there was Lon . . . He'd begged me to let him come with me that morning, and I'd foolishly told him no. Stubborn, he'd called me. He was frustrated and angry; but I insisted, and he didn't argue. This memory kick-started another round of tears. Everything he'd done for me, the time and work, the money he'd spent. It was all for nothing. Apart from that, I was losing him, and Jupe, and I'd only just found them. My aching heart shriveled.

Years of lukewarm relationships, noncommittal and joyless, lined my stomach like a lead weight. No happiness, no friends, no love, all because of my parents.

Hiding from the law, living a lie . . .

While they were running around scheming up crazy rituals to harvest some stupid power from me, I put my life on hold and lived in fear and silence. I ran from *their* enemies—the Luxe Order, Riley Cooper . . . I took the brunt of it for my parents. Their sins, not mine, but I paid for them. Me! How stupid was I?

"One minute," my father whispered to my mother as they took prearranged places in front of me.

I was out of options. Broken. They won. Nothing I could say or do would stop them.

But just as I'd accepted my fate, a light flashed. Not in my head, but out in the woods.

It floated and moved like a torch in the distance.

Flames bobbed and flickered.

It was a halo on fire.

37

I didn't know how, and I didn't care; hope sprang through me.

Oh, Lon, I thought, *please let that be you. My parents are crazy. They killed all those people and they're going to sacrifice me. I'm so sorry for dragging you into this mess.*

As soon as I finished my thought, the fiery halo went out.

I choked on a sob.

Maybe it wasn't him after all.

My father sauntered to the edge of chalk circle with something in his hands. Intoning a spell—not in Latin or English, but in some Æthyric language—he walked the circle. As he did, Frater Blue followed.

My father blew a breath onto the triangle that held the winged demon. The air around it got brighter. Then he walked behind me, repeating the incantation. Next was the watery female demon at the western point; he sprinkled liquid on her triangle to lighten it. Last, dirt was scattered on the demon with the barklike skin who represented earth. Not only did that triangle get brighter, but my father yelled out the spell and threw Heka down at the ground. The entire circle roared to life.

A blue glow emerged from the earth and spread over our heads like a gigantic umbrella, enclosing all of us inside a dome of light.

The circle was now fortified; it couldn't be breached from the outside. Not by a person, or even a gunshot.

"Let us begin," my father announced.

He dropped what he was holding and picked up the glass talon. My mother joined him and they approached me, strutting like deranged peacocks, both wearing horrible, repugnant smiles. Whatever image I'd once had of my parents, I couldn't reconcile it with the two alien beings standing before me. My family was gone. Lost. Dead. Worse: I'd never really had one at all.

Frater Blue's robed figure moved around the inner edge of the circle, vibrating with a low noise. A background spell, an underpainting to serve as the base for the layers of the main incantation.

My father began droning the Æthyric words to his ritual.

"*Oh-ele sohnef vorereh heg-heh. Goho-he iehadah bal eh teh.*"

I wriggled desperately against my bindings, then tried to rock the entire oracular bowl with my body. It gave ever so slightly, scraping against the rocky ground below me. My mother put her bare foot on top of the rim to still it. I growled at her, but neither one of them made eye contact with me.

"*Koh meh mateh—*"

"Fuck you!" I spat. "Fuck both of you . . . you . . . lunatics!"

"*Ah-deh nah gorgan-mal—*"

"I hope you both burn in hell." Angry tears ran down my face.

Movement outside the circle caught my eye. Three dark figures appeared at the top of the rocky hill outside the circle. My heart rammed against my chest. *Please . . .*

The caliph was the first. The head of the Luxe Order—Riley's father, Magus Zorn—was the second. And the third? Lon.

A wave of wild joy broke over me, but this was soon tempered when my mother turned her head to peer over her shoulder. She saw them, but she didn't react. Didn't care. All she did was nod at my father to continue. Cold terror trickled down my spine.

"*Oh-reh kalheh, zod a dehess—*"

The caliph was the first to approach the circle, calling out as he galloped down the hill. "Enola! Alexander! Stop this right now," he hollered.

My parents didn't look up. My mom just squeezed my dad's hand harder.

"This is lunacy!" the caliph said. A ghostly shape trailed him . . . his guardian. They stopped at the dome of light around the circle, and the caliph reached out to touch it with his hand. The fortified barrier sparked, and he flew backward, tumbling to the ground with a yelp, his guardian disappearing when he did.

"*Kahsah reh zod-heh bessmah—*"

"You can't breach it from the outside," I shouted.

Magus Zorn, the leader of our rival order and the man I'd believed to be my enemy all these years, reached to help the caliph back on his feet. Everything was wrong. Backward. I began to feel dizzy, until my focus shifted to the gold and green light behind them.

Lon walked the edge of the circle. We locked gazes. No pity darkened his face. No anger, either. No emotion at all. In the midst of all the craziness around me, the sight of his deadpan countenance calmed me. I took in shaky, labored breaths, forcing myself to extend them as long as I could, never taking my eyes off him.

"It can't be breached or broken from the outside." My voice was rough and strained as I spoke directly to him over the drone of the ritual words. "Not by anything physical. Nothing."

I tilted my head as something pierced the fog of my drug-addled brain.

"Not from the outside," I repeated. But if someone on the *inside* were to step out of the circle, it would break. I was bound, so I couldn't, and my parents would never step outside. Their eyes were shut. They were nearly in a trance, lost in the ritual.

Not me, not them . . . but what about Frater Blue? I hesitated, wavering. It was risky. Outside the circle, Lon was safe. I was already doomed, and there was no guarantee that he could save me, even if he was able to break the ward. What if they hurt him? They were psychotic killers and would clearly have no problem doing whatever it took to get my power. Maybe he would be better off if I just told him to leave.

But before I could weigh my uncertainty, Lon closed his eyes. A ripple distorted the blue light of the ward where he was standing. Like an ignited pyre, his halo flared up behind his head, and his horns began emerging. Zorn and the caliph looked up at him with a quiet awe. They couldn't see his halo, but they obviously spotted his horns. Yet they handled the transformation without fuss or protest; I wagered they'd already seen him do it.

He didn't look at me after he'd shifted. My nerves stretched like thin wire as he calmly marched around the outer edge of the circle and stopped near Frater Blue. It happened so fast. I saw Lon's mouth moving, and frantically wondered if he could he manipulate Frater Blue without touching him. The answer to that was reflected in Frater Blue's face when it drew up in fear.

"*Qeh-noh koheh dah—*"

My mother's eyes opened, drawing my attention away from Lon. She kneeled down in front of me. Her fingers lifted the hem of the shroud off the ground and gathered it up into her hands as she stood. If I hadn't been naked enough before, I was now. She pulled the shroud over my head like I was bride about to be kissed, exposed and humiliated, insult to injury. I spit in her face. Anger flared as she squeezed her eyes shut. But she merely wiped it away, then stepped back.

My attention flicked back to Lon. Frater Blue stood staring at him, his back to me. I couldn't tell what was going on. Lon's chest was heaving. He was mumbling something to himself. Frater Blue's head jerked around. He peered outside the circle at the caliph, eyes filling with panic.

My mother took the glass talon from my father's hand; the sharp point gleamed in the circle's charged light. She brought it to my breastbone and pressed down. The tip punctured my skin, stinging as she slowly slid it down between my breasts.

"*Oh-reh-reh-heh. Oh-reh-reh-heh,*" my father chanted, louder and louder.

Blood welled as the talon slashed. I gasped in pain. In shock. In disbelief. My hands tingled; my vision swam. I was on the verge of passing out when a sound roused me. With bleary eyes, I glanced beyond my mother to see Frater Blue smacking his hands against his ears. He abandoned his droning dirge and cried out, lunging forward with outstretched arms. The moment his foot crossed the circle, the domed blue ward fizzled, then broke into millions of tiny blue stars.

Like dying fireflies, they furiously blinked out of sync, then imploded.

Lon did it! He broke the fucking ward. Frater Blue was kneeling in front of Lon, pleading and crying. Whatever Lon had told him, he believed it. And I was so distracted by the spectacle that when my father's continued chanting registered in my ears—when I looked down and saw the glass talon still tearing through my skin—I was stunned.

My parents weren't stopping. Nothing had changed. Ward or no ward, they were going to finish this.

The crimson line between my breasts got longer. Warm blood streamed down my belly.

"*OH-REH-REH-HEH . . . KANILA.*"

An alarm beeped on my father's wristwatch.

Midnight.

38

It was a standard summoning. My father paused the incantation to perform it in the center of the circle, where I'd failed to recognize the large binding triangle and seal carved into the dirt, the channels filled with what was likely red ochre. Maybe even hematite powder, like Lon had used for my house ward.

A disturbance churned the air over the seal. The white demon was coming. Hot blood dripped down my legs as I waited for her to appear and answer my parents' bidding. To harvest me. I didn't want to watch the demon materialize, but I couldn't close my eyes either.

Then something clicked inside my head: If this Moonchild ability was so powerful that it was worth killing me to obtain, then *what exactly could it do*? Could it trump their summoning? Even without the glass talon in my possession? I had no idea, but it *was* after midnight, and what did I have to lose by trying? I'd already lost everything anyway . . .

I rallied my determination and tilted my face to the moon. The same way I reached out for electricity, I willed the ability to manifest.

And it came like a bullet.

Every hair on my head immediately lifted and whipped

around my face, charged with some sort of strange static; the red shroud, bunched around my shoulders and neck, fell away to the ground. Power hummed around me. My mother cried out. She flinched away from me, the bloodied glass talon gripped tight in her hand. Her eyes fixed on mine, and in that moment I saw realization . . . and fear.

The forest fell away into a black ocean. The rocky hill, gone; the ground below, swallowed. Only the people and the charged sigils remained. My mother, father, Lon—all of them—glowed like X-rays in the darkness, transparent as the Æthryic demons trapped at the cardinal points of the circle. They were stars floating in space.

Heka poured out of me, then like a crack of lightning, returned, kindled. It surged inside me, ready to be wielded. I couldn't have stopped it if I tried. Somewhere in front of me a bright pinpoint of light glinted in the black void. Vivid electric blue. A thrill rose up in my chest at the sight of it.

This was my power. This was what my parents wanted. Their new Aeon of magick. The summoning symbols didn't have to be written out by hand. I made them appear, just like I did back in the Hellfire caves with the incubus.

I spotted movement; Lon's transparent form was dashing toward me, his fiery halo crackling around his head like white fire. "Get back!" I warned. He stopped immediately, with Frater Blue cowering at his heels.

My father's charged summoning seal illuminated the ground; something was manifesting in the space above it, obscuring the sigils so that I couldn't read them. But it didn't matter. I pictured it clearly in my mind, just as I'd memorized it. And I willed it onto the blue circle of light. Black shapes fell away, leaving behind a scrolling map of bright blue ancient sigils.

The white demon's form was almost solid inside my father's summoning circle.

Time was up. I reached out with my mind . . . and pushed.

The blue seal spun on its side and crashed down onto the ground. Moon-kindled Heka streamed out of me, faster than the blood flowing down my body from the open wound on my breast.

"NIVELLA THE WHITE," I screamed at the top of my lungs.

The black void disappeared.

And when it did, Nivella flickered out of my father's seal, and reappeared smack in the middle of my blue trap.

A chorus of startled cries rang out around the circle.

Twice my height, she had skin so pale that her muscles and organs were visible beneath. She opened two large pink eyes and blinked. Her horns spiraled high over her head, just as they were drawn in the engraving in Lon's book. She stretched four arms out like Kali ready for battle. Long, thin fingers stretched on her hands, each tipped with white claws. But in the place of her index fingers were crystal talons. Three. The fourth hand bore a stump of hollow flesh, its missing talon in my mother's shaking hand.

"Who summoned me?" Nivella asked in an unfamiliar voice that skittered down my spine. I caught a glimpse of her serpentine tongue.

My father's neck craned to see the demon as my mother dropped the glass talon. It rolled on the ground near her feet, leaving a trail of my blood behind.

"I did," my father called out to the white beast.

Nivella tilted her head, puzzled, and looked at my father.

"No, you did not," she replied without emotion. "But I remember you, mage."

"I called you," I shouted.

Nivella's eyes blinked slowly, then fixed on me.

"Mother of Ahrimam," she said, bowing her head reverently. "How may I serve you?"

Holy fucking shit. How many times had I heard that phrase and assumed the worst? It wasn't a slur—it was a title of respect. What the hell had my parents drawn down from the Æthyr when they conceived me? Did they even know?

No time for that. The more pressing question was something much simpler: What in the world did I want from Nivella? Now that I had her, I didn't know what to request. My mind emptied, then flashed back on the original reason I'd spent the last couple of weeks hunting her ass down. She was a witness. And though I wished like hell that she could recount a story with a different ending, I had to hear it.

"Do you know the couple in front of me?" I asked.

She glanced at my father, then my mother. "Yes, I know them. They summoned me many times, years ago."

"For what reasons?"

"They questioned me the first two times I was summoned. The third time, they took my talon by force and trickery. The next three times, they called me to aid in the harvest of Æthyric energy."

"How?"

"The woman slaughtered three people with my stolen talon and I collected the energy at the moment of death and fed it into the couple."

"Enola," the caliph cried. "You were one of my favorite adepts. Your parents would roll over in their graves if they could see what you've become."

The Luxe leader stepped forward to stand beside the caliph. "I demand your parents' lives," Magus Zorn said in an icy voice, "as payment for the atrocities they've committed against the occult community."

"No," Nivella said, her voice sharp. "*I* demand the lives of this couple as payment for deformation and harm to my corporeal body. They stole what was mine. I want it back, and I want their lives with it."

My father backed away. Lon blurred past him, darted down, and scooped up the glass talon at my mother's feet. Her leg flew out to kick it from his hand, but he jerked back in time. Frater Blue, still under Lon's sway, put himself between them to defend Lon. With a wild growl, my mother's head snapped back in my direction.

"*OH-REH-REH-HEH!*" she screamed, her voice high and crazed.

One of her hands flew around my neck, choking me. She straightened the fingers on her other hand and reared back, as if she meant to crack open my bleeding wound and rip out my heart. But before she could, Lon grabbed her hair and snatched back her head violently. Her body snapped with it, as if her bones were made of rubber. He flung her roughly to the ground. The angry screeching sound she was making abruptly stopped. She didn't get up.

My father called out in anguish and ran to my mother's aid, but the caliph tripped him as he passed, sending my father skidding across the ground. He attempted to push himself up, but he was too slow. The caliph shoved his face into the dirt. Magus Zorn dropped to his knees, and together, he and the caliph both pinned my father to the ground.

"Hold still," Lon murmured near my side. He flipped the glass talon in his hand and crouched to slice through my bonds. Within seconds, my ankles and wrists sprung free. I stumbled and teetered on wobbly legs as Lon steadied me. I rubbed my wrists as Lon stripped the shroud off my head and threw it to the ground. He inspected my wound, stretching out his T-shirt to stanch the blood, then murmured a quick assessment. "Not deep."

Nivella's pink eyes peered down at me from a smooth face framed in white scales. "Give me the lives of these people as retribution, Mother. Those are the rules."

Were those the rules? I hadn't *personally* made a pact with Nivella; therefore, I had broken no pact. Right?

"Your occult community holds a child accountable for a parents' debts if the parents don't pay them," Lon whispered in my ear. He'd been listening to my thoughts. "It's the same in the Æthyr. This is an old demon who follows old rules."

My stomach knotted. I glanced at my mother's limp body on the ground. Her arm twitched and a soft groan fell from her lips as she tried to move her head. My father was still struggling under the caliph. Even then, despite everything that was happening—everything they'd revealed—I was desperately thinking of a way to justify what they'd done, to forgive them or excuse them. After all, they were clearly insane. It wasn't the first time I'd seen another magician derailed. All that power has a way of worming its way inside your head, making you feel invincible and above the law. And didn't I feel that way too? Hadn't I spent the last seven years living as fugitive? Maybe I was no better, so how could I judge them?

Lon gripped my chin and got in my face, anger blazing in his eyes. "No," he barked. "You are not like them. Hear me?"

"What do I do?" I whispered.

His face softened as he slowly shook his head. "I can't tell you that."

Of course he couldn't. I quickly sobered. This was my problem, not his. My responsibility. And there was no returning from this. My parents weren't just sick, they were beyond salvaging. No doctor would be able to rehabilitate them; they'd only escape. Hurt anybody who got in their way. The decision clutched my heart and wrung it dry, but I knew it was what had to be done.

"Magus Zorn," I asked as a swell of tears blurred my vision, "will the other orders consider their debt paid if I let the demon take them?"

"Yes, I will see to it," he said. "All blood debts will be void."

"Nivella the White," I shouted, "You can take the couple along with Frater Blue back to the Æthyr as payment on the condition that you consider the debt paid. Do we have a deal?"

Frater Blue squawked a protest and tried to bolt, but Lon grabbed him and forced him to the ground with my mother.

"What about my talon?" Nivella said.

"I'll keep it for now," I decided. If I had the talon, no one else could summon her; I reasoned that it was probably safer this way. "Do we have a deal?"

She paused for a long moment, considering, then nodded her head. "You have my word. Unbind me now and let me take what is mine."

Not really knowing if it would work, I willed the blue binding to break. Nothing happened at first; but after I strained harder, it finally loosened and disappeared, leaving behind the summoning seal.

Nivella's long white legs ghosted over the ground as she strode toward my mother's waking form. Lon bent down, unzipped my mother's robe, and unceremoniously wrenched it down over her shoulders, tugging it off her body. "She won't be needing this," he said, bringing it back to me. My mother groaned and protested groggily as Nivella picked up her nude body with all four arms and slung her over a broad, white shoulder. Lon whispered something to Frater Blue, who whimpered and went limp as Nivella grabbed him. I watched as the demon lugged them both back to my blue seal and tossed them inside one at a time. Then I had to look away.

Lon touched my elbow and held the robe out. My mother's scent lingered on the fabric, but it wasn't comforting, it was foreign. A stranger's scent.

"How did you find me?" I whispered as he helped me step into the robe.

"I lied. I had a dream last night. Your memories. I knew you wouldn't believe me until you saw it yourself, but I didn't know it would go this far."

I zipped up the robe and nodded.

"And like I told you this morning, Five is a much faster drive," he elaborated, with a weary grin.

As Nivella approached, the caliph and Magus Zorn both jumped off my father. The coward tried to get up and run, but the demon snagged him by the legs and dragged him toward the seal. She continued to hold onto him once she'd stepped inside.

She turned in my direction. "Summon me when you are ready to return my talon, Mother."

"Seléne!" my father screamed, his eyes crazed and filled with hate.

"My name is Arcadia now."

"We created you—you belong to us!"

"Not anymore," I murmured.

And with those words standing as my good-bye, I shouted a banishing spell.

Everything in the circle disappeared: the elementals, my parents, Frater Blue, and the white beast. All that was left behind was a cloud of shimmering blue light that fell to the ground like the last firework on the Fourth of July.

39

"What's that one there?"

"Which one?"

Jupe sighed impatiently, lying in the grass to my left. "Can't you see where I'm pointing? The one that goes in a straight line right there." His bent knee knocked against my leg, keeping time with his restless energy.

"That's part of Orion. She already told you that twice. You'd better be paying more attention in school than you are out here," Lon complained in the grass to my right. *His* bent leg, calm and still, pressed firmly against mine. His arm was also spread out beneath my neck, serving as a pillow. The three of us lay together in Lon's backyard at the edge of their rustic garden of Eden, looking out over the ocean.

Jupe reached over me to sucker-punch Lon in the gut. Retaliation came as a swift, fat pinch on Jupe's chest. He yowled and buckled, then snickered.

"Boys!" I chastised, grabbing both their arms. "Don't make me break this up or you'll be sorry."

"Pfft. I'm sorry already," Jupe said, grinning.

"Where's Mr. Piggy?" I asked.

"Oh, shit. I mean shoot. Wait, here he is." Jupe sat up

and reached down by his feet, picking up the hedgehog and placing him on his chest after he lay back down. Foxglove moved so that she could better watch the hedgehog; she was awfully suspicious of the miniature visitor on her turf. "Hey, do you think Mr. Piggy would be stupid enough to fall off the cliff if we just let him roam around out here?"

"Yeah, I do, and if I find out he's committed hedgie suicide, I'll be really angry and blame it on you."

Jupe lay his head on my shoulder as he moved Mr. Piggy closer to his face. "Calm down, woman. No need to get hysterical. I'm watching him."

I wrapped my arm around his head and smacked his forehead lightly. He giggled as I pushed his thick curls out of my face, combing them back with my fingers. I held one curl out—it tripled in length—then let it spring back into place.

"Why don't you just leave him here?" Jupe suggested. "He can stay in my room. I'll keep the door shut so he can't escape."

"No," Lon and I said together. Visions of Mr. Piggy being trampled under Jupe's dirty laundry filled my head.

"Go put him up in his crate," Lon said, checking his watch. "It's ten thirty. Why don't you get ready for bed?"

"Can he spend the night in my room if I promise not to let him out of his crate?"

"Okay," I agreed, "but just tonight. I'm taking him back home with me tomorrow."

Jupe stood and held Mr. Piggy in his hand. He rocketed toward the deck, clicking his tongue at Foxglove to follow.

"Don't run with him, Jupe. It makes him dizzy."

"Oops." He slowed and climbed the stairs, pausing midway. "Hey, are you coming up to watch the late shows?"

"Just until midnight." I stretched my legs out in front of me. "But only if you brush your teeth. Your breath smells like a sewer."

He laughed and headed inside.

Lon rolled to his side, grunting, and threw his free arm around my middle, his leg over my thighs. "You working a full shift tomorrow?"

"Yeah. For the next three nights. Did you take that shoot in Phoenix?"

"Hmm-mmm. I'm leaving tomorrow morning. I'll be gone two nights. If you could call and check in on Jupe after school, he'd appreciate it."

"Yep."

"Oh, and Mrs. Holiday has a doctor's appointment to-morrow. Can you take Jupe to school in the morning?"

"Christ, can't the boy get to school on his own?"

"The buses won't come up here. The city says the main road is dangerous. One stops at a house at the base of the cliff to pick up two other kids. You can drop him off there if you're willing to listen to Jupe bitch and whine."

"Not cool enough?"

"Only losers ride the bus, apparently. One week early this year I made him walk down the cliff to catch it as punish-ment, until I got a call from the principal's office. Two hours later I found him playing hooky at his friend Jack's house."

I pictured this in my mind and laughed.

"Hey, what about if you take him to school, then drop me off at the airport on your way back to your place," Lon suggested.

"Jeez, all I do these days is cart the two of you back and forth to the city, only to have Jupe complain about the lack of elbow room in my car."

Lon opened his mouth to smile against my neck.

"But I know what you're doing," I said quietly, "and I appreciate it."

"Do you?"

"You're trying to keep my mind off things by forcing me to help out with Jupe."

"Is it working?"

He knew it was.

It had been two weeks since San Diego. I'd like to pretend that I was over the whole mess, but, like Lon told me, I'd probably never be done with it completely. It probably wasn't fair of me, but during my darker moments I harbored an angry resentment toward other people who'd lost their parents in normal ways like car accidents or illness; at least the survivors knew that their parents had loved them. I didn't even have that. Sometimes I told myself that they might've loved me once, before they went crazy, but that was more painful than comforting.

Still, I didn't have any right to fall to pieces, and no one gave me time to do that anyway. Apart from Lon keeping me busy, there was work. I sat down with Kar Yee and Amanda after San Diego and told them more of the truth than I had before. I didn't reveal my real identity, but I admitted that I'd lied about my parents being dead before, and reported that they'd died when I went to San Diego. True enough.

I told the same story to Father Carrow. I'd already been harboring more than a little guilt about lying to him in the first place, and this was less of a lie, if not *quite* honest. I'm pretty sure he knew that, but he never held it against me. He brought me dinner a couple times when I wasn't staying with Lon and told me he prayed for me every night. I had my doubts regarding the amount of enthusiasm with which God received those requests, but, strange as it might sound, it gave me some amount of comfort.

Caliph Superior called me just about every day to check on me. He offered to visit and help me work on using my Moonchild ability. Said he'd send me everything he could find about it in the main lodge's library. But I was wary about using it. There were too many bad feelings associated with it, and, sure, maybe I was a little bit chicken. Wouldn't you be?

The caliph also told me that the Luxe Order had officially gone on record as maintaining a neutral relationship with our order again. Their leader, Magus Zorn, had told me after I'd banished Nivella in San Diego that he forgave me for what I did to Riley. Lon told him that he forgave Riley for what she did to Jupe, and that kind of shut Magus Zorn up. I think he was pretty damn scared of Lon, to be honest. Perhaps scared of me, too.

And he wasn't the only one. The head of the Hellfire Club, Mr. Dare, wanted to meet me. Through Lon, he'd sent a promise to have both David and Spooner punished; maybe they'd lose a turn with a succubus or be forced to fight it out in the demon ring. Mr. Dare also sent me a lovely hand-carved thirteenth-century caduceus. Impressive. Nothing says peace offering like a priceless medieval occult item, I supposed.

"Hey," I said to Lon, suddenly remembering, "the caliph told me today that you've refused the money he tried to give you for the talon."

"Mmm."

"Why?"

"I don't know. It just feels wrong. We've got the talon, so if I take his money, it's like I've sold it to him. And that makes me no better than Spooner. So let's just keep the damn thing locked up and call it even."

All right, then. I knew the caliph would keep hounding me, but whatever. I couldn't force Lon to take the money.

A long moment stretched out between us. I listened to the waves breaking against the rocks below until Lon finally spoke again.

"I haven't been asking you to haul Jupe around for grief therapy, you know," he said in a soft voice.

"Huh?"

"It's for my benefit too."

"Free babysitting?"

"No . . . familiarity creates bonds."

"Is that so?"

He nodded against my neck. "He grows on you. Right?"

"Like mold."

Lon chuckled deep and low, his chest vibrating against my shoulder. "Yeah, like mold."

An unseasonably cool ocean breeze fluttered our hair and seeped into my bones. I shivered and wedged myself further under him. He gathered me closer, kissed my neck, then spoke in a low voice next to my ear. "I figure, see, if you find yourself getting more attached to the two of us than you planned, maybe you won't think about picking up and leaving to start another life somewhere else."

"I haven't thought too much about that, not in the last few days," I admitted after a time.

"But you did at first—right after. I could hear it, you know." He fingers brushed over my clavicle, tracing the bone to my shoulder.

"I know," I said. "I'm sorry."

"I understand, but if you *did* want to do that, I hope

you'd be honest and tell me. I might try to talk you out of it, but I wouldn't stop you. I'm here for you . . . unconditionally."

Sadness crept over me. I tried to push it back, but it was persistent. "No one can be there unconditionally for someone else, Lon. There's no such thing."

"Sure there is."

"I gave my support to my parents unconditionally, and look where it got me."

"That's true, but it doesn't mean you should just give up on the whole damn concept. Believe me, I know a thing or two about pain and grief. I could be bitter at this point in my life and unwilling to trust anyone, but I'm not."

"Hmph."

"I'm older and wiser," he teased. "You should listen to me."

I laughed as the patio glass door slid open behind us. A frenzied rush of dog feet clamored down the redwood stairs. Foxglove whooshed by us, barking madly.

The sheen of black fur and fluorescent purple collar blurred past the edge of the cliff and into the adjacent woods where a narrow, dirt back road teetered down the mountain toward the rocky beach.

"What the hell?" I murmured as we sat up in the grass and watched her bound away.

Jupe stomped across the deck in pursuit.

"It's that mermaid ghost," he explained, breathless. "Below the sea stack. Can you see her? Foxglove always knows when she's down there."

We stood up, brushing off our clothes, and ambled across the yard together toward the cliff's rocky edge. Lon's "moat" lay at my feet: the circular house ward. Like the one he'd helped erect back at my house, it dimly glowed with charged Heka. I stood behind it like a bowler avoiding the foul line and peered over the cliff at the dark bit of rocky land jutting out from the Pacific. "Hmm . . . I don't see anything."

"Me neither," Lon agreed.

"Look, I know you both think I'm stupid and that neither of you believe in ghosts, but I *know* she's there. It's not an imp." Jupe padded up behind us in his pajama bottoms, a T-shirt, and bare feet. "I bet if we went down there right now, Foxglove would lead us straight to her."

I laughed. "There is no way in hell I'm walking down there right now. It's a twenty-minute walk down the side of the cliff."

"Not to mention the walk back up," Lon added. "Inside. Now." He loosely gripped the back of my neck and prodded me forward. "You too."

Jupe looked at me. "Will you come up and watch TV in my room?" He shivered once, wrapping his arms around his chest.

"Ye-e-e-s," I drawled, "for Pete's sake, I already told you I would five minutes ago."

"Just checking," he mumbled, grinning sheepishly.

I winked at him.

"Make sure the dog door is unlatched so Foxglove can get back in," Lon said.

As we climbed the stairs toward the house, I took one last look down at Mermaid Point, straining my eyes across the beach to the sea stack. Maybe it was just a trick of the moonlight or maybe Jupe was right, but I could've sworn I saw something. For a split second, I considered using my new ability to be sure; if there really was something out there, surely I'd be able to see it better in the black void that my power conjured up. Then I changed my mind—not because I was afraid that if I started using it I'd turn into my parents.

But if I used my ability and discovered that there *wasn't* anything there, then Jupe would lose his ghost, and I didn't want to take that away from him.

Besides, maybe he wasn't wrong. God knows I'd run into plenty of strange things that most people wouldn't believe existed. Just because you can't see something doesn't mean it's not there.

ACKNOWLEDGMENTS

My thanks and gratitude to:

Laura Bradford (the Dorothy Parker of literary agents), who believed in my voice long before I did, and who laughed—not winced—when I sent her a framed packet of Cock Soup;

Jennifer Heddle (the George Lucas of editors), who liked Arcadia enough to take a chance on her, and quietly made this book *far* better than it originally was;

Tony Mauro (the Tony Mauro of fantasy art), who graciously listened to my tedious vision of Arcadia and the Tambuku Tiki Lounge, and created a cover that is both gritty and beautiful;

Brian (the Mark Mothersbaugh of creative partners), whose cognitive skills are the stuff of legend. He let me bounce ideas off him, helped brainstorm plot solutions, and warned me when I was heading into Baroque Nightmare (a place all my books go sooner or later). But mostly he just told me to keep going when I didn't think I could. I love you dearly.

Additional thanks to my support teams: the Skunk Girls; the Bradford Babes (especially Jedi Master Ann); my lovely family (hands down, the nicest conservatives I know); my beautiful in-laws, who've always made me feel like a superstar; Bill Skeel, who volunteered to take photos of the least photogenic person in the world; and the generous people in the online writing/reading community, who befriended me without knowing what kind of writer I really am (I hope you're not sorry).

Kudos to everyone at Pocket Books, including Anne Cherry, Julia Fincher, and all the people behind the scenes who worked on this book. And my sincere thanks to librarians, book reviewers and bloggers, all booksellers (big and small), and supporters of genre fiction everywhere.

Read on for a sneak peek at
the next ARCADIA BELL novel,
coming in Summer 2012
from Pocket Books . . .

Jupe pinched himself on the arm and grinned at me from the passenger seat of my Volkswagen. "Yep, I definitely feel different."

I swiped my monthly pass through the card reader at the parking garage entrance down the street from my bar. It buzzed in acceptance, and the striped barrier arm began rising on the gate. "Well, you sure do *look* it," I agreed, stowing the pass in a pocket on the sun visor.

"Different how?" Jupe tugged at one of the long, espresso curls jutting out around his face. Like other Earthbound demons, his head and shoulders were crowned by a swirling halo of hazy light. His was an alluring spring-green that matched his remarkably pale eyes and gave off a lightning-bug luminescence in the shadowed interior of my car.

"You look older . . . more sophisticated," I teased.

"Really?"

I rolled my eyes and pulled through the raised gate into the dark garage. "No."

He punched me on the arm.

"Dammit, that hurt," I complained in the middle of a laugh, rubbing my shoulder. "See if I ever give you anything again, you ungrateful punk."

Jupe snickered as he stretched out long, wiry legs and examined the savings deposit receipt perched on his knee. He thoughtfully traced his finger along the indented ink. The deposit was for fifteen thousand dollars. It was originally a check made payable to me from Caliph Superior, the leader of my esoteric organization back in Florida. The money was payment for the black-market glass talon Jupe's father had bought to help me out a few weeks ago. My magical order was loaded, so I didn't feel guilty that they offered to reimburse Lon. But when he refused their check, I couldn't keep the money for myself, so the only logical solution was to give it to his son . . . while Lon was away in Mexico on a three-day photo shoot. Sneaky? Sure. But if you're going to lie to Lon, you have to do it while he's away on business. Otherwise, he'll just sense it before you can make it out the door. Jupe taught me that trick. He should write a book: *How to Outsmart an Empath.* The boy has skills.

But who knew giving money to an underaged kid would be so hard? Jupe and I spent almost an hour arguing with tellers inside my credit union: No, I did *not* want to put it in some giftable trust fund that Jupe couldn't touch until he was twenty-one. He already had a fat college fund and enough bonds and CDs to start a third-world country.

Problem was, the credit union didn't allow minors on a joint savings account without a parent or legal guardian co-signing, and I was neither. Girlfriend of the Boy's Father didn't qualify, apparently. The branch manager couldn't understand why I wouldn't wait until Lon was back in town to get his signature. Yeah, right. I wasn't about to tell the manager that Lon would refuse—which he would. After a blue-faced argument, the manager finally, inexplicably, gave in.

"By the way, I know you still don't believe me," Jupe said as he snooped inside the glove compartment, "but I really *did* do it. Me. I got the manager to make an exception and let us open the account."

God, he really wasn't going to give that a rest. I swatted his hand away from the glove compartment and steered the car down the ramp to the next parking level; the Metropark garage sticks the monthlies in the dregs on the bottom floor. "You're a charmer, don't get me wrong . . ." And he was. Witty, geek-smart, almost annoyingly outgoing, and well on his way to becoming drop-dead gorgeous. Just yesterday he bragged that he'd overheard some girl in his class referring to him as "totally hot." Did I mention he was cocky?

"I'm serious, Cady. I concentrated with my mind and twisted his thoughts around. I think it's my"—he leaned over the armrest and spoke in a lower voice, as if someone could hear us outside the car—"knack."

Knack. Earthbound slang for demonic ability. Most Earthbounds have one, but many knacks fall short of spectacular. A little foresight here, a little nighttime vision there. A whole hell of a lot of telepaths, most of whom are no more than bland party entertainment, unable to lift anything heavier than a freaking spoon a couple inches off the table. Don't get me wrong: the occasional impressive ability *did* exist. I'd met Earthbounds that could pick a lock with a touch, and others who could curse your unborn child. Those weren't exactly commonplace, though.

"You're crazy," I said, waiting for another car to back out. A large, sparkling jack-o'-lantern clung to the top of its antenna; less than two weeks to Halloween. "For starters, you've got a couple more years before your demonic ability will start expressing. And second, you'll probably end up with your dad's empathy. It's genetic, you know—you don't just get a new ability out of thin air."

"I know all that," Jupe complained. "Who's the demon here, me or you?"

"You."

"Yeah, and I got the stupid 'knack' speech along with the 'birds and the bees' from my dad when I was eight."

"Poor, poor Lon," I murmured. The car windows were fogging up; it was going to rain. I turned the dial to defrost and cranked up the compressor fan.

"All I'm saying is that I know about what's *supposed* to happen. But I'm telling you, Cady, I can make people do things. I can get inside their minds and change their thoughts. Permanently."

"Pfft. I've never even heard of a knack like that." Well, Lon could influence thoughts when he was amped up into his transmutated demon state, but that's nothing Jupe knew about, or would ever know. Not from me, anyway. Besides, Lon's influence was temporary, and he had to be touching the person. Plus it was more common for the inherited knack to be weaker than the parent's, not stronger.

"I think my knack is like"—he paused, as if he knew what he was about to say was going to sound ridiculous, but he just couldn't stop himself—"a Jedi mind trick."

I snorted.

"I'm serious!"

"Dream on." I shot him a sidelong glance as he snuck a couple fingers just beneath the waistband of his jeans and scratched—vigorously, with a teeth-gritting, pained look on his face. This was the third time today I'd caught him scratching. "What the hell is wrong with you? You have ants in your pants?"

He scratched harder and groaned. "I've got an injury."

Dear God, have mercy. I held up my hand to stop him

from saying more, waving away any mental images before they had a chance to pop into my head. "I don't *even* want to know."

Affronted, he made a face at me. "Not *there*. It's . . . nothing. Never mind."

No need to tell me twice. He could discuss it with the school nurse if he'd somehow managed to contract crabs from a gym towel in the boy's locker room. Not my job description. I promptly changed the subject. "So, what was all that jibber-jabber earlier about you wanting an Eldorado?"

He'd talked the branch manager's ear off, telling him what he was going to do with the savings account. Jupe swore to the guy—who couldn't have given a rat's ass—that he wouldn't touch his new money until he turned fifteen and could apply for a driver's learning permit . . . and buy a car. That's right: a year from now this ADHD mess of a boy would be plowing down the same roads I drove on. Heaven help us all.

"Umm, *Superfly*, duh. The Cadillac Eldorado is only one of the greatest cars in movie history—the original pimp mobile." He waggled his eyebrows. "Driven by Youngblood Priest, played by Ron motherfucking O'Neal."

I didn't even bother to curtail his obscenity-rich language anymore; getting honey out of a hornet would be easier. When I was his age, my parents would've slapped me for talking like that. Then again, my parents turned out to be evil, power-hungry serial killers, so what did they know? Compared to them, Lon was parent of the year. So I just stuck to the Butler house rule: no swearing around strangers. Unless Jupe was making an ass of himself in public, he could knock himself out.

"Yuck," I complained. "Didn't Boss Hog drive an Eldorado in the *Dukes of Hazzard*?"

His wince told me that I was right.

"Anyway, I seriously doubt your dad's going to go for a pimp mobile."

"Then how about a 1977 Firebird Trans Am?" He clicked the release on his seat belt several times. The boy was obsessed. He knew the make and model of every car that had been produced in the last fifty years—at least the ones featured in movies or on TV.

"Oh, *hell* no," I said. "Not a Trans Am."

"That's the Bandit's car. What's wrong with that?"

I puffed my cheeks out and made a puking noise.

"Hey, you're talking about Burt—"

"Yes, I know. Burt motherfucking Reynolds. Put your seat belt on, Snowman—we've still got two more levels to go."

He refastened the buckle. "Holy shit! I've never been this far down underground. There'd better be an elevator. This looks like the kind of place where you get stabbed and left for dead."

Ugh. Tell me about it. Parking here was the worst part of owning my bar, but it was better than leaving my car on the street. I once had my window broken and my car stereo stolen while parked in front of the bar. At least the garage had cameras and a guard on premises 24/7.

"If I had to choose, I guess I'd go for the Eldorado," I said, trying to distract both of us from a homeless guy sleeping in a dark corner by one of the stairwells. "But I'm kinda doubting that a measly fifteen-thou is going to buy you one."

"My dad knows a ton of car collectors. He'll get me a deal."

Mmm-hmm. Sure he would. We headed down the final ramp onto the monthlies level. I spotted a tight corner space, not too far from the elevator.

"We're parking here?" Jupe asked, wiping away the fog to peer out the window. "Gross."

"Welcome to glamorous big-city life."

"I bet the Snatcher would have a field day down in this dump."

"Who?"

"The Sandpiper Park Snatcher," he repeated, as if I were the dumbest person in the world. When I shook my head in confusion, he explained. "Some kid went missing in La Sirena a couple of days ago. Everyone at school says the Snatcher's back."

I grunted and warily glanced out the window. Leave it to me to get spooked by a teenager inside my own parking garage. "Look, you said you wanted to see my bar before it opens today . . ."

"I do, I do!" he confirmed, throwing off his seat belt.

"Then help me haul this shit out of the car and let's get going before the rain starts."

I popped the trunk as Jupe slammed his door shut and jogged around to meet me. The restaurant supply guy had screwed up our delivery yesterday, so that meant I had to take care of this weekend's garnish par-levels by tracking down mondo-sized sacks of lemons, limes, oranges, and pineapples. Jupe and I made a quick trip to the wholesaler's warehouse before the whole credit union fiasco. Along with the citrus, I let him pick out Halloween candy both for home and the bar, so we also had enough Tootsie Rolls, Pixy Stix, and severed gummy body parts to feed an army of demons.

While we unloaded the trunk, Jupe started in again about the Snatcher. In the oceanside town where he and Lon lived, this was apparently a local urban legend. A boogeyman whom no one had ever seen. When I pressed Jupe for details, all he could give me was a tangle of motley stories about young teenage Earthbounds who were picked off one by one at Halloween in the early '80s.

Great. That was the last thing I wanted to think about. It had been a month since Jupe had been held hostage and his arm broken. That memory sent a familiar pang of guilt through my gut. And from the worry shading his eyes right now, I guessed he wasn't all that keen on pondering the possibility of getting kidnapped again, either. Best not to talk about it.

"Smells like someone's been pissing all over the walls," Jupe complained, wrinkling his nose in disgust as we toted the bags of fruit and candy to the elevator.

"Someone probably has. Lots of someones." I glanced over my shoulder and scanned the dirty garage. The concrete floor shook with the dull boom of a car on the level above us driving over speed bumps. Otherwise, it was quiet. Usually was, during the daytime on weekends. "Inhale through your mouth," I suggested. "And stay sharp."

He followed my instruction as I stopped in front of the elevator and used a knuckle to press the cracked plastic up-arrow button. I started to ask Jupe a question but was interrupted when something hit me in the shoulder, knocking me sideways. Pain sparked as my cheek smacked into the concrete above the elevator button panel. A bag of limes fell out of my hand as Jupe yelled behind me.

"Against the wall!" a voice hollered near me. "Move!" A man in a bright blue hoodie towered in front of me, his face shrouded in sharp slices of shadow under the dim garage lights. No halo, so he was human, not Earthbound. His blond hair was shaggily cropped. He carried a curved hunting knife in one hand and stood with his legs apart, bouncing on the toes of his tennis shoes, ready for a fight.

I dropped the other bag I was holding and backed up against Jupe. The scrape on my cheek was on fire. My heart was racing so fast, it didn't feel like it was beating at all.

"Money. Now!" the man shouted. As he did, his head shifted out of the shadows to reveal a mouthful of yellow, rotting teeth. Meth head, I assumed, pairing his dental issues with the twitchy way he moved. Not exactly a man in his prime, that's for sure. On one hand, I might be able to take him down with a swift kick to his balls. Then again, I might get stuck with that dirty-ass knife.

"Credit cardth too," the man added with a lisp, looking me over with nervous eyes. He turned the knife over in his hand and blinked rapidly. His erratic, drug-primed pulse was probably a few pumps away from causing his heart to explode; I wondered if I could will it along a little faster.

Jupe made a soft mewing noise behind me as his hands gripped the back of my jacket. I thought of the magical seals on my inner forearm, white ink tattoos etched into my skin. I could charge one of them to make Jupe and I seem to disappear; we could run to the car and escape. But most of the seals require blood or saliva to activate, both rich with Heka, the magical energy needed to power spells. Not exactly practical at the moment; by the time I pushed my jacket sleeve up, the meth addict could easily shiv me in the gut.

What else? Not enough time to break out a hunk of red ochre chalk and scribble out a spell, and I couldn't very well knock the guy out with a sack of lemons. What in hell was I going to do?

"You got a wallet, boy?" the mugger asked.

"No fucking way," Jupe whispered in my ear. "He's not getting my car money."

"What did you say? You got money?" The man twisted

his head around, scanning the garage as another car drove through the level above us. "Let's get in your car and drive to the ATM."

I didn't answer. Like Jupe said, no fucking way.

"I don't mind hurtin' either one of you," the man warned. "Eat or be eaten. A big, bad thtorm's a-comin'. Can't you feel it in the air?"

From the psychotic glint in his eyes, I didn't think he was talking about the afternoon rain forecast. Stupid bastard was out of his ever-loving mind. Dirty, diseased, high, and crazy. Awesome.

A fluorescent light shone above the elevator. I was going to have to shock him; why was my last resort always my only option? Best not to kick a gift horse in the mouth, I supposed. Most magicians would probably give their right arm to be able to kindle Heka like I could; my sensitivity threshold to electrical shock was pretty high. "Stay away," I threatened, "or whatever god you pray to better help you, because I'm going to fry you to hell and back."

"Say what?" He narrowed his eyes and visually searched me for a weapon.

I tapped into the electrical current. My skin tingled with the familiar flow of foreign energy as I began to spool electricity into myself. No time to be gentle about it, so I pulled fast. Lights flickered. The descending elevator groaned in protest. Within a couple of seconds, my body hummed with enough charged Heka to shock the guy pretty badly. But I'd have to get close enough to touch him; the concrete floor was a poor conductor.

"Let go," I growled through gritted teeth, trying to shake Jupe off of me. He was gripping my jacket like death. If he didn't let go, I couldn't do this. Without a caduceus staff to even out the release, it was going to hurt all of us when I released the kindled Heka.

The garage elevator dinged.

The mugger yelped and swiveled wildly, searching for the source of the sound.

The elevator doors parted.

"Police are coming! Run!" Jupe shouted near my ear. I jumped in surprise, nearly losing control of the charged Heka.

Spooked, the mugger cried out incoherently, turned on his heels, and fled from Jupe's nonexistent police in the empty elevator car. We watched in disbelief as he raced his own heartbeat up the parking garage ramp toward the next level; I'd never seen anyone move so fast. But when he barreled around the corner, a large blue minivan sped down the ramp. It slammed on squealing brakes as Methbrain ran out in front of it. The disconcerting thump of metal on flesh echoed through the garage. The man's body jerked as he crumpled on top of the minivan's hood.

Jupe gasped.

The doors to the elevator closed.

Unable to hold the Heka any longer, I shoved a shaking hand into my inner jacket pocket until my fingers wrapped around a pencil. I pushed Jupe off of me forcefully, then thrust the pencil into the concrete wall, releasing a substantial volt of charged Heka through the small graphite lead. The wooden caduceus staves I normally use for magical work contain fat graphite cores that allow smooth releases of kindled energy. This puny pencil? Not so much. It overloaded and immediately shattered, wedging a wooden yellow splinter into my skin.

"Shit!" I stuck my injured finger in my mouth as a wave of post-magick nausea hit me and I swayed on my feet. The sound of car doors opening drew my attention to the minivan. Three people were running to help the meth head. Before I could scream for them to stop, he popped up from the hood like an unkillable video game character, briefly shook himself, and tore off again, farther up the ramp and out of sight.

Jupe's eyes were two brilliant circles of leafy green surrounded by white moons. "You okay?" I asked, putting my hands all over him like a soccer mom, as if there was a chance that all of his bones were crushed. Panicked thoughts of him needing another cast ran through my head: he'd only gotten out of the last one a couple of weeks ago.

"Whoa . . ." He was shaken, but otherwise fine. His eyes darted between me and the minivan. "We almost got mugged. Holy shit."

"Oh, God, Jupe. I'm *so* sorry." I wrapped my arms around him. A dark laugh vibrated his shoulders. I released him to study his face; he wasn't smiling.

"Do you believe me now?" he said. "I did that, Cady. Like I convinced the manager at the credit union."

"Jupe—"

He shook his head, dismissing my lack of belief, then said firmly, "I just made that mugger believe the cops were coming."

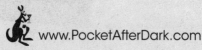

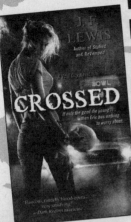

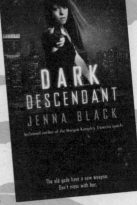